RUSSIAN
CLASSICS

NIKOLAI GOGOL

Dead Souls

Translated by CHRISTOPHER ENGLISH

RADUGA
PUBLISHERS
MOSCOW

Translation from the Russian

Edited by *Olga Shartse*
Designed by *Sergei Alimov*

ISBN 5-05-001128-0

CONTENTS

Foreword

The Enigmatic Gogol

Gogol's reputation in world literature has perhaps changed more radically in recent decades than that of any other great Russian writer. During Gogol's lifetime, in 1842, which saw the publication of Volume One of *Dead Souls*, his most important work, the well-known Russian critic Vissarion Belinsky wrote: "Where, show us, where in Gogol's works do we find that spirit of world history, that content which is common to all peoples and all ages? Tell us, what would happen to any of Gogol's works if they were translated into French, German or English?"

Belinsky was an ardent admirer of Gogol and regarded him as Russia's greatest writer, yet even he thought that the importance of the creator of *Dead Souls, The Government Inspector* and *The Greatcoat* was limited to Russia alone.

Today we know that this is not so. Gogol is translated into French, German, English, Japanese and many other languages. Articles and books about him are published all over the world. Symposia and seminars are held to discuss his work. In the past decade alone there have been several such discussions: a symposium in Venice (1976), a Soviet-Italian Colloquium in Rome organised by the Accademia Nazionale die Lincei (1981) and a Gogol Conference in Tokyo in April 1983. Of all the epithets currently used to describe this Russian writer's work, perhaps the most frequent is the word "enigmatic". People often speak of the enigmatic Gogol. In fact, a lengthy monograph published recently in England is actually entitled *The Enigma of Gogol*.*

The epithet "enigmatic" refers, of course, not so much to Gogol's unusual posthumous fate, the sudden growth of his fame throughout the world, but to the writer's life, his peculiar psychic and spiritual makeup, and the specific nature of his literary style.

It would be impossible to dwell at any length on these points in this introduction. We shall, however, attempt to indicate them at least, to provide the most essential information about the writer's life and work.

* * *

Nikolai Vasilievich Gogol was born on April 1 (March 20 Old Style), 1809, in the Ukrainian village of Velikiye Sorochintsi. His parents were members of the petty gentry. They possessed about four hundred serfs and the small estate of Vasilievka (also known as Yanovschina), not far from Velikiye Sorochintsi in Poltava province. It was in Vasilievka that the future writer spent his childhood.

The area was rich in legends, superstitions and strange stories which fired the imagination of the sensitive and impressionable boy.

At the age of twelve Gogol went to study at the Gymnasium of Higher Sciences, which had just opened in the small town of Nezhin in neighbouring Chernigov province. He spent seven years there, returning to Vasilievka only in the holidays. The rest of the time he boarded at the Gymnasium with a motley band of high-spirited and unruly boys.

Gogol did not find it easy to get on with his schoolmates. Even at this time he was regarded as strange and enigmatic. "I am considered an enigma by everyone, no one has managed to get to the bottom of me," Gogol wrote to his mother a few months before leaving the gymnasium. "Regard me as you like ... only believe that I am always inspired by noble feelings, that I have never debased myself spiritually and that I have dedicated my whole life to the common good."

*Richard Peace, *The Enigma of Gogol*, Cambridge University Press, 1981.

Very early on, in his teens, he began to prepare himself for important public service. No, he was not yet thinking of becoming a writer, although he began to write at the gymnasium, and according to some accounts even earlier, as a very young boy. The "field" to which Gogol referred in his letter to his mother, and to which he proposed to devote himself entirely, was the civil service. To be more precise, law, the administration of justice. "I saw that here there would be most work of all... Injustice, the greatest bane of all, distressed me more than anything else."

But things did not turn out as the young Gogol had planned. After leaving school and moving to St Petersburg in late 1828, he did indeed attempt to make a career in the civil service, working for a while as a junior clerk, but was not able to achieve anything of note in the sphere of justice. Government service with which Gogol soon became more and more disillusioned, gave way to other occupations—literary and pedagogical. Gogol began to teach, first at the Patriotic Institute, and later at St Petersburg University. And here, particularly in his literary pursuits, Gogol was brilliantly successful almost straightaway.

Whereas Gogol's first small book, the sentimental poem *Hanz Küchelgarten* published under the pseudonym of V. Alov in 1829, met with ridicule in the press, his next one, the two-volume collection of tales called *Village Evenings near Dikanka* (1831-1832) immediately placed the author among the leading Russian writers of his day. Gogol's writing now showed mastery, maturity and originality of style. He had transformed artistically the experience drawn from his native soil—his remarkable knowledge of Ukrainian folklore, life and customs. Thanks to him thousands of Russian readers literally fell in love with the Ukraine, and the imaginary publisher of the book, the cunning bee-keeper Rudy Panko (the author did not reveal his own name), was thought by many to be a real person.

Shortly after reading the first part of Gogol's book, Alexander Pushkin wrote, "I have just read *Evenings near Dikanka*. It astounded me. Here is real gaiety, sincere, spontaneous, without stiffness or affectation. And in places what poetry! What sensitivity! All this is so extraordinary in our present-day literature that I have not yet recovered from it."

Meanwhile another surprise awaited readers. In the tales which followed *Evenings* and were published in two new collections entitled *Mirgorod* and *Arabesques* (both 1835) Gogol now appeared not as an inspired romantic, but as a strict recorder of everyday life, a penetrating analyst of its baseness and triviality (although the profoundly poetic basis retained its force in these tales, as in all of Gogol's work, of course). In some stories, such as *Story of How Ivan Ivanovich Quarrelled with Ivan Nikiforovich*, Gogol looked from a different angle at the provincial life which he had known since childhood, his beloved Ukraine. In other works, the so-called *St. Petersburg Stories* (*Nevsky Prospekt, Diary of a Madman*, etc.), his portrayal of life in the Russian capital is penetrating and merciless. His ability to detect and convey acute social conflicts and contradiction between dream and reality, the unique fantastic quality of his writing, his profound and mature lyricism, all this gave a remarkable vitality and authenticity to Gogol's portrayal of St Petersburg.

In the tales from *Mirgorod* and *Arabesques* Gogol's comic gift, the richness and brilliance of his irony, were revealed to the full. And it was then, as he himself admitted, that he decided, "If one is going to poke fun at something, it is better to poke fun mercilessly at something that really deserves universal ridicule" (*Author's Confession*). Thus the idea of "state service" was combined with the idea of a literary career. Gogol had reached a crucial decision which was to determine all his subsequent life, namely, that he must seek to be socially useful not in the civil service, for example, but as an author, a comic author writing about the society of his day.

The year 1836 saw the appearance on the stage and in print of the famous *The Government Inspector* which portrayed life in a small provincial town as if under a magnifying glass. The image of this town was so profound and vivid, yet at the same time so full of symbolical meaning, that the comedy made a very strong impact and brought the author not only the approval of friends, but also the abuse of enemies. Deeply wounded by this abuse, Gogol nevertheless did not turn aside from his chosen path, but embarked upon the realisation of an even more grandiose plan, the creation of the poem *Dead Souls*. This work was begun almost at the same time as *The Government Inspector* around 1835. The subjects for both works were suggested to Gogol by Pushkin.

Later in his *Author's Confession* Gogol described the circumstances in which Pushkin gave him the subject for *Dead Souls*. "He had been urging me to embark upon a big work for some time and finally, one day, after I read him a short description of a small scene, which however impressed him more than anything else I had read to him before, he said to me: 'With this ability to see a person and portray him completely in a few strokes, as if he were alive, with such an ability it is simply a sin not to write a big work!' Afterwards he began talking about my weak constitution, my ailments which could bring my life to an early end; as an example he quoted Cervantes, who, although he wrote several very fine and delightful stories, would never have won the place he now holds among writers had he not written *Don Quixote*, and, in conclusion, presented me with a subject of his own, which he had been proposing to use for some sort of a narrative poem and which, as he told me, he would never have given to anyone else. It was the subject of *Dead Souls*."

There is a reference in some memoirs which confirms that Pushkin's attention was drawn to a case of speculation in dead souls.*

The bibliographer and publisher P. Bartenev in his footnotes to the memoirs of the writer Count Vladimir Sologub wrote: "One day Pushkin was at the races in Moscow with an acquaintance of his. A certain P (an old dandy) was there also. Pointing the latter out to Pushkin, the acquaintance told him how P had bought up dead souls and mortgaged them for a lot of money. Pushkin was delighted by this.

---

*It should be explained that under serfdom a peasant could be bought and sold like a commodity or real estate. The number of each landowner's peasants was recorded in special registers which were compiled and submitted once every few years. Peasants who died in the interval were still counted as being alive, and the landowner had to pay taxes on them. It is this situation which the main character in *Dead Souls*, Chichikov, seeks to use to his advantage: a landowner would readily let him have his dead peasants in order not to pay tax on them, and he, Chichikov, would mortgage them if they were still alive and get a handsome sum of money for them.

'You could write a novel about that,' was one of the things he said." But as in the writing of *The Government Inspector* Gogol may have been influenced by other sources as well: many cases of fraud involving dead souls were known. One of them, as M. Anisimo-Yanovskaya, a distant relative of the writer, recalled, took place in Gogol's native parts, the Mirgorod district, and was well-known to the writer.

As Gogol himself stated (in his "Four Letters to Various Persons apropos of *Dead Souls*", letter 3), the original drafts of the poem were written in somewhat different, more sombre tones, and the characters were like "monsters". Gogol became aware of the need to change this treatment after reading the poem to Pushkin (at the end of 1835 or in the first half of 1836). "...When I began to read Pushkin the first chapters from D(ead) S(ouls) in their original form, Pushkin, who always laughed during my readings (he liked a good laugh), gradually became gloomer and gloomer, until he was quite morose. When the reading ended, he said in a weary voice: 'Dear Lord, how sad our Russia is!' This astonished me... Afterwards I began to think how I could soften the painful impression which *Dead Souls* might make."

According to Gogol's new plan the work was to deal not only with the dark aspects of Russian life. Instead of depicting Russia "from one side only", Gogol was now talking about "the whole of Russia appearing in it".

That *Dead Souls* was to consist of several parts, Gogol announced in his letter to Mikhail Pogodin of November 28, 1836. He compared Volume One to the "porch of the palace which is being built within me" (Letter to Pyotr Pletnyov of March 17, 1842).

The story of the writing of Volume Two is complex and in many respects unclear. Of the surviving chapters the oldest in terms of being written is the concluding chapter. It is a fragment of the 1843-1845 draft, the draft which Gogol burnt in the summer of 1845.

Concerning his reasons for destroying the manuscript, Gogol wrote: "There are times when you cannot direct society or even a whole generation to great and noble things until you have shown the full extent of its present baseness; there are times when you should not speak of what is noble and splendid, without first showing as clear as daylight the ways and paths to it for each and every one. The latter aspect was developed only slightly and weakly in Volume Two of _Dead Souls_, whereas it should have been almost the main thing: and that is why it was burnt" ("Four Letters to Various Persons apropos of _Dead Souls_", Letter 4). The difficulties which he encountered were thus connected with the main aim of Volume Two: he had to retain the "meaningfulness" of the characters, yet avoid them being far-fetched and idealised, to bring the "noble and splendid" closer to the reader.

From June 1836 to April 1848 Gogol lived abroad (in Germany, Switzerland, France and Belgium, but most of the time in Italy). He made short visits to Russia of a few months, once in 1839 to make arrangements for his sisters, who had just graduated from the Patriotic Institute, and again in 1841 to supervise the publication of Volume One of _Dead Souls_, which came out in 1842.

Although during the 1840s Gogol published new works (including such masterpieces as the story _The Greatcoat_, and the dramatic works _The Wedding_ and _The Gambler_), his whole life was subjected to his main task, the completion of _Dead Souls_. Here again the words "enigmatic" and "enigma" appear, this time in relation to his poem. For _Dead Souls_ was meant to reveal the enigma of Russian life, Russia's mission in modern history.

His work on the poem cost him an almost superhuman effort. On the night of 11 February, 1852, in the Moscow house in Nikitsky Boulevard where he was living, Gogol deeply dissatisfied burnt the fair copy of the draft for Volume Two. A few days later, on the morning of February 21, he died.

The "enigma" of the poem's continuation, its far-ranging, all-embracing content the writer carried with him to the grave.

* * *

Gogol's "enigmatic" quality stems from the fact that outwardly he appears to be a very simple writer, yet in terms of inner meaning he is a very complex one. Gogol must be read extremely carefully, not restricting oneself to the subject and the plot, but paying attention to the smallest details. The well-known Russian writer, poet and literary critic Andrei Bely said that Gogol's content is buried in detail. This applies above all to _Dead Souls_, of course, Gogol's most complex work. Here, too, the way to an understanding of the deeper levels of meaning is through the mass of small detail.

We shall illustrate this by one example only.

In the chapter about the landowner Manilov there is the following passage: "Sometimes, as he gazed from the porch into the yard or on to the pond he would say how fine it would be if they were to dig a subterranean passage from the house, or to erect a stone bridge across the pond, with stalls along both sides, where merchants would sit and ply those petty wares so essential to the peasants."

A stone bridge over a pond! One might think (and statements to this effect do in fact exist in the literature on Gogol), that this detail was suggested to the writer by real impressions which he received while living in Italy—the Rialto Bridge in Venice or the Ponte Veccio in Florence. Yet the passage quoted above was written by Gogol before he went to Italy.

Gogol's description has a meaning of its own, and this meaning is determined by the whole content of the poem.

The above-mentioned bridges in Florence and Venice have a definite point. A bridge over a river (or canal) is a centre of communication: several times a week (and perhaps even a day) the townsfolk will cross the bridge and are bound to notice the trading booths on either side of it. Moreover these bridges are beautiful, very beautiful, as anyone who has seen them will know.

Gogol's image is charged with the opposite meaning, however. Is it pure chance that the bridge in Manilov's imagination is not over a river, but over a pond, which does not need it, of course? The merchants and customers (who are peasants, incidentally, also an important detail for Gogol) would have to go onto the bridge specially in order to make the necessary purchases. And aesthetically a large bridge over a pond (Manilov wants to build it of stone) is a ridiculous, absurd sight. Thus, the meaning of Manilov's bridge is precisely that it serves no purpose at all, that it is void of meaning.

This passage is most characteristic of the structure of the poem as a whole. We might even say that it is the quint-essence of its style, for it deliberately records two kinds of absurd inexpediency in the world of the Manilovs and Chi-chikovs—purely economic (practical) and aesthetic. In *Dead Souls* they flow along in two streams, occasionally merging.

An example of practical pointlessness is the house of the selfsame Manilov, which stands "in isolation on the brow of a hill exposed to all winds that might ever chance to blow". And an example of aesthetic inexpediency is the house of another landowner, Sobakevich. Everything about this building is solid, but at the expense of beauty and symmetry. "The pediment could not be fitted into the middle of the building however hard the architect tried, because the owner ordered that one column on the side should be scrapped, with the result that there were not four columns, as intended, but only three."

Both buildings are absurd. In *Dead Souls* the grotesque poetics of the absurd is developed to the limits of artis-tic perfection. This poetry lies in a deliberate, sometimes stressed, but more often unaffected, insinuating, involun-tarily naive, subtle and as it were unintentional violation of the norm. For example, the description of the dining-room in the hotel. Everything here was "just as it is everywhere, the one difference being that one of the pictures depicted a nymph with breasts so enormous that the reader has probably never seen their like."

The spheres for the manifestation of the absurd are the external appearance of objects, incidents during a journey, reflections and utterances of the characters, etc. Human stupidity, the absence not only of elementary common sense, but of the most primitive logic, advance from vic-tory to victory. When the postmaster (during his discussion with the chief of police in Chapter Ten) concludes that Chichikov is Captain Kopeikin, totally ignoring the fact that Kopeikin has an arm and a leg missing, whereas Chi-chikov is all in one piece, praise be, he is erecting a kind of absurd mental construction analogous to Manilov's bridge.

The poetics of the absurd is directly linked with the plot and subject of the work, the buying and selling of "dead souls".

But the main point is that everything that happens in

the poem, its central event (the speculation with dead souls), is rather ambivalent and problematic. Problematic not only in the elevated sense of the public good (there is no doubt as to Chichikov's parasitism), but even from the point of view of personal gain, the individual success of the speculator. Within the framework of the poem Chichikov's "negotiation" did not lead to the desired success: he had to leave the town of N in a hurry, although without being exposed. In the subsequent parts, judging from the material available, not only new transgressions, but also new and even more devastating failures awaited him. However considerable the sums which Chichikov gets hold of from time to time, his main goal recedes further and further away from him, like a mirage in sun-scorched desert, and this mirage, if you like, is also akin to Manilov's fantastic construction.

Gogol rises to the heights of generalisation, extending the grotesque formula of the absurd to the whole of human life. Hence the bitter philosophical lines about human error and confusion: "How crooked, dark, narrow, impassable, and misleading have been the paths followed by mankind in its striving after the eternal truth... And however often they have had the way pointed out to them by the good sense that descends from heaven, still they managed to fall by the wayside and wander from the true path, to stray once again in broad daylight into the impassable thicket, to confuse one another and, dragging themselves in pursuit of will-o'-the-wisps, succeeded in reaching the edge of the abyss to ask each other in horror: where is the way out, where is the road?"

We see a direct link, a direct correspondence between the micro-images, such as the description of Manilov's bridge and the major constructions of the work. We see the mainspring behind Gogol's poem, the passionate dream of a straight, honest, true path for mankind. And the passionate denunciation of false steps, of everything that leads to fatal deviation from this path.

Gogol the writer kept the promise which he made at the very beginning of his life's path: "...believe me, I have dedicated my whole life to the common good."

Yuri Mann

Dead Souls

VOLUME ONE

CHAPTER ONE

Into the gates of the inn in the provincial capital NN there drove a rather smart smallish sprung chaise of the kind affected by bachelors: retired lieutenant colonels, junior captains, landowners possessed of about a hundred souls—in a word, by all those regarded as gentlemen of average means. In the chaise sat a gentleman neither handsome, nor yet of an unpleasing aspect, neither too fat, nor too thin; not exactly old, and yet not what you would call over-young either. His arrival caused absolutely no stir in the town and was not accompanied by anything unusual; only two peasants, standing by the doors of the pub opposite the inn, made a few remarks, pertaining, to be sure, more to the carriage than the man sitting in it. "Take a look over there," said the one to the other, "see that wheel! What do you reckon, would a wheel like that make it to Moscow if it had to or not?" "Course it would," answered the other. "But no Kazan, would it?" "No, not Kazan," answered the other. Whereupon the conversation ended. And then, when the chaise drove up to the inn, they passed a young man dressed in white dimity breeches, very short and tight, a tail-coat with pretensions to fashion, and beneath it a dicky secured with a Tula pin in the form of a bronze pistol. The young man turned on his heels, surveyed the carriage, caught hold of his cap, which the wind had almost blown off, and continued on his way.

When the carriage drove into the courtyard the gentleman was met by the waiter, a character so lively and fidgety that it was impossible to make out what he looked like.

He darted out, a napkin over his arm, his lanky form clad
in a long, wool mixture tailcoat, the collar almost touching
the back of his head, tossed back his hair and nimbly led
the gentleman upstairs and along the entire length of the
wooden gallery to show him the room God had sent him.
The room was of the familiar kind, for the inn was also of
the familiar kind, that is to say, precisely the kind found
in provincial capitals where for two rubles a day travellers
are given a quiet room complete with cockroaches staring
like prunes from every corner, and a door permanently
blocked by a chest of drawers which leads to the adjoining
room, occupied by another traveller, a taciturn and placid
man, but exceptionally inquisitive, eager to learn every
detail about his new neighbour. The outer facade of the
inn matched its interior: it was very long and two storeys
high; the lower one was unplastered, leaving exposed the
dark red bricks, rendered even darker than they already
were by the sharp changes in the weather; the upper one
was painted the inevitable yellow; on the ground floor
were little shops selling harness, ropes and bread rolls. In
the corner shop, or, to be more precise, at the window of
it, a honey-tea vendor stood beside his copper samovar,
his face just as coppery as his samovar, so that from afar
one might have thought there were two samovars standing
in the window, had not one of them sported a pitch black
beard.

While the new arrival was surveying his room his chattels were borne in: first his suitcase of white leather, its
battered state indicating that it had been on the road
before. The suitcase was carried in by the coachman Selifan, a squat little chap in a sheepskin, and the valet Petrushka, a surly-looking fellow of about thirty with very
large lips and nose, in a too-large old frock-coat, clearly
his master's hand-me-down. The suitcase was followed by a
box of mahogany inlaid with Karelian birch, a pair of boot-
trees and a roast fowl wrapped in blue paper. When all this
had been carried in, the coachman Selifan withdrew to
the stables to attend to the horses, while the valet Petrushka settled in the little hallway, a dark kennel of a room
where he had already brought his overcoat and with it a
special smell of his own, which in its turn was imparted to
the sack he then brought containing his valet's parapherna-

lia. In this cubby-hole he propped a narrow three-legged
bed up against the wall, covering it with a wretched little
palliasse, that was flat as a pancake, and perhaps as greasy
as the pancake he had wheedled from the inn-keeper.

While his servants attended to their business, our gentleman set off for the dining room. Just what these dining
rooms are like every traveller knows only too well: the
same oil-painted walls which, higher up, were stained
brown with tobacco smoke and, lower down, were discoloured by the rubbing backs of various travellers, and even
more so by the backs of the local merchants who, on market days, came here in sixes and sevens for their customary
round of tea; the same smoke-blackened ceiling; the same
smoked chandelier with its multitude of glass pendants
which bounced and tinkled when a waiter hurried along
the shabby oil-cloth runners, deftly balancing his tray,
stacked with tea-cups as densely as sea birds on a stretch
of beach; the same oil paintings stretching the length of
the wall,—in a word everything just as it is everywhere, the
one difference being that one of the pictures depicted a
nymph with breasts so enormous that the reader has probably never seen their like. A similar freak of nature can be
seen, to be sure, in various historical pictures, brought to
us here in Russia no one knows when, from where, or by
whom, some of them even by our noble lovers of art,
who bought these chef-d'oeuvres in Italy on the advice of
their coachmen.

The gentleman took off his cap and unwound from his
neck the bright woollen muffler of the type a husband has
knitted for him by his wife, and presented with appropriate
instructions on how to wrap himself up in it, and a bachelor—well, I cannot really say how he comes by them, God
alone knows: I have never worn such mufflers. Once the
muffler was unwound, the gentleman called for his supper.
In due course he was brought the fare usually served in
such inns: cabbage soup with a meat pie, a stock of which,
lasting for several weeks, is kept specially for travellers;
calves' brains with peas, sausages with cabbage, roast chicken, salt gherkins, and that faithful friend of travellers,
the inevitable jam tart, and while all this was served to him,
some of it reheated, some of it cold, he prevailed upon the
waiter to tell him this and that: who had kept the inn

before and who kept it now, how much profit it brought, and was their master a big rogue; to which the waiter gave his customay answer: "Oh a big rogue, sir, a proper scoundrel." Just as in enlightened Europe, so too in enlightened Russia there are now a great many distinguished people who simply cannot dine in an inn without striking up a conversation with his waiter, and sometimes even pulling his leg. To be sure, our guest was not just asking idle questions; with extraordinary sharpness he inquired after the names of the governor, of the President of the Chambers, of the public prosecutor; in a word, he did not overlook a single prominent official; but with even greater sharpness, if not with eagerness, he asked about all the prominent landowners: how many souls each of them owned, how far they lived from the town, even what sort of people they were and how frequently they visited the town; he also inquired concernedly about the state of the province: had there been any illnesses, epidemics, any deadly fevers, smallpox and the like, displaying a thoroughness and sharpness that betokened more than mere curiosity. The gentleman's manner was that of a man of substance, and he blew his nose extremely loudly. It is unclear how he did it, but his nose sounded like a trumpet. This seemingly quite innocent distinction did, however, earn him the considerable respect of the waiter, so that every time he heard this sound he tossed back his hair, straightened up for greater alacrity, and, bowing his head, asked if the gentleman required anything. After dinner the gentleman drank a cup of coffee and sat down on the divan, stuffing behind his back the cushion which in Russian inns is stuffed not with springy wool but with something uncommonly like bricks and cobblestones. At this point he began to yawn and asked to be conducted to his room; he lay down on his bed and slept for two hours. When he had rested, he wrote down on a scrap of paper, at the request of the inn-keeper, his rank and name in full for the information of the appropriate quarters, the police. As the servant descended the staircase he haltingly read the following: "Collegiate Councellor Pavel Ivanovich Chichikov, landowner, on private business."

While he was still deciphering the note syllable by syllable, Pavel Ivanovich Chichikov set off to view the town, with which he was, it appeared, satisfied, for he discovered that the town was in no way inferior to the other provincial capitals: the stone houses dazzled the eye by their yellow paint, while the wooden houses were a modest and dingy grey. The houses were one, two, or one-and-a-half storeys high, with the inevitable attic, a very elegant feature in the opinion of the local architects. Some of these houses appeared lost amidst the wide expanse of the street and the unending wooden fences; others were grouped in tight clusters, and here one saw more movement and colour. There were shop signs depicting breadrolls and boots, almost totally washed away by the rain, a sign with blue trousers painted on it and the signature: Arshavsky, Tailor; there was a shop with caps of various kinds, and written above it: The Foreigner Vasily Fyodorov; somewhere else there was a sign showing a billiard table with two players in tailcoats like those worn by the guests who appear on stage only at the finale. The players were depicted aiming their cues, their arms twisted slightly back, a leg still in midair as after an entrechat. Beneath all this was written: "Step this way." Here and there tables had been simply set up in the street, selling nuts, soap and gingerbread that looked like soap; somewhere else there was an eating-house under a sign showing a fat fish impaled on a fork. Still, the most noticeable signs and most frequently recurring were those bearing the tarnished imperial eagles, which have now been replaced by the laconic inscription: "Wine Shop." The roadway was in poor condition throughout.

He also glanced into the town garden, which consisted of a few spindly trees, which had not properly taken root, their trunks propped up by triangular supports, most attractively painted a dark green. Moreover, although none of these trees stood any higher than a reed, the newspapers, reporting on the town's festive illumination, said of them that: "Our town has been embellished, thanks to the concern of the governor, with a garden, consisting of shady, spreading trees, affording coolth on a sultry day", and that "it was a joy to behold how the hearts of our citizens trembled from an overflow of feeling, and how the tears streamed down their faces, tears of gratitude to our honoured governor." Having established, after detailed enquiry of a constable, the shortest route, should he need to visit the cathedral, the municipal offices, or the governor, he set off to have a look at the river, which flowed through the centre of the town, on the way tearing off a playbill nailed to a post with the intention of reading it more closely when he got home, stared hard at a lady of not displeasing aspect who was passing by on the wooden pavement, with a boy in train dressed in military livery, a bundle in his hand, and, casting one last glance all round him as if to commit to memory the disposition of the place, he repaired home, making directly for his room, gently assisted up the stairs by the servant. After having his tea he seated himself at the table, called for a candle, took the playbill from his pocket, held it up to the candle and began to read it, slightly screwing up his right eye. To be sure, the playbill contained little of any interest: A drama by Mr Kotzebue was being performed, in which Rollo was to be played by Mr Roplyovin, Cora by Miss Zyablova, the other parts were even less memorable; nevertheless he read them all, descending even as far as the price of seats in the stalls and ascertained that the playbill had been printed at the printing-shop of the provincial board; then he turned it over to see whether there might not be something on the other side, but, finding nothing he wiped his eyes, neatly folded it and placed it in the little box, into which he customarily placed everything that came his way. His day, it seems, was concluded by a helping of cold veal, a bottle of sour kvass and a deep sleep "with his bellows full open" as the expression goes in various parts of the extensive Russian land.

The whole of the next day was devoted to visits; Chichikov set off to pay his respects to all the local dignitaries. He made his obeisances to the governor, who, as it turned out, like himself was neither fat nor thin, wore a St Anna order round his neck and, so it was rumoured, had even been nominated for a star; to be sure he was a splendid fellow and sometimes even did a spot of embroidery on tulle. Next, he repaired to the vice-governor, then called upon the public prosecutor, the President of the Chambers, the chief of police, the monopolist, the director of the state factories... Unfortunately it is rather hard to remember all the great men of this world; suffice it to say that our visitor evinced a remarkable assiduity in the matter of visits:

he even went to convey his respects to the inspector of the Medical Board and the town architect. Thereafter he remained seated in his chaise for a long time, wondering whom else he might visit, but there simply were no more officials to be found. In his conversations with each of these worthies he demonstrated great skill in the art of flattery. To the governor he said *en passant* that entering his province was like entering Paradise, the roads were smooth as velvet, and that those administrations which appointed wise men to positions of authority deserved high approbation. He said something most blandiloquent to the police chief about the local constabulary; while in his conversation with the vice-governor and the President of the Chambers, who had the rank of mere state councellors, he even mistakenly twice said: "Your Excellency", which pleased them greatly. This had the result that the governor requested the honour of his company that same day at a private gathering, the other officials also invited him, some to dinner, some for a little game of Boston, some to take tea.

Our visitor appeared loath to divulge much about himself and if he did speak it was somehow in clichés, delivered with obvious diffidence, and on such occasions his speech acquired rather bookish turns of phrase: he was but an unworthy worm of this earth who merited not that others should be incommoded on his account, that he had endured much in his journey through life, had suffered for truth in his career, that he had many enemies, and attempts had even been made on his life, and that now, in his quest for peace, he hoped at last to select a domicile and that, having arrived in this town, he regarded it as his immediate duty to pay his respects to its leading dignitaries. This was all that became known in the town about the new arrival, who lost no time in taking the governor up on his invitation. Preparations for this event occupied rather more than two hours, and here our visitor displayed a rare punctiliousness in the matter of his toilet. After a brief after-dinner nap he called for hot water and spent an extraordinary amount of time lathering both cheeks, pushing his cheeks out with his tongue; then, taking his towel from the shoulder of the servant, he thoroughly wiped his fleshy face with it from all directions, commencing from behind his ears and first snorting twice right into the servant's face. Then he donned his shirt-front before the mirror, plucked out two little hairs which had peeped out of his nostril, and immediately after that was helped into a cranberry-red, shot-silk tailcoat. Thus attired, he drove forth in his own carriage along the endlessly wide streets, faintly illuminated by a dim gleam from the occasional lighted window. The governor's house, however, was lit up as for a ball; carriages with lanterns, two uniformed men before the entrance, the cries of coachmen in the distance—in a word, all *comme il faut*. Entering the hall, Chichikov had to screw up his eyes for a minute, so terrible was the glare from the candles, the lamps and the ladies' dresses. Everything was bathed in light. The black tailcoats flashed and whizzed about, singly and in groups, like flies around a dazzling white sugar loaf in the heat of a July afternoon which the old housekeeper, standing before an open window, chips and divides into sparkling chunks, while the children stand around gazing in curiosity at the movements of her sinewy arms, wielding the hammer, and the airborne squadrons of flies, buoyed up by the light air, swoop bravely in as if they own the place, and taking advantage of the old woman's purblindness and the sun glaring into her eyes, scatter over the succulent morsels, either singly, or in dense squads. Already sated with the richness of summer, which anyway sets out such dainties at every step, they have swarmed in with absolutely no desire to eat, but merely to flaunt themselves, to promenade up and down the sugar loaf, to rub their hind or forelegs together, or to scratch beneath their wings, or, stretching forth their arms, to rub these above their heads, to turn around and take to the air once more, only to return with new, importunate squadrons. Chichikov had scarcely had time to get his bearings before his elbow was seized by the governor, who at once presented him to his wife. Here, too, our visitor was nothing discomposed: he delivered a compliment, most appropriate from a man of middle years, of a rank neither too high nor too low. When the dancing couples, taking the floor, pressed everyone else to the wall he put his hands behind his back and studied them for about two minutes with close attention. Many ladies were finely and fashionably dressed, others wore what God had sent to their provincial capital. The men here, as everywhere, fell into two types: those belonging to the first type were slender men, forever hovering around the ladies; some of these were such that they could hardly be distinguished from their St Petersburg counterparts: they had the same whiskers, neatly, very cleverly and tastefully trimmed, or simply pleasant, clean-shaven oval faces; they seated themselves just as nonchalantly beside the ladies, talking French and making the ladies laugh just as is done in St Petersburg. The other type of men were the fat ones, or those like Chichikov, that is to say those who were not over-fat, nor yet exactly thin. These, by contrast, warily shied away from the ladies and only glanced around to see whether the governor's footman had set out the green baize tables for whist anywhere. Their faces were full and round, some even had warts, and one or two were pockmarked; they wore their hair neither in tufts, nor in curls, nor in the _Que diable_ manner, as the French put it: their hair was either cut short or slicked down, and their features were mostly prominent and strong. These were the town's august dignitaries. Alas! The fat are better able to conduct their affairs in this world than the thin. Thin men serve mostly on special assignments or their jobs exist only on paper, whilst they flit about from place to place; their very existence is somehow too light, airy and totally unreliable. Fat men, on the other hand, never occupy peripheral positions, but only central ones, and if they do take a chair somewhere, they will do so firmly and solidly, so that even if it cracks beneath them and crumbles they will still remain firmly installed. They disdain outward sparkle; their tailcoats are not so smartly cut as those of their thin brethren, yet their coffers are full of God's plenty. After three years a thin man will not possess a single unmortgaged soul; but before you know it the fat man will have acquired a house at one end of the town, bought in his wife's name, then another house at the other end of town, then a little hamlet near the town, then a village, too, with serfs and everything. Finally, the fat man, having served God and the Tsar and earned universal regard, leaves the service, moves to his new home and becomes a landowner, a hospitable Russian country gentleman, and there he lives, and prospers. After his demise his thin heirs gallop through their patrimony in the true Russian manner. It was reflections of practically this kind that occupied Chichikov while he observed the company, and in consequence he finally joined the fat men, among whom he encountered almost exclusively familiar faces: the public prosecutor with his thick, coal-black eyebrows and a slightly drooping left eyelid that seemed to wink and say: "Here, old chap, let's slip into the next room and I'll tell you a story"—but who was, in fact, a serious and taciturn man; the postmaster, a squat fellow, but a wit and a philosopher; the President of the Chambers, a most sagacious and congenial man,—all of whom greeted him like an old friend, which honour Chichikov returned with a slightly oblique bow, delivered, however, not without pleasantness. Here he also made the acquaintance of the most courteous and obliging landowner Manilov and the rather clumsy-looking Sobakevich, who there and then stepped on his toes, saying, "Beg your pardon." Here, too, he was presented with an invitation to whist, which he accepted with an equally gracious bow. They sat at the green baize table and did not rise again until supper. All conversation totally ceased, as always happens when people at last get down to real business. Although the postmaster was a most garrulous man, even he, once the cards were dealt, put on a pensive expression, covering his upper lip with his lower and retaining this aspect throughout the game. When making his play he slapped the card hard down on the table, exclaiming, if it were a queen, "Off with you, you old priest's wife!" if a king: "Go to it, you Tambov peasant!" While the president reiterated: "That'll be one on his nose! That'll be one on her nose!" Sometimes as the cards hit the table the players exclaimed: "Come what may! If you've nothing better, lead diamonds!" or else: "Hearts of Gold!" or: "Spades! Spadrillo! Spadrango!" and even simply: "Spads!" calling out the names they had christened the various suits in their company. At the end of the game they argued, as was their custom, fairly heatedly. Our visitor argued too, but somehow with great adroitness, so that the others could see that he was arguing, yet arguing agreeably. He never said: "You led", but: "you were so good as to lead," "I had the honour to beat your deuce" and so forth. In

order to reconcile his opponents still further, he would
then invite them all to take a pinch from his silver enamelled
snuff-box, at the bottom of which they noticed two violets
placed there for their aroma. Our visitor's attention was
particularly caught by the landowners Manilov and Sobakevich, whom we have mentioned above. He at once made
enquiries about them, drawing the president and the postmaster slightly to one side. The few questions he put evi-
denced not idle curiosity, but rather a thoroughness: for,
first of all, he asked how many serfs each of them had, and
what state their properties were in, and only then did he
ask after their first names and patronymics. In a brief time
he succeeded in totally charming both of them. The landowner Manilov, a man still in the vigour of youth, with
eyes as sweet as sugar, which he screwed up when he smiled,
was quite smitten by Chichikov. He shook his hand hard
and long and implored him to honour him with a visit
to his estate, which, in his own words, was a mere fifteen
versts from the town gate. To which Chichikov retorted,
most graciously inclining his head and sincerely squeezing
Manilov's hand, that he was not only willing to comply,
but even regarded it as his most sacred duty. Sobakevich
also added rather laconically, "Come to my place too",
scraping his foot, which was shod in a boot of such gigantic
dimensions that it is most unlikely a foot could be found
anywhere to fit it, particularly in this day and age, when
giants are becoming extinct even in Russia.

The next day Chichikov repaired for dinner and a soirée
to the police chief, where after dining they sat down to
whist, playing solidly from three in the afternoon until
two in the morning. There, by the way, he made the
acquaintance of the landowner Nozdryov, a man of about
thirty, a dashing fellow, who after three or four words
began calling Chichikov by his first name. Nozdryov was
also chummy with the police chief and the public prosecutor, and was most affable towards them, but when they
sat down to play, the police chief and the public prosecutor studied his bids with suspiciously close attention and
scrutinized practically every card he played. The following
evening Chichikov spent at the home of the President of
the Chambers, who entertained his guests in his rather
stained dressing-gown, though there were two ladies

present. Then he attended a soirée at the vice-governor's, a large dinner at the monopolist's, a small dinner at the public prosecutor's, which in fact was as big as a large dinner; he was at a light luncheon after the midday service, given by the mayor, which was also as heavy as a dinner. In a word, he did not have to tarry at home for a single hour and he returned to his hotel only to sleep. Our visitor somehow managed to find his feet everywhere, and proved himself to be an experienced man of the world. Whatever the topic of conversation he was always able to hold his own: if the conversation turned to stud farms, he too would talk of stud farms; if they talked about hounds, here too he contributed very apposite remarks; should they touch on a prosecution brought by the revenue board—he showed that he was not altogether ignorant of legal chicanery either; if the subject raised was billiards—he was always on the ball; when they discussed virtue, he, too, deliberated most movingly on the subject of virtue, actually with tears in his eyes; if it was the preparation of mulled wine, he knew his stuff here, too; if the talk turned to customs inspectors and officials—he held forth as if he himself had been both an inspector and an official. But the remarkable thing was that he knew how to invest all this with a certain dignity, and was able to conduct himself so well. He spoke neither loudly nor too quietly, but exactly as was appropriate. In a word, whichever way you look at it he was a very proper man. All the officials were pleased with the arrival of a new person in their midst. The governor delivered himself of the opinion that Chichikov was a law-abiding man; the public prosecutor that he was a practical man; the colonel of gendarmes declared that he was a man of learning; the President of the Chambers that he was a knowledgeable and honourable man; the police chief that he was an honourable and civil man; and the police chief's wife that he was a man of the utmost civility and courtesy. Even Sobakevich himself, who rarely found anything good to say about anyone, upon returning late from town and, having undressed and lain down on the bed beside his scrawny wife, said to her: "I spent the evening at the governor's, dear heart, and had dinner at the police chief's, and made the acquaintance of Collegiate Councellor Pavel Ivanovich Chichikov: a most engaging man!" To which his good wife retorted: "Hm!" and gave him a kick.

Such was the opinion, most flattering to our visitor, that was formed of him in the town, and it remained in force until a peculiar trait of this visitor and the undertaking he launched, about which the reader shall learn forthwith, plunged almost the entire town into total bewilderment.

CHAPTER TWO

By now our visitor had been in the town for more than a week, visiting and going out to dinner, and in general having a most congenial time, as they say. Finally he decided to transfer his visits to outside the town and to pay the promised calls on the landowners Manilov and Sobakevich. Perhaps he was prompted here by some other more cogent reason, by a business more serious and closer to his heart. But the reader will be apprised of all this gradually and in good time, if he has the patience to read through the story we offer him, long though it be, which will grow in breadth and scope as it nears the end and culmination of the affair. The coachman Selifan had received instructions to harness the horses early in the morning to the chaise; Petrushka was ordered to remain at home and keep an eye on the room and the case. At this point the reader might well make the acquaintance of these two serfs of our hero. Although, of course, they are not such prominent characters, being of the kind termed secondary or even tertiary, although the main moves and springs of our poem repose not on them, even if they do touch them in odd place and involve them slightly—but the author likes excessively to be circumstantial in all things, and in this respect, despite the fact that he is himself a Russian, he wishes to be as punctilious as a German. This will not take up much time, or space, however, because little need be added to that which the reader already knows, namely that Petrushka sported a too-large brown frockcoat (one of his master's cast-offs) and, like people of his class, had a large nose and lips. By character he inclined more to the taciturn than to the loquacious; he even had a noble aspiration towards enlightenment, that is towards the reading of books, the content of which bothered him not in the slightest: it was absolutely immaterial to him whether he read the adventures of an amorous hero, or simply an ABC book, or a prayer book—he read everything with equal attention; hand him a manual of chemistry and he would not demur. He enjoyed not so much what he read as the act of reading, or to be more precise, the very process of reading, the remarkable way those letters combined to produce some word or other, a word which sometimes meant the devil only knows what. This reading was usually done in a supine position in the hallway, on the bed, the paliasse on which had been worn in consequence to the thinness and flatness of a pancake. Besides his passion for reading he had two other habits, which constituted his two remaining characteristics: he did not undress to sleep, but lay down as he was, complete with frockcoat, and he carried about with him his own particular aura, a special miasma, suggesting a long lived-in room, so that he only needed to roll out his bedding somewhere, be it in a hitherto unoccupied room, and to lug in his overcoat and chattels, and it would at once seem as though people had been sleeping here these past ten years. Chichikov, being a most pernickety, finicky man and even squeamish in certain instances, taking a fresh noseful of air in the morning would frown, shake his head, and say: "What's the matter with you, damn you, d'you sweat a lot or something? I wish you'd go to the bath-house sometimes." To which Petrushka would not reply, but would immediately make a show of great activity: he would either advance on his master's coat with a clothes brush, or set about tidying things up. There is no knowing what he was thinking while he thus remained silent—perhaps he was saying to himself: "You're a fine one yourself, not sick of saying the same thing forty times over"—God knows, it is hard to tell what thoughts are passing through a house serf's head while his master is delivering an admonition. So this is all I can say about Petrushka for the time being. The coachman Selifan was quite a different kettle of fish... But the author feels somewhat ashamed to be occupying his readers at such length with people of low rank, knowing from experience how loath they are to acquaint themselves with the lower

classes. For such is the Russian character: a passionate longing to rub shoulders with those who are if only one notch
higher on the scale of ranks, and a nodding acquaintance
with a count or a prince is worth more than any number
of intimate friendships. The author even feels some anxiety over his own hero, who is a mere collegiate counsellor.
Court counsellors may perhaps stoop to such an acquaintance, but as for those who have already scrambled their
way up to generals,* they, God knows, might even cast
one of those contemptuous glances which a man cast
proudly on anything crawling at his feet or, even worse,
might pass by with killing disregard. But however regret-
table are both such attitudes we must anyway return to
our hero. Thus having issued the necessary instructions the
previous evening and waking very early in the morning,
sponging himself down from head to toe, something he did
only on the Sabbath—for it was indeed Sunday—shaving in
such a manner that his cheeks acquired the softness and
lustre of satin, donning his cranberry-red, shot-silk tailcoat and then a greatcoat lined with bearskin, he descended the staircase, supported now on one side, now on the
other, by the servant, and took his seat in his chaise. The
chaise thundered out of the hotel gates on to the street.
A priest walking by doffed his cap; a gaggle of urchins in
grubby shirts stretched out their hands, intoning: "Sir,
something for a poor orphan!" The coachman, observing
that one of these was a great adept at jumping on the
running board, took a swipe at him with his whip, and the
chaise bounced away along the cobblestones. The striped
barrier in the distance, was a joy to espy, for it proclaimed
that this roadway, like all earthly torment, would soon
come to an end; after knocking his head a few more times
fairly hard against the carriage roof Chichikov at last felt
the carriage rolling along soft ground. Hardly was the town
behind them when the vegetation on both sides of the road
gave way to the sort of shrubs and scrub that are normal in
our country; tussocks, a fir-wood, mangy, low clumps of
young pines, the scorched trunks of old ones; wild heather

* A reference to the Table of Ranks, instituted in 1722 by Peter the
Great for civil servants, army officers and courtiers.
   There were fourteen ranks in all, the first being the highest.

and similar rubbish. They encountered villages strung along
the roadside, the houses like so many stacks of old firewood, topped by grey roofs whose intricately carved eaves
hung beneath them like embroidered hand-towels. Groups
of peasants wearing sheepskin coats sat yawning, in their
customary manner, on the benches in front of the gates.
Women with fat faces peered out of the upper windows;
the occasional calf gazed from a lower window or a pig
thrust out its blunt snout. In a word, all the usual sights.
After covering fifteen versts Chichikov thought that he
should by now have reached Manilov's village, but the six-
teenth verst flew by too, and there was still no sight of the
village and if they had not come upon two peasants they
probably would never have found their bearings. To the
question, was it far to the village of Zamanilovka, the peasants doffed their hats, and one of them, the more intelligent of the two, who sported a wedge-shaped beard, answered:

"Manilovka, not Zamanilovka by any chance?"

"Ah yes, Manilovka."

"Manilovka! Well you go another verst, and there you
have it, straight to the right, that is."

"To the right?" repeated the coachman.

"Aye to the right," said the peasant, "that'll be your
way to Manilovka; but there's no Zamanilovka round
these parts. That's what they call it, see, I mean its name
is Manilovka, but there's no Zamanilovka round here.
You'll see the house there, right up on the hill, a brick
house two storeys high, the manor house, the one the
master himself lives in, that is. That's your Manilovka, but
there's no Zamanilovka here, and never has been."

They set off in search of Manilovka. After driving for
two versts, they came to a turn on to a country track,
but went on for what seemed a further two, then three,
then four versts, and still could see no brick, double-sto-
reyed house. Then Chichikov remembered that if a friend invited you to call on him in his village fifteen versts from
town, you could be fairly certain you would have a good
thirty to travel. The village of Manilovka could have
lured few by its setting. The manor house stood in isolation on the brow of a hill exposed to all winds that might
ever chance to blow; the slope of the hill on which it

stood was clothed in a lawn. Scattered about it after the English manner were clumps of lilac bushes and yellow acacia; half a dozen birch trees raised their mangy foliage aloft. Two of them shaded a summer-house with a flattened green dome, pale blue wooden columns and the inscription "Temple of Solitary Contemplation"; further down there was a pond, covered with duckweed, something, moreover, which is no oddity in the English gardens of Russian landowners. At the foot of this eminence and partly on the slope itself, a number of shabby dark huts stood this way and that, and our hero, for some obscure reason, at once sat about counting them, arriving at over 200: between them there was not a single tree nor a scrap of greenery, nothing but the ugly log walls staring him in the face. The scene was enlivened by two peasant women, who, with their skirts picturesquely gathered up and tucked in on all sides, waded kneedeep about the pond, dragging behind them by two wooden yokes a tattered drag-net, in which they had snared two crawfish and a stray shimmering roach; the women seemed to be quarrelling amongst themselves and bickering about something. Afar off to one side lay the forest, a dark dreary blue. Even the weather contributed to the general effect: it was not a bright day, nor exactly was it overcast, but a sort of pale grey colour like that only found in the old uniforms of those regular garrison soldiers, a peaceful force, but inclined to drunkenness on the Lord's day. To complete the picture a cockerel was also in evidence, that herald of changeable weather, who, for all that his head had been pecked through to the brain by the beaks of other cocks for the usual reasons of philandering, crowed throatily and even flapped his wings, as tattered as old bast mats. Chichikov now observed the owner himself standing on the porch in a green Châlons frockcoat, his hand held to his brow to shade his eyes, the better to see the carriage that had driven up. As the chaise rolled up to the porch his eyes sparkled with joy and a smile spread across his countenance.

"Pavel Ivanovich!" he exclaimed at last, when Chichikov clambered out of the chaise. "So you remembered us at last!"

The two friends embraced fervently and Manilov led his guest inside. Although the time it will take them to traverse the vestibule, anteroom and dining-room is rather limited, we shall nonetheless try to make good use of it and to say something about the master of the house. But here the author must confess that such an undertaking is very difficult. It is much easier to describe big characters: there you have only to hurl the paints on to the canvas—black burning eyes, beetling eyebrows, a furrowed brow, a cloak, black or flame-red, thrown over the shoulder—and the portrait is complete; but as for all these gentlemen who are legion in the world, who in appearance are much like one another, yet when you look closer at them you notice many highly elusive yet distinctive features— these gentlemen are terribly hard to portray. Here you have to concentrate your mind, if all these subtle, almost invisible features are to come into focus before your eyes, and eyes even adept in the science of observation have to be strained to the utmost.

God alone might just have been able to say what Manilov's character was like. There is a type of nondescript men, neither one thing nor the other, neither fish nor fowl, as the proverb has it. Perhaps we should rank Manilov amongst their number. To look at he was a handsome man; his features were not unpleasing, but this pleasantness seemed to be overloaded with sugar: his mannerisms and turns of phrase contained something that besought favourable disposition and acquaintance. His smile was alluring, he was fair, with pale blue eyes. In the first minute of conversation with him you could not help thinking: "What a nice, kind person he is!" You would not think anything in the second minute, but in the third you would curse inwardly: "Drat him!" and you would move further away, for if you did not move away you would be bored sick. You would never hear from him a single lively or challenging word of the sort you would hear from practically anyone else when you spoke on a subject that touched him to the quick. Everyone has such a pet subject: with one it is borzoi dogs; another will fancy himself a great music-lover, amazingly sensitive to its hidden profundities; a third is known for his fondness of good food; a fourth likes to play a role if only one tiny notch higher than that properly assigned to him; a fifth, whose desires are more limited, dreams of going for a stroll arm-in-arm with an aide-de-camp to the Emperor, showing off to his friends, acquaintances and even strangers; a sixth was born with the sort of hand that feels a supernatural longing to bend back the corner of some ace, or a deuce of diamonds for a quarter-stake, while the hand of a seventh is itching to enforce proper order, to get at the face of a station master or a cab-driver—in a word, everyone has a pet subject, but Manilov had none. At home he spoke very little and spent most of the time in thought and reflection, but as for what he was thinking of, that, once again, the Lord alone perhaps knew. You could not exactly say he took an interest in running his estate: he never even drove out to his fields, and the estate more or less looked after itself. When his bailiff said: "Well, master, it would be a good idea to do such-and-such," he would usually respond, "Yes, not a bad idea", drawing on his pipe, a habit he had acquired while still in the army, where he was considered a most modest, tactful and well-educated officer. "Yes, not a bad idea at all," he would repeat. When a peasant came up to him, scratching the back of his head to ask, "Master, may I go off and do a job to earn some tax money", "Go, by all means," he would say, pulling on his pipe, and it would never even enter his head that the peasant was going on a binge. Sometimes, as he gazed from the porch into the yard or on to his pond, he would say how fine it would be if they were to dig a subterranean passage from the house, or to erect a stone bridge across the pond, with stalls along both sides, where merchants would sit and ply those petty wares so essential to the peasants. As he said this his eyes would take on an expression of extraordinary sugariness and his face a look of utter contentment; nevertheless all these projects began and ended with his words. A book always lay in his study with a book-mark at page fourteen, a book he had been reading continuously for the past two years. In his house there was permanently something lacking: his drawing-room was furnished with a fine suite, upholstered in foppish silk which had clearly not been cheap; but there had not been enough of it for the last two armchairs, which were covered in coarse matting; he would invariably warn his guests, year after year: "Pray do not sit in those chairs, they are not quite ready yet." In one room there was no furniture at all, although it had been his habit to declare in the days immediately after his wedding: "Sweetheart, tomorrow we really must get down to it and have some furniture put in this room, if only temporarily." In the evenings a most ornate candelabra of dark bronze adorned with the three Graces and an ornate mother-of-pearl base would be set on the table, and beside it a simple brass invalid of a candlestick, lopsided and covered in tallow-grease, and this was not noticed by the master, by his lady, or by the servants. As for his wife... *à propos*, they were totally content with each other. Although more than eight years of married life had elapsed, each of them would still bring the other some tidbit: a morsel of apple, a sweetmeat, or perhaps a little nut and would say in a touchingly tender voice, expressive of perfect love: "Open mouthies, sweetie, and I'll pop in this morsel." Needless to say, mouthies would open at this suggestion most gracefully. For birthdays special surprise gifts were prepared: such as a miniature toothpick case sown with beads. And very often, as they sat on the settee, suddenly for no apparent reason, the one would lay aside his pipe and the other her work, if indeed it was in her hands at that moment, and they would plant upon each other's lips a kiss of such languor and duration that you could smoke a small cheroot from beginning to end while it lasted. In a word, they were, what is known as a happy couple. Of course, we might remark that there are many other things to do in a house apart from exchanging lengthy kisses and surprise gifts, and there are many different questions we might ask. For instance, why did stupidity and waste prevail in the kitchen? Why was the larder so empty? Why have a thief for a housekeeper? Why were the servants slovenly and drunken? Why did all the house servants sleep so late and carouse wildly all the rest of the time? But all these are base matters, and Mrs Manilov had been properly brought up. And a proper upbringing is, of course, received in boarding schools for young ladies. And in boarding schools for young ladies, as everyone knows, three main subjects constitute the basis of all human virtue: French, essential to the happiness of family life; piano playing, to provide pleasurable minutes for the husband; and finally the house-keeping proper, that is, knitting tiny purses and other surprise gifts. However, the methods do change and improve, especially nowadays; all this depends more on the good sense and abilities of the ladies who run the boarding schools. In some boarding schools piano playing may come first, then French, and finally housekeeping. And occasionally you find that they start with the housekeeping part, that is, the knitting of surprise gifts, then move on to French, and only then to the piano. Procedures differ. It would not be amiss to note here, too, that Mrs Manilov... But I must confess I greatly fear talking about ladies, and besides it is time I returned to our heroes, who have now been standing for several minutes before the doors of the sitting-room, each inviting the other to proceed.

"Pray, do not discommode yourself on my account, I shall follow," said Chichikov.

"No, Pavel Ivanovich, no, you are my guest," said Manilov, gesturing towards the door.

"I beg you, please do not trouble yourself. Please, after you," said Chichikov.

"Now you must forgive me, I cannot allow such a charming and educated guest to follow behind me."

"Why educated?... No, please, after you."

"But no: please be so kind as to lead the way."

"But why?"

"Well, because!" said Manilov with a pleasant smile.

Finally the two friends entered the doorway sideways and slightly squashed each other.

"Allow me to present my wife," said Manilov. "Sweetheart! It's Pavel Ivanovich!"

Chichikov did indeed see a lady, whom, while exchanging civilities in the doorway with Manilov, he had not noticed at all. She was not unattractive and was becomingly dressed. She looked well in a pale silk morning-dress; with her small, slender hand she tossed something hastily onto a table, and crumpled a batiste handkerchief with embroidered corners in her fingers. She rose from the settee, and Chichikov stepped up to her and kissed her hand, not without pleasure. Mrs Manilov averred, slurring her 'r's elegantly, that his visit was a great source of joy to them, and that never a day passed without her husband mentioning him.

"Ah, yes," said Manilov, "indeed she herself is foreve

asking me: 'Now why doesn't your friend come to see us?'
—'Just wait, sweetheart, he'll come.' And now at last you
have favoured us with your visit. Indeed, you've given us
such pleasure ... a May day ... a celebration for the heart..."

Upon hearing that things had already reached a celebration for the heart, Chichikov was somewhat embarrassed
and modestly replied that he had neither an exalted name
nor even a prominent rank.

"You have everything," interrupted Manilov with the
same pleasant smile, "you have everything, even more than
everything."

"How did you find our town?" chimed in Mrs Manilov.
"Did you have a pleasant time there?"

"A very fine town, an excellent town," replied Chichikov, "and I spent my time most pleasantly: the most
charming society."

"What do you think of our governor?" asked Mrs Manilov.

"Is he not the most distinguished and amiable of men?"
added Manilov.

"Indeed he is," concurred Chichikov, "a most distinguished man. How well he exercises his duties, how well
he understands them! One could only wish there were
more like him."

"How well he can receive anyone, you know, and conduct himself *avec délicatesse*," adjoined Manilov with a
smile, and from the sheer pleasure of it he screwed up his
eyes, almost completely, like a cat that is being gently
tickled behind the ears.

"A very charming and pleasant man," continued Chichikov, "and so skilful! I would never even have imagined it.
How well he embroiders those pretty things for the home!
He showed me a purse he had made himself: rare are the
ladies who can embroider with such skill."

"And the vice-governor? Is he not a dear man?" asked
Manilov, once again narrowing his eyes slightly.

"A very, very worthy man," agreed Chichikov.

"But might I enquire: what were your impressions
of the chief of police? Did you not think him a most pleasant man?"

"Extraordinarily pleasant, and such a clever, such a
ell-read man! We played whist at his house with the

public prosecutor and the President of the Chambers till cockcrow; a very, very worthy man."

"Well, and what is your opinion of the police chief's wife?" asked Mrs Manilov. "A most delightful woman, would you not say?"

"Oh indeed, she is one of the most worthy women I know," answered Chichikov.

Thereupon they discussed the President of the Chambers and the postmaster, and in this manner worked their way through almost all the officials in the town, who all turned out to be the most worthy people.

"Do you spend all your time in the country?" Chichikov enquired, at last, in his turn.

"Mostly in the country," answered Manilov, "we do occasionally visit the town, but for the sole purpose of enjoying the society of well-educated people. You grow a bit rusty, you know, living shut up here all the time."

"How true, how true," echoed Chichikov.

"Of course," continued Manilov, "it would be quite a different matter if one had a better class of neighbours, if one had the sort of person with whom, so to speak, one could talk about refinement, about good manners, with whom one could follow some science or other, don't you know, that would stir up the soul, so to say, and send it soaring and soaring..."

Here he was about to voice something more, but perceiving that he had rather let his tongue run away with him, he merely dug the air with his hand and continued:

"To be sure, the country and solitude would be very enjoyable then. But there is positively no one... All one can do is to read the occasional issue of *Son of the Fatherland*."

Chichikov expressed his full agreement with this sentiment, adding that nothing could be more pleasant than living in retirement, delighting in the spectacle of nature and occasionally reading some book or other...

"But do you know," adjoined Manilov, "without a friend, with whom one can share things, all this..."

"Why, how true, how very, very true!" interjected Chichikov. "What are all the treasures of the world wor~ in comparison! For, as one wise man has said, 'Seek ~ money, seek the society of good people.' "

"And then, you know, Pavel Ivanovich!" exclaimed Manilov, his face taking on an expression that was not merely sweet, but actually cloying, like that cough mixture which a cunning society doctor has mercilessly sugared to the expected delight of his patient. "You feel something, in a manner of speaking, like spiritual delight... Such as, for example, now, when fortune has granted me the happiness, I might say, the exemplary beneficence of talking to you and delighting in your pleasant conversation..."

"Oh come, my pleasant conversation?... I am a man of utter insignificance, that's all," replied Chichikov.

"Oh no, Pavel Ivanovich! Allow me to be frank: I would gladly give up half my fortune in exchange for a portion of those merits which you possess!"

"On the contrary, I, for my part, would consider it the most extreme..."

We can only guess where this mutual effusion of sentiment by the two friends would have led, had not the servant entered to announce that dinner was served.

"Shall we go in?" said Manilov. "You must forgive us if we do not serve the kind of dinner you will find in fine houses and in the capitals: we eat simple fare here, our Russian cabbage soup, to start with, but it's offered from the heart. Shall we go in?"

Here they disputed a little while longer about who would be the first to proceed, and finally Chichikov sidled past his host into the dining-room.

Two boys stood waiting in the dining-room, Manilov's sons, who were already old enough to eat at the table, but still on high chairs. Attending them was a tutor, who bowed politely and with a smile. The lady of the house sat down behind the soup tureen; the guest was seated between his host and hostess, and the footman fastened napkins round the necks of the children.

"What darling children," said Chichikov, looking at them, "and how old would they be?"

"The elder is seven, and the younger had his sixth birthday only yesterday," said Mrs Manilov.

"Themistoclus!" said Manilov, addressing the elder, who was endeavouring to free his chin from the napkin which the footman had tied round it.

Chichikov slightly raised his eyebrows, hearing this partly Greek name, to which, for some unknown reason, Manilov had appended the suffix "us", but instantly tried to compose his features to their usual expression.

"Themistoclus, tell me, which is the best city in France?"

Here the tutor turned his full attention on Themistoclus and fixed him with a ferocious stare, but relaxed and nodded his head when Themistoclus said:

"Paris."

"And which is our best city?" enquired Manilov further. Once again the tutor fixed the boy with his stare.

"St Petersburg," answered Themistoclus.

"And which other one?"

"Moscow," answered Themistoclus.

"What a clever boy, the darling!" exclaimed Chichikov, and, turning a look of amazement upon the Manilovs, continued: "Really, I must say! Such knowledge at such a tender age! I am bound to tell you that this child will display great abilities."

"Oh you do not know him yet," replied Manilov, "he has a remarkable wit. Now the younger one, Alchides, he's not so quick, but as for this lad, when he sees something, a bug or a little beetle, his darling eyes will start to dance at once; he will run after it and watch it. I'm putting him down for the Diplomatic Service. Themistoclus," he continued, turning to the boy, "do you want to be an ambassador?"

"I do," replied Themistoclus, chewing a piece of bread and wagging his head from left to right.

At this moment the footman standing behind him wiped the ambassador's nose, and his was a very good timing, too, for otherwise a sizeable foreign droplet would have fallen into his soup. A conversation was now begun at the table about the pleasures of a quiet life, interrupted by the hostess's remarks about the local theatre and its actors. The tutor most attentively watched the speakers and, the moment he noticed that they were about to laugh, he at once opened his mouth and laughed with gusto. He was probably a grateful man and wished thereby to repay his employer for the good treatment accorded him. On one occasion, however, his face took on a severe look and he fiercely thumped the table with his fork, glaring at the children sitting opposite him. This was when Themistoclus bit Alchides's ear, and Alchides, screwing up his eyes, opened his mouth to emit a wail, but sensing that this action was very likely to cost him his dinner, he recomposed his features and with tears in his eyes set about gnawing a mutton bone, which caused both his cheeks to glisten with fat. The hostess repeatedly addressed herself to Chichikov with the words:

"You are not eating anything, you have taken very little."

To which Chichikov would invariably reply:

"I thank you most humbly, I'm full, a pleasant conversation is better than any dish."

They had already left the table. Manilov was extremely contented, and with his hand supporting Chichikov's back he was about to guide his guest into the drawing room, when the guest suddenly announced with a look of great significance that he intended to discuss a most important matter with his host.

"In that case allow me to invite you into my study," said Manilov and conducted him into a smallish room, whose window looked out on to the distant forest.

"This is my little den," said Manilov.

"A delightful little room," said Chichikov casting his eyes around.

The room was indeed rather attractive: the walls were painted a greyish pale-blue, there were four upright chairs, one armchair, a desk on which lay the inevitable book with its bookmark that we have already had occasion to mention, and some papers covered with writing, but what there was most of was tobacco. It was to be found in a variety of forms: in paper bags and in a tobacco jar, and simply, poured in a heap on the desk. On both sills were little mounds of ash, knocked out of the pipe and stacked with a measure of care in most attractive little rows. It was evident that this was something of a pastime for the master of the house.

"Do please seat yourself in this armchair," said Manilov. "You will find it most comfortable."

"I'll sit on a chair if I may."

"Please allow me not to allow you," said Manilov with a smile. "This armchair is specially assigned for my guests: you simply must sit in it like it or not."

Chichikov sat down.

"Please allow me to fill you a pipe."

"Thank you, I do not smoke," answered Chichikov softly, with a look of seeming regret.

"Why is that?" enquired Manilov as softly and with a look of regret.

"I never formed the habit, I'm afraid; they say a pipe dries one up."

"Please allow me to point out that that is a prejudice. I would even submit that smoking a pipe is much more healthy than taking snuff. In our regiment there was a lieutenant, a most excellent and cultivated gentleman, who never removed his pipe from his mouth, not only at meals, but even, would you believe it, in all other places too. And now he is already over forty, but, with the grace of God, to this day in perfect health."

Chichikov observed that such things did indeed happen and there were many things in nature which were beyond the comprehension of even a broad intellect.

"But please allow me first to make one request..." he ventured in a voice which rang with a strange or almost strange note, and for some unknown reason looked round. Manilov also looked round for some unknown reason. "How long ago did you submit your census list?"

"Well, a long time ago. Truth to tell, I don't recall exactly."

"And since that time have many of your peasants died?"

"Well, I couldn't say; I think we would have to ask my bailiff that." He called out to his manservant: "Fetch the bailiff, he should be here today."

The bailiff appeared. He was a man nearing forty, beardless, clad in a frockcoat and, visibly, enjoying a most peaceful life, because his face looked plump and chubby, whilst the sallowness of his skin and his bloated little eyes betrayed his excessive familiarity with feather beds and pillows. It was at once evident that he rose to his position as did all estate bailiffs: he started as servant boy who could read and write, then he married the housekeeper or, perhaps, the maid who was the mistress's favourite, became the steward and then the bailiff. Once promoted bailiff, he naturally did like all bailiffs: he mixed with the wealthier villagers and stood god-father to their children, upped the rents of the poorer one, slept late in the morning, until after eight o'clock, then called for the samovar and had breakfast.

"I say, my good man, how many of our peasants have died since we put in the census list?"

"How many? Well... Lots have," replied the bailiff and thereupon hiccupped, half covering his mouth with his spade-like hand.

"I must admit I thought so myself," said Manilov, "Yes, indeed, a great many have died!" Here he turned to Chichikov and added for good measure, "Indeed, a great many."

"But how many exactly?" asked Chichikov.

"Yes, how many?" repeated Manilov.

"How can I say? No one knows how many died, nobody counted them."

"Yes, precisely," said Manilov, turning to Chichikov. "I also presumed the mortality was high. It's quite unknown how many have died."

"Count them up, will you," said Chichikov to the bailiff, "and make a detailed list of all their names."

"Yes, of all their names," said Manilov.

The bailiff said, "Yessir!" and withdrew.

"And for what purpose might you want this?" asked Manilov when the bailiff had left.

This question appeared to incommode his guest; his face took on a somewhat strained expression, causing him to flush—from the strenuous effort to express something that could not be easily put into words. And to be sure, Manilov was to hear such strange and extraordinary things as had never before been heard by the ear of man.

"You ask, for what purpose? My purpose is this: I would like to buy some peasants..." said Chichikov, stammering to an abrupt halt.

"But allow me to enquire," said Manilov, "how would you like to buy the peasants: with the land, or to take away, that is, without the land?"

"No, what I want are not exactly peasants," said Chichikov. "It's the dead ones I want..."

"Oh? I beg your pardon... I'm a little hard of hearing, I thought I heard a very strange word..."

"I propose to acquire the dead ones, who, however, figure in the census as alive," said Chichikov.

Manilov thereupon dropped his pipe on the floor and gaped at Chichikov in wide-mouthed astonishment for several minutes. The two friends, who had been discoursing so agreeably on the gratifications of a convivial life, were now frozen, staring into each other's eyes, like those portraits which in days gone by were hung opposite each other on the two sides of a mirror. Manilov bent down to pick up his pipe and glanced up at Chichikov, trying to see if there was a smile on his lips, implying that he had been joking; but there was nothing like this to be seen; on the contrary, Chichikov's features were even more composed than usual; then Manilov wondered whether his guest might not suddenly have lost his wits and he peered at him in alarm; but his guest's eyes were perfectly clear, they did not burn with a wild, restless fire, such as dances in the eyes of a madman, everything was proper and in order. No matter how Manilov racked his brains, wondering how to react and what to do, he could think of nothing other than to exhale the remaining smoke from his mouth in a very fine stream.

"So, I would like to know if you would transfer to me those serfs who are not in reality alive but are alive in legal terms, sell them to me, or make over in whatever manner you think best?"

But Manilov was so taken aback and nonplussed, that he could only stare.

"I believe you are in two minds about this?" observed Chichikov.

"I?... No, it's not that," said Manilov, "it's just that I can't quite grasp... I'm sorry... Of course, I did not receive such a brilliant education as, so to speak, can be seen in your every movement; I lack the lofty art of eloquence... Perchance here ... in the explanation which you have just expressed ... there is some hidden meaning... Perhaps you expressed yourself thus for the sake of eloquence?"

"No," interjected Chichikov, "no, I mean exactly what I said: I want the souls which are indeed dead."

Manilov was utterly at a loss. He felt that he ought to do something, to ask something, but the devil only knew what. But all he did was exhale smoke once again, this time not from his mouth, but through his nostrils.

"Well then, since you have no objections, let us get

down to the drawing-up of the deed of purchase," said Chichikov.

"How do you mean, a deed for dead souls?"

"Ah, you're wrong there!" said Chichikov. "We shall put them down as living men, just as it is stated in the census list. I make it a rule never to deviate from the laws of the land, although I suffered for this in the service, such is my custom, with your permission an obligation is something sacred to me, and the law—I turn awe-struck before the law."

These last words were much to Manilov's liking, but he still could not fathom what was going on and instead of replying set about puffing on his pipe with such vigour that it finally started to wheeze like a bassoon. It was as if he were trying to draw from it an opinion pertaining to such an unheard-of circumstance; but the pipe wheezed and nothing more.

"Perhaps you have some doubts?"

"Oh! Heavens no, none at all! I say that not because I have any, so to speak, critical prejudice about you. But forgive me for suggesting it, only would not such as undertaking or, to put it more precisely, negotiation, be somewhat at odds with the civic decrees and Russia's further prospects?"

Here Manilov with a slight motion of his head cast a very significant look at Chichikov's face, all his features and his pursed lips taking on an expression of such profundity as had perhaps never before been beheld on a human face, excepting perhaps for some too clever minister, and even then when he was puzzling over a hopeless brain-twister.

But Chichikov declared quite simply that such an undertaking, or negotiation, would not be at odds with the civic decrees and Russia's further prospects, and a moment later added that the treasury would even derive a profit therefrom, for it would receive the legal dues.

"Do you think so?..."

"I believe that it will be a good thing."

"Ah, if it is a good thing, that is another matter: I have no objections," said Manilov, feeling completely reassured.

"It only remains now to agree on the price."

"What do you mean on the price?" Manilov began and stopped. "Surely you are not suggesting that I would take money for souls which in a certain sense have finished their existence? If indeed such a, shall we say, fantastic desire has arisen, then for my part I shall simply give them to you and I shall pay the transfer fees myself."

The historian of the events described would be greatly at fault if he omitted to say that our guest was overcome with delight when he heard these words uttered by Manilov. Rational and moderate creature though he was, he nearly jumped like a goat, something which is generally known only to happen at the most powerful surges of joy. He twisted so violently in his seat that the woollen upholstery of the cushion burst; Manilov cast him a look of some bewilderment. Motivated by gratitude, Chichikov at once delivered himself of so many terms of appreciation that his host was quite overcome with confusion, he flushed all over, made a gesture of disavowal with his head, and assured his guest that it was an absolute trifle, that indeed he wanted to find some way of demonstrating his heartfelt attraction, the magnetism of the soul, so to say, and that, in a certain sense, dead souls were utter rubbish.

"Not rubbish at all," said Chichikov, squeezing his host's hand. Thereupon a deep sigh escaped him. He appeared to be in the mood for an outpouring of the heart; not without emotion did he at last utter the following words: "If only you knew what a service you are doing with what appears to you as rubbish to someone without kith or kin! For indeed, what have I not suffered? Like a barque tossed on the stormy seas... What persecutions, what victimizations have I not endured, what sorrow have I not tasted, and for what? For standing by the truth, for keeping my conscience clean, for reaching out my hand both to the helpless widow and to the sorrowing orphan!..." At this point he actually dabbed at an escaping tear with his handkerchief.

Manilov was profoundly moved. The two friends squeezed each other's hands at great length and stared long and silently into each other's eyes, eyes brimming with tears. Manilov was most loath to release the hand of our hero, and continued to squeeze it with such ardour that Chichikov was quite at a loss how to disengage it. Finally, having gradually worked it free, he said it would be just as well if they drew up the purchase deeds as soon as possible, and it would be excellent if Manilov himself would come into town. Then he took his hat and started to make his farewells.

"What? You want to leave so soon?" asked Manilov, suddenly coming to his senses with something close to alarm.

At this moment Mrs Manilov entered the study.

"Lizanka," said Manilov with a woebegone look. "Pavel Ivanovich is leaving us!"

"We must have bored Pavel Ivanovich," answered Mrs Manilov.

"Madam!" protested Chichikov. "Here, right here," he placed his hand on his heart, "yes, here there will always remain the delightful memory of the time I spent in your company, and believe me, there could be no greater bliss for me than to live with you, if not in the same house, then at least in the closest contiguity."

"Why, you know, Pavel Ivanovich," said Manilov, who found this idea greatly to his liking, "indeed how excellent it would be to live thus together, under one roof, and to philosophise about this and that in the shade of some elm-tree or something, to get to the very heart of things..."

"Oh! That would be paradise on earth!" said Chichikov with a deep sigh. "Farewell, dear madam!" he continued, stepping up to kiss Mrs Manilov's hand. "Farewell, most honourable friend! Do not forget my request!"

"Oh, rest assured!" answered Manilov. "We shall be parted for no more than two days."

They all went out into the dining-room.

"Farewell, darling sparrows!" said Chichikov to Alchides and Themistoclus who were playing with a wooden hussar, already missing one arm and his nose. "Farewell, my little dears. Please forgive me for not bringing you a present, because I must confess I did not even know of your existence in this world, but now, when I come again, I shall certainly bring something. I shall bring you a sabre: do you want a sabre?"

"Yes," answered Themistoclus.

"And for you a drum—would you not like a drum?" he continued, with a bow towards Alchides.

"Dwum," answered Alchides in a whisper, lowering his eyes bashfully.

"Good, I'll bring you a drum. A wonderful drum, and you'll go: turum-ru, tra-ta-ta, ta-ta-ta. Farewell, my sweet child! Farewell!" He kissed him on the head and turned to Manilov and his spouse, with a little chuckle, such as is usually addressed to parents as an indication of the innocence of their children's desires.

"Pavel Ivanovich, you really must stay!" said Manilov, after they had stepped out on to the porch. "Just look at those thunderclouds."

"They are only little thunderclouds," answered Chichikov.

"But do you know the way to Sobakevich's?"

"I wanted to ask you about that."

"Allow me to explain to your coachman at once." Manilov thereupon explained everything to the coachman most obligingly, addressing him in terms of great courtesy.

The coachman, hearing that he had to pass two turnings and take the third, said: "We'll get there all right, Your Honour", and Chichikov departed, sped on his way by much bowing and waving of handkerchiefs from his tiptoeing hosts.

For a long time thereafter Manilov remained standing on the porch, watching the chaise disappear into the distance, and even when it was quite lost to sight he still remained there, smoking his pipe. Finally he went back indoors, sat down on a chair and fell into reverie, rejoicing in spirit at the small pleasure he had been able to afford his guest. Then his thoughts imperceptibly strayed to other matters, and were borne off in heaven knows what direction. He thought about the happiness of a life of friendship, about how nice it would be to live with his friend on the bank of some river, then in his mind he saw a bridge built across this river, then there appeared a most enormous house with such a lofty belvedere that from it they could see as far as Moscow and they could sit there in the evenings, drinking tea in the open air and discussing various pleasing subjects. Then, that he and Chichikov arrived together in fine carriages at some social gathering, where they charmed all the guests with their courteous manners, and that the Tsar himself, learning of this great friendship, promoted them both to the rank of general, and then his thoughts became so hazy that Manilov himself could not sort them out. Suddenly Chichikov's strange request interrupted his dreams. Somehow his mind was especially incapable of grasping the idea; he turned it over this way and that but he simply could not understand it, and thus he sat smoking his pipe, right through till supper.

CHAPTER THREE

Meanwhile Chichikov sat in a mood of contentment in his chaise, which had already travelled far along the highway. It is already apparent from the preceding chapter what constituted the main object of his taste and inclinations, and it is therefore small wonder that he was soon thoroughly absorbed in this object, in body and in soul. The assumptions, estimates and considerations which wandered across his face were clearly most agreeable, for every minute they left behind them the traces of a smug smile. Thus occupied, he paid no attention to his coachman, who, pleased with the treatment Manilov's servants had accorded him, was making extremely business-like remarks to the dappled trace-horse harnessed on the right. This dappled horse was most cunning and made a mere show of pulling, while in fact the shaft-horse, a bay, and the other trace-horse, a light-chestnut, called Assessor because he had been bought from one, toiled away for all they were worth, so much so that their eyes betrayed the pleasure they received from this toil.

"You think you're smart! But I'll outsmart you," said Selifan, rising from his coach-box and lashing the shirker with his whip. "You do your job, you German pantaloon! The bay's an honourable horse, he does his duty, I'll gladly give him an extra bagful, because he's an honourable horse, and Assessor's also a good horse... What's this? Shaking our ears, are we? Listen when I talk to you, blockhead! Don't think I'll teach you bad habits, you dunce. Look at him, crawling along!" At this he gave him another lash with the whip, crying: "My, what a barbarian! A damned Bonaparte!" Then he shouted at them all: "Giddyap, my beauties!" and cracked his whip across all three, not by way of chastisement, but to show that he was pleased with them. Having thus conveyed his pleasure, he addressed himself to the dappled trace-horse again: "You think you can fool me? Oh no, you do the job properly if you want to be shown respect. Now those were good people at that house. I'm always happy to talk to a good man. I always get on well with a good fellow, we're fine friends: drink tea together or have a bite to eat—with pleasure, if he's a good man. Everyone respects a good man. Like our master now, everyone respects him, because, d'you hear, he's done his civil service, he's an allegiate consessor..."

Deliberating thus, Selifan finally strayed into the farthest realms of abstraction. If Chichikov had bent an ear, he would have learnt many details pertaining to his own person; but his thoughts were so taken up with his own subject that only a loud clap of thunder was able to make him come to his senses and look around him; the sky was entirely covered with thunderclouds and the dusty postroad was spattered with drops of rain. Then there was an even louder and closer thunderclap and the rain suddenly came pouring down in buckets. First, it took an oblique path through one window of the carriage, then it lashed down through the other, then changing its angle to an exact perpendicular it drummed on the roof; and now splashes started to spray him in the face. This obliged him to draw the leather blinds, with their two little peepholes, designed for the scrutinizing of the roadside views, and to bid Selifan drive faster. Selifan, also interrupted in the very middle of his discourse, twigged that this really was no time for lingering, promptly pulled out an ancient grey coat from under his coach-box, thrust his arms into the sleeves, seized up the reins in both hands and chivvied up his troika, which had been languidly ambling along, feeling pleasantly relaxed by his admonitory speeches. But Selifan could not for the life of him remember whether they had passed two or three turnings. Straining his memory, he realized that he must have gone past a great many turnings, all of which he had missed. Since a Russian will always figure what to do at moments of crisis without engaging in any lengthy deliberations, he turned right at the first crossroads and shouted: "Hey you, my honoured friends!" and whipped the horses into a gallop, giving little thought to where the road he had taken would lead.

The rain, however, seemed to be the persistent kind.

The dust on the road soon turned into mud and with every minute it became harder for the horses to drag the chaise forward. Chichikov was already becoming highly alarmed, as they had come this far without seeing Sobakevich's village. By his calculations they should have arrived long ago. He peered to either side, but it was so dark he could not see the nose before his face.

"Selifan!" he called at last, leaning out of the chaise.

"What is it, master?" answered Selifan.

"See if there's a village in sight!"

"No master, can't see one anywhere!"

Whereupon Selifan, with a swipe of his whip, gave voice to something, not exactly a song, but long and seemingly endless. It contained everything: all the exclamations and interjections used to spur horses on throughout all the length and breadth of Russia, adjectives of every kind taken completely pell-mell, as they came to his tongue. Things came to such a pass that in the end he was even calling the horses secretaries.

Meanwhile Chichikov noticed that the chaise was lurching from side to side and dealing him violent jolts; this suggested to him that they must have strayed from the road and were probably ploughing through a furrowed field. Selifan seemed to have made the same deduction, but he held his tongue.

"Hey, you rogue, what road do you think you've taken?" said Chichikov.

"But what can I do, master, it's the time of day: you can't see the whip it's that dark!" Saying this, Selifan caused the chaise to list so far to one side that Chichikov had to hold on with both hands. Only then did he notice that Selifan had been tippling.

"Hold tight, hold tight, you're going to tip us over!" he shouted.

"No, master, how could I do a thing like that," said Selifan. "Tipping us over would be bad, don't I know it, I'd never do that." He then started slightly to turn the chaise turning it more and more and finally turned it right over on its side. Chichikov measured his length in the mud. Selifan did, however, stop the horses, although they would in fact have stopped by themselves because they were totally exhausted. This so unforeseen an eventuality completely

astounded him. Clambering down from the box he stood
before the chaise, arms akimbo, while his master floundered
in the mud, trying desperately to extricate himself, and
after some consideration he declared:

"Well, what do you know, we did come a cropper!"

"Why, you're drunk!" said Chichikov.

"No, master, how could I be drunk? I know it's a bad
thing to be drunk. I had a chat with a friend, because you
can chat with a good man, there's nothing wrong in that;
and we had a bite together. There's no harm in having a
bite; it's not wrong to have a bite with a good man."

"And what did I tell you last time you got drunk? Hey?
Have you forgotten?" said Chichikov.

"No, Your Honour, how could I have forgotten? I know
my business. I know it's not proper to be drunk. I had a
chat with a good man because..."

"You wait and I'll give you such a whipping that you'll
soon find out how to chat with a good man!"

"As your worship sees fit," answered the all-accepting
Selifan, "if whip you must, then whip you must; I'll not
say nothing against that. And why shouldn't you whip me,
if there's cause, that's for the master to decide. There has
to be whipping because a peasant will get out of hand, and
you've got to keep order. If there's cause, whip me: why
shouldn't you?"

This line of argument left his master at a loss for an
answer. But at this moment it seemed fate itself had decided to take pity on him. Dogs could be heard barking somewhere. Overjoyed, Chichikov ordered Selifan to whip up
the horses. The Russian coachman has a keen sixth sense
in place of sight: with his eyes shut tight, he will tear along
blindly and yet will always arrive somewhere. Selifan,
unable to see a thing, pointed the horses so straight at the
village that he only stopped when the shaft of the carriage
collided with a fence and they simply could go no further.
All Chichikov could see through the thick blanket of pouring rain was something that looked like a roof. He sent
Selifan in search of the gate, a quest that would certainly
have been of long duration were there not in Russia, in
place of porters and gate-keepers, fierce dogs, who announced him so clamorously that he was forced to stop his
ears with his fingers. A light appeared in a little window,

casting a feeble beam as far as the fence, and revealing the whereabouts of the gate to our travellers. Selifan started knocking and shortly a little door in the gate opened. A figure emerged draped in a man's cloth coat, and the master and his servant heard a hoarse female voice:

"Who's knocking? What are you up to?"

"We're travellers, my good woman. Let us in for the night," said Chichikov.

"Well I never, shameless, aren't you," said the old woman, "what a time to arrive! This isn't an inn, you know, this is a lady's house."

"But what can we do, we lost our way. We can't spend the night in the steppe in weather like this, can we?"

"Yes, it's dark time, a bad time," added Selifan.

"Shut up, fool," said Chichikov.

"But who are you anyway?" asked the old woman.

"A nobleman, my good woman."

The word "nobleman" seemed to give the old woman cause for thought.

"Just wait, I'll tell the mistress," she announced and in about two minutes she was back again bearing a lamp.

The gates were opened. Now a faint light could be seen in another window too. The chaise drove into the yard and stopped before a small house which was hard to see properly in the darkness. Only one half of it was illuminated by the light emanating from the windows; they could also see a puddle before the house, directly in the path of that faint beam of light. The rain drummed on the wooden roof and poured in rivulets into the barrel set out to catch it. In the meantime the dogs went on barking in chorus: one, craning his head upwards, howled so assiduously as if he were earning God knows what fee for his toil; another rapped out his responses impatiently, and between the two rang, like a postman's bell, the indefatigable shrill yapping of no doubt a young puppy, and all this was drowned by a bass, probably that of an old patriarch, possessed of a sturdy canine nature, because he wheezed the wheeze of the choir counterbass, when the concert is in full swing: the tenors stand on tip-toe in their anxiety to hit a high note and everything around strives upwards, with heads thrown back, while he alone, his unshaven chin thrust into his cravat, crouches almost to the ground and from there raises his own note, which causes the windows to tremble and rattle. From the very barking of this choir, composed of such musicians, one had reason to think that it was a decent-sized village; but our drenched and frozen hero could think of nothing other than bed. Even before the chaise came to a complete standstill he had already alighted nimbly on to the porch, where he lurched and almost fell. Another woman stepped out on to the porch, younger than the first, but very similar to her. She led him inside. Chichikov stole two glances about him: the room had shabby, striped wallpaper; there were pictures of birds; between the windows hung ancient little mirrors in dark foliated frames; a letter, an old deck of cards, or a stocking was stuffed behind each mirror; a wall clock, its face decorated with flowers ... he had not the strength to observe anything more. His eyelids felt so sticky as if they had been smeared with honey. A minute later the mistress of the house entered, a lady of middle age, wearing some sort of night cap, donned in haste, with a flannel shawl about her neck, one of those smalltime landowners, who are forever whining about poor harvest and losses, who hold their heads somewhat inclined to one side, and in the meanwhile collect a bit of money in small calico bags, distributed in various chests of drawers. Into one bag they put all the silver rubles, in another all the fifty-kopek pieces, in a third the quarters, stuffing a small bag here and another one there so that there appears to be nothing in the drawers besides undergarments and bed jackets, and skeins of yarn, and a ripped old cape which will one day be made into a dress if ever a hole should be burned in an old one during the cooking of pancakes or meat pies on a holiday, or should it simply wear out by itself. But the dress will not be burnt nor wear out by itself; the old lady is thrifty and the cape is destined to lie many a year in its ripped form, then to be bequeathed in the deceased's will to the niece of a third cousin with all sorts of other junk.

Chichikov apologized for troubling her with his unexpected arrival.

"Never mind!" said the good lady. "Fancy travelling in this weather! Roaring and blowing and what not... You should have something to eat after your journey, of course, but at this time of night we can't start cooking."

Her words were interrupted by a strange hissing which caused our guest considerable alarm; it sounded as though the entire room was suddenly full of snakes; but looking up he realised that it was simply the wall clock taking a notion to chime. The hissing was followed by a wheezing, and finally, with an utmost exertion the clock chimed two o'clock with a noise like someone striking a broken pot with a stick, whereupon the pendulum resumed its quiet swinging from right to left.

Chichikov thanked his hostess, avowing that he needed nothing to eat, begging her not to worry about anything, that all he wanted was a bed for the night, and he merely wanted to know where he had strayed and how far it was from here to Sobakevich's estate, to which the old lady retorted that she had never heard the name and that there was no such landowner.

"You do at least know Manilov?" ventured Chichikov.

"And who's Manilov?"

"A landowner, madam."

"No, never heard of him, there's no such landowner."

"And what landowners are there hereabouts?"

"Bobrov, Svinin, Kanapatyev, Kharpakin, Trepakin, Pleshakov."

"Are they wealthy people or not?"

"No, sir, none of them are any too wealthy. One may have twenty souls, and another thirty, but you won't find any as have a hundred."

Chichikov realised he had strayed into a real backwater.

"Well, is it far, to the town, at least?"

"Must be sixty versts. How sorry I am that there's nothing to eat! But wouldn't you like a cup of tea, sir?"

"No thank you, madam. I need nothing, besides a bed."

"That's true, after a journey like that you do need a good rest. Make yourself comfortable, on this sofa, right here. Hey, Fetinya, bring a feather bed, pillows and sheet. What weather the good Lord has sent us: such thunder—I've kept a candle burning before the icon all night long. Goodness gracious, man, your whole back and side are covered with mud, just like a hog! Where, might I ask, did you get yourself into such a mess?"

"I can only thank God it was only a mess, I have to be grateful I didn't break all my bones!"

"Saints above, what calamities! But wouldn't you like something rubbed into your back?"

"Thank you, no. Please don't worry about it, only ask your servant to dry and clean my clothes."

"Do you hear, Fetinya?" called the lady, turning to the woman who had stepped out on to the porch with a candle and now brought a feather bed which she had plumped up on both sides with her hands, filling the entire room with a cloud of feathers. "Take the gentleman's coat and his underclothes and first dry them out before the fire like you used to do for the late master, and then give them a good rub and beat the dirt out."

"Yes, missus!" said Fetinya, spreading a sheet over the feather bed and laying out the pillows.

"So's there's your bed ready for you," said the lady. "Farewell, sir, I wish you a good night. But do you not need anything more? Perhaps, you're used to having someone tickle your heels at night? My dear departed could never go to sleep without it."

But her guest declined the tickling of heels too. His hostess left the room and he at once set about undressing, handing over all his clothes, outer and inner, as he removed them, to Fetinya, who, also wishing him a good night, took away all this wet armour. Left alone, he gazed not without pleasure at his bed which reached almost to the ceiling. Fetinya, it appeared, was a great adept at plumping up featherbeds. When, after pushing up a chair, he climbed onto the bed, it sank beneath him almost to the floor, while the feathers which his weight had squeezed through the seams, flew all round the room. He blew out his candle, covered himself with the patchwork quilt, curled up under it, and instantly fell asleep.

He awoke the following day quite late in the morning. The sun blazed straight into his eyes and the flies, which the previous night had slept peacefully on the walls and ceiling, now all turned their attention on him: one alighted on his lip, another buzzed about hoping to land on his eyeball, and the unfortunate one which had the lack of forethought to position itself close to his left nostril was promptly inhaled by the half-awakened Chichikov, who thereupon set about sneezing violently—and it was this circumstance that finally brought him to full consciousness.

Casting his eyes about the room, he now noticed that the pictures did not only depict birds; amongst them hung the portrait of Field-Marshal Kutuzov and an oil-painting of some old man with red lapels on his uniform, as was the fashion under Emperor Paul. The clocks once again began their hissing and struck the hour of ten; a woman's face peeped in at the door and promptly disappeared, for Chichikov had cast off absolutely everything that covered him. The face which peeped in seemed slightly familiar. He wondered who it might be—and at last remembered that it was his hostess. He put on his undershirt; his clothes, by now dry and clean, lay beside him. Once dressed, he walked up to the mirror and sneezed once again so loudly that a turkey cock, strolling up to the window, which was very close to the ground, gabbled something in response to his sneeze in its strange language at great speed, no doubt something like, "Take good care of yourself", and was called a fool by Chichikov. Stepping up to the window, he inspected the views that unfolded before him: the window appeared to overlook a chicken-run; at any rate the narrow yard before it seethed with poultry and all sorts of domestic creatures. Turkeys and chickens there were beyond number; a cock strutted amongst them with measured strides, shaking his comb and turning his head to one side, as if listening out for something; right under his nose there was a sow and her family, and as this sow rooted through a heap of rubbish she devoured a young chicken in passing and went on consuming watermelon rinds as before. This small yard, or chicken-run, was partitioned off by a plank fence, beyond which stretched extensive vegetable gardens with cabbages, onions, potatoes, beets, and other farm crops. Scattered about the garden were a few apple-trees and other fruit trees, covered with nets to protect them from magpies and from the sparrows, which flocked like massive slanting storm clouds from one place to another. For the same purpose several scarecrows had been erected on long poles, with outstretched arms; one of them wore the lace bonnet that had once graced the mistress herself. Beyond the vegetable garden stretched the peasants' huts, which although they were scattered helter-skelter and not arranged in streets, did, as Chichikov remarked, demonstrate the prosperity of their occupants, for they were properly maintained: the dilapidated planks on the roofs had all been replaced with new ones; none of the gates hung askew, and in some of the covered sheds facing him he could see a practically new spare cart, and in others, even two. "Well, this little village of hers is quite a size," he said, promptly determining to become better acquainted with the lady herself. He peeped round the slightly open door where she had earlier poked her head, and seeing her sitting at her tea table, stepped in with a cheerful and courteous look.

"Goodday to you, sir. Did you sleep well?" she asked, rising slightly from her chair. She was better attired than on the previous night—in a dark dress and no longer wearing a night-cap, but she still had something wound around her neck.

"Very well, thank you," said Chichikov, seating himself in an armchair. "And yourself, madam?"

"Badly, badly."

"Why so?"

"Couldn't sleep. My spine's aching something terrible and my leg, just above the knee, is throbbing and throbbing."

"It'll pass, it'll pass. There's nothing to worry about."

"I would to God it did. I rubbed in some pig fat, then I dabbed it with turpentine. Will you have a little nip of something with your tea? There's some fruit vodka in the flask."

"That's not a bad idea, madam, a nip of fruit vodka will be fine."

I expect the reader has already noticed that Chichikov, despite his courteous look, was speaking far more freely here than he had with Manilov, and was not standing on ceremony at all. I should say here, that whilst we in Russia may in certain respects still lag behind foreigners, we have far outstripped them in our skills of behaviour. It would be impossible to enumerate all the nuances and subtleties of our behaviour. A Frenchman or a German will never fathom or comprehend all these particularities and distinctions in a lifetime; he will employ almost the same tone and language when speaking with a millionaire or with a tobacco peddler, although, of course, in his soul he will fawn to a degree on the former. It is not so with us:

amongst us there are people of such cleverness that they will speak with a landowner who owns two hundred souls in a manner quite unlike the way he will speak with the owner of three hundred, while with him of three hundred souls he will again talk quite differently than with him who has five hundred, and with him who has five hundred quite differently than with him who has eight hundred—in a word, even if you go up to a million, further nuances will still be found. Let us imagine, for example, a government office somewhere—not here, but over the hills and far away, and in this office let us suppose there sits the head of the chancellery. I invite you to look at him while he sits amongst his subordinates—why, you will be struck dumb from sheer terror! Pride, nobility, and heaven knows what else is expressed by his face! He is simply asking to be painted: a Prometheus, a veritable Prometheus. He glowers like an eagle, he stalks with measured step. Yet this same eagle, the moment he leaves his office and nears that of his own superior, begins to scurry along for all he's worth like a partridge with papers tucked under its wing. In society and at a soirée, so long as no high rank is present, Prometheus remains Prometheus, but should there appear someone ever so slightly senior to him, Prometheus undergoes a metamorphosis such as Ovid himself could never imagine: he becomes a fly, less than a fly, he is reduced to a grain of dust!

"But that's not Ivan Petrovich," you will say, looking at him. "Ivan Petrovich is taller, and this man is short and puny; Ivan Petrovich talks in a loud, deep voice, and never laughs, while this chap sounds nothing like him: he squeaks like a bird and cackles all the time." You go up a little closer and look, why—it is Ivan Petrovich after all!

"Dear, oh dear!" you think to yourself...

However, let us return to our dramatis personae. Chichikov, as we have already seen, had decided not to stand on ceremony at all and therefore, taking up his cup of tea and pouring in a tot of fruit vodka, he embarked on the following discourse:

"Now, madam, you have a fine little village here. How many souls in it?"

"There must be, well now, nigh on eighty," said his hostess, "but times are bad, and last year there was such a terrible harvest, may God preserve us from another such."

"Still the peasants look a sturdy lot, their little huts are nice and strong. Might I ask your surname? Remiss of me not to have asked before, but I arrived at night..."

"Korobochka, widow of a Collegiate Secretary."

"I thank you most humbly. And your name and patronymic?"

"Nastasya Petrovna."

"Nastasya Petrovna? Now that's a nice name, Nastasya Petrovna. I have an aunt, sister to my mother, Nastasya Petrovna."

"And what would your name be?" asked his hostess. "For I presume you must be an assessor?"

"No, madam," answered Chichikov with a chuckle, "no, indeed, I'm not an assessor; I am merely travelling on private business."

"Ah, so you're a buyer! Dear me, it's such a pity I sold my honey so cheaply to the merchants, or you would have bought it from me, sir, I'm sure."

"No: honey I wouldn't have bought."

"But what then? Hemp perhaps? But I don't have much hemp: no more than half a pood."

"No madam, my merchandise is rather different: tell me, have any of your peasants died?"

"Oh, sir, eighteen of them!" said the old lady with a sigh. "And they were all fine chaps the ones who died, good workers. After this, of course, more have been born: but what good are they: all such small fry; and then the assessor comes—and says I've got to pay revenue duty on them. The men are dead, but I've got to pay as if for live ones. Last week my smith was burnt to death, such a skilful smith too, he wasn't a bad plumber either..."

"So did you really have a fire, madam?"

"The Lord preserve us from such a disaster: a fire would have been even worse; no, my good sir, he burnt himself up. He just caught fire inside, somehow: he'd had too much to drink and all that came from him was a blue flame, he glowed and smouldered away and turned black like charcoal, and he really was such a skilful smith! And now I can't go for a drive: there's no one to shoe the horses."

"It's all the will of God, madam!" said Chichikov, with a sigh. "There's no gainsaying the wisdom of God... Let me have them, Nastasya Petrovna."

"Have whom, sir?"

"Why, all the ones that died."

"How do you mean: let you have them?"

"Just like that. Or if you like, sell them to me. I'll give you money for them."

"But how? I don't think I quite understand—surely you don't mean to dig them up out of the ground?"

Chichikov could see that the old girl was getting such wrong ideas that he would have to explain to her what he was about. So, in a few words he told her that the transfer or purchase would only figure on paper and that the souls themselves would be registered as if alive.

"But what do you need them for?" asked the old lady, her eyes popping out at him.

"Now that's my business."

"But they're dead!"

"So who's saying they're alive? And it's for that very reason that they're a liability to you, because they're dead: you have to pay for them, and now I'm going to spare you the trouble and the expense. Do you understand? And I'm not only going to rid you of them, I'm going to pay you fifteen rubles on top. Is it clear now?"

"I must say I don't know," declared his hostess, speaking slowly and deliberately. "After all, I've never sold dead ones before."

"I should think not! That would be nothing short of miraculous if you had sold them to anyone, or do you think there really might be some profit in them?"

"No, I don't think that. What profit would there be in them, there's no profit. What gives me pause is that they're dead."

"What a blockhead of a woman!" thought Chichikov.

"Now, just listen, madam. Work it out properly for yourself: you're ruining yourself paying duty for them just like for the live ones..."

"Goodness yes, don't even mention it!" interrupted the old lady. "To think that a couple of weeks ago I handed over more than a hundred and fifty. And I greased the assessor's palm too."

"So you see? And now just consider that you'll never have to grease the assessor's palm again, because I'll be paying for them; me, not you. I take all the dues upon myself. I'll even pay for the purchase deed out of my own pocket, do you understand now?"

The old lady fell to thinking. She could see that it did seem a good deal, only there was something too new and unusual about it, and so she very much feared that this buyer might be pulling a fast one on her; God only knows where he had come from, and at night too.

"Well, then, madam, do we shake on it?" said Chichikov.

"Really, I've never had occasion to sell deceased folk before. Living ones I did sell of course; the year before last I let the archpriest have two girls, one hundred rubles apiece, and he was very grateful, they turned into fine workers; they weave their own napkins."

"Yes, but we're not talking about the live ones. Don't worry about them. I want your dead."

"I admit, it does frighten me, being the first time, I wouldn't want to bear a loss. What if you're cheating me, my good sir, and they're ... and somehow they're worth more."

"Listen, madam... Dear, oh dear, what are you on about? What could they cost? Just look: they're dust and ashes. Do you see? Dust and ashes. You take any old piece of rubbish, for example, even an ordinary rag, and that rag will have its price; they'll at least buy it for the paper factory—but those souls are totally useless. I mean, tell me yourself, what use are they?"

"Well yes, that is true, of course. Of course they're no earthly use at all; but there's only one thing which troubles me: they are already dead, you see."

"What a blockhead!" said Chichikov to himself, beginning to lose patience. "Try and do business with her! She's put me all in a sweat, the cursed old hag!" Thereupon he took his handkerchief from his pocket and mopped his brow, which was indeed beaded with sweat. Chichikov's anger, however, was unfounded: there are highly respected persons, almost statesmen, but in actual fact they are just another Korobochka. With people like that once they get an idea into their heads nothing will drive it out; no matter how many arguments you put forward as clear as day they all bounce off them like a rubber ball off a wall. Mopping his brow, Chichikov resolved to try and approach her from a different tack.

"Now then, madam dear," he said, "either you don't want to understand my words, or you're just saying that on purpose, for the sake of saying something... I'm giving you money: fifteen rubles in banknotes. Do you understand? That's money, you know. You won't find it growing on trees. Now tell me: how much did you sell your honey for?"

"Twelve rubles the pood."

"A little sin on your conscience there, madam. You didn't sell it for twelve rubles."

"As God is my witness, I did."

"Well, do you see now? But then, that was honey. You've been collecting it for perhaps a year, with all sorts of effort and bother; you had to go and smoke the bees, then feed them in your cellar the whole winter; but dead souls are not of this world. Here you have not had to expend any energy, for it was the will of God that they should leave this world, to the detriment of your estate. There, for your work, for your effort, you received twelve rubles, but here you're getting money for nothing, and not twelve but fifteen rubles, and not in silver, but in banknotes." After such persuasive arguments Chichikov hardly doubted that the old woman would not give in.

"It's true," answered Korobochka. "I'm such an inexperienced old widow! It would be better if I waited a little; perhaps some other buyers will come along, and I'll be able to compare prices."

"Shame on you, madam! Shame! Just think what you're saying! Who's going to buy them? What possible use could they have for them?"

"Who knows, maybe they could come in useful round the farm some time..." objected the old lady, but did not finish her sentence. Her jaw dropped and she gazed at him almost with terror, waiting to hear his reply.

"Use the dead round the farm! What are you talking about! You mean to scare the sparrows away from your vegetable patch at night, or something?"

"O Lord, have mercy on us! What terrible things you are saying!" muttered the old lady, crossing herself.

"But where else did you want to use them? Anyway, you can keep all the bones and the graves; the transfer will only take place on paper. So what is it to be? Well?

You might answer me at least."

The old lady again fell to thinking.

"What's on your mind, Nastasya Petrovna?"

"I must say, I still can't decide what to do; I think I should rather sell you some hemp."

"Why hemp? For heavens' sake, I am asking about something else entirely, and you push your hemp at me! Forget about your hemp; the next time I come I'll take your hemp too. So what is it to be, Nastasya Petrovna?"

"Truly, it's such a strange thing to sell. I've never heard its like!"

Here Chichikov quite reached the end of his tether. In his anger he pounded a chair against the floor and threatened her with the devil.

The good lady harboured an uncommon fear of the devil.

"Oh no, you must not mention him, God preserve us from him!" she shrieked going quite pale. "Only a couple of days ago I dreamt of the accursed one all night. I'd been reading my fortune-telling cards after I'd said my prayers, and obviously God sent him to me as a punishment. He looked so horrible, with horns longer than a bull's."

"I'm only surprised they don't haunt your sleep in dozens. I only wanted to help you out of a Christian love of my neighbour; here was a poor widow suffering, undergoing hardship ... but you can go and rot with all your village!"

"Oh! What terrible curses!" said the old lady, staring at him with terror.

"You've driven me to them! You know you're just like the dog in the manger, if you'll excuse me for saying so. I was going to buy some of your farm produce, because I also buy in supplies for the government..." Here he told a little fib, quite off the cuff, admittedly, and without any further thought, but—to his surprise—a most felicitous one. The government supplies had a powerful effect on Nastasya Petrovna, at any rate she uttered in an almost pleading voice:

"But why do you get so vexed? If only I'd known earlier how vexatious you are I would never have said a word to cross you."

"I'm not vexed a bit! The whole deal isn't worth a thought, so why should I get vexed about it!"

"Well, all right then! I'm ready to let you have them for fifteen rubles! Only remember about the supplies, sir: if you need any rye flour, or buckwheat, or groats, or slaughtered bullocks, don't pass me over."

"No madam, I shan't pass you over," he said, wiping his hand across his face, down which the sweat poured copiously. He asked whether she had an attorney in the town, or an acquaintance whom she could authorize to draw up the purchase deed and so forth.

"Well yes, the son of Father Kyril, the archpriest, he clerks in the Chambers," said Korobochka.

Chichikov asked her to write him a letter of authorization and, to avoid any further complications, offered to draw it up himself.

"It would be nice," thought Korobochka in the meanwhile, "if he were to buy some flour and cattle from me for his supplies. I must get round him somehow: there's some dough left from last night, so I'll go and tell Fetinya to bake pancakes; it would also be nice to make an egg-pie, my cook makes really tasty ones and they don't take long!" She went out to put into effect her plan about the egg-pie and probably supplement it with other home baked concoctions; while Chichikov returned to the drawing-room where he had spent the night, in order to take the necessary papers from his box.

Everything had long since been tidied up in the drawing-room, the luxurious feather bed had been borne away and before the settee there now stood a table, covered with a tablecloth. Setting his box upon it he rested for a moment, for he was drenched with sweat: every scrap of clothing on his body, from his shirt to his stockings, was soaking wet. "Cursed old fool, I'm quite done in!" he said, feeling somewhat rested, and opened his box. The author is convinced that there are some readers so curious that they would like to know the design and inner lay-out of the box. Ah well, why should we not satisfy their curiosity! And so, for the inner lay-out: at the very centre was a soap box; behind the soap box there were six or seven narrow compartments for razors; then rectangular nooks for a sand-box and an inkwell, with a runner cut between them to hold the quills, sealing-wax and other longer instruments; then there were all sorts of compartments with and

without little lids, for the shorter objects, crammed full of
visiting cards, memorial cards, theatre tickets and so forth,
which had been kept as souvenirs. The entire upper drawer
with all its compartments could be removed to reveal
beneath it a space filled with piles of papers, then there
was a small secret drawer for money, cunningly fitted to
one side of the box. It was always opened and shut with
such alacrity by the owner that it was impossible to say for
certain how much money it contained. Chichikov at once
set to work, sharpening a quill and starting to write. At
this moment his hostess entered the room.

"That's a nice box you have," she said, sitting next to
him. "I suppose you bought it in Moscow?"

"Yes, in Moscow," answered Chichikov, busy writing.

"I knew it; you can tell by the quality. The year before
last my sister brought back from Moscow some warm
boots for the children: so solidly made they're still wearing them. My goodness what a lot of official stamped
paper you have!" she continued, peeping into his box.
Indeed, there was a considerable quantity of stamped
paper. "Couldn't you give me one little sheet? I'm so short
of official paper; sometimes you have to submit an application to the courts and there's nothing to write it on."

Chichikov explained to her that this was a different sort
of paper, that it was intended for purchase deeds and not
for applications. To appease her, however, he gave her one
with a ruble stamp value. When he had finished his letter
he gave it to her to sign and asked for a list of the peasants.
It transpired that the old lady did not keep any records or
lists, but knew practically everyone by heart; so he prevailed
upon her to dictate the names to him there and then. Some
of the peasants rather surprised him with their names and
even more with their nicknames, causing him to pause each
time before writing them down. He was particularly struck
by one Pyotr Savelyev Neuvazhay-Koryto (Don't-Respect-
the-Trough), so that he could not forbear to remark: "What
a long one!" One had the tag attached to his name: "Cow's
Brick", another was simply "Ivan the Wheel". When he
had finished writing he took a fairly deep breath and caught
the tantalizing smell of something frying in butter.

"Be so kind as to partake of this humble fare," said his
hostess.

Chichikov looked round and saw the table already set with mushrooms, pies, dumplings, doughnuts, muffins, pancakes, pastries with all sorts of fillings: onion, poppy-seed, cream-cheese, sprats and the Lord knows what else besides.

"Have some egg-pie," said the hostess.

Chichikov made for the egg-pie and promptly devoured a good half of it with fulsome expressions of praise. Indeed, it was a tasty pie, and after the fuss and bother with the old lady it seemed all the tastier.

"How about some pancakes?" asked his hostess.

In reply to this Chichikov raked up three pancakes together and, dunking them in melted butter, steered them into his mouth, and wiped his lips and hands dry with a napkin. After repeating this procedure about three times he asked his hostess to order his carriage. Nastasya Petrovna at once despatched Fetinya, directing her at the same time to bring some more hot pancakes.

"I must say, madam, your pancakes are very good," said Chichikov setting about the hot ones that had been brought in.

"Yes, my girls cook them well, but the trouble is the harvest was poor, and the flour is not so good... But why are you in such a hurry, sir?" she asked seeing Chichikov take up his hat. "Your chaise has not been brought round yet."

"Oh, they'll bring it round. It doesn't take my man long to get it ready."

"But please, don't forget about the supplies."

"No, no, I shan't forget," said Chichikov, stepping out into the hallway.

"Do you not want to buy any pork fat?" asked his hostess, walking behind him.

"Yes, why not? I'll buy some, only later."

"I'll have some pork fat ready at Christmas time."

"We'll buy some, we will, we'll buy a bit of everything, and we'll buy some pork fat too."

"Perhaps you need some bird's feathers? I will have some bird's feathers too, by St Philipp's fast."

"Fine, fine," said Chichikov.

"There you see, your chaise is not ready yet," said his hostess, when they were out on the porch.

"It'll be ready in good time. Just tell me how to get to the main road."

"Now, how shall I do that?" asked Korobochka. "It's hard to explain, there are so many turnings: it would be better if I gave you a girl to guide you there. I expect there's room for her, up on the coach-box?"

"Of course there is."

"I will give you a girl, I think. She knows the way, only don't you let her get stranded; some merchants once did that to a girl of mine."

Chichikov assured her of the girl's safety and Korobochka, her mind put at rest, turned her attention to everything going on in her yard; she goggled at the housekeeper, emerging from the cellar bearing a wooden cask full of honey, then at a peasant who appeared in the gateway, and little by little she became absorbed in her usual household cares. But why do we spend so long on Korobochka? What do we care for Korobochka's or Mrs Manilov's thrifty or not thrifty households, let us press on! What does make us marvel is the way things are arranged in this world: joy will instantly turn into sadness if you linger too long before it, and then God only knows what manner of thing will stray into the mind. Perhaps you will even start thinking: come now, does Korobochka really stand so low on the endless ladder of human self-improvement? Is there really such a great abyss separating her from the grand lady, securely protected by the walls of an aristocratic house with its fragrant wrought-iron stairways, its gleaming brass, its mahogany and carpets, yawning over an unfinished book and looking forward to some visitor from the world of wit and fashion, when she will be able to display her intellect and give utterance to various hackneyed sentiments, which in accordance with the laws of fashion occupy the town for a whole week, not thoughts about the affairs of the house and the estate, reduced to a state of neglect and disorder thanks to the general ignorance of management, but about what political upheaval was imminent in France, which direction has been taken by fashionable Catholicism? But let us press on, let us press on! Why speak of this? But then why is it that amidst these carefree, mindless moments quite another, wonderful stream of thought should suddenly flash past, quite by itself; the laughter has hardly died on a man's face but he has become different amongst the same people, and his face is already illuminated by a different radiance...

"Ah, there's the chaise! There's the chaise!" exclaimed Chichikov when at last he saw his chaise driving up. "What kept you so long, you blockhead? It seems you haven't quite shaken off yesterday's binge?"

Selifan gave no answer to this.

"Farewell, madam! And where's this girl of yours?"

"Hey, Pelageya!" called the old lady to a girl of about eleven loitering by the porch in a home-dyed dress and in bare feet which from a distance could have passed for boots so caked were they with fresh mud. "Show the master the way."

Selifan helped the girl onto the coachbox; placing one foot on the running-board, she spattered mud all over it, and then clambered up on top and seated herself beside him. After her Chichikov hoisted his own foot onto the running-board, and tilting the chaise to the right because he was a little on the heavy side, finally installed himself, declaring:

"Ah, that's better now! Farewell, madam!"

The horses set off.

Selifan was moody throughout the journey and at the same time exceptionally attentive to his duties, as he always was when he had committed some peccadillo or had been drunk. The horses had been splendidly groomed. The collar on one of them, which previously had almost always been put on in a tattered state, with oakum sticking out of the leather, had been skillfully sewn together. He remained silent throughout the journey, only cracking his whip occasionally and not delivering any admonitions to the horses, although the dappled trace-horse would of course have liked to hear some words of edification, for at such times the loquacious driver would always idly relax his hold on the reins and the whip would only play above their backs for form's sake. But on this occasion the only sounds to issue from those sullen lips were the monotonous and unpleasant exclamations: "Now there, now you old crow, yawn away!"—and nothing further. Even the bay and Assessor were disgruntled never once to hear the words: "My lovelies" or "Your honours". The dappled horse received some extremely unpleasant blows on his plump and broad haunches. "What's got into him!" he said to himself, flattering his ears. "He certainly knows where to aim his whip! He doesn't hit right across the back, but manages to find the spot where it hurts most: he gets you on the ears or lashes you under the belly."

"Right, is it?" Selifan asked the girl sitting by his side, as he pointed with his whip to the rain-blackened road between the bright green, fresh-smelling fields.

"No, no; I'll tell you when," answered the girl.

"But where, then?" asked Selifan, when they had driven up closer.

"That way," answered the girl, pointing.

"Oh, you!" said Selifan. "But that *is* right: she doesn't know her right from her left!"

Although it was a very fine day the ground had become so muddy that the wheels of the chaise were soon thickly caked as if with felt, and this considerably impeded their progress; furthermore the soil was loamy and extraordinarily sticky. In consequence it was after noon before they were clear of the cart tracks. Without the girl it would have been hard to do even that, because the roads forked off in every direction, like captured crawfish when they are shaken out of the sack, and Selifan would have floundered for hours through no fault of his. Soon the girl pointed at a building looming in the distance and announced:

"There's the highway!"

"And the building?" asked Selifan.

"The inn," said the girl.

"Well now we can go on by ourselves," said Selifan. "You run along home."

He stopped and helped her alight, muttering through his teeth: "Just look at those filthy feet!"

Chichikov gave her a copper coin and she wandered off homewards. Just sitting on a coach box had been happiness enough.

CHAPTER FOUR

As they drove up to the inn Chichikov called a halt for two reasons. On the one hand he wished to rest the horses, and on the other he himself wanted a bite to eat and some liquid sustenance. The author feels bound to confess that he is most envious of the appetite and digestion of such people. He has absolutely no thought to spare all the grand folk of St Petersburg and Moscow, who spend an age deliberating what they'd like to eat tomorrow and what they might fancy for dinner the day after tomorrow, never embarking on this dinner without first gobbling a pill, after which they swallow their oysters, sea spiders and other horrors and then go off to Karlsbad or the Caucasus for a cure. No, these gentlemen have never excited his envy. But middle-class people, who at one post-house order ham, at the next—suckling pig, at the third—a good piece of sturgeon or sausage fried with onions, and then, quite as if they had not eaten all day, sit down at any time you like and tuck into the sterlet soup with burbot and soft roe, which hisses and burbles between their teeth, followed by kedgeree pie or a sheat-fish pasty, just watching them makes your mouth water. These people are truly blessed with a most enviable gift from heaven! Many a gentleman of quality would, without a moment's hesitation, sacrifice half his serfs and half his estates, mortgaged and unmortgaged, complete with all improvements in the foreign and the Russian manner, to have such a digestion like that, but the sad thing is that no amount of money, no estates, with or without improvements, can buy the kind of digestion generally enjoyed by people of the middle-class.

The weathered, swarthy timber inn received Chichikov beneath its narrow but welcoming canopy, supported by chiselled wooden posts, not unlike antique church candlesticks. The inn was built somewhat in the manner of a Russian peasant house, only on a larger scale. The carpenter's lace carved from new wood that surrounded the windows and ran along the eaves vividly brightened up its dark walls; the shutters were embellished with painted jugs of flowers.

As he climbed up the narrow wooden staircase into the wide vestibule a door creaked open and Chichikov saw a fat old woman, clad in a gaudy cotton print, who announced: "This way, please!" In the room he found all the old friends, familiar to anyone who has put up in inns of this kind so common along our roads, to wit: a discoloured samovar, smoothly planed pine walls, a triangular tall boy in the corner with teapots and cups, gilt porcelain eggs hanging under the icons on blue and red ribbons, a cat that has recently kittened, a mirror, reflecting not two, but four eyes and some sort of a pancake instead of a face; and finally, little bunches of fragrant herbs and carnations tucked behind the icons, but so desiccated that anyone wishing to smell them would only sneeze and nothing more.

"Do you have suckling pig?" enquired Chichikov of the woman standing before him.

"We do."

"With horseradish and sour cream?"

"With horseradish and sour cream."

"Let's have some then!"

The old woman went off and brought out a plate, a napkin, starched so stiff that it humped like a piece of dried bark, then a knife with a yellowed bone handle and a blade as thin as a penknife, a two-pronged fork, and a salt-cellar which simply would not stand upright on the table.

Our hero, following his custom, at once struck up a conversation with her, enquiring whether she herself were the innkeeper, or if there was a landlord, and what sort of income the inn brought in, and whether her sons lived with them, and was the eldest son a bachelor or married, and what sort of wife he had taken, with a big dowry or not, and was her husband content, or had he been angry because he did not receive more gifts at the wedding—in a word, he omitted nothing. Needless to say, he also satisfied his curiosity as to the local landowners, and learnt that there were many: Blokhin, Pochitayev, Mylnoy, Colonel Cherpakov, and Sobakevich. "Ah! You know Sobakevich?" he asked and thereupon learnt that the old woman knew not only Sobakevich, but also Manilov, and that Manilov was the more particular of the two: he would at once demand a boiled chicken, and would also ask for some veal; now if there was some mutton liver he would order that too, but would only just taste everything, while Sobakevich would only order one thing, but would eat it all up and even shout for a second helping without paying extra for it.

While he was thus conversing, and consuming his suckling pig, of which only the last morsel remained to be eaten, he heard the rattle of a carriage driving up outside. Looking through the window he espied a light chaise that had drawn up before the inn, pulled by three handsome horses. Two men were alighting from the carriage. One was fair and tall; the other not quite so tall, and swarthy. The former was clad in a dark blue dolman jacket, the latter more simply attired in a striped caftan. Another scruffy carriage was still on its way, in the distance, empty and dragged along by a shaggy foursome with tattered collars and rope harness. The fair-haired gentleman at once ascended the staircase, whilst his swarthy companion remained behind, groping for something in the chaise, at the same time talking to the servant and waving to the carriage that was coming up. His voice struck Chichikov as somehow familiar. While he was thus inspecting him, the fair-haired traveller managed to find the door and open it. He was a tall man, with a gaunt face or what would be called a dissipated look, and a small ginger moustache. From his darkish face one could conclude that he was no stranger to smoke, at least to the tobacco, if not the gunpowder, variety. He made a courteous bow to Chichikov, which the latter returned in a like manner. They would have gotten to talking and become well acquainted in a matter of minutes, as the foundations had already been laid, with them both almost simultaneously expressing their pleasure at the way the dust on the road had been completely laid by the previous day's rain and how cool and agreeable it had been to drive, had not his swarthy comrade entered just then, flinging his cap onto the table, and rumpling up his thick black hair with a dashing stroke of the hand. This was a well-built fellow of medium height, with full, ruddy cheeks, teeth white as snow and whiskers black as pitch. He seemed to be in the pink of health.

"Well, well, well!" he exclaimed suddenly, throwing out both arms on seeing Chichikov. "What brings you here?"

In him Chichikov recognised Nozdryov, the very same Nozdryov he had met at the dinner given by the public prosecutor and who in the space of a very few minutes had assumed the most intimate familiarity with Chichikov, although the latter had not given him any cause to do so.

"Where've you been?" demanded Nozdryov, and without waiting for a reply continued: "I've just come from the fair, brother. Congratulate me, I'm clean as a whistle!

Would you believe it, never in all my life have I been cleaned out like that! I even had to come home in a hired cart. Just have a look through the window!" Here he thrust Chichikov's head round so violently that he well nigh struck it against the window frame. "Look at that junk! They only just made it here, confound them, and so I had to climb over into his chaise." As he said this, Nozdryov pointed a finger at his comrade. "But don't you know each other yet? My brother-in-law Mizhuyev! We've been talking about you all morning. 'Just you wait,' I said, 'I bet we meet Chichikov.' If you knew how they cleaned me out, old chap! Would you believe it, I not only blew my four trotters, I lost the shirt off my back: I've neither a chain, nor a watch to hang on it..." Chichikov looked and saw that he did indeed have neither watch nor chain. It even seemed to him that one of Nozdryov's whiskers was shorter and less bushy than the other. "And yet if I had only had twenty rubles in my pocket," continued Nozdryov, "not a kopek more, I could have won it all back, and over and above what I would have won back, I tell you, as an honest man, I would have come away with thirty thousand in my wallet."

"But that's what you said at the time," objected the fair-haired traveller, "and when I gave you fifty rubles you promptly lost the lot."

"But I wouldn't have! Honest to God, I wouldn't have blown that fifty! If I hadn't been so stupid, I really wouldn't have blown it. If I hadn't raised on the confounded seven after we had doubled stakes I could have broken the bank."

"But you didn't break it," said his fair-haired companion.

"I didn't break it because I put up the stake too early. Do you really think that major of yours plays well?"

"Well or not, he still beat you."

"Bully for him!" said Nozdryov. "But I'll beat him yet. No, just let him try doubling and then we'll see what sort of a player he is! But then, my dear Chichikov, those first few days were one marvellous binge! I must say, the fair was most excellent. Even the merchants were saying they'd never seen such a crowd before. All the stuff we brought from the village we sold at the very best prices. Oh,

brother, what a binge! Even now, when I remember...
Damn and blast! I mean, it's such a pity you weren't with
us. Would you believe it, there was a regiment of dragoons
stationed only three versts from the town. Just imagine:
those officers, the whole bang lot of them, forty officers at
least, were all in the town; and then, brother, the wine
really started to flow... Staff Captain Potseluyev ... now
there's a fine chap! Brother, you should see his whiskers!
Bordeaux—he calls bored crow! 'Hey, waiter, one bored
crow!' he orders. Lieutenant Kuvshinnikov... Ah, brother,
now there's a first-rate fellow! A binge is the break of life
for him! We were together the whole time. You should see
the wine we bought off old Ponomaryov! I should warn
you that he's a scoundrel and you mustn't buy anything
in his shop; he puts all sorts of rubbish in the wine: sandal-
wood, burnt cork and even elderberries, the rogue! But
then if you can get a bottle out of his little room at
the back, his special store he calls it—now then, brother,
that's soaring in the Empyrean fields. That champagne we
had: after it the governor's stuff is kvass! Just imagine,
that was no mere Cliquot, but some sort of Cliquot Matra-
dura, that means double Cliquot. And he got us another
bottle of French stuff called Bon-Bon. And the bouquet?
Pure roses. That was some binge!.. After us some prince
or other arrived, sent to the shop for champagne, and there
wasn't a bottle left in town, the officers had drunk the lot.
Would you believe it, I alone got through seventeen bottles of champagne during a single dinner!"

"Come now, not seventeen bottles," objected his fair-
haired companion.

"I'm telling you on my word of honour that I drank
seventeen bottles," insisted Nozdryov.

"You can say what you like, but I'm telling you you
couldn't even drink ten bottles."

"Do you want to wager that I can't?"

"Wager what?"

"Well, that gun, which you bought in town."

"No, not that."

"Go on, try!"

"I don't want to try!"

"If you did it'd be the last you saw of your gun. Damn
it, Chichikov, my dear chap, I mean what a pity you weren't

there. I know you and Lieutenant Kuvshinnikov would have really hit it off. Yes, you'd have got on like a house on fire. That's no public prosecutor, or any of our provincial skinflints who grudge every kopek. This one, brother, will take you on at bezique or faro or what you will. Hell, Chichikov, why couldn't you have come? You're a real swine, a swineherd! My dear chap, give me a kiss, you know how I love you! Hey, Mizhuyev, isn't it marvellous how fate has brought us together? I mean, what's he to me or I to him? He's come here from the devil knows where, I live here too... And, brother, you should have seen all the carriages, millions of them. I had a crack at the old lucky wheel: I won two jars of pomade, a china tea-cup and a guitar; then I put it all on once more and lost the lot, damn and blast, plus, six rubles on top. But that Kuvshinnikov fellow, you should see him, such a skirt-chaser! He and I went to practically every ball in the place. There was one doxy, dressed up like a doll, you know, all frills and flounces and God knows what else besides... There was me saying to myself: I'll be damned! And old Kuvshinnikov, he's such an old goat, goes and sits next to her and spouts all these compliments in French... Believe it or not, he just couldn't keep his hands off even the peasant women. He calls it sampling the local fruit. They brought in some amazing fish, and fillets of smoked sturgeon. In fact I brought one with me; it's a good thing I thought of buying it while I still had the money. Where are you bound for now?"

"I have to go and see a chap I know," said Chichikov.

"To blazes with your chap! Come to my place!"

"No I cannot, I have business to do."

"Ha! Business, is it now? What a pack of lies! Four-flusher Ivanovich!"

"It's true, I do have business, and important business too."

"I'll wager you're lying! So tell me, whom are you going to see?"

"Well, Sobakevich."

Here Nozdryov burst into peals of ringing laughter that can come only from a healthy man, with all his sugar-white teeth revealed and his jowls trembling and shaking, the kind of laugh that makes the neighbour sleeping somewhere behind double doors three rooms away wake up with a violent start, rub his eyes and mutter: "Something's tickling him!"

"But what is so funny?" asked Chichikov, somewhat discomposed by this hilarity.

But Nozdryov continued to hoot with laughter, repeating:

"Have mercy on me, you're killing me!"

"There's nothing funny about it: I gave him my word," said Chichikov.

"You'll be sorry you ever saw the light of day when you get to his place: he's a thorough skinflint! Remember, I know your character, and you're grievously mistaken if you're hoping for a game of bezique and a nice bottle of Bon-Bon when you get there. You listen to me, brother: to the devil with Sobakevich, come to my place! I'll treat you to a superb sturgeon! Ponomaryov, the old swine, bowing and scraping, said: 'Specially for you, you can search the whole fair, you won't find another like it.' But he's a terrible rogue. I told him so to his face: 'You and our monopolist,' I said, 'you're the biggest thieves in town.' He just laughed, the swine, stroking his beard. Kuvshinnikov and I took our breakfast at his stall every day. I say, I forgot to tell you: I know you'll never give up trying, but you won't get it from me even for ten thousand, I warn you in advance. Hey, Porfiry!" going to the window, he summoned his man, who was clutching a little knife in one hand and in the other a crust of bread and a chunk of sturgeon, which he had contrived to slice off whilst unloading something from the chaise. "Hey, Porfiry!" shouted Nozdryov, "bring me that puppy! What a puppy!" he continued, turning to Chichikov. "Stolen, you know; the owner said he wouldn't sell him to save his own life. I offered him my chestnut mare, the one I swapped from Khvostyryov you remember..." Chichikov, however, did not know Khvostyryov from Adam, nor had he ever seen the chestnut mare.

"Master! Nothing to eat for you?" asked the old woman, entering at this moment.

"No, nothing. Phew, brother, what a binge we had! In fact you could bring me a glass of vodka; what kind have you?"

"Aniseed," answered the old woman.

"Bring me some aniseed then," said Nozdryov.

"And bring me a glass too!" called the fair-haired friend.

"In the theatre there was an actress, damn her, who sang like a canary! Kuvshinnikov was sitting next to me and you know what he said: 'How about tasting that little strawberry!' I reckon there must have been a good fifty booths. Old Fenardi kept turning somersaults for four solid hours." At this point he took his glass from the old woman, who handed it to him with a low bow. "Aha, bring him here!" he cried, seeing Porfiry coming in with the puppy. Porfiry was dressed just like his master in a sort of quilted, but somewhat grubby, caftan.

"Bring him here, put him down here!"

Porfiry put the puppy down and it stretched out on its four legs and started sniffing the floor.

"Now there's a puppy!" said Nozdryov, catching it by the scruff of the neck and lifting it up. The puppy gave a rather plaintive squeal.

"But you didn't do what I told you," said Nozdryov, addressing himself to Porfiry and carefully inspecting the puppy's belly. "You didn't give him a brushing, did you?"

"Yes I did."

"So where do all these fleas come from?"

"I wouldn't know. Perhaps they somehow got on him from the chaise?"

"You're a lying scoundrel, you never brushed him; if you ask me you've given him some of yours as well. Now just take a look, Chichikov, just look at those ears, just feel them with you hand."

"No why, I can see them like this: a fine breed!" answered Chichikov.

"No, just take a firm hold of an ear and feel it!"

To humour him Chichikov felt the puppy's ears and agreed: "Yes, he'll grow into a fine dog all right!"

"Now just feel his nice cold nose. Touch it with your hand." Anxious not to offend him, Chichikov also felt the puppy's nose, declaring: "He'll have a good scent."

"He's got a good jaw on him," continued Nozdryov, "and I must confess, I've been hankering after one just like him. All right, Porfiry, you can take him away now!"

Porfiry picked up the puppy and carried it back to the chaise.

"Listen, Chichikov, you must come away with me immediately, it's only five versts, we'll get there in a brace of shakes and then you can go on to Sobakevich's."

"Oh well," thought Chichikov "why not go to Nozdryov's after all? He's no worse than any of the others, cast in the same mould, and he's lost money. He seems game for anything, so who knows, I might be able to wheedle something out of him for nothing."

"Very well, let's go," he said, "but I must not tarry long, my time is precious."

"Now that's more like it, my dear chap! That's splendid, let me give you a kiss for it." Here Nozdryov and Chichikov embraced. "First class: we shall drive on, all three together!"

"No, if you don't mind, I'll be excused," said the fair-haired companion, "I must be getting home."

"Stuff and nonsense, brother, I shan't let you go."

"Honestly, my wife will be angry; and now you can move into this gentleman's chaise."

"No, no, no! I won't hear of it."

The fair-haired companion was one of those people whose characters seem at first to contain a streak of stubbornness. No sooner have you opened your mouth to speak than they are preparing to dispute what you say and will apparently never agree with anything that is manifestly contrary to their own manner of thinking nor will they ever call stupidity wisdom, nor in particular, will they ever agree to dance to another man's tune; but the end result is always the same: they always turn out to be soft, they agree to the very idea they have denied, they do call stupidity wisdom, and they turn out to be very good at dancing to someone else's tune: in a word, what starts with a riot ends in quiet.

"Nonsense!" snapped Nozdryov in answer to some argument of his fair-haired friend, putting on his hat for him and—and the friend tagged along with them after all.

"Master! You haven't paid for the vodka," said the old lady.

"Ah yes, of course. Listen, brother-in-law, settle up, will you? I haven't a kopek in my pocket."

"How much do we owe you?" asked the brother-in-law.

"Only twenty kopeks."

"Nonsense. Give her fifteen, that's more than enough for her."

"It's not really enough, master," protested the old woman, nevertheless accepting the proffered money with gratitude and eagerly bustling forward to open the door for them. She had not made a loss as she had asked four times what the vodka cost.

The travellers took their places. Chichikov's chaise travelled alongside the chaise bearing Nozdryov and his brother-in-law, and thus all three were able to chat with one another the entire length of the journey. They were followed at an inexorably increasing distance by Nozdryov's little buggy, pulled by scrawny hired horses. In it sat Porfiry and the puppy.

Since the conversation between our voyagers would not be of great interest to the reader, we will do better by telling something more about Nozdryov, who will perhaps be destined to play not the least significant role in our story.

People of Nozdryov's type are no doubt already fairly familiar to the reader. We have each of us had occasion to encounter a great many like him. They are called dashing fellows even as children and at school they are known for good friends, and yet they come in for quite painful beatings. Their faces always display something open, direct and devil-may-care. They are quick to make friends, and in no time are on the most intimate terms. The friendship is to last forever, it would seem, but somehow it invariably happens that the new friends quarrel that very same evening, at their first binge together. They are always line-spinners, carousers and dashing blades, they like to be seen and noticed. At the age of thirty-five Nozdryov was exactly the same as he had been at eighteen and twenty: a great one for carousing. Marriage had not changed him one whit, the more so since his wife soon quit him for a better world, leaving behind two babes, who were of no need to Nozdryov at all. The children were, however, taken care of, by a pretty young nanny. He was quite incapable of staying at home for more than one day at a time. His keen scent could detect from dozens of versts away where a fair was being held, with all its gatherings and balls; in the twinkling of an eye he would transport himself there, to enter battle at the green tables, for like all such men, he had a great passion for cards. His card playing, as we have already seen in the first chapter, was not entirely sinless and clean, since he knew many different little tricks and other refinements, and therefore it very often ended with a different sort of game: either he was given a sound drubbing or his luxuriant and most excellent side-whiskers received a very good tugging, so that he sometimes returned home with just one side-whisker and at that a rather mangy one. But his full and healthy cheeks were so well constituted and had such growing power that the side whisker soon grew back and was even better than the old one. But strangest of all, and this is something only possible in Russia, after a little while he would be playing cards again with the friends who had thrashed him, they would meet as if nothing had happened, and he would think nothing of it, and they would think nothing of it.

In a sense, Nozdryov was a history-making man, for no gathering at which he was present could go off without an *histoire*. Either he was escorted out of the room by constables, or was kicked out by his own companions. If it was not this, it was something else, such as never happens to anyone else: he would either get so plastered in the refreshment room that he could only giggle foolishly, or he would tell such tall tales that in the end he would himself feel ashamed. He would lie quite without any reason, suddenly announcing that he once had a horse with a blue or pink coat, and similar rubbish, finally driving all his listeners away, who would mutter as they retreated: "Really, brother, the yarns you spin!" There are people who have a passion for doing the dirty on their fellow men, sometimes for no reason at all. You will even find a gentleman of rank, with a noble mien, a star on his chest, who will shake your hand, converse with you on matters profound and thought-provoking, and then, to your astonishment, right before your very eyes, will do the dirty on you. And he will do it just like some paltry collegiate registrar, and not at all like a man with a star on his chest, capable of conversation on matters profound and thought-provoking, so that you can only stand in wonderment, shrugging your shoulders and nothing more. Noz-dryov had this very same quirk. The closer a friend of his a person became, the more he would single this same friend out for his malice: he would spread some unimagi-nably ridiculous slander, break up a betrothal or a busi-ness deal and yet would not in any way regard himself as your enemy; on the contrary, if fate were to bring you together again he would treat you as an old friend and even say: "Aren't you a scoundrel, never calling on me!" Nozdryov was a man of diverse interests, and anything was good for sport. At one and the same moment he could offer to go with you anywhere you liked, even to the end of the world, to embark on any business venture, to exchange anything at all for whatever you wished. His gun, dog, horse—to him they were all objects for barter, with no profit in mind at all, and the exchange proceeded en-tirely from his irrepressible esprit and vitality of character. If he had the good fortune to come across a simpleton at the fair and clean him out at cards he would buy up a pile of whatever he clapped his eyes on: horse collars, wax tapers, kerchiefs for the nanny, a stallion, raisins, a silver wash-stand, Dutch sailcloth, flour, tobacco, pistols, salt-ed herring, pictures, a grindstone, pots, boots, crockery—until the money ran out. However, these purchases rarely reached home; perhaps that very same day they would all be lost to another, luckier player, sometimes with the ad-dition of his own pipe complete with tobacco pouch and mouth-piece, or even with his coach-and-four together with the coachman, so that the owner himself would set off in his short coat or kaftan in search of some friend or other who would let him share his carriage. For such a one was Nozdryov! Perhaps people will call him an obsolete type, asserting that there are no Nozdryovs today. Alas! Those who say this are mistaken. Nozdryov will be around in this world for a long time to come. He is everywhere amongst us, except possibly that he wears a different kaf-tan; but people are careless and lacking in perspicacity, and to them a man in a different kaftan seems a different man.

Meanwhile the three carriages had already rolled up to the porch of Nozdryov's house. Nothing had been pre-pared in the house for their arrival. Two wooden trestles had been placed in the middle of the dining room, and on these stood two peasants who were whitewashing the walls and intoning some interminable song; the floor was thoroughly bespattered with whitewash. Nozdryov at once ordered the men to make themselves scarce with their trestles and dashed into the next room to issue instructions. His guests heard him order the cook to make luncheon; realising the implications of this Chichikov, whose appetite had started to revive, calculated that they would not sit down to table earlier than five o'clock. Nozdryov meanwhile returned and took his guests on a conducted tour of his estate, but in a little over two hours he had shown them absolutely everything, as there simply was nothing more to show. First of all they went to inspect the stables, where they saw two mares, one a piebald grey, the other a chestnut, and then a bay stallion, not particularly prepossessing to look at, but for which Nozdryov swore to have paid ten thousand.

"You never paid ten thousand for him," remarked the brother-in-law. "He isn't even worth one."

"I swear to God, I paid ten thousand," said Nozdryov.

"You can swear until you're blue in the face," retorted the brother-in-law.

"Well then, let's take a wager on it!" said Nozdryov. The brother-in-law declined this offer.

Then Nozdryov showed them some empty stalls, where previously there had been other fine horses. In this same stable they also saw a billy-goat, which was kept with the horses in accordance with an old superstition, and which appeared to be on good terms with them, strolling about blithely beneath their bellies. Then Nozdryov took them to see a wolf-cub which he kept on a chain.

"Now there's a wolf-cub!" he said. "I deliberately feed him raw meat because I want him to grow into a fierce beast!"

They went to view the pond in which, according to Nozdryov, there were fish of such gigantic size that it took two men to pull out a single one and that with great difficulty, another story about which his brother-in-law was quick to express reservations.

"Now Chichikov," said Nozdryov, "I shall show you a superb pair of borzois: the strength of their thighs is simply incredible, and their muzzles—pointed like needles!"

And he led the way to a very elegantly constructed little house, surrounded on all sides by a large walled yard. Entering this yard they saw a great variety of dogs, shaggy and smooth-coated, of every possible shape and colour: dark red, black with white flecks, dun-skewbald, spotted-skewbald, brown-skewbald, black-eared, grey-eared... All the known canine names were represented: Shooter, Scolder, Glitter, Blaze, Squinty, Chopper, Pest, Scorcher, Northy, Prize. With them Nozdryov was like a father amongst his children; they all at once lifted high their tails, and dashed across to greet the guests. A good ten of them jumped up and put their paws on Nozdryov's shoulders. Scolder bestowed the same sign of favour on Chichikov and, standing on his hind legs, licked him full in the mouth, making him spit in disgust. They inspected the dogs, the strength of whose thighs provoked their incredulity— they were indeed fine dogs. Then they set off to view a Crimean bitch, which was already blind, and according to Nozdryov would soon die, although only two years ago she had been a fine bitch; they viewed the bitch, and the bitch, indeed, was blind. Then they set off to inspect the windmill, which was missing the sprocket holding the upper mill-stone—the "whizzer", in the marvellous expression of the Russian peasant, because of the way it "whizzes" round its axle.

"We shall soon come to the smithy!" said Nozdryov.

Walking on a little way they did indeed come to the smithy, and duly inspected it.

"Now in this field here," said Nozdryov, pointing, "there are so many hares, you can't see the ground for them; I actually caught one by its hind legs with my bare hands."

"Come now, you'll never catch a hare with your bare hands!" objected the brother-in-law.

"I did catch it, I did!" retorted Nozdryov, and turning to Chichikov said: "And now I shall take you to see the boundary, where my land ends."

Nozdryov led his guests through a field which in many places was covered with tussocks. His guests were obliged to pick their way between strips of fallow and harrowed land. Chichikov was beginning to feel weary. In many places their feet squelched in water, so low-lying was the terrain. At first they tried to step carefully over these areas, but then, realising the futility of this, they ploughed on regardless, not bothering to ascertain where the mire was deeper and where shallower. After covering a considerable distance they did indeed see the boundary, consisting of a wooden post and a narrow ditch.

"There's the boundary!" announced Nozdryov. "Everything you see on this side is mine, and even on the other side, the whole of that forest you can see way over there in the distance, and everything beyond the forest, that's all mine too."

"Since when has that forest been yours?" asked the brother-in-law. "Do you mean you've recently bought it? It used not to be yours."

"Yes, I bought it recently," said Nozdryov.

"How did you manage to do that so quickly?"

"No problem, I bought it the day before yesterday, and paid a fortune for it too, confound it."

"But you were at the fair then."

"For goodness' sake, Sofron! Are you saying it's impossible to be at the fair and buy land at the same time? Yes, I was at the fair, and my steward bought it here in my absence."

"Your steward—of course!" said the brother-in-law, and shook his head in doubt.

The guests returned by the same disagreeable route to the house. Nozdryov led the way into his study, which, however, lacked any trace of the usual appurtenances of such places, to wit, books and paper; on the walls hung sabres and two guns, one costing three hundred, the other eight hundred rubles. The brother-in-law only shook his head as he inspected them. Then Nozdryov showed his guests some Turkish daggers, on one of which the words "Craftsman Savely Sibiryakov" had been engraved by mistake. After these the guests were shown a barrel-organ. Nozdryov at once gave them a tune. The barrel-organ emitted a not unpleasant sound, but something must have come unstuck inside it, because the mazurka ended off as the song "Marlborough s'en va-t-en guerre", and this suddenly ended with some popular old waltz. Nozdryov had stopped turning the handle, but the organ had one very large pair of bellows inside, and this showed no sign of abating, whistling away by itself for a long time. Then they were shown pipes—wooden, clay, meerschaum, smoked-in and not yet smoked-in, suede covered and uncovered, a chibouk with an amber mouthpiece which he had recently won at cards, a tobacco pouch, embroidered by some countess who had fallen head-over-heels in love with him at some post-house, and whose little hands, in his own words, were most sublimely *superflescence*—a phrase which with him appeared to signify the summit of perfection. After an hors d'oeuvre of smoked sturgeon they waited for dinner until five o'clock. Dinner, it appeared, was not the most important thing in Nozdryov's life; some of the dishes were burnt, others were sadly underdone. It was apparent that the chef guided himself by some sixth sense and threw in the first ingredients that came to hand: if the pepper was near at hand in would go a dash of pepper, if some cabbage was handy he would stick in the cabbage, also milk, ham, peas—in short, any old thing would do, so long as the dish was hot, for there was bound to be some sort of taste in the end. Nozdryov did, however, set great store by his wines: even before the soup had been served he had already poured large glasses of port and similarly large glasses of "Haut Sauterne", for plain Sauterne is not to be had in our provincial and district capitals. Then Nozdryov called for a bottle of Madeira, declaring that the Field Marshal himself had never drunk better. The Madeira did indeed burn on the tongue, for the merchants selling it, familiar as they were with the taste of landowners, mercilessly laced it with rum, and on other occasions even poured in some aqua regia trusting in the Russian constitution to stand anything. Then Nozdryov called for another special bottle of something or other, which according to him was a blend of Champagnon and Bourgognon. He lavishly poured it out, right and left, into the glasses of his brother-in-law and Chichikov; but Chichikov noticed that Nozdryov did not pour much for himself. This told him to be cautious, and whenever Nozdryov became absorbed in what he was saying or was busy filling his brother-in-law's glass, Chichikov would promptly empty his own into his plate. Before long some rowanberry vodka was served, which, according to Nozdryov, had the smoothness of cream, but which in fact startingly tasted of rot-gut at its potent worst. Then they drank a balsam with a name too difficult to even remember, so much so that Nozdryov himself called it something else the second time round. Dinner was long over, and all the varieties of liquor had been sampled, but the guests remained seated at table. Chichikov was quite unable to broach his main subject in the presence of the brother-in-law. For the brother-in-law was after all an outsider, and Chichikov's subject demanded confidential and friendly discussion. The brother-in-law, however, would hardly have posed much of a threat, because it seemed he had sampled to his heart's content, and still seating in his chair, kept nodding and startling up guiltily. Finally realising that he was no longer entirely *compos mentis*, he started to talk of going home, but in an extremely lethargic and listless manner.

"No, no, no! I won't hear of it!" said Nozdryov.

"No my friend, I really must go," said the brother-in-law. "I'll mind very much if you won't let me."

"Nonsense, nonsense! We'll get a game of cards going right away!"

"No, you go ahead, and play it, but I can't join you, the wife will be terribly annoyed, she will, I really have to tell her all about the fair. No I must, brother, I must give her that pleasure. No, no, don't detain me!"

"Well confound her, your wife, to hell with her! I can just imagine what important business you two have to do!"

"No brother! She's so respectable and true! She does me such favours... Believe me, it's bringing the tears to my eyes. No, don't try and keep me; honestly I must go. It's the honest truth."

"Let him go, what use is he anyway?" interjected Chichikov quietly.

"How very true!" agreed Nozdryov. "I can't abide wet rags like him!" And to his brother-in-law he said: "Well, confound you, go and knit stockings with your wife, you nanny-goat!"

"No, brother, don't you call me a nanny-goat," answered the brother-in-law. "I owe her my very life. She's truly so kind and sweet, she does such nice things ... it brings tears to my eyes. She'll ask me what I saw at the fair, I must tell her everything. She's so sweet, truly she is."

"Well, go then, and tell her your load of claptrap! Here's your hat."

"No, brother, you really shouldn't talk of her in that tone; that way you're hurting my feelings, you know, she is so sweet."

"Run to her then, run!"

"Yes brother, I shall, and forgive me for not being able to stay. I would be sincerely delighted if I could, but I cannot."

The brother-in-law continued in this apologetic vein for a long time, not even noticing that he had in fact long been seated in his chaise, had long since driven out of the gates and that before him there had long been only empty fields. We cannot but surmise that his wife was not vouchsafed many details about the fair.

"What a rotter!" said Nozdryov, standing before the window and gazing at the departing carriage. "Just look at him crawling along! The trace-horse is not bad, I've wanted to get my hands on him for ages. But it's quite impossible to come to an agreement with him. A nanny-goat, that's what he is!"

Thereupon they returned inside. Porfiry set out candles, and Chichikov noticed that in his hands his host had a pack of cards that had appeared from God knows where.

"How about it?" asked Nozdryov, arching the pack so that the wrapping snapped. "Just to pass the time, I'll hold the bank at three hundred rubles."

But Chichikov pretended not to have heard the suggestion, and as if he had suddenly remembered said: "Ah! Before I forget: there's something I want to ask you."

"What?"

"But first give me your word you'll do what I ask."

"But what's the request?"

"First give me your word!"

"Very well."

"On your word?"

"On my word."

"This is my request: I dare say you have a great number of peasants who have died but have remained in the census lists?"

"I dare say I have, so what?"

"Transfer them to me, to my name."

"What do you want with them?"

"Well, I just need them."

"What for?"

"I just need them ... it's my business, anyway,—in a word, I need them."

"You've got some scheme, I can see it. Own up, what is it?"

"But what scheme could I have? What could you scheme with rubbish like that?"

"So why do you need them, then?"

"Oh, isn't he inquisitive! He has to pick up every bit of rubbish, finger it and sniff it, too."

"Why won't you tell me?"

"But what will you gain by knowing? All right, it's simply a whim."

"I won't play until you tell me, and that's that!"

"Now you see, that's not honest of you: you gave your word, now you're trying to back out."

"Have it how you will, but I won't play until you tell me what it's about."

"What can I tell him?" thought Chichikov and after a minute's reflection declared that he needed the dead souls to gain some weight in society, that he did not own any large estates, so in the meantime he would like to have some souls at least.

"You lie! You lie!" said Nozdryov, cutting him short. "You're lying, brother!"

Chichikov himself could see that he had not thought up a very clever excuse, and that his pretext was rather feeble.

"Well in that case I'll be more frank," he said, recovering his aplomb. "Only I beg you not to breathe a word of it to anyone. I've decided to marry; but I must tell you that my betrothed's mother and father are extremely ambitious people. I'm in such a predicament, you know, I'm sorry I started the whole thing. They absolutely insist that the husband-to-be should have no less than three hundred souls, and seeing that I am short by almost a hundred and fifty..."

"Liar! You lie!" shouted Nozdryov again.

"Oh no, this time I haven't lied even this much," said Chichikov and demonstrated the top joint of his little finger with his thumb.

"I'll bet my life that you're lying!"

"This is really becoming insulting! Who do you think I am? Why are you so certain I'm lying?"

"Ah, but I know you, you see: you're a terrible rogue, allow me to tell you that as a friend! If you were subservient to me I should hang you from the very first tree!"

Chichikov took umbrage at this remark. Indeed, any remark that was ever so slightly coarse or injurious to good breeding, was upsetting to him. He even was not prepared to let pass any over-familiar behaviour unless it originated from one of very high rank. And for this reason he now took great offence.

"I swear, I would hang you," repeated Nozdryov, "I'm telling you quite frankly, not to offend you, but simply as a friend."

"There's a limit to everything," said Chichikov with dignity. "If you wish to flaunt such threats in your conversation, the barrack-room is the place for you," and then added, "If you won't give them away you might sell them."

"Sell them! But I know you, you rogue, you won't give much for them."

"You're a fine one yourself! Look at that! Are they made of diamonds or something?"

"There you are. I just knew it."

"I beg your pardon, brother, but you argue like a Jew! You should simply hand them over to me."

"Well, just to prove that I'm not some sort of skinflint, I won't take a thing for them. Buy a stallion from me and I'll give you them into the bargain."

"What on earth do I need a stallion for?" said Chichikov, genuinely astonished at this proposal.

"What for? But do you realise I paid ten thousand for him and I'll let you have him for four?"

"But I have no need of a stallion. I do not run a stud farm."

"Listen, I don't think you understand: all I'm asking you for now is three thousand, and you can give me the remaining thousand later."

"But I do not need any stallion, confound it!"

"All right, buy the chestnut mare."

"Nor do I need any mares."

"For the mare and that grey horse I showed you I'd be

prepared to accept a mere two thousand."

"I tell you I do not need a horse at all."

"You can sell them, you'll get three times as much at the very first fair."

"In that case you would do better to sell them yourself, since you're so sure you'll get triple."

"I know I'll make a profit, but I want you to benefit as well."

Chichikov thanked him for his consideration and adamantly refused both the grey horse and the chestnut mare.

"In that case buy some dogs. I'll sell you a couple that'll send a shiver down your spine! Shaggy beasts with big whiskers and thick, bristly coats. You have to see the rib-cage to believe it, and such trim paws, they hardly touch the ground."

"But what do I need dogs for? I'm not a hunter."

"I'd like you to have some dogs. Listen, if you don't want any dogs, why don't you buy my barrel-organ? It's a wonderful organ, and I tell you on my word of honour, I paid one and a half thousand for it: I'll let you have it for nine hundred."

"But what do I need a barrel-organ for? I'm no German, to lug it around the streets begging money."

"But this is not the sort of barrel-organ that Germans use. This is the real thing; just take a close look: it's solid mahogany. Let me play it to you again!"

Here Nozdryov, seizing Chichikov's hand, started to pull him into the next room, and despite the latter's resistance and remonstrations that he already knew what the organ was like, he still had to hear once again how Marlborough betook himself to war. "If you don't want to pay money I've got another idea, listen: I'll give you the organ and everything else I have, dead souls too, and you give me your chaise and three hundred rubles into the bargain."

"Excellent idea! And in what, pray, am I to travel?"

"I'll give you another chaise. Let's go into the shed, I'll show it to you! All it needs is a coat of paint and it'll be a beauty."

"What confounded ideas the devil has put into his head!" thought Chichikov and determined at whatever cost to keep safe from any chaises, barrel-organs or dogs of whatever breed, regardless of their unimaginable rib-cage and trimness of their paws.

"But I'm offering the chaise, the barrel organ, and dead souls too, the whole lot!"

"I don't want them," said Chichikov yet again.

"Why don't you want them?"

"Because I just don't want them, and that's the end of it."

"You're a rare specimen and no mistake! There's no dealing with you like with a decent friend or comrade, not you, oh no!... Now I can see how double-faced you are!"

"What sort of fool do you take me for? Think for yourself: why on earth should I acquire something I have absolutely no use for?"

"No, I beg you, say no more. Now I see right through you. What a thorough scoundrel! Well now, listen, if you like I'll stake them at cards. I'll stake all my dead souls, and the barrel-organ too."

"By staking everything you are subjecting yourself to uncertainty," said Chichikov with a sideways glance at the cards in Nozdryov's hands. Both packs looked as though they might well have been doctored and even the pattern on the jackets looked decidedly suspicious.

"What do you mean uncertainty?" demanded Nozdryov. "There's nothing uncertain about it! You only need luck on your side and you can win the devil of a lot. That's the thing! It's all luck!" he said, dealing and working himself up into a fever of excitement. "It's all luck! Just luck! You never know when it'll strike! Now there's that cursed nine on which I blew the lot! I had a feeling that it would let me down, but I screwed up my eyes and thought: 'All right, you swine, go on and let me down, damn you!' "

While Nozdryov was saying this Porfiry brought in a bottle. But Chichikov firmly refused both to play and to drink.

"And why will you not play?" asked Nozdryov.

"Because I do not feel like it. And to be perfectly honest, I'm no great lover of cards anyway."

"Why not?"

"I'm just not." Chichikov shrugged.

"Now, aren't you a rotter!"

"I can't help it. That's the way God made me."

"A nanny-goat, that's what you are! I used to think you had some decency in you, but you have simply no idea how to behave. It's impossible to talk to you as a good friend ... you've no honesty, no sincerity! You're just like Sobakevich, a real swine!"

"But why do you insult me? Is my not playing cards an offence? Why won't you just sell me the souls, if you're the sort of person who grudges such rubbish?"

"You'll get damn all, that's what you'll get! I wanted to give you them for nothing, I really did, but not now, oh no! You can offer me three kingdoms and I still won't let them go. What a swindler! From now on I do not wish to have any dealings with you. Porfiry, go and tell the stable boy not to give his horses any oats, let them eat hay only."

This last instruction quite took Chichikov by surprise.

"I only wish I had never set eyes on you!" said Nozdryov.

However, the host and his guest sat down to sup together, despite their quarrel. True, this time there were no wines with exotic names on the table. There was only one bottle containing some sort of Cyprus sherry, of the kind universally regarded as pure unadulterated vinegar. After supper Nozdryov said to Chichikov, taking him to a side room in which a bed had been prepared for him:

"That's your bed! I don't even want to wish you a good night!"

Nozdryov departed and Chichikov was left in the worst possible mood. He was vexed with himself and chided himself for coming to this place and thus wasting his time. But he cursed himself still more for having broached his subject with Nozdryov, for having acted without discretion, like a child, like a fool: for this was no matter to be entrusted to Nozdryov... Nozdryov was a bouncer, Nozdryov might talk, exaggerate, spread the devil knows what lies, the gossips would make much of the scandal—it was bad, very bad. "I'm a plain fool," he said to himself. He slept very badly that night. Some exceptionally nimble little insects inflicted such unbearably painful bites on him that he scratched away at the bites with all his fingers, muttering: "Damn and blast you, together with Nozdryov!" He awoke early on the following morning. Without further ado he donned his dressing gown and boots and went across the courtyard to the stables to order Selifan to harness the chaise at once. On his way back across the yard he encountered Nozdryov, who was also in his dressing gown, and with his pipe between his teeth. Nozdryov greeted him most cordially and asked if he had slept well.

"So-so," answered Chichikov very drily.

"As for me, brother," said Nozdryov, "I had such horrible dreams all night, too sickening to recount, and I have such a foul taste in my mouth as though a squadron of horses has been camping in it. Just imagine: I dreamt I was being whipped, I swear! And guess by whom? You'll never guess: Staff Officer Potseluyev together with Kuvshinnikov."

"Hm," thought Chichikov, "if only they really would whip you!"

"Honest to God! The whip stung! I woke up: and blow me down if I'm not really itching—sure enough, it's those cursed fleas. Well, you run along now and get dressed and I'll join you shortly. First I must go and bawl out that scoundrel of a steward."

Chichikov withdrew to his room to dress and wash. When he emerged into the dining room he found the table set for breakfast with a bottle of rum. The room retained traces of the dinner and supper the day before; it appeared to be quite untouched by any form of brush or broom. The floor was strewn with breadcrumbs, and there was tobacco ash even on the tablecloth. Our host himself, who promptly joined Chichikov, wore nothing but a dressing gown open on his chest, on which a sort of beard was growing. Clutching a long pipe in his hand and slurping tea from his cup he presented a fine subject for the painter who cannot abide well-groomed and pomaded gentlemen, like those on barbershop signs, or those with fancy haircuts.

"Well now, what have you decided?" asked Nozdryov, after a brief silence. "Do you not wish to play for the souls?"

"I've already told you, my friend, that I do not play; as for buying them, I'll buy them with pleasure."

"I would not like to sell them, that would not be friendly. I'm not one to derive profit from worthless rubbish. But staking them in a game—that's quite another story. Let us at least play one round!"

"I have already said no."

"Will you not swap them?"

"I will not."

"Listen then, let's play draughts, and if you win they're all yours. After all, I have a lot of those which should be removed from the census list. Hey, Porfiry, bring us the draughts board."

"You're wasting your time, I will not play."

"But this is not gambling; there's no question of good or bad luck here: it's pure skill; I can even assure you that I'm a hopeless player, and you might perhaps give me a small handicap."

"Maybe I really should play a game of draughts with him!" thought Chichikov. "I used to be a fair player, and it will be hard for him to pull a fast one here."

"Very well, so be it: I'll play you draughts."

"The souls stand at one hundred rubles!"

"That much? Fifty will be quite enough."

"No, what sort of a stake is fifty? For that amount I might just as well throw in a middlish puppy or a gold watch fob."

"Very well!" said Chichikov.

"What sort of handicap will you give me?" asked Nozdryov.

"Why on earth should I? None at all, of course."

"At least let me make the first two moves."

"Certainly not, I'm a poor player myself."

"I know the sort of poor player you are!" said Nozdryov, moving a piece.

"It's ages since I held a draughts piece in my hand!" said Chichikov also moving forward a piece.

"I know the sort of poor player you are!" said Nozdryov, moving a piece.

"It's ages since I held a draughts piece in my hand!" said Chichikov, moving forward a piece.

"I know the sort of poor player you are!" said Nozdryov, moving a piece, and at the same time nudging forward another piece with the cuff of his sleeve.

"It's ages since I... I say, what's all this! Put it back!" cried Chichikov.

"Put what back?"

"That piece, of course!" said Chichikov and even as he said this he could see before his very nose another piece which was well on its way to becoming a king. "No," said Chichikov, rising from the table, "it's quite impossible to play with you! That's no way to play: moving three pieces at a time."

"What do you mean, three pieces? That was a slip. One was pushed accidentally, and look, I'll move it back."

"Then where did the other one appear from?"

"What other one?"

"This one, about to become a king."

"I like that, as if you didn't remember!"

"No, I've been counting all the moves and I remember everything: you've only just slipped it in there now. That's where it should be!"

"What do you mean, where?" asked Nozdryov, flushing. "You're quite a fibber, I see!"

"No, brother, it's you who are a fibber and not a very successful one."

"Who do you take me for?" cried Nozdryov. "Cheat, would I?"

"I do not take you for anyone, but one thing is for sure: I shall never play with you again."

"No, you cannot refuse now," said Nozdryov, incensed, "the game has started!"

"I have the right to refuse because you are not playing as befits an honest man."

"No, you lie, you cannot say that!"

"No, brother, *you're* the liar!"

"I was not cheating, and you cannot withdraw, you have to finish the game!"

"You will never force me," said Chichikov coolly and, standing up, scattered the pieces.

Nozdryov flared up and stepped so close to Chichikov that the latter recoiled a couple of paces.

"I *will* force you to play! It makes no difference that you've scattered the pieces, I can remember all the moves. We'll set them out just as they were."

"No, brother, the matter's closed; I shall not play any more with you."

"You mean you will not play?"

"You can see yourself that it's impossible to play with you."

"No, tell me straight out: you do not want to play?" said Nozdryov, advancing on him.

"I do not want to play!" said Chichikov, but to be on the safe side he raised his hands to his face, for things were getting very hot indeed.

This precaution was, as it happens, very timely, because Nozdryov swung an arm—and one of our hero's agreeably plump cheeks might well have been ineradicably stained with ignominy; fortunately enough, he parried the blow, gripped the irrascible Nozdryov by both hands and held him firmly.

"Porfiry! Pavlushka!" Nozdryov yelled in a frenzy, trying to wrench himself free.

On hearing this Chichikov, who did not wish to make the servants witnesses to such a corrupting scene and at the same time sensed the futility of holding Nozdryov, released his arms. At that very moment in came Porfiry and Pavlushka, a strapping fellow to tangle with whom would have been most ill-advised.

"So you do not wish to finish the game?" said Nozdryov. "Give me a straight answer!"

"It's quite impossible to finish the game," said Chichikov, with a glance through the window. He could see his chaise, which was all ready, with Selifan waiting, apparently, for a wave before driving up to the porch, but he had not a chance to escape from the room with the two hefty idiot serfs standing in the doorway.

"So you do not wish to finish the game?" repeated Nozdryov, his face flushing a fiery red.

"I would if you played as befits an honest man. But now I cannot play."

"Ah, you can't, you scoundrel! You're losing so you can't! Give him a beating!" he shrieked in a frenzy, turning to Porfiry and Pavlushka, while he himself reached for a long cherry-wood pipe. Chichikov went as pale as a sheet. He tried to say something, but he felt his lips moving without making a sound.

"Beat him up!" shouted Nozdryov, lurching forward, brandishing his pipe, flushed and covered with sweat, as if pitting himself against an invincible fortress. "Go for him!" he shouted in the voice of a reckless lieutenant urging his platoon on to some great exploit; a lieutenant whose manic daring has already attained such notoriety that special orders have been issued for him to be held by the arms during the heat of battle. But the lieutenant is already fired with bellicose fervour, his head is spinning; the image of Suvorov hovers before him, he longs for glory. "Forward, lads!" he shouts in a frenzy, not realising that he is upsetting the general plan of attack, and that millions of gun barrels are being levelled at him through the embrasures of unassailable fortress walls, dissappearing into the clouds, and that his helpless platoon is about to vanish into the air like so much fluff, and that a fateful bullet is already whistling through the air, on its way to plug his clamorous throat once and for all. But whilst Nozdryov may have resembled a desperate, madcap lieutenant storming a fortress, the fortress on which he marched looked anything but unassailable. On the contrary, the fortress was stricken with such terror, that its heart was in its mouth. Even the chair, with which he had prepared to defend himself, had been wrested from his hands by the servants, and with his eyes screwed shut in a dead funk, he was waiting to be hit by his host's Circassian pipe, and the Lord only knows what would have become of him. The fates, however, saw fit to preserve from injury the limbs, shoulders and other well-bred parts of our hero. Suddenly, out of the blue, came the jingling of bells and the rattle of a trap sweeping up to the porch, and even inside the room they could hear the heavy breathing and laboured snorting of the overheated horses outside. Everyone involuntarily looked through the window: a man with a moustache, in a half-military frock-coat, was alighting from the trap. Making enquiries in the hall, he entered the room at the very moment, when Chichikov, still unable to recover from his fright, was in the most pitiful state a mortal has ever found himself in.

"Might I enquire which of you gentlemen is Mr Nozdryov?" asked the stranger, looking with some bewilderment at Nozdryov, brandishing his pipe, and at Chichikov, who had barely begun to recover.

"Might I first make so bold as to enquire with whom I have the honour to speak?" asked Nozdryov, stepping closer up to him.

"Captain of police."

"And what can I do for you?"

"I have come to convey to you information that has

been imparted to me, namely that you are on trial until such time as a decision is reached in your case."

"What's all this nonsense, what case?"

"You have been implicated in an affair, concerning the infliction on landowner Maximov of personal injury with a birch rod when you were in a state of inebriation."

"You're lying! I've never clapped eyes on landowner Maximov!"

"Sir! Allow me to remind you that I am an officer. You may say such things to your servant, but not to me."

At this point Chichikov resolved not to wait for Nozdryov's reply, and snatching his hat slipped behind the police captain's back out onto the porch, climbed into his chaise and ordered Selifan to whip the horses on for all they were worth.

CHAPTER FIVE

Our hero certainly took a terrible fright. Although his chaise raced along like a bat from hell and Nozdryov's village had long been lost from sight behind the fields and rolling countryside, he continued to glance back with fear, as if expecting to be overtaken at any moment. His breathing was laboured and when he pressed his hand to his heart he felt it fluttering like a quail in a cage. "Goodness, what a drubbing he nearly gave me! Thinks he can get away with anything!" Here, many unpleasant and strongly desired things were wished on Nozdryov; certain indecorous words were even uttered. But who can blame him? He was Russian, and angry besides. And then, this was no joking matter. "Whichever way you look at it," he said to himself, "if that captain of police hadn't turned up in the nick of time I might have breathed my last in this world! I would have vanished without a trace, like a bubble on the water, leaving no descendants, leaving neither a fortune nor an honourable name to my future children!" Our hero was most concerned about his descendants.

"My, what a mean gentleman, that one!" Selifan was thinking. "I've never seen a gentleman like him! I'd like to spit in his face! All right, don't give a man anything to eat, but you've got to feed a horse, because a horse loves his oats. That's his provisionals, see: what's tack to us that's oats to him, that's his provisionals."

The horses also, it appeared, had formed a poor opinion of Nozdryov: not only the bay and Assessor, the dappled horse too was out of spirits. Although he usually got the worst share of the oats and Selifan could not fill his trough without first muttering: "Oh you, shirker!" all the same, it was still oats, and not plain old hay, and he would chew it with relish, frequently thrusting his long face into his comrades' troughs to check what sort of provisions they had been given, especially when Selifan had left the stable, but here all they had had was hay ... that was not good; everyone was disgruntled.

But soon all the disgruntled were interrupted in the midst of their fulminations in the most sudden and unexpected manner. Every one of them, not excepting the coachman himself, only came properly to his senses when a carriage drawn by a team of six horses bore down upon them and the air right above their heads was rent by the shrieks of the ladies inside it, and the oaths and threats of its coachman: "Hey you, there! Didn't you hear me yelling at you, you half-wit, to get off the road, to keep to the right! Are you drunk or what?" Selifan was aware of his own culpability, but like any Russian who hates to admit to others that he is in the wrong, he at once riposted, in high dudgeon: "And just who do you think you are, belting along like that? Got blind drunk at the pub?" He then started tugging back his team, to free them from the harnesses of the other horses, but it was not to be, for they were hopelessly entangled.

Then dappled horse was sniffing with great curiosity at his new friends, who were now on both sides of him. All the while the ladies seated inside the carriage looked on with fear written large on their faces. One of them was an old lady, the other a pretty girl, no more than sixteen, with golden tresses, deftly and charmingly smoothed down over her head. Her sweet face was oval like a fresh egg and glowed with that same translucent whiteness that you see in a freshly-laid egg when it is held up against the light in the swarthy hands of the housekeeper, who wants to see whether it is fresh; the girl's little ears were also translucent, and rosy from the warm light that shone through them. All this, plus the alarm on her parted lips and the tears in her eyes, made such a charming picture that our hero stared at her for some minutes, oblivious of the imbroglio in which the horses and coachmen were caught. "Back your horses, do you hear, you Nizhny Novgorod half-wit!" shouted the other coachman. Selifan tugged back his reins, the other coachman did likewise, the horses recoiled slightly and then collided once again, stepping over each other's traces. In this new configuration the dappled stallion was so pleased with his new acquaintance that he was quite determined not to step out of the rut into which he had landed in this unforeseen manner, and placing his muzzle against the neck of his new friend appeared to be whispering something right into his ear, no doubt some utter rubbish, for the newcomer constantly twitched his ears.

This fracas, however, drew a crowd of local peasants whose village, fortunately, was in the vicinity. Since such a spectacle is manna from heaven to a Russian peasant, as much a delight as newspaper or his club are to a German, soon such a multitude of them had gathered round the carriage that only the old women and small children were left in the village. They disentangled the traces; a few prods on the dappled horse's muzzle persuaded him to retreat; in short, they disengaged and separated them. But whether from pique, because they had been parted from their friends, or from sheer stupidity, however much the other coachman whipped his horses, they refused to budge and remained rooted to the spot. The peasants' participation had by now attained ridiculous proportions. Each of them pushed forward in turn with his advice: "Go on, Andryushka, you lead away the trace-horse on the right, and let old Mityai get up on the shaft-horse and ride it away! Up you get, Uncle Mityai!" The tall and lean ginger-bearded Uncle Mityai, duly climbed up on the shaft-horse and, once mounted, looked like a village bell-tower, or, even better, like the long crook they use to pull up the bucket from a well. The coachman whipped the horses, but to no avail, Uncle Mityai was unable to provide any assistance. "Stop, stop!" shouted the peasants. "You get on the trace-horse, Uncle Mityai, and let Uncle Minyai get up on the wheeler!" Uncle Minyai, a broad-shouldered peasant with a coal-black beard and a belly as round and full as the gigantic samovar in which they make enough honey-tea for the entire frozen populace at the market, gladly mounted the shaft-horse, whose back practically buckled to the ground. "Now things will start moving!" cried the peasants. "Give him stick! Let him have a taste of your whip—that one over there, the light bay, look at him balking like a great gallinipper!"* But when they saw that things were not moving and that no amount of stick helped, both Uncle Mityai and Uncle Minyai got on the shaft-horse's back and they seated Andryushka on the trace-horse. Finally, the thoroughly exasperated coachman drove away both Uncle Mityai and Uncle Minyai, and it was just as well he did, for the horses were giving off such a steam as if they had galloped an entire stage without drawing breath. He gave them a minute to rest, whereupon they moved off by themselves. Throughout all these proceedings Chichikov had remained raptly gazing at the pretty young girl. He essayed several times to engage her in conversation, but somehow nothing came of it. In the meantime the ladies drove off, the girl with the delicate features and the slender figure was lost from sight, like a vision, and once again there was only the road, the chaise, the equine threesome so familiar by now to the reader, Selifan, Chichikov, the smooth expanse and the emptiness of the neighbouring fields.

Everywhere, in all walks of life, whether amongst the hard and rough, untidy and rousty lower orders or amongst the uniformly cold and tediously proper upper classes, everywhere a man will encounter, at least once in his life, a phenomenon quite unlike anything he has seen hitherto, which at least that once will inspire in him a feeling quite unlike anything he has been fated to feel all the days of his life. Everywhere, despite all the sorrows from which our lives are woven, there will flash a glittering dream of joy, just like a glittering carriage with gold trappings, fairy-tale horses and sparkling windows which suddenly appears

---

Gallinipper—a large, long-legged, lethargic mosquito; it occasionally flies into a room and perches alone somewhere on the wall. You can easily walk up to it and grab it by the leg, in response to which it will only resist by spreading wide its legs, or balking, as the people put it. (Note by N. V. Gogol).

from nowhere and flashes past some wretched village out in the sticks, which has never seen anything other than a farm cart, and for a long time after the peasants remain standing, mouths agape, caps still doffed, although the wondrous carriage has long since passed from view. Thus too did the fair-haired beauty suddenly appear from nowhere in our story and just as suddenly vanish. Imagine if, instead of Chichikov this had been some twenty-year-old youth, a Hussar, say, or a student, or simply some fellow just starting out on his chosen career—and merciful God! What turmoil, what a fever would have raged in him! Long would he have stood insensate, rooted to the spot, his eyes fastened blankly on the distance, having quite forgotten his journey, and with it all the reprimands that awaited him, and the dressing-down for being late, having forgotten himself, his career, the world, and everything in it.

But our hero was already a man of middle age and of a temperate and circumspect character. He also grew pensive, but his thoughts were more positive, not so uncontrolled and in some respects even very practical. "A nice wench!" he said, opening his snuff-box and taking a pinch of snuff. "But, come to think of it, what's so nice about her? The best thing about her is that she's fresh from some boarding school for young gentlewomen, and that there is as yet no female affectations about her, in other words none of that which is most unpleasant about ladies. She is just like a child now, she does everything simply: she says whatever comes into her head and laughs when she wants to. She can be shaped into anything, she can become something marvellous, and she can just as easily turn into a nasty piece— which is what she will do! Just wait until all those mamas and aunties get to work on her. In one year she'll be so crammed full of genteel stuff and nonsense that her own father won't recognise her. Suddenly, before you know it, she'll go all prim and haughty, dumbly following the rules that had been drummed into her, calculating with whom and how, or how much she should speak, whom she should look at, and, living in constant fear of saying more than she should, finally getting so confused that she will end by quibbling all the time and turning into the devil knows what!" At this point he fell silent for a little while before adding: "Yet it would be intriguing to know who her people are? Who her father is, what he's like? Is he a rich and respectable landowner or simply some right-thinking chap with a bit of capital that he has acquired in the service? For if, let us suppose, this young girl should have a dowry of some two hundred thousand settled on her, she would make a very, very tasty morsel indeed. In fact it would be enough to secure the happiness of a decent man, you might say." The two hundred thousand now started to assume such an attractive shape in his mind that he became quite vexed with himself for having omitted, during all the bother with the carriages, to ascertain from either the postillion or the coachman the identity of the travellers. Soon, however, these vexatious thoughts were dispelled by the appearance of Sobakevich's village, and his mind was forced back to its customary subject.

The village struck Chichikov as fairly large; two woods, one of birch and the other of pine, bounded it on the left and on the right, like two wings, the one darker, the other lighter; in the middle stood a wooden house with an attic, a red roof and dingy grey, or rather, unpainted walls—a house like those built in Russia for military settlements and German colonists. It was evident that during its construction the architect had constantly warred with the owner's taste. The architect was a pedant and desired symmetry whereas the owner sought only comfort, and this had evidently caused him to board up all the matching windows on one side of the house, replacing them with just one small window, which was presumably necessary for the dark larder. The pediment also could not be fitted into the middle of the building, however hard the architect tried, because the owner ordered that one column on the side should be scrapped, with the result that there were not four columns, as intended, but only three. The yard was enclosed by a strong and extraordinarily thick wooden trellis. The owner, it seemed, was greatly concerned with solidity. The stables, sheds and cookhouses were constructed of thick and heavy logs, designed to last a hundred years. The peasants' huts were also a wonder to behold: there were no planed walls, carved ornamentation or other fanciful touches but everything had been firmly and properly joined. Even the shaft of the water well was made of the sort of strong oak that is normally only used for wind-

mills and ships. In a word, everything Chichikov set eyes
on was rugged and sturdy, inelegantly but solidly built. As
they drove up to the entrance, he saw two faces, which
glanced out of the windows almost simultaneously: a
female face, in a lace bonnet, long and narrow like a
cucumber, and a man's face, broad and round like a Molda-
vian pumpkin from which balalaikas are made in Russia,
the light two-stringed balalaika that is the passion and
adornment of every spirited young buck of twenty or so,
of every young blade and gallant winking and wolf-whistl-
ing at the girls with their lily-white bosoms and necks, who
have gathered round to listen to his soft-stringed strumming. After one glance both faces instantly vanished. A
footman in a grey jacket with a stiff, pale blue collar came
out onto the porch and conducted Chichikov into the hall,
where he was joined by the master of the house who
brusquely said: "This way please!" and led Chichikov
inside the house.

When Chichikov stole a sidelong glance at Sobakevich
he thought him remarkably like a medium-sized bear. To
complete the likeness, the suit he was wearing was exactly
bear-coloured, with sleeves and trousers too long for him;
he walked with a lumbering, awkward gait and constantly
trod on other people's toes. His complexion was a deep,
burnished red, the colour of a copper coin. As we all
know, there are many such faces in this world, faces over
whose finish Mother Nature wasted little time or effort,
disdaining to use fine instruments such as files, gimlets and
so forth, but has merely gone hacking away: one swipe of
the axe—and there's the nose; another swipe, and there's
the mouth, she gouges out the eyes with a great big brace
and bit, and without smoothing it off she pushed it out
into the world, saying: "Done!" Such was the very powerful and astonishingly rough-hewn countenance of Sobakevich: he held his head down more than up, never twisted
his neck at all, and, as a result, rarely looked at his interlocutor, staring instead at a corner of the stove, or at the
door. Chichikov cast him another sidelong glance, as they
walked through the dining-room: "A bear! A perfect bear!"
But imagine the strange coincidence: like the bears of folk-
tale he was even called Mikhail Semyonovich. Knowing his
host's tendency to tread on people's toes, Chichikov placed

his own feet with great care and allowed him to lead the way. Sobakevich appeared to be aware of this deficiency in himself and at once enquired: "Have I perhaps discomforted you?" But Chichikov thanked him and said that there had been no discomfort so far.

Entering the drawing-room, Sobakevich pointed at a chair and said again: "Please!" Chichikov sat down and glanced at the pictures hanging on the walls. They all depicted dashing warriors, all Greek generals, portrayed full length: there stood Mavrocordato in his red trousers and uniform, spectacles on his nose, Miaulis, Kanaris. All these heroes had such massive haunches and fabulous moustaches that it sent a shiver down his spine. Squeezed between these redoubtable Hellenes, heaven knows how or why, was our own Bagration,* thin and scrawny, with a few small battle standards and cannon at his feet, and provided with the narrowest of frames. Then came the Greek heroine Bobelina, with legs so massive that one of them would have exceeded in bulk the body of any of those dandies who throng our drawing-rooms today. The master of the house, himself a powerful and sturdily-built man, seemed to wish his room to be adorned likewise with powerful and sturdily-built people. Beside Bobelina, in the very corner, hung a cage, out of which peered a dark, speckled thrush, also very like Sobakevich. The guest and his host had not been silent for more than two minutes together before the door to the drawing-room opened and the lady of the house entered, a personage of inordinate height, wearing a lace bonnet with home-dyed ribbons. She made a stately entrance, bearing her head up high, like a palm tree.

"This is my Feodulia Ivanovna!" said Sobakevich.

Chichikov stepped up to kiss Feodulia Ivanovna's hand, which she practically thrust against his lips, allowing him to observe that her hands had been washed in cucumber brine.

"Dear heart, may I present," continued Sobakevich, "Pavel Ivanovich Chichikov! I was favoured to make his

---

Prince Bagration (1765-1812)—a Russian general in the Patriotic War of 1812 against Napoleon's invasion. He was mortally wounded in the battle of Borodino.

acquaintance at the governor's and the postmaster's soi-
rées."

Feodulia Ivanovna asked him to be seated, also saying:
"Please!" with a motion of her head like that made by
actresses playing the parts of queens. Then she disposed
herself on the settee, wrapped her merino wool shawl
around her and made no further movement, either of her
eye or even her eyebrow.

Chichikov once again raised his eyes and once again saw
Kanaris with his large haunches and immeasurable whiskers, Bobelina and the thrush in its cage.

A general silence was maintained for almost a full five
minutes; all that could be heard was the tap-tap of the
thrush's beak against the wooden floor of the cage, on
which it angled for grains of wheat. Chichikov cast another
glance around the room and saw that everything in it was
solid and exceedingly awkward in design, bearing an uncanny resemblance to the master of the house himself; in
the corner of the room stood a paunchy walnut bureau
on four most absurd legs: a perfect bear. The table, chairs,
arm-chairs—they all possessed this same cumbrous and
uneasy property—in a word, each piece, each chair, seemed
to be saying: "I, too, am Sobakevich!" or "I, too, am very
like Sobakevich!"

"We were talking about you at the house of the President
of the Chambers, at Ivan Grigoryevich's," said Chichikov
at last, seeing that no one was inclined to initiate a conversation, "last Thursday. We had a most pleasant time."

"No, I was not at the president's that time," answered
Sobakevich.

"What an excellent man!"

"Who's that?" asked Sobakevich, staring at the corner
of the stove.

"The president."

"Well, perhaps that's how he seemed to you: to be sure
he's a mason, but otherwise he's the biggest fool the world's
ever seen."

Chichikov was somewhat taken aback by this rather
harsh appraisal, but then, recovering himself, continued:
"Of course, we all have our failings, but then the governor
is such an excellent man!"

"The governor—an excellent man?"

"Why yes, is he not?"

"The biggest brigand in the world!"

"What, the governor a brigand?" said Chichikov, quite unable to comprehend how the governor could be classed as a brigand. "I must confess, I would never have thought it," he continued. "But with your permission I might point out that he does not act at all like one, on the contrary, there is even something very gentle about him." Here he produced as evidence the purses which the governor embroidered with his own hands, adding words in praise of the latter's affectionate mien.

"He has the face of a brigand too!" said Sobakevich. "Just give him a knife and let him loose on the highway and he'll cut your throat, he'll cut it for a kopek! He and the vice-governor together—they're a proper Gog and Magog!"

"No, he's not on good terms with them," Chichikov said to himself. "But I'll try talking about the police chief: I believe he's a friend of his."

"Anyhow, it's no concern of mine," he said. "I must admit I was most taken with the police chief. Such an upright, honest character, somehow you can see real candour in his face."

"The rogue!" said Sobakevich, with great sangfroid. "He'll deceive you, betray you and then eat dinner with you! I know them all: they're all rogues, the whole town's the same, all rogues to a man. They are all Judases. There's one decent man amongst them, the public prosecutor, and even he, if the truth be told, is a swine."

After such eulogistic, if somewhat abridged, biographies Chichikov could see there was little point in mentioning any other officials, and he recalled that Sobakevich did not like to express a good opinion of any man.

"Come, dear heart, dinner is served," Sobakevich's wife said to him.

"Please!" said Sobakevich.

At a table which had been set with hors d'oeuvres guest and host drank their statutory glass of vodka each, chased it down with an hors d'oeuvre, just as vodka is chased down throughout the length and breadth of Russia, in towns and villages alike, that is, with every kind of salty titbit and other appetite-whetting dainties, and then proceeded into the dining-room; the procession was led by the hostess, sailing along like a goose. The small dining table was set for four. The fourth place was soon taken, but it is difficult to say exactly by whom, whether a lady or a girl, a relative, housekeeper, or simply someone living in the house; a creature, around thirty years of age, and wearing not a bonnet but a brightly coloured kerchief on her head. There are some characters who exist in this world not like objects in their own right, but like foreign markings or blobs on other objects. They remain sitting in one place, holding their heads in exactly the same way, so that one could easily mistake them for pieces of furniture, and it is hard to imagine that such lips could ever have uttered a human word; but somewhere in the maids' quarters or the pantry they are quite a terror.

"The soup, dear heart, is very good today!" said Sobakevich, slurping his cabbage soup and helping himself to a massive chunk of nanny-pie, a dish served with cabbage soup and consisting of sheep's stomach-bag stuffed with buckwheat, sheep's heart and trotters. "You won't find nanny-pie like this in town," he continued, turning to Chichikov, "the devil only knows what rubbish they'll serve you there!"

"The governor keeps a pretty good table I must say," said Chichikov.

"But do you know what goes into all that food? You wouldn't touch it if you knew."

"I do not know how it is cooked, I would be no judge of that, but his pork cutlets and steamed fish were excellent."

"That's what you thought. After all I know they buy everything at the market. That rascal of a cook, who was apprenticed to a Frenchman, he'll buy a cat, skin it and serve it up as hare."

"Ugh! How can you say such nasty things!" said Madame Sobakevich.

"It's true, dear heart, that's how they do things, and I'm not to blame if they do. All refuse, such as our Akulka throws into the slop-pail, if you'll pardon me saying so, they'll put in the soup! Yes sir, in the soup!"

"Why must you always discuss these things at table?" objected Madame Sobakevich again.

"Why not, dear heart," said Sobakevich, "it's not as if I

were doing that myself; but let me tell you straight that I refuse to eat filth. You can coat a frog with sugar and I still won't stick it in my mouth, nor will I touch oysters: I know what oysters are like. Take some mutton," he continued, turning to Chichikov, "this is a side of mutton with buckwheat! This isn't one of those fricassees which they make in fashionable houses out of mutton that has been lying around at the market for at least four days! All that rubbish was concocted by a lot of French and German doctors, and I'd string them all up for it! Inventing this diet, to cure people by starving them! Because they have that wishy-washy German constitution, they imagine they can get the better of a Russian stomach! No, it's all wrong, it's all a lot of bunkum, it's all..." Here Sobakevich even shook his head angrily. "They are always on about their enlightenment, enlightenment this, enlightenment that, but what is this enlightenment?—Pshaw! I would have used another word, but it would not be proper at table. It's not like that in my house. What I say is: if you want pork—put the whole pig on the table; you want mutton, bring on the whole sheep; a goose—take the whole goose! I'd rather eat only two dishes, but eat a proper amount, to my heart's content." Sobakevich showed himself to be as good as his word: he tipped half the side of mutton onto his plate, devoured it all, gnawed the bones, and sucked them clean.

"Yes," thought Chichikov, "this one certainly knows what's good."

"It's not like that in my house," repeated Sobakevich, wiping his hands with a napkin. "I don't believe in living like some Plyushkin: he owns eight hundred souls, but he lives and eats worse than my goatboy."

"Who is this Plyushkin?" asked Chichikov.

"A rogue," answered Sobakevich. "You could never imagine such a skinflint. The convicts in prison live better than him: he's starved all his serfs to death."

"Really!" interjected Chichikov with enthusiasm. "Do you mean to say that his serfs are really dying in large numbers?"

"Dying like flies."

"Like flies! Goodness! Might I ask how far from you he lives?"

"Five versts."

"Five versts!" exclaimed Chichikov and actually felt his heartbeat quicken slightly. "Now if one were to drive out of your gate, would one turn to the right or the left?"

"I wouldn't even advise you to know the way to that dog!" said Sobakevich. "It would be more pardonable to visit some house of ill-repute than him."

"Oh no, I'm not asking for any specific reason, but only because I always take an interest in learning the lie of the land," countered Chichikov.

The saddle of mutton was followed by curd tarts, each one of which was much bigger than a plate, then came a turkey the size of a calf, stuffed with all manner of good things: eggs, rice, liver and goodness knows what else, and all that was lumped heavily into one's stomach. With this the meal ended; as they rose from the table Chichikov felt he had gained a good stone in weight. They proceeded to the drawing-room where saucers of jam were awaiting them; it was not pear, nor plums nor any berry, but neither guest nor host touched it anyway. The hostess departed, in order to fill more saucers. Availing himself of her absence Chichikov turned to Sobakevich, who, recumbent in an armchair, was able only to wheeze after such a massive repast and to emit certain indistinct noises from his mouth, crossing himself and covering his mouth with his hand every few seconds. Chichikov turned to him with these words:

"I would like to discuss a small business matter with you."

"Here's some other jam," said the hostess, returning with a dish. "This is radish, stewed in honey!"

"We'll have some later!" said Sobakevich. "You run along into your own room now, Pavel Ivanovich and I want to remove our coats and have a little breather!"

Their hostess had already expressed her readiness to send for feather bolsters and pillows, but her husband said: "Never mind, we'll stretch out in the armchairs", and Madame Sobakevich withdrew.

Sobakevich bent his head slightly forward as he prepared to learn the nature of this small business matter.

Chichikov stated in a most roundabout way, first touching on the entire Russian state in general, waxing lyrical about its great expanse, declaring that even the most ancient monarchy of Rome had not been so vast and that it was with good reason that foreigners were so impressed (Sobakevich listened, his head bent) ... and that by the existing laws of this state, unequalled in its glory, registered souls who had reached the end of their journey through life, still continued to count, until the next census, alongside the living, lest the authorities be burdened with a mass of trivial and useless reports which would only further complicate the already sufficiently complex machinery of state (Sobakevich listened away, his head bent) ... and that, nonetheless, however justified this measure it was sometimes onerous for many landowners, obliging them to pay taxes just as they would for living serfs, and that he, out of a feeling of respect, was prepared to take upon himself a portion of this truly burdensome obligation. His main subject Chichikov treated with great caution: he scrupulously avoided referring to the souls as dead, describing them merely as non-existent.

Sobakevich listened as before, his head inclined and without displaying anything that could remotely be described as an expression. You might have thought his was a body entirely devoid of a soul, or that if he did have one he kept it not where it should be, but like the miser of folklore, the immortal Koshchei, somewhere at the back of beyond and covered with such a thick shell that whatever stirrings there might have been within it they produced absolutely no tremor on the surface.

"Well?..." asked Chichikov, waiting for the answer in some trepidation.

"You want dead souls?" asked Sobakevich very simply, without the slightest surprise, as if they were discussing wheat.

"Yes," answered Chichikov, and at once softened the expression adding: "the non-existent ones."

"Should be some, why not..." said Sobakevich.

"And if there are, then you would surely ... be pleased to disburden yourself of them?"

"Why not, I'll sell," said Sobakevich, now lifting his head slightly as he tumbled to the fact that the buyer must surely be going to derive some profit from this.

"What the devil," thought Chichikov, "this one's already selling before I've even broached the subject!" and he continued aloud: "Now what sort of price did you have in mind?... Although, of course, with merchandise of this nature ... to talk about price is rather strange..."

"I don't want to overcharge you, so a hundred rubles a piece!" said Sobakevich.

"A hundred!" shrieked Chichikov, gaping wide-mouthed at Sobakevich, uncertain whether he had misheard or whether Sobakevich's unwieldy tongue had twisted the wrong way and blurted out one word in place of another.

"So you think that's too dear?" declared Sobakevich and then added: "What's your price then?"

"My price! I think we must have made a mistake, or be talking at cross-purposes, or perhaps we have forgotten the nature of the merchandise. For my part all I can suggest in all honesty is eighty kopeks a soul, that's the best I can offer!"

"Eighty kopeks? You're way out."

"Why, in my opinion, as I see it, you could not ask more."

"What I'm selling are not bast sandals, you know."

"But see for yourself: they're not people, either."

"Do you think you'll find the kind of fool who'll sell you registered souls for twenty kopeks a piece?"

"I crave your pardon: why do you call them registered when these souls have themselves passed away long ago, and all that remains is the impalpable sound of the word? However, to obviate further discussion of the subject I'm prepared to give you a ruble fifty each, but that's my last word."

"You should be ashamed to mention such a sum! If you want to do business, name a proper price!"

"No, Mikhail Semyonovich, on my word of honour, believe me, I cannot: what cannot be done, cannot be done," said Chichikov, but promptly added another fifty kopeks.

"Why be so stingy?" asked Sobakevich. "They're cheap at the price! Another scoundrel would cheat you, selling you a lot of rubbish and not souls; but mine are the real thing, the pick of the best: either clever craftsmen or strapping peasants. See for yourself: take Mikheyev the carriage-maker for instance! You know, he never made any carriages that weren't properly sprung. And this wasn't any of your Moscow workmanship, good for one hour only: this was solid work, he'd upholster them himself and put on the varnish too!"

Chichikov opened his mouth, about to point out that Mikheyev had, however, long since departed this life; but Sobakevich was just getting into his stride and, as they say, there was no stopping him in his eloquence:

"And Probka Stepan, the carpenter? I wager my own head you'll never find another to match him. The strength of that man! He could have been a guardsman with his build! Seven foot in his socks he was!"

Once again Chichikov was about to observe that Probka had also departed this life, but there was no stopping Sobakevich now: such torrents of words poured out that he could only sit and listen. "Milushkin, the bricklayer! He could build a stove in any house you like. Maxim Telyatnikov, the cobbler: a few stabs of his awl and there's a pair of boots for you, and never a drop of liquor! And Yeremei Sorokoplyokhin! That fellow is a match for the best of them, he plied his trade in Moscow and paid me five hundred rubles in quit-rent alone. That's the sort of men they are! Not the rubbish some old Plyushkin would sell you."

"But pardon me for saying so," said Chichikov finally, astonished by this overwhelming flood of words to which there appeared to be no end, "why do you enumerate all their merits when there is no use in them now anyway, as they are all dead? A dead man's only good for propping up a fence, as the proverb says."

"Yes, of course, they're dead," said Sobakevich, as if coming to his senses and realising that they were indeed all dead, but then added: "But then look at it this way: what of those people who count as being alive? What sort of people are they? They're flies, not people."

"Nonetheless they do exist, whereas these are only imaginary."

"Oh no, no, not imaginary! Allow me to inform you what sort of a chap Mikheyev was, you'll never find his equal anywhere: such an ox of a man, he wouldn't fit through this door; no, no: that's not imaginary! And in his shoulders he had more than the strength of a carthorse; I'd like you to tell me where else you think you can find someone imaginary like that!"

These last words he addressed to the portraits of Bagration and Kolokotroni hanging on the wall, as often happens when the speaker, for some unknown reason, suddenly addresses not the person to whom his words are directed, but someone else who has unexpectedly entered the room, perhaps even a total stranger, from whom the speaker knows he will receive neither a reply, nor an opinion, nor a confirmation, yet on whom he fixes his stare as if asking him to be an intermediary; and the stranger, somewhat bewildered at first, does not know whether to venture an answer on a matter about which he has heard nothing, or merely to stand there, preserving a proper decorum, and then to take his leave.

"No, I cannot go higher than two rubles," said Chichikov.

"All right then, since I would not wish you to say that I had overcharged you, and since I do not want to do you any special favours, so let us say seventy-five rubles per soul, but in bank-notes, and even that price is only for the sake of our friendship!"

"Does he really take me for a fool?" Chichikov wondered, adding aloud:

"I must say this seems very odd to me: it is as if we were acting out some theatrical performance or comedy, I cannot see any other explanation... I do believe you to be a person of considerable intelligence, endowed with the knowledge conferred by education. After all this merchandise is sheer rubbish. What is it worth? What use is it to anyone?"

"Well, you're the one buying it, so it must be of use to you."

Here Chichikov bit his lip at a loss for an answer. He started to mention certain family circumstances and concomitances, but Sobakevich abruptly retorted:

"I have no wish to learn about your circumstances. I do not interfere in family matters, that's your own business. You require souls, so I am selling them to you, and you'll regret not having bought them."

"Two rubles," said Chichikov.

"Now aren't you like the proverbial parrot: once you've set your mind on two rubles nothing will shift you. Name a proper price!"

"The devil confound him," thought Chichikov, "I'll put on another fifty kopeks for the swine, and that'll clinch it!"

"Very well, I'll add another fifty kopeks."

"Then allow me also to say my last word: fifty rubles! Admittedly, I'm selling at a loss, you will not get such fine serfs anywhere at that price!"

"What a money-grubber!" said Chichikov to himself, and then continued aloud in some vexation:

"Now really, this is quite ridiculous, you can't mean it; I could get them for nothing somewhere else. Indeed, most people would be only too glad to let me have them, if only to get rid of them the quicker. Only a fool would wish to hold on to them and pay taxes for them!"

"But are you aware that purchases of this nature, and I say this just between you and me, out of friendship, are not always permissible, and if I, or someone else, were to talk, the buyer would be denied trust if he tried to make a contract or any advantageous commitment."

"So that's the line he's taking, the knave!" thought Chichikov, and thereupon announced with an air of complete nonchalance:

"Please yourself; I'm not buying them for any particular purpose, as you think, but for no reason at all, for a mere whim. If you won't take two and a half—I bid you farewell!"

"He won't give in, he's stubborn!" thought Sobakevich.

"Very well then, give me thirty a piece and you can have them!"

"No, I see you do not wish to sell, goodday!"

"Hold on a minute," said Sobakevich, taking the hand Chichikov offered in farewell and leading him back into the drawing-room. "Let me put something to you."

"There's no need. I've said everything I wish to say."

"Now, just a moment!" said Sobakevich, keeping hold of his hand and treading on his toes, for our hero had omitted to take precautionary action, in punishment for which he was forced to hiss in pain and hop about on one leg.

"I crave your pardon! I seem to have discomforted you. Please, take a seat over here!" He seated his guest in an armchair with quite some dexterity, just like a bear which has been well schooled can turn somersaults and perform various tricks in response to the commands: "Now, Misha, show us how ladies take their bath" or: "How do little children steal peas, Misha?"

"Seriously, I am wasting my time here, I must hurry on my way."

"Just stay for another minute and I'll tell you something that you'll like to hear." Here Sobakevich moved his chair up close and said into his ear, as if imparting a secret: "How about a quarter?"

"Do you mean twenty-five rubles? Not on your life, I wouldn't ever give a quarter of that; I will not add a single kopek."

Sobakevich fell silent. Chichikov also remained silent. This silence lasted some two minutes. Bagration with his aquiline nose surveyed this transaction from his perch on the wall with the closest attention.

"What then is your final price?" asked Sobakevich at last.

"Two fifty."

"I must say, you've got a boiled turnip in place of a heart. At least you could give me three rubles!"

"I cannot."

"Very well then, have it your way. I'm losing money, but that's just my blasted good nature, I can't help giving pleasure to my fellow-man. And now, I suppose, I have to make out the deed of purchase, so that everything will be in order."

"Naturally."

"There, you see, it means I shall have to go into town."

And thus the deal was concluded. They agreed to meet the very next day in town and to settle the deed of purchase. Chichikov asked for a list of the serfs. Sobakevich acquiesced willingly, and promptly repaired to his study, where he set about transcribing in his own hand not only all their names, but even a dossier of their laudable qualities.

Meanwhile Chichikov kept himself occupied, as he stood behind Sobakevich, by studying his host's massive frame. As he gazed at his back, as broad as that of a squat Vyatka cart-horse, and at his legs, as solid as the cast-iron bollards which are placed on pavements, he could not help exclaiming inwardly: "My, what a solid job God made of you! A real case of 'roughly hewn but toughly sewn', as they say!... I wonder, were you born a bear, or has this backwoods life turned you into one, with its sowing and reaping, bother with the peasants, all of which has made you so tough and tight-fisted? On second thoughts, no: I believe you would have been like that even with a fashionable education, and given a start in life in St Petersburg and not in these backwoods. The only difference is that now you tuck away half a saddle of mutton with buckwheat, chasing it down with a plate-sized curd tart, whereas then you would have eaten dainty little cutlets with truffles. And now you have serfs under your authority: you get along with them, and naturally, you do not maltreat them because they are yours, for if you did things would only be worse for you; whereas there you would have had underlings, whom you would have bullied because they were clerks and not your own serfs; or else you would have embezzled funds! No, no: once a man's a tight-fisted bully he'll never unclench his fist! And if he does prize open one or two fingers, things will only be the worse for him. Just let him get a smattering of some science or other and later, when he holds some more important office, he'll squash the real experts. And he might even say to himself, later on: This will make everyone sit up and take notice! And he'll concoct a directive of such wisdom that many will squirm... Just imagine if everyone was like that!..."

"The list is ready," said Sobakevich, turning round again.

"It is? Ah, let's have a look!" Chichikov ran his eyes over it and marvelled at its accuracy and precision: not only had the trade, title, age and family status of each been recorded in detail, but in the margin there were even special comments on their conduct, sobriety and so forth: in a word, it was a pleasure to behold.

"Now let's have a little something in advance!"

"What do you want an advance for? You shall receive all the money in a lump sum in town."

"All the same, you know, that's the way it's done," objected Sobakevich.

"I don't know how I can pay you, I didn't bring any money with me. Well, I do have ten rubles."

"Ten! Give me at least fifty!"

Chichikov began to remonstrate that he did not have the money; but Sobakevich was so insistent that Chichikov produced another banknote, saying:

"As you will, here is another fifteen, making twenty-five in all. Only, may I have a receipt?"

"But why should you want a receipt?"

"All the same, you know, it's better to have a receipt. You never know, anything might happen."

"Very well, let's have the money!"

"What's the hurry? Here it is in my hand! As soon as you write out your receipt you'll get it right away."

"Really now, how can I write a receipt before I've seen the money?"

Chichikov released the notes from his hand. Sobakevich stepped up to the table, and placing the fingers of his left hand on the money, with his other hand wrote on a scrap of paper that he had received in full the deposit of twenty-five rubles in state banknotes in payment for souls. After writing the receipt he re-examined the notes.

"This is a rather old note!" he declared, holding one of them up to the light, "and it's a little tattered, but as friends we need not worry about that."

"What a tight-wad!" thought Chichikov to himself. "And a knave into the bargain!"

"Don't you want females?"

"No, thank you."

"I'd let you have them cheap. As a friend: a ruble a piece."

"No, I don't need any females."

"Well if you don't need them, then there's no point discussing it. There's no accounting for taste; some love the priest, others the priest's wife, as the proverb says."

"There is one more thing I wanted to ask you," said Chichikov, taking his leave. "I trust this transaction can remain strictly between us."

"Why, that goes without saying. There's no point in involving a third person in this: what happens between close friends out of the sincerity of their hearts should remain within the bonds of their friendship. Farewell! Thank you for visiting us; please do not neglect us in the future: if you have a spare hour or so, pop out for dinner, spend some time with us. Perhaps we'll be able to do each other a further good service."

"Yes, mightn't we indeed!" thought Chichikov, as he took his seat in the chaise. "Extorting two and a half rubles for a dead soul, the tight-fisted devil!"

He was displeased with Sobakevich's conduct. After all, whichever way you looked at it, he was an acquaintance, they had met at the governor's, and at the police chief's, yet he had behaved like a complete stranger, taking money for such rubbish! As the chaise drove out through the gates, he turned round and saw Sobakevich still standing on the porch and, so it seemed, peering after his guest, anxious to know whither he was bound.

"Blast him, he's still standing there!" Chichikov muttered through his teeth, and ordered Selifan to turn towards the peasants' huts and drive off in such a way that the chaise would not be visible from the master's house. He wished to call on Plyushkin, whose serfs, if Sobakevich was to be believed, were dying like flies, but he did not wish this to be known to Sobakevich. Once the chaise had reached the very end of the village, he called out to a peasant who had found an enormous log somewhere on the road and was now lugging it home on his shoulders, like the indefatigable ant.

"I say, beardy! How do we get to Plyushkin's estate from here, without going past the master's house?"

The peasant appeared to be at a loss for an answer.

"Well, don't you know?"

"No, sir, I don't know."

"Tsk, tsk! An old greybeard like you! You mean, you don't know the miser Plyushkin, the one who does not feed his serfs properly?"

"Ah! Old Patches!" exclaimed the peasant.

He also annexed an adjective to the word "patches", a very appropriate epithet, but one not employed in fashionable conversation, and therefore we shall omit it here. However, one could divine that it was singularly apt, for Chichikov, even when they had travelled some distance and the peasant had long since been lost from sight, still sat chuckling away in his chaise. How strongly the Russians express themselves! And once they bestow an epithet on someone, it will stick to his kith and kin, he will take it with him to his office, and into retirement, and to St Petersburg, and to the four corners of the earth. And no matter how cunningly he might try to ennoble his sobriquet, even if he hires learned scribblers to derive its etymology from some ancient princely line, it will avail him nought: the name will scream for itself at the top of its ugly voice and will make it quite plain from where this bird has come. Something aptly spoken is as good as something written: it is there to stay. And there is nothing more apt than the expressions coined in the heart of Russia, where there are no German, or Finnish, or any other tribes, but only your native folk, the quick and agile Russian wit, which does not have to hatch the right word, like a broody hen her chicks, but stamps it on one swiftly, like a passport to be borne for ever, and there's no point in adding later what sort of nose or mouth you have: your likeness has been drawn, from head to toe, in a single stroke!

Just as there is a countless multitude of churches, of monasteries, with domes, cupolas and crosses, scattered across the devout expanse of holy Russia, so does a countless multitude of tribes, generations and nations jostle one another in colourful confusion across the face of the earth. And every nation, endowed with strength, creative abilities, its own vivid individuality and other gifts of God, has distinguished itself with its own particular word, which, no matter what object it describes, reflects a facet of the nation's own character. The word of the Briton will resound with worldly wisdom and knowledge of the human heart; the short-lived world of the Frenchman will sparkle like a carefree dandy only to disappear forever; the German will think up his intricate, skimpily clever word, not understandable to all; but there is no word so pert and quick, so spontaneously bursting from the heart, so seething and bubbling with life, as the aptly spoken Russian word.

CHAPTER SIX

Long, long ago, in the years of my youth, in the years of my childhood, which flitted past so irrecoverably I loved to drive up for the first time to an unfamiliar place: it mattered not whether this was a small village, a wretched little provincial town, a hamlet or a settlement—the child's inquisitive eye uncovered much of interest in each of them. Every building, everything which suggested at least some trace of the peculiar or the remarkable—it all

caught my attention and amazed me. Be it an official
building, designed in that certain style with half its
windows false, towering over the woodpile of one-storeyed
dwelling houses, be it a perfectly rounded cupola, totally
covered with sheets of zinc, raised up above a new snowily
whitewashed church, be it a market, or a provincial dandy,
I happened to see in town—nothing escaped my fresh, keen
attention, and, thrusting my nose out of the carriage, I
would stare at a frockcoat cut in a style I had never before
seen, or at the wooden boxes filled with nails, with yellow
sulphur, with raisins, or with soap, seen through the doors
of greengrocer's shops, alongside jars of dried-up Moscow
sweets. I would stare too at the strolling infantry officer,
cast from God knows where into this provincial boredom,
and at the merchant, smart in his *sibirka**, in a racing gig,
and in my thoughts I would be carried away into their
trivial life. Should a local official walk past, at once I
would be lost in thought: where was he bound, to a soirée
perhaps at a cousin's house, or was he on his way home,
where, after sitting for half an hour on the porch until the
last glow of dusk had faded, he would sit down to an early
supper with his good mother, his wife, his wife's sister, and
all his family, and I would wonder what they would converse about, when, not until after the soup, a tallow candle
in an ancient, plain holder was brought in by the house-
maid wearing beads or the house boy in a padded jacket.
As we drove up to the village of some landowner I would
gaze with interest at the tall, narrow wooden bell-tower or
the old broad, dark wooden church. The red roof and
white chimneys of the manor house would wink enticingly
at me from afar through the leafy branches, and I would
wait impatiently for the gardens before the house to open
up on both sides and the house itself to be revealed in its
glory, which in those days—unlike today, alas!—was far
from vulgar; and I would try to judge from the house what
sort of landlord lived in it: was he fat, did he have any
sons, or three full brace of daughters, filling the house
with their ringing girlish laughter and games, and was the
youngest girl, as always, a pretty one, and were they black-
eyed, and was he a jovial fellow himself, or sullen as the

Sibirka—a long cloth overcoat with a standing collar and gathered at the
waist.

last week of September, studying his calendar and talking about such dull subjects for young people as rye and wheat?

Today I drive up to an unfamiliar village with indifference, and just as indifferently do I survey its vulgar aspect; it is disagreeable to my cool gaze, I do not find it amusing, and what in earlier years would have stirred lively animation in my face, laughter and incessant chatter, now slips past me and my immobile lips preserve an impassive silence. Oh my youth! Oh my innocence!

While Chichikov was chuckling over the nickname the peasants had bestowed upon Plyushkin, he failed to observe that they had driven into the centre of an extensive village with a large number of houses and streets. He was soon made aware of this, however, by a most violent jolt, caused by the log paving, compared to which the cobblestones of a town are nothing to grumble about. These logs jumped up and down like piano keys, and the incautious traveller will get either a bump on his crown, or a bruise on his forehead, or even bite off the tip of his tongue very painfully. He noticed something particularly dilapidated about all the buildings: the log walls of the cottages were old and dark; the roofs were in such a state of disrepair that in some all that remained were the cross-piece and the rib-like side beams. It was as if the owners themselves had removed all the shingles and planks, reasoning, of course quite correctly, that a house cannot be roofed when it pours and when it shines there's no rain anyway, and why stay cooped up at house like an old woman, when there was plenty of space in the inn and in the open— in a word, anywhere you wished. The windows in the cottages were unglazed, some had been stuffed up with rags or an old coat, the little balustraded balconies beneath the roofs, which for some unknown reason are built on to some Russian peasant cottage, stood askew and had turned so sullenly black that they were not even picturesque. In many places huge ricks of corn, which had evidently stood there for a long time, stretched in rows behind the houses; they had taken on the colour of old, badly fired bricks, whilst all sorts of weeds were growing on top of them and bushes had even rooted in the sides. The grain clearly belonged to the squire. Two village churches came into sight behind the ricks of grain and the dilapidated roofs, now on the right, now on the left, as the chaise negotiated the turns; one was an abandoned wooden church and next to it was a brick church, with dingy yellow walls, cracked and stained. Then parts of the squire's house came into view, and finally it was all visible where the line of cottages came to an end, giving way to a large empty vegetable plot, or cabbage patch, encircled with a low partly broken fence. This strange castle, immensely, inordinately long, looked like some decrepit invalid. In places it had one storey; in others two; from its dark roof, which did not everywhere provide secure protection for its ancient interior, two belvederes protruded, one opposite the other, already leaning over to the side and bare of whatever paint had once covered them. The walls of this house, with the plaster crumbled away to the bare stuccoed wattle beneath, had clearly suffered badly from every manner of storm, rain, whirlwind and inclement autumn weather. Of the windows only two were open, the others being shuttered or even boarded up. And even these two windows were half-blind; a triangular dark-blue piece of sugar-paper had been stuck over one of them.

A large old garden, stretching away behind the house, beyond the village and eventually merging with the fields, overgrown and choked with weeds, appeared to be the only source of greenery in this vast village and was the single vivid feature in all its picturesque desolation. The crowns of the untended trees merged together to form a mass of green clouds and trembling, asymmetrical arboreal cupolas along the horizon. The colossal white trunk of a birch tree, decapitated by violent winds or storms, towered above this mass of greenery like a gleaming, perpendicular marble column; the sharp-pointed, slanting tip with which the tree ended, instead of a capital, showed black against the snowy whiteness of the bark, like a cap, or a black bird. The hop-plants, which choked the bushes of elder, rowan and hazel growing below, ran along the top of the entire fence before starting upwards to wreathe around the half-destroyed birch trunk. On reaching the halfway point it swung down again, either to catch on to the tops of other trees or to hang in the air, plaiting its slender, sticky tendrils into ringlets that swung in the breeze. In places the green thickets, which caught the rays of the sun, fell apart to reveal a shadowy hollow between them, yawning like the dark maw of some beast; it was entirely enveloped in shadow, and only the faintest impressions could be gleaned of its darksome depths: a narrow, winding path, a broken balustrade, a sagging gazebo, the hollow trunk of an ancient willow, a clump of hoary shrubbery, thrusting out its twigs and leaves, dried up in the terrible density of undergrowth, from behind the willow and, finally, the bough of a young maple, reaching out its green leafy palms, one of which was transformed by a shaft of sunlight, which penetrated hither by some mysterious chance, into something translucent and fiery, glowing miraculously amidst this thick darkness. To one side, at the very edge of the garden, a group of tall aspens rising above the other trees, lifted enormous crows' nests aloft on their trembling summits. Branches that had been torn off, but not totally detached, hung down with their dried-out leaves. In a word, it was all somehow barrenly splendid, in a way that neither nature nor art could devise by itself, but as can only happen through their union, when the accumulated and often purposeless labours of man are given a finishing touch by nature's chisel, removing the massive accretions, destroying the crudely obvious symmerty and beggarly rents, through which the naked, unconcealed plan is revealed, and imparting a marvellous warmth in everything created in the coolness of calculated neatness and cleanness.

After making one or two turns our hero finally found himself right in front of the house, which now struck him as even more wretched. A green mould had already spread over the ancient timbers on the fence and gate. A profusion of buildings: cottages, barns, cellars, all visibly dilapidated, crowded the courtyard; to left and right beside them were gates leading to other courtyards. Everything suggested that once there had been an extensive farming business flourishing here, but now everything had an air of utter gloom. There was nothing in evidence to enliven the picture: neither open doors nor any people merging from within: none of the lively fuss and bustle of a home! Only the main gates were open, and that merely to admit a peasant with a loaded cart, covered with bast matting, who arrived as if on cue to liven up this lifeless scene; otherwise the gates too would have been securely fastened, as was evident from the massive padlock hanging from an iron staple. By one of the buildings Chichikov soon espied a figure, squabbling with the peasant who had arrived with the cart. For a long time he could not decide whether this figure was a man or a woman. Its garb was quite indeterminate, very similar to a woman's capote with a tall cap like that worn by village serving wenches, only the voice struck him as a little husky for a woman. "Oh, it's a woman!" he said to himself and at once added: "No, it's not!" "A woman, of course!" he said at last, when he had had a closer look. For her own part the woman stared back just as hard at him. Guests must have been rare here, for she scrutinized not only him, but also Selifan, and the horses, starting with the tail and continuing to the head. From the keys hanging from her belt and from the way she scolded the peasant in rather abusive language, Chichikov concluded that this was surely the housekeeper.

"Listen, my good woman," he said, climbing from his chaise. "Is the master at home?"

"Not at home," interrupted the housekeeper, without waiting for him to finish his question, and then, a minute later, added: "And what do you want?"

"I have business!"

"Go inside!" said the housekeeper, turning round to show him a back dusted with flour and with a great rent in the skirt.

He entered the large, dark hall, as cold and draughty as a cellar. From this hall he passed into a room, also dark, but ever so slightly illuminated by the light filtering in through a large chink at the bottom of the door. Opening this door he finally found himself in the light and was astounded by the disorder which confronted him. Perhaps it was floor-scrubbing day in the house, and so all the furniture had been stacked in here for the time being. On one table there stood a broken chair, and next to it a clock with a motionless pendulum, to which a spider had already affixed its web. Here too, leaning against the wall, stood a cupboard full of old silver, decanters and Chinese porcelain. On top of a bureau, inlaid with mother-of-pearl, chinks of which had already fallen out to expose yellowed grooves, filled with glue, lay a mass of assorted rubbish: a pile of papers covered in a fine scrawl and held down by a marble paper-weight, shaped like an egg on top and green with mould, an ancient leather-bound book with red edging, a lemon, completely dried up, shrivelled to the size of a hazelnut, the broken off arm of a chair, a wine-glass containing some sort of liquid and three flies, covered with a letter, a little piece of sealing wax, a scrap of rag picked up somewhere, two quill pens, stained with ink and as dried-up as a consumptive, a tooth-pick, completely yellowed, with which the owner had perhaps picked his teeth even before the invasion of Moscow by Napoleon's army.

The walls were hung with pictures in crowded confusion: a long, yellowed engraving of some battle, with enormous drums, shouting soldiers in tricorns and drowning horses, hung in a glassless mahogany frame with thin bronze strips along the side and little bronze discs at the corners. Alongside this an enormous time-darkened picture occupied half the wall, painted in oils and depicting flowers, fruit, a watermelon cut in half, the head of a boar and a duck hanging head down. From the centre of the ceiling hung a chandelier in a canvas sack, so layered with dust that it resembled a silk cocoon around a large worm. Heaped on the floor in the corner were various grosser items which were unsuitable to be placed on tables. What exactly was to be found in this heap it was hard to discern, for it was covered with such a thick layer of dust that any hand that touched it would be instantly clad in a brown glove; more prominent than the rest were a broken-off piece of a wooden spade and the sole of an ancient boot. One would never have thought that this room was inhabited by any living creature if this fact had not been proclaimed by an old, worn night-cap lying on the table. While Chichikov was engaged in surveying these strange furnishings, a side door opened to admit the housekeeper he had seen outside. But now he saw that this was sooner the steward than the housekeeper: a housekeeper, at any rate, would not have to shave her beard, whereas this one did shave, and it would seem, somewhat infrequently, for his entire chin from the cheeks downwards had the appearance of a wire curry-comb such as is used in stables to groom the horses. Chichikov, adopting an interrogative mien, waited with impatience for the steward to speak. For his part, the steward also waited for Chichikov to say something. Finally the latter, taken aback by this strange bewilderment, brought himself to ask:

"So where's the master? In his room, is he?"

"The master's here," said the steward.

"Where here?" repeated Chichikov.

"Are you blind or something?" asked the steward. "Right here! Can't you see, I'm the master!"

At this our hero involuntarily stepped back and stared closely at the figure before him. In his time he had seen many people of every different kind, even such as the reader and I may never have occasion to see; but one like this he had never seen before. There was nothing remarkable about his face; it was practically identical to that of many scrawny old men with the exception that the chin was extremely prominent, forcing its owner to keep on covering it with a handkerchief lest he beslobber it; his little eyes still had not lost their gleam and darted about beneath his tufted eyebrows like mice when they stick their sharp little noses out of their dark mouseholes, their ears pricked up and their whiskers twitching, on the lookout for a lurking cat or a mischievous small boy lying in wait, and suspiciously sniff the air. What was far more remarkable was his attire: by no efforts or devices could one possibly divine of what his dressing-gown was concocted: the sleeves and upper skirts were shiny and greasy to a point where they shone like boot-leather; in the back hung not even two, but four skirts, from which the cotton stuffing dangled in lumps. Wound round his neck was something similarly mysterious: a stocking, perhaps, or a knitted sash, or even a stomacher, but most definitely not a necktie. In a word, if Chichikov had met him thus attired somewhere by the doors of a church, he would probably have given him a kopek. For, to our hero's credit, let it be said that his heart was compassionate and he would never walk past a beggar without giving him a kopek. Yet standing before him was not a beggar but a landowner. This landowner had more than a thousand souls, and you would be hard put to find another landowner with as much wheat in grain, flour and stooks, or whose barns and drying sheds were so crammed with linens, bolts of cloth, cured and uncured sheepskins, dried fish, and every kind of comestibles. Anyone glancing into his work-yard, with its stores of timber and never-used pots and pans, would imagine that this was, in fact, the woodcraft market in Moscow, to which all the mothers-in-law, followed by their cooks, bustle along each morning to do their household shopping and where you find mountains of wooden utensils—jointed, chiselled, dovetailed, or wattled: barrels, vats, piggins, skeels, pitchers with spouts and without spouts, two drinking cups, bast punnets, trugs, into which country women put their yarn and thread and other rubbish, kists made from aspen slats, pyxes of plaited birch-bark and much else besides, of the sort used by both rich and poor Russia. But what possible use could Plyushkin have for such a mountain of these artefacts? In the course of an entire human life he could not have found employment for them on even two estates like his—but he still thought them insufficient. Not content with what he had he patrolled the streets of his village every day, peering under the footbridges, and beneath the fences, and everything he saw—be it an old sole, a woman's rag, an iron nail, a clay shard—he carried it home to add to the pile Chichikov had seen in the corner of the room. "There goes the fisherman out to his nets!" the peasants would say, seeing him setting off in search of booty. After him there was really no need to sweep the streets: a passing officer once lost one of his spurs—this same spur instantly made its way to Plyushkin's pile; if a peasant woman stood gawking at the well and took her eyes off her bucket, he would ferret the bucket away too. However, if an observant peasant caught him in the act he would not argue and would promptly surrender the purloined object; but once it had found its way to the pile it was gone for good: he would swear till he was blue in the face that the thing was his own, bought sometime or other, from someone or other or inherited from his grandfather. In his room he would pick up everything he saw on the floor: a little piece of sealing wax, a scrap of paper, a quill pen, and all this he would place on his bureau or on the window-sill.

And yet there was a time when he was simply an economical squire! He had a wife and a family, and a neighbour would come for dinner, to listen to his advice and learn from him the skills of farming and sagacious thriftiness. Everything ran briskly and smoothly: the windmills and fulling mills, the clothmills, spinning mills and joiners' lathes all worked; nothing eluded the master's keen eye, and like the sedulous spider he scurried everywhither, bustling but efficient, to all four corners of the web of his husbandry. His features bore no trace of excessive emotions, but his eyes revealed an astute mind; his speech was imbued with experience and knowledge of the world and it was a pleasure to hear him talk; his affable and garrulous spouse was renowned for her hospitality; a guest would be met by two attractive daughters, both fair-haired and fresh as roses; his son would come running out, a lively young lad who would give everyone a welcoming kiss, whether the guest liked it or not. All the windows in the house were kept open, in the mezzanine lived the French tutor, a splendid exponent of the art of shaving and a fine marksman: he invariably brought home a brace of black-cock or duck for the table, though sometimes only sparrows' eggs, which the cook would fry for him, for no one else in the house would eat them. The mezzanine was shared by his countrywoman, governess to the two girls. The master himself would appear at dinner in a frockcoat, albeit somewhat worn, but still neat, with the elbows whole and not patched. But the good lady died; a portion of the keys, and with them certain trifling chores, now devolved upon him. Plyushkin became more anxious, and like all widowers, more suspicious and niggardly. He would not let himself depend in all things on his elder daughter Alexandra Stepanovna, and, as it happens, rightly so, because Alexandra Stepanovna soon eloped with a staff-captain from God knows what cavalry regiment and concluded a hasty marriage with him in some village church, knowing that her father nursed some strange prejudice against officers, regarding them all as inveterate card-sharps and spendthrifts. Her father cursed her for a valediction, and did not bother to pursue her. The house became even emptier. He started to display more obvious signs of miserliness; and this developed further as the grey streaks, which are the faithful friend of miserliness, began to appear in his coarse hair; the French tutor was dismissed because the time had come for his son to enter the civil service; the governess was banished, because she proved to have been not entirely blameless in the abduction of Alexandra Stepanovna; the son, having been dispatched to the provincial capital in order to learn what his father considered worthwhile service in the Civic Chambers, instead elected to join a regiment, and wrote to his father only after receiving his commission with a request for money to kit himself out; as might have been expected, he received what in common parlance is called a fig. Finally his second daughter, the last to remain at home, died, and the old man was left alone as watchman, custodian and proprietor of his riches. The solitary life provided ample nourishment for miserliness, which is known to have the hunger of a wolf; the more it devours the more insatiable its appetite grows; the common human feelings, which anyway were not profound in him, started to evaporate altogether and every day something else was lost in this worn-out ruin of a man. And as ill-fortune would have it, as if in confirmation of his views on officers in general, his son lost a fortune at cards; he sent the lad his heartfelt paternal curse and never again sought to discover whether he was still alive or not. Every year more and more windows were shuttered up in his house; finally only two were left, and one of these, as the reader has already seen, was papered over; with every year more and more important areas of his husbandry were lost to his sight, and his petty attention was turned to the papers and quill pens which he collected in his room; he became increasingly more unyielding to the merchants who came to buy his farm produce; the buyers would haggle and haggle, but finally they abandoned him altogether, saying that this was no man but a devil; his hay and wheat rotted, his grain bins and ricks turned into pure compost, ideal for the cultivation of cabbages, the flour in his cellars turned into stone and had to be chipped away, the cloths, linens and other home-spun textiles disintegrated at the touch. He had already forgotten how much of everything he owned and could only remember where in which cupboard he had placed a small decanter containing the remains of some liqueur, on which he made a nick so that no one should thievishly pour himself a drop of it; or where he had placed his quill pen and sealing wax. Meanwhile income continued to accrue on the farm just as before: each peasant had to pay the same amount of quit-rent, every woman contributed her due share of nuts, each weaver woman wove for him her prescribed quantity of linen; all this was piled in storerooms, where it became mouldy and full of holes, and finally the owner himself degenerated into a hole in humanity. Alexandra Stepanovna visited on two occasions with her little son in the hope of getting something out of him; evidently her peripatetic life with her officer husband was not so rosy as she had pictured it before the elopement. Plyushkin did in fact offer her his pardon and even gave his little grandson a button that was lying on the table to play with, but he would not part with any money. The next time she came with both her children she brought her father an Easter cake she had baked him, and a new dressing gown, because the one he wore was not just shameful but even disgraceful to behold. Plyushkin caressed both his grandsons, and seating them one on his right knee and the other on his left, jigged them up and down just as if they were riding horses; he took the cake and the dressing gown, but he gave his daughter not a bean, and there ended Alexandra Stepanovna's visits.

Such, therefore, was the manner of landowner that stood before Chichikov! It must be said that his is a rare breed in Russia, where the tendency is rather for the open hand than the closed fist, and the occurrence of such a one is all the more remarkable for the fact that he is bound to have as a neighbour a landowner who carouses and revels in the grand Russian manner, burning the candle, as they say, at both ends. The uninitiated visitor will stop with amazement at the sight of his demesne, marvelling that such a potentate should suddenly be encountered here amongst the petty, parochial householders! His white stone houses look like palaces, with their countless abundance of chimneys, belvederes, weather-vanes, surrounded by flocks of outbuildings and every manner of accommodation for visiting guests. What more could he want? He gives theatrical shows, balls, his garden is illuminated all night long with a riot of torches and lampions, and reverberates with thunderous music. Half the province comes in its finery to stroll beneath the trees, and no one finds it weird or threatening when in this violent light an artificially illuminated branch springs theatrically out of the midst of the foliage, bereft of its own bright greenery, and darker and more severe on top and twenty times more awesome looking against the night sky, with its leaves rustling above at a great height, where they disappear in the impenetrable gloom, as the stern crowns murmur their indignation at this tawdry brilliance that lights up their roots below.

Plyushkin had now been standing for several minutes without saying a word, while Chichikov was still unable to open a conversation, distracted both by the appearance of his host and by everything else in his room. For a long time he could not think in what terms to explain the reason for his visit. He was on the point of saying that having heard much of the virtue and rare qualities of his host's soul, he regarded it as his duty to offer him the personal tribute of his respect, but he came to his senses in time, realising that this was a little excessive. Casting another sidelong glance at everything in the room he sensed that such words as "virtue" and "rare qualities of the soul" could most successfully be replaced by the words "economy" and "orderliness"; and therefore, having revised his speech accordingly he said that having heard of his host's economy and rare skills in the management of his estates, he regarded it as his duty to make his acquaintance and to pay his respects in person. Of course he could have adduced another, better reason, but nothing else would come to his mind.

In response Plyushkin muttered something through his lips, for lack of teeth, the exact sense of which is unknown but probably of the following tenor: "To the devil with you and your respects!" But since hospitality is such a tradition with us that even a miser is unable to defy its laws, he at once added somewhat more distinctly: "Please be seated!"

"I have not received guests for quite some time," he continued, "and, to be quite honest, I see little point in them. People have developed a most despicable custom of calling on one another whilst their estates go to rack and ruin ... and you even have to feed your hay to their horses! I have long since had my dinner, and my kitchen is a vile place: the chimney has completely collapsed, so when you start a fire you expect the whole house to go up in flames."

"How nice!" thought Chichikov. "It's a good thing I had that curd tart and that chunk of mutton at Sobakevich's."

"And unfortunately it so happens that there's hardly a tuft of hay on my entire farm!" continued Plyushkin. "Anyway, how could one store it? It's only a little place, my peasants are lazy, they don't like to work, all they think about is slipping off to the inn ... the next thing I know I'll be reduced to wandering around begging for a living in my old age!"

"But I was told," ventured Chichikov diffidently, "that you have more than a thousand souls."

"Now who told you a thing like that? Why, my good sir, you should have spat in the eye of the man who said it! He is a jester, clearly, liking to make fun. Imagine, a thousand souls, but just you go out and count them for yourself and you'll see there are none! In the last three years the cursed fever has carried off a good number of my peasants."

"Indeed! And were many carried off?" exclaimed Chichikov with enthusiasm.

"Yes, plenty were carried to the graveyard."

"If I might make so bold as to enquire: how many in fact?"

"A good eighty souls."

"Never!"

"I don't tell lies, sir."

"Allow me to ask another thing: I suppose these must be souls that you are counting from the day of the last census?"

"If only they were," said Plyushkin, "but the worst of it is that there's a good hundred and twenty since that day."

"Goodness! A hundred and twenty?" exclaimed Chichikov, even gaping somewhat in amazement.

"I'm too old to start lying, sir: I'm past sixty!" said Plyushkin. He appeared to take umbrage at Chichikov's almost joyous exclamation. Chichikov realised that such insouciance about another's misfortune was indeed improper, and he therefore sighed promptly and expressed his condolences.

"But you cannot put condolences in your wallet," said Plyushkin. "Now take the captain who lives close to me; the devil knows where he sprung from, calls himself a relative: 'Uncle! Uncle!' he says, and kisses my hand, and when he starts on his condolences he makes such a song and dance you have to block your ears. He's bright red in the face: he must hit the bottle something dreadful. I dare say he squandered his money while serving in the army, or let himself be fleeced by some actress, and that's why he's so full of condolences now."

Chichikov endeavoured to explain that his own condolences were of quite a different kind from the captain's, and that he was prepared to demonstrate them not through empty words but in action and, not wishing to delay matters further and without any beating about the bush, at once expressed his readiness to take on himself the obligation to pay the taxes for all the peasants who had met such unfortunate deaths. This proposal appeared to flummox Plyushkin totally. His eyes starting from his head he stared long and hard at Chichikov and finally asked:

"Did you yourself serve in the army?"

"No," answered Chichikov, with a certain slyness, "I was in the civil service."

"The civil service?" repeated Plyushkin, and started to chew his lips, as if eating something. "But what do you mean? It would mean a loss to you?"

"For your pleasure I am prepared to endure even a loss."

"Ah, sir! Ah my benefactor!" shrieked Plyushkin, failing to notice in his delight that a thick drop of snuff the colour of strong coffee had oozed from his nose in a most unpicturesque manner, and that the skirts of his dressing gown had parted to reveal underclothes that were not entirely suitable for public scrutiny. "Now there's comfort for an old man! Praise the Lord and His saints above!" Plyushkin was at a loss for more words. But before even a minute had passed this same joy which had so suddenly transfigured his wooden features, disappeared just as suddenly, as if it had never been at all, and his face once again took on its look of concern. He even mopped his brow with his handkerchief and, rolling it into a ball, started to rub his upper lip.

"Allow me to enquire, without wishing to anger you in any way, are you undertaking to pay the tax on them every year? And are you going to give me the money, or the treasury?"

"Well shall do it like this: we'll draw up a deed of purchase, just as if they were alive and as if you had sold them to me."

"Ah yes, a deed of purchase..." said Plyushkin, growing pensive and once again chewing his lips. "But deeds—they all cost money. Those chancery clerks have no shame! In the old days, you know, you used to be able to get off with half a ruble in brass and a bag of flour, but now you've got to hand over a whole cartload of grain, and a ten-ruble note into the bargain, they're such money-grubbers! I cannot understand why the priests don't do something about it; they should bring it up in their sermons: after all, whichever way you look at it, there's no going against the word of God."

"Oh no, you'd never go against it, would you!" thought Chichikov, and promptly announced that out of his respect for his host he was even prepared to take all these expenses upon himself.

Hearing this Plyushkin concluded that his guest was a complete fool and was lying when he said he had been in the civil service; he had probably been an officer chasing after chorus girls. Despite all this, however, he was still unable to conceal his delight, and he wished his guest every possible blessing and the same for his little children, without even ascertaining whether he had any children or not. Stepping up to the window he rapped on the pane and shouted: "Hey, Proshka!" A moment later they could hear someone running breathlessly into the anteroom, fussing around there for some time with a loud stamping of boots, before the door finally opened to admit Proshka, a lad of about thirteen, in such huge boots that his feet almost came out whenever he took a step. Why Proshka had such big boots can be easily explained: for all his domestic servants, however many there were in the house, Plyushkin kept only one pair of boots, which always had to remain in the anteroom. Anyone summoned into the master's presence had to skip barefoot across the yard, put on the boots once inside the house and appear before the master thus shod. On his departure from the room he would leave the boots in the anteroom again and walk back on his own tender soles. If a visitor were to glance out of the window in autumn, and especially when the light morning ground-frosts had started, he would see the entire household staff describing leaps that would have put the most accomplished dancer in any theatre to shame.

"Just take a look at that mug!" said Plyushkin to Chichikov, pointing at Proshka's face. "As dumb as a stump, but you leave anything lying around, he'll steal it in a flash! Well, why have you come in, you fool, eh, why?" This he followed with a brief silence, which Proshka answered with a similar silence. "Put on the samovar, d'you hear, and take this key to Mavra so she can go to the pantry: she'll find some dry Easter cake on the shelf in there, the one Alexandra Stepanovna brought, for us to have with our tea! Wait, where are you going? Numbskull! Fathead! Can't you keep your feet still, you imp! Hear me out first: the crust might be a bit mouldy, so tell her to scrape it off, but mind she doesn't throw away the crumbs, she can feed them to the chickens. And you look out, young fellow, don't you go poking your nose in the pantry or you'll get what for! I'll give you a taste of the birch rods! I know you've a fine healthy appetite, that way it'll get better still! Just you dare go into the pantry, I'll be watching all the while from the window here. You can't trust them with anything," he continued, turning to Chichikov, after Proshka had removed himself and his boots. And now he started to peer suspiciously at Chichikov too. This extraordinary show of magnanimity began to seem highly improbable to him and he said to himself: "How the devil do I know, may be he's just another loud-mouth, like all these wasters and squanderers; he'll tell you a lot of lies for his tea, and be off." And therefore, partly out of caution and partly wishing to test Chichikov a little, he suggested it would be no bad thing to conclude the transfer as swiftly as possible, because human life is an uncertain thing: today a man may be alive and well, but only God knows what tomorrow will bring.

Chichikov declared himself ready to settle the matter that very minute if need be and requested only that he be given a list of all the peasants' names.

This set Plyushkin's mind at rest. It was apparent that he was considering some course of action, and sure enough, he took up his keys, walked across to a cupboard, opened the door, rummaged about amongst the cups and glasses, and finally announced:

"I can't seem to be able to find it, but I had a splendid liqueur in here somewhere, if only someone hasn't already drunk it! The servants are such thieves! Ah now, I think this is it!" Chichikov saw in his hand a decanter, covered in a thick jacket of dust. "This was made by my late wife," continued Plyushkin, "and my rogue of a housekeeper was all for throwing it away, and didn't even cork it up, the wretch! In no time it was full of all sorts of dead flies and bugs, but I got all the rubbish out and it's quite clean now; I'll pour you a little glass."

But Chichikov declined the "splendid" liqueur, saying that he had already drunk and eaten.

"You have already drunk and eaten!" said Plyushkin. "Yes, of course, you can always tell a man of breeding: he doesn't eat, but he's not hungry. Now take some thieving ne'er-do-well, no matter how much you feed him... Like the captain, he comes here and says: 'Give us something to eat, Uncle!' And I'm no more uncle to him that he's grandpa to me. There's probably not a bite to eat in his own home, so he comes scrounging round here! So, you want a little list of all those idlers? Well, as luck could have it I wrote all their names down on a separate piece of paper, so that I could have them struck off the census at the very next opportunity."

Plyushkin put on his glasses and started to rummage through his papers. He united countless bundles of documents and in the process treated his guest to such a helping of dust that the latter sneezed. He finally extracted a scrap of paper, scrawled all over. Peasants' names covered it as densely as midges. There were all sorts of names: Paramonov was there, and Pimenov, and Panteleimonov, and Chichikov even spotted some Grigory Doyezzhai-ne-Doyedesh— in all, some one hundred and twenty plus. Chichikov's face beamed at the sight of such abundance. Stuffing the list in his pocket he remarked to Plyushkin that to conclude the deal it would be necessary for him to travel into town.

"Into town? But how can I? How can I leave my house?

My peasants are either thieves or rogues: they'll pick this place so clean in a day there won't even be anywhere to hang a coat."

"In that case do you not have an acquaintance who could do it?"

"What acquaintance? All my acquaintances have either croaked or become unacquainted. But wait a moment, what am I saying, of course I have!" he exclaimed. "The president himself is an acquaintance, in the old days he even used to drive out to visit me, how could I forget! We were trough-mates at school, we used to climb over fences together! What do I mean, no acquaintances? And what an acquaintance! Why not write to him?"

"Why not, indeed."

"Fancy forgetting him, an acquaintance like that! We were great friends at school."

And a ray of warmth suddenly flitted across those wooden features, as they expressed—not feeling, but some pale reflection of feeling, reminiscent of the sudden reappearance of a drowning man on the surface of the water, provoking a shout of joy from the crowd standing along the bank. But it is in vain that the delighted brothers and sisters cast a rope from the bank or wait for his back to emerge again, or his hands exhausted by the struggle: that appearance was the last. Everything is silent and the calm surface of the unresponsive element now seems all the more ghastly and desolate. Thus, too, did Plyushkin's face, after the brief flash of feeling across it, become still more unfeeling and more crass.

"There was a quarter square of clean paper lying here on the table," he said, "I can't think where it's got to: these servants of mine are such rogues!" He promptly set about looking under the table and on top of the table, rummaging through everything and finally shouted: "Mavra! Hey, Mavra!"

His summons was answered by the appearance of a woman bearing a plate on which lay a piece of dry cake, with which the reader is already familiar. The following conversation ensued between them:

"Where did you put that paper, you robber?"

"Honest to God, master, I never saw any paper, excepting a tiny little scrap which you used to cover the wine glass."

"And I can see by your eyes that you swiped it."

"Now why would I want to swipe it? It's no use to me: I can't read or write."

"You liar, you took it to the sexton's boy: he's learnt to write, so you gave it to him."

"But the sexton's boy, if he wants, can get his own paper. He has no use for your piece of paper!"

"Just you wait: on the Day of Judgement the devils will give you a good thrashing with their steel rods for this! You'll see what a thrashing you'll get!"

"But why will they thrash me when I never took your piece of paper in my hand? Let them thrash me for some other female weakness, but no one's ever had reason to accuse me of stealing."

"But those devils will thrash you anyway! They'll say: 'Take that, you scoundrel, for deceiving your master!' and they'll thrash you with red-hot rods too!"

"Then I shall say: 'I've done nothing, honest to God, I've done nothing, I never took nothing...' Look, there it is on the table! You're always blaming me for no reason!"

Plyushkin saw the quarter piece of paper was, indeed, there, and he stopped for a moment, chewing his lips, before announcing:

"So what's all the fuss about? What a nag! Say one word to her, and she answers with ten! Run along and fetch a candle so I can seal the letter. No, wait: you're bound to bring a tallow candle and that tallow melts fast: once you've lit it that's the end of the candle, it burns to nothing: better you bring me a taper!"

Mavra went off and Plyushkin seated himself in the armchair and took up a quill pen; for a long time he turned the quarter piece of paper round and round, wondering whether he might not make two eighths out of this one quarter, but he finally decided it was impossible; he plunged his pen into the inkwell containing some mould-covered liquid and a mass of dead flies on the bottom and started to write, describing letters like musical clefs, continually having to restrain the eager motion of his hand which skipped across the paper, and stingily cramming the lines close together, thinking the while with some regret that there would still be a lot of empty space left on the paper.

To what a nadir of paltriness, despicableness and nastiness a man can sink! How could he change so! But is this true to life? Everything is true to life, anything can happen to a man. Your ardent youth of today would recoil in horror if you were to show him his very own portrait as an old man. Once you set off on life's journey, once you take your leave of those gentle years of youth and enter the harsh, embittering years of manhood, remember to take with you all your human emotions, do not leave them by the wayside, for you will not pick them up again! Grim and terrible is the old age which awaits us, and nothing does it give in return! The grave itself is more merciful than old age, on the grave stone you find written the words: "Here a man lies buried!" but you cannot read anything in the cold, unfeeling features of inhuman old age.

"You don't happen to have a friend who might need some fugitive souls?" asked Plyushkin, folding up the piece of paper.

"Do you have fugitives as well?" Chichikov asked quickly, awaking from his reverie.

"I'm very much afraid I do. My son-in-law made some enquiries, he reckons we've lost track of them now, but then he's a military man: an expert at jingling his spurs, but when it comes to legal matters..."

"But how many of them are there?"

"Well, there must be up to seventy."

"Really?"

"Yes, there must be! There's never a year passes without some of them scarpering. My peasants are a terribly greedy lot, in their idleness they've developed the habit of guzzling, and I don't even have any food myself... I'd take anything I was offered for them. So this is my advice to your friend: even if he only tracks down a dozen of them, his money will be well spent. After all, a registered soul is worth a good five hundred rubles."

"No, my friend will not get even a sniff of this," said Chichikov to himself, and then explained that such a friend would be impossible to find, and that the expenditure incurred in such a business would make it not worthwhile, one would have to sell one's birthright and worse; but if Plyushkin really was in such straits, he was prepared to offer ... but it would be such a trifle it was hardly worth discussing.

"How much would you offer?" asked Plyushkin, with the eagerness of a Jew: his hands started to tremble like quicksilver.

"I would give twenty-five kopeks per soul."

"And how would you pay, in cash?"

"Yes, the money's here."

"Out of pity for my poverty, would you make it forty kopeks each?"

"My most respected sir!" said Chichikov. "Not only forty kopeks would I give but five hundred rubles apiece! I should be delighted to pay that, for I can see a respected and kind old man being forced by his own magnanimity to endure adversity."

"Why yes, that's how it is! Honestly, that's the truth!" exclaimed Plyushkin, hanging his head and shaking it in desolation. "It all stems from my own magnanimity."

"There, you see, I comprehended your character at once. Therefore, why should I not give you five hundred rubles per soul, but alas ... I lack the means; with your pardon I might be prepared to add another five kopeks, thereby bringing the price of each soul to thirty kopeks."

"As you wish, but could you just stick on another two kopeks per soul?"

"Very well, another two kopeks I shall add. How many of them do you have? You did say seventy, I seem to recall?"

"No, in all there are seventy-eight."

"Seventy-eight, seventy-eight, at thirty kopeks each, that will be..." Here our hero thought for a second, no longer, and promptly declared: "That will be twenty-four rubles and ninety-six kopeks!" Chichikov was good at arithmetic. He at once made Plyushkin write a receipt and handed over the money, which his host received with both hands and took over to his writing-desk as gingerly as if he were carrying a bowl of liquid and afraid of spilling it. Reaching his desk he counted the money again and deposited it, still with extraordinary caution, in a drawer, where, no doubt, it was destined to lie until the day when Father Karp and Father Polikarp, the two priests in the village, would lay him to his earthly rest, to the unbounded joy of his daughter and son-in-law and, perhaps, also of the captain who claimed kinship with him. After hiding the money Plyushkin seated himself in an armchair and appeared at a loss for a topic on which to discourse.

"What, are you going already?" he said, observing the slight movement made by Chichikov, who was only trying to take his handkerchief out of his pocket.

This question reminded our hero that there was indeed no purpose in lingering any longer.

"Yes, I must be away!" he announced, taking up his hat.

"And the tea?"

"Thank you, but I think perhaps we'll leave the tea for another time."

"But I've called for the samovar. I myself, to be quite honest, am no great lover of tea: it's a costly beverage, and the price of sugar has gone up mercilessly. Proshka! We don't need the samovar. Take the cake back to Mavra, do you hear: tell her to put it back where it was,—no, on second thought, bring it here, I'd better put it away myself. Farewell, kind sir, and may God bless you, and be sure to give my letter to the president. Yes! Let him read it, he's an old friend of mine. Imagine! He and I were school-fellows once!"

Thereupon this weird apparition, this shrivelled old miser saw Chichikov off from the yard, after which he ordered the gates to be locked at once, and then he toured his storerooms to check whether the guards were at their posts; they stood at every corner, drumming with wooden spoons on an empty barrel, rather than the customary iron bar; after this he peered into the kitchen, where, on the pretext of ascertaining whether his servants were enjoying their supper, he ate his fill of their cabbage soup and porridge and, after scolding them all roundly for thieving and general misconduct, returned to his own room. Once on his own he even started to consider how he could thank his guest for such truly unprecedented generosity. "I shall present him my pocket watch. It is a good one, after all, real silver, and not some pinchback alloy or bronze; a little damaged, but then he can have it repaired; he is still a young man, he needs a pocket watch to please his betrothed! On second thoughts, no," he added after a few moments' considertaion; "better I leave it to him after my death, in my will, so that he remembers me."

But even without a pocket watch our hero was in the best possible spirits. Such an unexpected acquisition was a most fortuitous windfall. Imagine, not only did he have dead souls, but also fugitives, all in all some two hundred souls and more! True, when he was only approaching Plyushkin's estate something told him that there would be some gain in his visit, but he never expected to make such a killing. All the way he remained in uncommonly high spirits; whistling away, pursing his lips and putting his fist to his mouth as if blowing a trumpet, and finally bursting into a song so outlandish that even Selifan, after listening for some time, said, with a slight shake of his head: "Just listen to the master sing!" The gloom of dusk had already fallen by the time they reached the town. Light and shade had merged completely and it seemed as if the objects themselves had blended into one another. The striped turnpike had taken on a strangely indeterminate colour; the moustache on the soldier standing on guard appeared to grow on his forehead, high above his eyes, whilst his nose seemed to be altogether missing. From the rattling noise and lurching motion it was apparent that the chaise was now driving on cobblestones. The street lamps had not yet been kindled, lights burned in only a few windows as yet, while in the side-streets and alleys various scenes and conversations were taking place as they inevitably do at this evening hour in all towns where there are large numbers of soldiers, cabmen, workers, and of that particular genus of red-shawled and stockingless ladies who can be seen darting about the crossroads like bats. Chichikov did not notice them and was even oblivious to the many slender young officials brandishing thin canes, who were probably homeward bound after taking the air outside town. Every now and again certain exclamations, apparently feminine in origin, reached his hearing: "You're lying, you drunkard! I never allowed him any such liberties!" or: "Don't you hit me, you brute, let's go to the police station and I'll show you what's what!" In a word, those utterances which suddenly, like a cloud of steam, scald some day-dreaming twenty-year-old youth, who, emerging from the theatre, still retains the image of a street in Spain, night, and a wondrous beauty with a guitar and curly locks. There are no bounds to his flights of fancy: he is in heaven and is paying his compliments to Schiller himself—when suddenly the fateful words ring out above him, like thunder, and he sees that he has returned to earth with a bump, and more precisely to Sennaya Square, and even to the vicinity of an inn, and once again real life has resumed its prosaic strutting before him.

Finally the chaise, after a hefty jolt, plunged through the gates of the inn, as if into a pit, and Chichikov was met by Petrushka who helped his master out of the carriage with one hand, while with the other he held down one skirt of his coat, for he did not like the skirts to separate. The inn-servant also came running out, bearing a candle in his hand and a napkin over his shoulder. Whether the arrival of his master was a source of joy to Petrushka we do not know, but he and Selifan did at least exchange winks and his normally severe expression did seem to brighten somewhat on this occasion.

"Your Honour was gone a long time," said the inn-servant, lighting the way up the stairs.

"Yes," said Chichikov, climbing the steps. "And how are things here?"

"God be praised," answered the inn-servant, with a bow. "Yesterday a lieutenant from some regiment or other arrived, he took room number sixteen."

"A lieutenant?"

"I don't know the regiment, but he's from Ryazan, with bay horses."

"Good, good, be sure and keep up the good work!" said Chichikov, repairing to his room. As he crossed the anteroom he wrinkled up his nose and said to Petrushka: "You could have at least opened the windows!"

"But I did open them," said Petrushka, telling a barefaced lie. Indeed, his master knew perfectly well he was lying, but he no longer felt like objecting. After his journey he was overcome with fatigue. Calling for an extremely light supper, consisting only of some suckling pig, he immediately undressed and, climbing under the quilt, fell fast asleep, sinking into that wondrous sleep that is enjoyed only by those lucky people who are not worried by piles, fleas, or excessive cerebral abilities.

CHAPTER SEVEN

Happy is the traveller who, after a long, tedious journey with its cold, slush, mud, groggy station-masters, jingling bells, breakdowns, wrangling, coachmen, blacksmiths and highway rogues of every description, at last espies a familiar roof and lights in the windows, and then he enters the familiar rooms, hears the joyous cries of the servants running out to meet him, the happy excitement of the children and his wife's comforting, quiet speeches, interrupted by ardent embraces, capable of annihilating the most dismal memories. Happy is the family man, who has such a nook, but woe betide the bachelor!

Happy is the writer who, by-passing tedious and repulsive characters, the very misery of whose lives is a source of amazement, comes to characters who manifest man's lofty dignity, the writer who out of the great maelstrom of images that spin past him every day has selected but a few rare exceptions, who has never once varied the elevated refrain of his lyre, has never descended from his heights to his wretched and paltry fellowmen and, without even touching the ground, is completely absorbed in his remote and exalted images. Doubly enviable is his excellent lot: he remains amongst them as amongst his own family; yet at the same time his glory is spread far and wide. He has clouded men's eyes with his intoxicating smoke-haze; he has flattered them marvellously, concealing from them all that is wretched in life and displaying to them Man in all his splendour. He drives his triumphal chariot in a tumult of applause followed by admiring crowds. He is acclaimed a great poet, soaring high above all other geniuses of this world, as the eagle soars high above the other lofty flying creatures. At the very mention of his name young and ardent hearts are all a-flutter, all eyes glisten with responsive tears... He is unequalled in his power: he is a god! But this is not the lot, and different is the destiny of the writer who dares to summon forth all that is constantly before our eyes, yet that which indifferent eyes do not see: all the terrible, shocking mire of trivia which enmesh our lives, the full depth of the cold, fragmented, humdrum characters, who are legion on our earthly path, so often tedious and bitter, the writer who has dared with a bold stroke of his remorseless chisel to display them in full and vivid relief to the eyes of all men! He will not reap the reward of popular applause, he is not destined to see tears of gratitude and the unanimous rapture of the souls he has moved; a sixteen-year-old maiden, dizzy with heroic passion, will not rush to embrace him; he is not fated to lose himself in the sweet fascination of the sounds he has himself uttered; nor can he escape the contemporary judgement, that hypocritical, unfeeling judgement which will condemn as paltry and base the creations he has lovingly nurtured, will assign to him a contemptible corner amongst those writers who have defamed mankind, will ascribe to him the qualities of his own heroes, will deny him his heart, his soul and the divine flame of his talent. For contemporary judgement does not recognize that lense through which we can view the stars and those through which we can watch the movements of insects are equally wonderful; that a great spiritual depth is required if one is to illuminate a picture taken from despicable life and to elevate it to a pearl of creation; that elevated, rapturous laughter deserves to stand beside exalted lyric flow, and that there is an enormous divide between such laughter and the clowning of a fair-booth jester! None of this is recognized by contemporary judgement, which turns everything into a reproach and vilification of the unrecognized writer; denied sympathy, response and understanding, he remains alone on the road like the bachelor wayfarer. Cheerless is his calling, and bitterly does he feel his solitude.

For a wondrous power ordains that I shall walk hand-in-hand with my strange heroes for a long time yet, viewing life in all its enormousness and swiftness, viewing it through the laughter that the world sees and the tears that it neither sees nor knows of! And far off as yet is that time when the dread blizzard of inspiration shall lift itself aloft in a different key from a head enveloped in holy terror and radiance and men shall list with bewildered trepidation to the majestic thunder of other speeches.

Let us take to the road! To the road! Begone the frown that flits across the brow and the severe, gloomy mien! Let us once and for all plunge into life with all its soundless chatter and little bells, and let us see what Chichikov is up to.

Chichikov awoke, stretched his arms and legs, and felt

that he had had a good night's sleep. Remaining supine
for a moment or two longer, he snapped his fingers and
beamed all over his face as he recalled that he was now the
owner of well nigh four hundred souls. He at once sprang
from his bed and without even pausing to examine his
face, something he loved most frankly and whose most
attractive feature he thought the chin, for he would most
frequently boast of it to his friends, particularly if he
was shaving at the moment. "See what a perfect rounded
chin I have!" he would usually say, stroking it. But now he
did not glance at his chin or at his face, just pulled on his
morocco leather boots, with their multi-coloured tooled
design, of the sort in which the town of Torzhok does such
a brisk trade owing to the chronic indolence of the Russians, and attired *à l'écossaise,* clad only in his shirt, and
forgetting his staid nature and mature age, described two
leaps across the room, adroitly kicking himself with his
heel as he did so. Thereupon he at once got down to business: standing before his box he rubbed his hands with all
the relish of an unbribable district magistrate who has travelled out to hear a case and is about to partake of refresh-
ments, and then removed some papers from inside it.
He was anxious to conclude everything as swiftly as possible and not shelve it for some later date. He decided to
draw up the deeds of purchase himself, writing down the
names and making copies, so as not to have to pay any
scriveners. He was entirely familiar with these formalities:
he boldly inscribed in large letters: "The Year One Thousand Eight Hundred and N", then after this in smaller letters: "Landowner such-and-such" and all the rest as appropriate. Within two hours all was ready. When afterwards he
looked at these sheets of paper, at the peasants who had
indeed once been peasants, working, ploughing, drinking,
carting, deceiving their masters, or who perhaps had simply
been good peasants, he was overcome by a strange sensation,
one he could not comprehend himself. Each little list
seemed to have its own special character, and through this
it was as if the peasants themselves acquired their own
special character. The peasants who belonged to Korobochka practically all had appendages to their names and
sobriquets. Plyushkin's list was remarkable for its terseness:
frequently only the initials of the names and patrony-

mics were given, followed by two dots. Sobakevich's roll struck him with its extraordinary fullness and circumstantiality, with not one of the peasants' qualities overlooked: about one he had written: "Good joiner", about another: "Knows his business and doesn't touch liquor." He also included detailed information about the identity of the mother and father and indicated how these latter had conducted themselves; only of one fellow called Fedotov had he written: "Father unknown, born to house-girl Kapitolina, but has good morals and not a thief." All these details lent a particular air of freshness: it was as if the peasants had been alive only yesterday. As he gazed long at the list, he felt spiritually moved and declared with a sigh: "Heavens above, what a lot of you crammed in here! Tell me, my dear chaps, what did you do in your lives? How did you make ends meet?" And his eyes involuntarily came to rest on one name: that of our old friend Pyotr Saveliev Neuvazhay-Koryto who had once belonged to Korobochka. Again he could not restrain himself from saying: "Phew, what a mouthful, sprawling across a whole line. So were you a master craftsman, or a simple peasant, and what manner of death took you off? Did it come in the inn, or were you run over by a train of unwieldy carts, as you slept in the middle of the road? Probka Stepan, carpenter, of exemplary sobriety. Ha! So this is he, that Stepan Probka, that giant of a man, who would have made a fine guardsman! You probably walked the length and breadth of all the provinces, your axe in your belt and your boots over your shoulder, eating a farthing's worth of bread and two farthings' of dried fish, always coming home, no doubt, with a hundred silver rubles in your pouch, and perhaps with a thousand-ruble note sewn into your hempen breeches, or stuffed into your boot—where did death overtake you? Did you climb up right under the church dome, for a bigger profit perhaps, or even hoist yourself onto the cross, to slip from the cross bar and crash down to the ground, with only some old uncle Mikhey there to see it and, scratching the back of his head, to sigh: 'Poor Vanya, you're gone and done it!' and then, tying the rope round him and climbing up into your place. Maxim Telyatnikov, cobbler. Huh, cobbler! 'Drunk as a cobbler,' goes the saying. Yes, I know you, my good fellow; if you like

I'll tell your whole story: you were apprenticed to a German, who used to feed all his lads together, beating you with a leather strap across the back for slipshod work and not allowing you out of the house to gad about in the streets, and you would have made a marvel of a cobbler, and your German couldn't praise you too highly, when talking to his wife or Kamerad. And I know how your apprenticeship ended: 'See if I don't start my own little business,' you said to yourself, 'and not like a German, saving up kopek by kopek; I shall get rich right away.'

"So, paying your master a tidy sum in quit-rent, you set up a little shop, collected a big pile of orders and set to work. You got hold of some rotten old leather for a third of the price and, to be sure, you made double profit on each boot, but after a fortnight all your boots fell apart and you were cursed as an out-and-out swindler. No customers came to your shop now, and you took to drinking or loafing around the streets, intoning: 'No, it's a rotten world! There's no life for a Russian, the Germans are always getting in the way.' Now what peasant do we have here? Yelizaveta Vorobei. A woman! How did she get in here? You rogue, Sobakevich, sneaking this one in!" Chichikov was right: this was indeed a woman. How she got in here we do not know, but her name had been so skilfully written that from a distance she could be mistaken for a man, and the feminine suffix had even been omitted from her name, which read: Yelizavet. Chichikov was not impressed by this amendment, however, and promptly scratched out her name. "Grigory Doyezzhai-ne-Doyedesh! What sort of a man were you? Were you a carrier by trade, and did you one day harness up your troika to your bast-covered wagon, and turn your back for ever on your home, on your native lair, and set off with the merchants on the long drive to a fair? Was it on the road that you gave up your soul to God, or did your very own friends dispatch you, over some plump, red-cheeked grass widow, or did a forest tramp take a fancy to your leather guantlets and your troika of squat, sturdy horses, or perhaps you yourself, lying up there on your bunk, thought and thought and then, suddenly made for the pub and then straight into an ice-hole, and that was that! Ah, my Russian people! You don't like dying a natural death! And what about you, my good lads?" he continued, his eyes moving across to the list of Plyushkin's fugitive souls. "You may still be alive, but what use are you? You're as good as dead, but where are your fleet feet carrying you now? Was it that bad with Plyushkin or did you simply prefer to take to the forests and rob wayfarers? Are you now rotting in prison somewhere or have you found new masters whose land you are now tilling? Yeremei Karyakin, Nikita Volokita, his son Anton Volokita—these are expert fugitives: you can tell by the names. Popov, house-serf, he must have had schooling: I bet he never brought a knife into play, and did all his thieving in a gentlemanly manner. But then you were caught with no passport by a police captain. You faced him boldly. 'Who do you belong to?' asks the captain, taking advantage of the situation to abuse you with some strong epithet. 'I belong to landowner so-and-so,' you answer readily. 'So why are you here?' asks the police captain. 'Released on quit-rent,' you answer without hesitation. 'Where's your passport?' 'With my master, the merchant Pimenov.' 'Call Pimenov.' Are you Pimenov?' 'I'm Pimenov. 'Did he give you his passport?' 'No, he never gave me any passport.' 'So you're lying?' says the captain, appending a particularly strong epithet. 'That's correct, sir,' you reply boldly, 'I didn't give it to him, because I came home late, so I gave it for safekeeping to Antip Prokhorov, the bell-ringer.' 'Call the bell-ringer! Did he give you his passport?' 'No, I never received any passport from him.' 'So you're lying again!' says the captain of police, embellishing his utterance with another strong epithet. 'So where's your passport?!' 'I did have it,' you reply adroitly, 'but I must have mislaid it somewhere on the road.' 'Then why,' continues the captain, once again for good measure affixing a choice epithet, 'did you steal a soldier's greatcoat? And a cash-box full of coins from the priest?' 'No, no,' you say, without batting an eyelid, 'not me: I've never been one for pinching and that.' 'So how come the greatcoat was found on you?' 'I couldn't tell you: perhaps someone else brought it.' 'Huh, you devil! You devil!' says the police captain, shaking his head, his arms akimbo. 'Put him in stocks and march him to gaol.' 'Why certainly! With pleasure,' you reply. And then, taking your snuff-box from your pocket, you hospitably extend it to the two invalids, busy fastening the stocks on your legs, and you enquire how long they have been in retirement and which war they fought in. And then you settle into prison life until your case comes up in court. The court decrees: you are to be transferred from Tsarevokokshaisk to such and such a gaol, and the court there decrees: you are to be transferred to some place called Vesyegonsk, and so you travel from gaol to gaol saying, as you inspect your new abode: 'No, the Vesyegonsk gaol was a bit cleaner than this: there was enough space even for a game of knucklebones, there was plenty of room, and more company too!' Abakum Fyrov! And who might you be, brother? Where, in what part of Russia are you? Have you strayed to the Volga and come to love the free life, joining the boatmen?" Here Chichikov paused and grew slightly pensive. What was he thinking about? Was he thinking of the fate of Abakum Fyrov, or had his thoughts been carried away by themselves, as happens to every Russian, of whatever age, rank and station, when he reflects on the joys of the free life? Indeed, where was Fyrov now? Carousing noisily and merrily at the grain wharf, after striking a bargain with the merchants? Flowers and ribbons in their hats, the entire gang of boatmen makes merry, as they take their leave of sweethearts and wives, tall and slender, adorned with ribbons and necklaces; there is dancing and singing; the entire wharf is a frenzy of activity, and all the while the stevedores go about their business, amid a din of shouting, cursing and goading, hoisting nine poods—a good three hundred-weight—on to their backs with their hooks, noisily dumping the peas and wheat into the deep holds, rolling massive bags of oats and barley along, while all around tower piles of sacks, stacked like cannon-balls into pyramids, and this whole grain arsenal looks hopelessly enormous until everything has been loaded into the deep wheat barges which then proceed in an endless single file through the spring ice-floes. Now comes your turn to sweat, Volga boatmen! Go to it all together as you had just made merry together, and haul the boats to the strains of a song as endless as Russia herself.

"Goodness me! Twelve o'clock!" said Chichikov at last, glancing at his watch. "How can I have tarried so? It would be one thing if I had been doing business, but first I started talking a lot of nonsense, and then fell into a reverie. Really, what a fool I am!" Having said this, he exchanged his Scottish costume for something more European, drew in his ample paunch by tightening his buckle, splashed Cologne over himself, picked up his winter cap and placing his papers under his arm set off for the Chambers to effect the transfer of souls. He hurried on his way not because he was afraid of being late—he had no fear of that, for the president was a personal friend and could extend or curtail receiving hours as he wished, in the manner of Homer's Zeus of old, who would lengthen the days and send down short nights when he wished to bring to an end the hostilities of his favoured heroes or enable them to fight to the finish, but he felt an inner need to bring matters to their conclusion as swiftly as possible; until this was done things would seem awkward and unstable: he could not quite suppress the thought that the souls were not entirely real and that in such situations the sooner one had the business over the better. Nor sooner had he set foot outside the inn, reflecting on all this and simultaneously pulling a bearskin coat faced in brown cloth around his shoulders, when at the first turning into a side-street he bumped into another gentleman wearing a bearskin coat, similarly faced with brown cloth, and in a winter cap with ear flaps. The gentleman cried out in surprise: it was Manilov. They at once fell into each other's arms and remained in this position in the street for fully five minutes. The kisses on both sides were of such force that for most of the day they both suffered from aching front teeth. Such was Manilov's joy that only his nose and lips remained visible in his face, his eyes completely disappearing. For a good quarter of an hour he clutched Chichikov's hand in both of his own, warming it terribly. Employing the choicest and most agreeable locutions, he recounted how he had flown to embrace Pavel Ivanovich; this oration was concluded with a compliment such as it might only be proper to bestow upon the lady with whom one is about to dance. Chichikov opened his mouth, still not knowing how to express his gratitude, when Manilov suddenly produced a document from inside his overcoat, rolled up and secured with a little pink ribbon, and handed it over, holding it most adroitly with two fingers.

"What is that?"

"Peasants."

"Ah!" Chichikov at once unrolled it, ran his eyes over it and marvelled at the neatness and beauty of the hand. "Splendidly written," he said, "there's no need even to write it out again. With a special border too! Who made such an expert border?"

"Now, you mustn't ask me that!" said Manilov.

"You?"

"My wife."

"My word! I must say, I feel somewhat ashamed that I have caused so much trouble."

"Anything we do for Pavel Ivanovich cannot be trouble."

Chichikov bowed in gratitude. Hearing that he was bound for the Chamber to conclude the business, Manilov announced his desire to accompany him there. The two friends linked arms and proceeded together. At every slight incline, or elevation, or little step, Manilov supported Chichikov, and practically lifted him up bodily, averring with a pleasant smile that he would in no circumstances permit Pavel Ivanovich to hurt his dear feet. Chichikov was greatly embarrassed and did not know how to thank him, for he was aware that he was a trifle on the heavy side. Performing such mutual services, they finally arrived at the square where the government offices were situated: a large, three-storeyed building, painted as white as chalk, presumably to reflect the purity of the souls of the officials within; the other structures round the square were dwarfed by this imposing brick building. These were: a sentry box, by which a soldier stood, holding a rifle; a couple of cab-stands, and, finally, long fences adorned with the usual dirty words and drawings, scribbled with a piece of charcoal or chalk; there was nothing more to be seen on this desolate, or as they are usually described, beautiful square. The incorruptible heads of the priests of Themis sometimes stuck out of the second and third floor windows, only to disappear at once within: presumably at that moment their superior had entered the room. The friends did not walk up the staircase, but ascended it at a run, because Chichikov, anxious to free himself from Manilov's solicitous arm, had quickened his pace, while Manilov also flew ahead, endeavouring to prevent Chichikov from growing fatigued, and thus they were both considerably out of breath when they finally entered the dark corridor. Neither corridors, nor the rooms themselves struck them as impressively clean. No one was much concerned about cleanliness at that time, and whatever became dirty remained dirty, without being given a decorous appearance, and Themis received her guests informally, in a dressing gown, so to say. We should now proceed to a description of the offices through which our heroes passed, but the author must confess to a great timidity with regard to any offices. Even on those occasions when he chanced to pass through gleaming and ennobled offices, with polished floors and tables, he would endeavour to hurry through as swiftly as possible, his eyes humbly and modestly downcast, and for that reason he does not know at all how the business flourishes there. Our heroes saw much paper, both rough copies and fair copies, they saw bowed heads, broad necks, tail coats, frock-coats of a provincial cut and even one plain, light grey shortcoat, which stood out conspicuously, as, with its head inclined to the side and resting almost on the paper, it transcribed in a bold and florid hand some report on the sequestration of land or confiscation of an estate, seized by some peace-loving landowner, quietly living out his days while the case continued, accumulating profits for himself and his children under protection of the courts, and they heard someone saying brusquely in a hoarse voice: "Allow me, Fedosey Fedoseyevich, to see case No. 368!" "You're always mislaying the cork from the office ink-well!" Sometimes a more imperious voice, no doubt that of one of the superiors, would ring out peremptorily: "Here, copy that out again, or else I'll have your boots taken away and you can sit here in the office for six days running without a bite to eat!" The noise of the pens was considerable and sounded like several carts of brushwood scrunching their way through a forest over a deep carpet of dry leaves.

Chichikov and Manilov approached the first desk, at which sat two youthful officials, and enquired:

"I wonder if you could tell us where deeds of purchase are dealt with here?"

"What do you want?" asked both officials, looking around.

"I wish to submit an application."

"So what have you bought?"

"First I would like to know where is the purchase desk, here, or somewhere else?"

"But you tell me first what you have bought and for how much, then we can tell you where, otherwise we don't know."

Chichikov could see at once that the officials were merely inquisitive, like all young officials, and that they wished to attach greater importance and weight to themselves and their activities.

"Listen, my good fellows," he said, "I know perfectly well that all purchase matters, at whatever price, are dealt with in one and the same place, and therefore I request that you show me the desk, and if you do not know what goes on in your office then we shall enquire elsewhere."

The officials made no answer to this, one of them merely pointed to one corner of the room, where an old man sat at a desk, making marks on sheets of paper. Chichikov and Manilov strode between the desks right up to him. The old man was intent on his work.

"Allow me to enquire," said Chichikov with a bow, "is this where purchase deeds are dealt with?"

"No purchase deeds here."

"Where then?"

"You must go to the purchase department."

"And where is this purchase department?"

"That's Ivan Antonovich's section."

"And where is this Ivan Antonovich?"

The old man pointed to another corner of the room. Chichikov and Manilov made their way across to Ivan Antonovich. Ivan Antonovich had already peeped round and given them a sideways glance, but the moment they approached him he buried himself even more intently in his copying.

"Permit me to enquire," said Chichikov with a bow, "is this the purchase desk?"

Ivan Antonovich appeared not to hear and remained totally immersed in his papers, vouchsafing no reply. It was at once evident that this was a man of prudence and maturity, not some young loudmouth and scatter-brain. Ivan Antonovich, it appeared, was already well over forty years of age; his hair was black and thick; the entire central section of his face protruded and grew into his nose—in other words, it was one of those faces which in common parlance is known as a "jug-snout."

"Permit me to enquire, is this the purchase department?" said Chichikov.

"It is," said Ivan Antonovich, turning his jug-snout back, and applied himself once more to his copying.

"My business is as follows: I have purchased peasants for transfer from various landowners in this district: I have the deeds of purchase, they only need to be finalized."

"Are the sellers present?"

"Some are present, others have given power of attorney."

"Have you brought the application?"

"I have indeed. I should like to... I am in rather a hurry... Would it not, for example, be possible to conclude the matter today?"

"Today! Quite impossible," said Ivan Antonovich. "We also need to investigate whether there remain any distrains."

"In fact, with regard to speeding things up I might say that Ivan Grigorievich, the president, is a close friend of mine..."

"But remember, Ivan Grigorievich is not alone: there are others," riposted Ivan Antonovich severely.

Chichikov understood the innuendo and said: "The others will have no cause for complaint either, I used to be in the service myself, I know the form..."

"Go and see Ivan Grigorievich," said Ivan Antonovich in a slightly more amenable voice, "let him issue a pertinent order, and we will speed things up all we can."

Chichikov now produced a banknote from his pocket, and placed it before Ivan Antonovich, who took absolutely no notice of it and promptly covered it with a book. Chichikov was on the point of bringing this to his attention, but with a movement of his head Ivan Antonovich gave him to understand that such action was unnecessary.

"He will take you to Ivan Grigorievich's office!" said Ivan Antonovich, with a nod of his head, and one of the acolytes in their immediate vicinity, who had been offering his sacrifice to Themis with such zeal that both sleeves had burst at the elbows and the lining had long since fallen out, for which service he had at the time been promoted to the rank of collegiate registrar, now waited upon our friends, as once Virgil had waited upon Dante, and conducted them into the office, where the president sat in solitary splendour, in the only armchair there, behind a desk on which stood a glass pyramid, displaying Peter the Great's edicts, and two fat tomes. Our modern-day Virgil felt such veneration before this place that on no account would he presume to set foot within, and he turned around, to reveal a back as threadbare as a bast mat and with a chicken feather stuck to it. As Chichikov and Manilov entered the office, they discovered that the president was not in fact alone, for next to him sat Sobakevich, totally obscured by the pyramid. The entry of the visitors provoked an exclamation, and the presidential armchair was noisily pushed back. Sobakevich also half-rose from his seat and was now visible from all sides with his too-long sleeves. The president welcomed Chichikov into his embrace, and the office resounded with the noise of osculation; they enquired after each other's health; it transpired that they both suffered somewhat from lumbago and this was ascribed to a sedentary life. The president, it seemed, had already been apprised by Sobakevich of the purchase, because he set about offering his congratulations, and at first rather embarrassed our hero, particularly when he realised that Sobakevich and Manilov, two sellers with whom he had conducted his business secretively, were now standing face-to-face. Nonetheless, he thanked the president and turning at once to Sobakevich enquired:

"And how is your health?"

"Thank the Lord, nothing to complain about," said Sobakevich.

And to be sure, there can have been nothing to complain about: an iron bar would be more likely to catch a cold and start coughing than this miraculously robust gentleman.

"But then you've always been renowned for your good health," said the president, "and your late father was also a strong man."

"Yes, he used to take on a bear single-handed," answered Sobakevich.

"I reckon, however," said the president, "that you would also fell a bear if you took one on."

"No, I wouldn't," answered Sobakevich, "the old man was stronger than me," and, with a sigh, he continued; "No, you don't get people like that any more; take my life, for example, what sort of a life is it anyway? Pretty run-of-the-mill..."

"In what way is your life deficient?" asked the president.

"It's no good, no good at all," said Sobakevich, shaking his head. "Judge for yourself, Ivan Grigorievich: I'm over forty, and I've never once been ill, not so much as a sore throat or a boil... No, it's not a good sign! Sooner or later I shall have to pay for all this." Whereupon Sobakevich sank into melancholy.

"Honestly," thought Chichikov and the president as one man, "what a thing to moan about!"

"Here's a letter to you from someone," said Chichikov, taking Plyushkin's letter from his pocket.

"From whom?" asked the president and, opening the letter, exclaimed: "What! From Plyushkin? So he's still dragging out his miserable existence? There's fate for you, to think what a brilliant, wealthy man he was! And now..."

"He's a cur," said Sobakevich, "a scoundrel, he's starved all his serfs to death."

"Why, certainly, certainly," said the president, reading the letter, "I am quite happy to be his attorney. When would you like to conclude the deal, now or later?"

"Now," said Chichikov, "in fact, if possible I would even request that we do it today, because I was hoping to leave town tomorrow; I've brought both the deeds of purchase and the applications."

"That's all very well, but say what you will, we shall not let you go so soon. The deeds of purchase will be completed today, but you simply must stay on with us for a while. I shall give the order right away," he said opening a door into the clerical department literally packed with clerks, who were not unlike so many industrious bees buzzing round their hives, if one might presume to liken clerical affairs to bee-hives.

"Is Ivan Antonovich here?"

"He's here," answered a voice from within.

"Send him in!"

The jug-like snout of Ivan Antonovich, with which the

reader is familiar by now, appeared in the office, and he bowed deferentially.

"Here, Ivan Antonovich, take all these purchase deeds..."

"Now don't forget, Ivan Grigorievich," interrupted Sobakevich, "we need witnesses, at least two on each side. Send for the public prosecutor: he's an indolent man and is probably sitting at home while all his work is being done for him by his scrivener Zolotukha, the world's worst bribe-taker. The sanitary inspector is another loafer and also at home, no doubt, unless he's headed off somewhere to play cards, and there are plenty of others even nearer at hand—Trukhachevsky, Begushkin, they are all surplus ballast on earth's voyage!"

"Quite so! Quite so!" said the president and promptly dispatched the messenger to fetch them all.

"Could I also ask you," said Chichikov, "to send for the attorney of a certain gentlewoman, with whom I also did some business, the son of the archpriest Father Kiril; he works here in your department."

"Why of course, let's send for him too!" said the president. "All will be done, and please do not give the officials any money, I beg you. My friends should not have to pay." Having said this he at once gave some instruction to Ivan Antonovich, which appeared not to please the latter. The purchase deeds seemed to have a benign effect on the president, especially when he saw that the transactions amounted to a total of almost one hundred thousand rubles. For several minutes he gazed into Chichikov's eyes with a look of genuine delight and finally declared: "Well, so that's that! So there, Pavel Ivanovich! So you've made some acquisitions."

"I have," answered Chichikov.

"An excellent thing, to be sure, an excellent thing!"

"Indeed, I can see it myself that I could not have undertaken a more excellent thing. Say what you will, but man's purpose in life remains uncertain unless he plants his feet firmly on solid ground and does not cling to some frivolous chimera of youth." At this point he most appositely scolded all young people for their liberalism, and serves them right too. But the curious thing was that his words betrayed a certain irresolution, as if at the same time he were saying to himself: "Tsk, brother, what lies you tell, and real whoppers too!" He even avoided Sobakevich's and Manilov's eyes, lest he read something in their expression. But his apprehensions were unfounded: Sobakevich's face was totally impassive, whilst Manilov was so enchanted by this sentiment that he could only rock his head from side to side in approbation and pleasure, sinking into the position struck by a music lover when the soprano outdid the violin itself, squeaking so high a note that it would be beyond the reach of even a songbird.

"Yes, why do you not tell Ivan Grigorievich," rejoined Sobakevich, "exactly what it is you've bought; and you, Ivan Grigorievich, why do you not ask what acquisition has been made? Let me tell you, those are first class men! Solid gold. Would you believe it, I sold him my coach-builder Mikheyev."

"No, surely you haven't sold Mikheyev?" said the president. "I know Mikheyev the coach-builder: a splendid craftsman, he refurbished my droshky. Only, just a second, surely... Did you not tell me he had died?"

"Why, Mikheyev dead?" said Sobakevich, not batting an eyelid. "It's his brother who died, but he's alive and kicking, and even healthier than before. The other day he knocked together a chaise better than any you would find in Moscow. To be quite honest, he should really only work for the Tsar."

"Yes, Mikheyev's a fine craftsman," said the president, "and I'm only amazed you could part with him."

"And it's not as if Mikheyev's the only one! There's Stepan Probka, the carpenter, Milushkin, the bricklayer, Telyatnikov Maxim, the cobbler—they've all gone, I've sold them all!" But when the president asked how he could have sold them when they were all indispensible serfs for the house and workshops, Sobakevich answered with a wave of his hand: "Ah! It's simple, a moment of folly: 'Why don't I sell them,' I said, 'I'll sell them', and like the fool I am I sold them!" Then he hung his head, as if repenting of his deed, and added: "You see, wisdom does not come with grey hairs."

"But allow me to ask, Pavel Ivanovich," said the president, "how can you be buying peasants without land? Are they to be transferred?"

"Yes, that is correct."

"Ah well, that's a different matter. And where to, might I ask?"

"To, er... to Kherson province."

"Ah, there's some excellent land there!" said the president and delivered fulsome praises about the height of the grass in those parts. "And is the property sufficiently large?"

"It is indeed; there is enough for the number of peasants I have bought."

"Does it have a river or pond?"

"A river. In fact, there is a pond too." Having said this, Chichikov glanced inadvertently at Sobakevich, and although Sobakevich was as impassive as ever, Chichikov seemed to read in his face: "Oo, you liar! I bet there's no river, nor pond, nor any land at all!"

While this conversation was in progress the witnesses were gradually assembling: the readers' old friend the winking prosecutor, the sanitary inspector, Trukhachevsky, Begushkin and the others, who, in Sobakevich's phrase, were all surplus ballast on earth's voyage. Many of them were quite unknown to Chichikov; the missing numbers and reserves were made up there and then, from the ranks of the department clerks. They had also brought not only the son of the archpriest Father Kiril, but even the archpriest himself. Each of the witnesses signed his name complete with all his honours and ranks, some in a back-slanting hand, some slanting forward, some writing practically upside down, inserting letters the like of which have never been seen in the Russian alphabet. Our friend Ivan Antonovich dispatched his functions most expeditiously: the deeds of purchase were signed, noted, registered in a book and wherever necessary, with the levying of half percent and fees for publication in the *Gazette*, and Chichikov was obliged to pay only the merest trifle. The president even gave instructions that he should only be charged half the payable duties, and the other half, in some incomprehensible manner, was charged to another applicant.

"So," said the president, when all was completed, "there remains only the matter of celebrating the purchase."

"I'm quite ready," said Chichikov. "All you have to do is set the time. It would be a serious transgression on my part if I were not to uncork two or three bottles of sparkling wine in such delightful company."

"No, no, the sparkling wine we shall supply ourselves," said the president, "that is our duty, our obligation. You are our guest: we must treat you. You know what, gentlemen! This is what we shall do: let us all of us, just as we are, go round to the chief of police; he's a real miracle-worker: he only needs to wink as he walks past a fish-stall or a wine-cellar and we shall all have a feast to remember! And while we're about it we can have a little game of whist."

This was a suggestion no one could decline. The witnesses could feel an appetite stirring at the very mention of the words fish-stall: they all at once reached for their hats and caps and the official business was over. As they passed through the office Ivan Antonovich, a jug snout, with a most respectful bow, said *sotto voce* to Chichikov:

"You bought peasants to the value of one hundred thousand, but for all the work gave a measly twenty-five ruble note."

"But you should see the peasants," replied Chichikov, also *sotto voce*, "the most useless and worthless lot, they're not worth the half of what I paid."

Ivan Antonovich guessed that this client was a strong character and would give no more.

"How much did you get Plyushkin's souls for?" whispered Sobakevich in his other ear.

"And why did you slip Vorobei on to the list?" whispered Chichikov in reply.

"Which Vorobei?" asked Sobakevich.

"That woman, Yelizaveta Vorebei, and you dropped the -a off her name."

"No, I never added any Vorobei," said Sobakevich and went to join the other guests.

The guests eventually arrived in a big crowd at the police chief's. The chief of police was, indeed, a miracle-worker: no sooner had he heard what was going on than he summoned his constable, a nimble young fellow in patent leather boots, and seemed to whisper no more than two words in his ear, adding only "Got me?" and lo and behold! in the next room, while the guests were playing whist, a table was served with dishes of beluga, sturgeon, salmon, pressed caviare, fresh-salted caviare, salted herring, cheeses, smoked tongue—all this being the contribution of the fish-stalls. These were followed by domestic offerings from the host's own kitchen: fish-head pie, made of the gristle and cheeks of a nine-pood sturgeon, another pie stuffed with mushrooms, then meat patties, dumplings, and berries stewed in honey. The chief of police was to a certain extent a father figure and benefactor to the town. He moved amongst his citizens as amongst his own family, and dropped in on the shops and market place as into his own pantry. He sat firmly in the saddle and knew his job in and out. It was even hard to say whether he had been created for the job or the job for him. He performed his duties with such wisdom that he made twice as much profit as all his predecessors, and at the same time earned the love of the entire town. The merchants loved him dearly for the very reason that he was not proud; and, to be sure, he stood godfather to their children, fraternized with them, and although at times he might fleece them terribly he somehow always did it with great adroitness: with a slap on the back, a friendly laugh, a drink of tea, a promise to come and play draughts, an enquiry about business and everything. And if he learnt that some child had fallen ill he would recommend medicine—in a word, he was a first class chap! As he drove through town in his droshky he saw that order was kept and at the same time drop a word to one man and another: "Hey, Mikheich! You and I must get together sometime to finish that game of ours." "Yes, Alexei Ivanovich," Mikheich would reply, doffing his cap, "we must." Or else: "I say, brother, Ilya Paramonich, come round and have a look at my trotter; he'll beat yours in any race, so put yours in racing harness; let's give it a try." The merchant, who was obsessed with trotters, would grin and welcome this most eagerly, stroking his beard and saying: "Let's give it a try, Alexei Ivanovich!" Even all the stall-keepers usually doffed their caps at such moments, and exchanged glances as if to say: "He's a good man, Alexei Ivanovich is." In other words, he managed to make himself universally popular, and the merchants held the opinion that Alexei Ivanovich "might take a wee bit, but then he'll never play you false".

Observing that the food was ready, the chief of police suggested to his guests that they continue their whist after they had lunched and they all proceeded into the next room, the aromas from which had long since been tickling their noses and through whose door Sobakevich had already been peeking, having espied in the distance a whole sturgeon, lying on a large dish. The guests, after drinking a glass of vodka of a dark olive colour, like that only found in the translucent Siberian stone from which engraved seals are cut in Russia, surrounded the table, and here each revealed his own character and predilections, one going for the caviare, another for the salmon, a third for the cheese. Sobakevich, scorning all these trifles, addressed himself to the sturgeon, and while the others drank, conversed and ate, he, in the course of little more than a quarter hour, polished off the entire fish, so that when at last the chief of police remembered about it and asked: "And what, gentlemen, is your esteemed opinion of this product of nature?" approaching the fish, fork at the ready, he saw that of the product of nature there remained only the tail; but Sobakevich pretended that it wasn't him, and moving across to another dish, standing as far away from the sturgeon as possible, started to poke his fork at a small dried fish. Having thus dispatched the sturgeon, Sobakevich went and sat in an armchair and neither ate nor drank any more and only blinked his eyes and all but purred. The chief of police, it appeared, did not like to stint on the wine; toasts were endless. The first toast was drunk, as the readers may have already guessed, to the health of the new Kherson landowner, then to the welfare of his serfs and their successful re-settlement, then to the health of his future wife, a great beauty, at the thought of whom an agreeable smile was teased from the lips of our hero. Well-wishers came up to him from all sides and started persuasively to entreat him to remain in the town if only for another fortnight:

"No, Pavel Ivanovich! We won't take no for an answer! You know how it's said; it's just a waste of firewood opening the front door only to close it after the guest. No, you must spend some time with us! You'll see, we shall find you a wife: we shall marry him off, Ivan Grigorievich, shall we not?"

"We'll marry him off, all right!" echoed the president. "No matter how hard you dig in your feet, we'll get you to the altar! No, my good sir, you brought yourself here, so don't complain. We do not like to joke."

"Why not? Why should I dig in my feet?" said Chichikov with a chuckle. "I've nothing against marriage, you know, provided the bride's the right one."

"We'll find you a bride, never fear, everything will be just as you wish!"

"Well, in that case—"

"Bravo, he's staying," they all chorused. "Vivat, hooray for Pavel Ivanovich! Hooray!" And they all stepped up to clink glasses with him.

Chichikov touched everyone's glass. "Again, again!" called those who were more enthusiastic, and they all clinked again; then they called for a third round, and they clinked glasses a third time. In a short time everyone felt uncommonly merry. The president, a most charming man when in his cups, embraced Chichikov several times, exclaiming in an excess of emotion: "My dear soul! My very dear soul!" and even, clicking his fingers, executed a little jig around him, singing the well-known Kamarinsky song. After the champagne they uncorked some Tokay, which infused even greater energy and high spirits into the company. They had totally forgotten their whist; they argued, shouted, talked about anything and everything: about politics, even about military matters, expounded the sort of free-thinking ideas that at another time they would have whipped their own children for professing. There and then they resolved a great number of highly vexatious issues. Chichikov had never before felt so jolly, already imagining himself a real Kherson landowner, describing the various improvements he planned for his estate: the three-field system of crop rotation, the happiness and blissful coexistence of two souls, and he started to recite to Sobakevich Werther's letter in verse to Charlotte, which recitation Sobakevich received sitting in his armchair and staring blankly in reply, for after his meal of sturgeon he felt a strong inclination to sleep. At last Chichikov sensed that he had started to unwind a little too much, so he called for a carriage and availed himself of the prosecutor's droshky. The prosecutor's coachman, as luck would have it, was a sturdy chap of some experience, for he was able to drive with only one hand, leaving the other free to support the gentleman behind him. And so Chichikov arrived back at the inn in the prosecutor's droshky, and here for a long time he continued to prattle all sorts of nonsense: about a fair-haired bride with rosy cheeks and a little dimple on her right cheek, the villages in Kherson province, capital investment. Selifan was even given certain managerial instructions: to gather together all the peasants that were being resettled and to take a roll-call. Selifan listened in silence for a long time and then left the room, remarking to Petrushka: "Go in and undress the master!" Petrushka set about removing his master's boots and nearly pulled him down on to the floor with them. But at last the boots were off; the master undressed properly and, tossing and turning for a little while on the bed, which creaked unmercifully, he finally fell asleep and slept the sleep of a Kherson landowner. Meanwhile Petrushka took his breeches and cranberry shot-silk tailcoat out into the corridor, hung the coat on a wooden hanger and pounded it with a stick and a brush, sending the dust flying down the corridor. As he was about to take back the garments he glanced down from the gallery and saw Selifan on his way back from the stables. Their eyes met and an unspoken message passed between them: namely, the master is fast asleep, we can pop in you-know-where. So Petrushka immediately returned the coat and breeches to the room, then hurried downstairs, and the two set off together, saying not a word about the purpose of their journey and chatting away as they walked about totally extraneous matters. They did not have far to go: to be precise, only across the street, to the building opposite the inn, and they entered through a low, smoke-blackened, glass-paned door, which led almost into the cellar, where they found a great variety of people already sitting at the wooden tables: men with and without beards, some in country sheepskin coats and others in shirts, and one or two even in frieze greatcoats. What exactly Petrushka and Selifan did once inside, God only knows, but they emerged from there an hour later, arms linked, preserving a total silence, being most attentive to each other and warning each other about any corners in their path. Hand in hand, neither letting go, they clambered up the porch steps for fully a quarter of an hour, finally gaining the top step and entering the inn. Petrushka paused for a moment before his low bed, considering how

he might most decently lie down, and then flopped dov
right across it, so that his feet were propped against the
floor. Selifan also lay down on the same bed, reposing his
head on Petrushka's belly and quite forgetting that he was
not supposed to sleep here at all, but in the servants' quarters, if not in the stables next to his horses. They both fell
asleep instantly, snoring with a sonority never heard here-
tofore, to which their master in the adjacent room responded with a thin nasal whistle. Soon everyone else there was
settled down, and the inn was embraced by the sleep of
the dead; light remained in but one room, occupied by a
lieutenant who had come from Ryazan, clearly a great
amateur of boots, because he had already ordered four
pairs, and was trying on a fifth, time and time again. He
walked up to the bed, meaning to pull them off and lie
down, but he just could not do it: the boots were so well
made, that for a long time he sat raising his foot and admiring the smartly and wondrously tapered heel.

CHAPTER EIGHT

Chichikov's purchases became the subject of discussion.
Rumours, views and opinions were aired in the town on
the advisability of buying peasants for transfer. Many accomplished experts on the subject emerged from these
debates. "Of course," reasoned some, "it is true, and one
cannot deny it: the land in the southern provinces is fine
and fertile; but how will Chichikov's serfs fare without
water? There is not a single river there." "That's not the
worst of all, I say, not the worst, at all, Stepan Dmitrievich,
but re-settlement as such is a chancey business. You know
our peasants: in new lands, having to till the fields, and the
man has nothing of his own—no home, no household,
nothing, so what does he do? He scarpers, as sure as eggs is
eggs, he runs so fast you can't see him for dust." "No, no,
Alexei Ivanovich, forgive me, but I cannot agree with you
that Chichikov's peasants will run away. The Russian peasant is capable of anything, and he will adapt to any climate. Send him to Kamchatka if you like, give him only a
pair of warm mittens, and he'll spit into his hands, grab his
axe and go and chop himself a new house." "No, Ivan Gri-

...rievich, you overlook an important consideration: you have not asked what sort of serfs Chichikov has. You have forgotten that a landowner will not sell a good man; I would be prepared to stake my life that Chichikov's serfs are thorough-going thieves and drunkards, lay-abouts and trouble-makers of the blackest hue." "Yes, yes, I agree, it's true, no one will sell a good man, and Chichikov's peasants are drunkards, but you must bear in mind that this is the whole point, this is where the moral lies: now they are scoundrels, but re-settle them in new lands and they may suddenly become first-class subjects. There have already been a great number of such cases: in the world in general, and in the course of history." "Never, never," said the superintendent of the government manufactories, "believe me, this can never happen. For Chichikov's serfs will now have two powerful enemies. The first is the proximity of the Ukrainian provinces where, as you know, wine is freely on sale. Let me assure you: in two weeks they'll all become drunkards. The other enemy is the predilection for the nomadic life which the peasants will inevitably acquire during re-settlement. The only way is for Chichikov to keep a sharp eye on them constantly and to rule them with a rod of iron, he must punish them for the slightest little thing, and he mustn't rely on someone else, he must do it himself, and when necessary step in and slap them right and left." "But why should Chichikov have to go round slapping people himself, when he can find a bailiff to do it for him?" "Oh yes, you try finding a bailiff: they're all thieves!" "They're thieves, because their masters don't manage their estates themselves." "That's true," joined in many others. "If the squire himself knows something about farming and is a good judge of people, he will always have a good bailiff." But the superintendent said that for less than five thousand you would never find a good bailiff. The president said that you could find one even for three thousand. But the superintendent said: "Where are you going to find him: right up your nose I suppose?" But the president said: "No, not up my nose, but in our own district, namely: Pyotr Petrovich Samoilov, that's the bailiff that Chichikov needs for his peasants!" Many of them felt strongly for Chichikov, and the ardours of re-settling such an enormous number of peasants totally scared the wits out of them; they began to be greatly afraid that there might even be a riot amongst men as restless as Chichikov's peasants. To this the chief of police countered that a riot was nothing to fear, that to suppress riots there was the authority of the local police captain, that the police captain did not even need to go himself, he need merely send his uniform cap along in his place,. and this cap alone would drive the peasants to their new place of residence. Many wondered how to eradicate the rebellious spirit that had so gripped Chichikov's peasants. There were views of every kind: some smacked altogether too strongly of military severity and cruelty that was, perhaps, excessive; some, on the contrary, were imbued with mildness. The postmaster observed that Chichikov faced a sacred obligation, that he could become something of a father to his peasants, that he could even, in the postmaster's phrase, introduce the benefits of enlightenment, and he took the opportunity to express fulsome praise of the Lancaster school of mutual instruction.

Thus did the town folk talk and deliberate, and·many of them, out of a feeling of sympathy, went so far as to impart certain of these counsels to Chichikov in person, even recommending a convoy as the safest means of transporting the peasants to their new place of residence. Chichikov thanked them for their advice, assuring them that he would not miss an opportunity to avail himself of their wisdom, but he rejected the idea of a convoy most resolutely, saying that this was quite unnecessary, that the peasants he had purchased were of a markedly submissive character, were themselves well-disposed to the idea of re-settlement and that there simply could not be any riot amongst them in such circumstances.

All these discussions and debates did, however, have the most fortuitous consequences for Chichikov. To be precise, rumours started to spread that he was no more nor less than a millionaire. The inhabitants of the town had already, as we have seen in the first chapter, quite lost their hearts to Chichikov, but now, after such rumours, they lost their hearts even further. To be sure, if the truth is to be told, they were a good lot, they lived in concord amongst themselves, addressed each other in the most cordial terms, and their discourse bore the stamp of a remarkable ingenuousness and intimacy: "My dear friend, Ilya Ilyich." "Listen, brother, Antipator Zakharievich!" "You're talking through your hat, dear Ivan Grigorievich." When addressing the postmaster, who was called Ivan Andreyevich, they would invariably add: "Sprechen Sie Deutsch, Ivan Andreich?" rhyming Deutsch with Andreich—in a word, they were like one big family. Many of them had a certain amount of education: the president of the Chamber knew Zhukovsky's *Lyudmila* by heart, a poem which was then still fresh off the presses, and he would masterfully declaim many passages, particularly "The forest sleeps, the vale reposes", and pronounce the word "Hush!" so that one could really see the vale reposing; for greater verisimilitude he would even screw up his eyes at this point. The postmaster had devoted himself more to philosophical pursuits and was a most assiduous reader, even at night, of Young's *Night Thoughts* and Exkartshausen's *Key to the Mysteries of Nature*, from which he would copy out very long extracts, but of what sort no one ever knew; he was a witty fellow, by the way, florid in his speech and fond, as he put it himself, of embellishing his language. He would embellish his speech with a liberal sprinkling of parentheses, like: "Allow me, my good sir, if I may say so, you know, you understand, you can imagine, with regard so to say, in a manner of speaking." He would also rather felicitously embellish his speech with sly winking, a crinkling of one eye, which lent a most acerbic expression to many of his satirical innuendos. The others were also to a greater or lesser extent men of enlightenment: one read Karamzin,* another the *Moscow Gazette*, some even read nothing at all. One was a sluggard, that is to say a man who had to be kicked into action; another was such a lie-a-bed that it was useless even trying to rouse him; for nothing in the world would make him stir. As far as God appearance is concerned, we have already seen that they were all securely-built men and that there was not a single consumptive amongst them. All of them were the sort of men to whom their wives, in moments of tender intimacy, give pet-names such as tubby, fattykins, pumpkin, joujou, and so forth.

Nikolai Karamzin (1766-1826)—Russian author and historian. His major work was *A History of the Russian State*.

But on the whole they were good folk, full of hospitality, and any man who had once shared their repast or spent an evening with them at whist was already regarded as a friend. How great a friend, therefore, was Chichikov, with his enchanting qualities and manner, a man possessed of the great secret of pleasing others. They grew to love him so dearly that he could see no way of escaping from their town; he heard nothing but: "Do stay with us a week, one little week more, Pavel Ivanovich!"—in brief, he was, as they say, lionised. But this was as nothing in comparison to the impression Chichikov (the object of utter amazement!) made on the ladies. To explain this at all it would be necessary first to dwell at some length on the ladies themselves, on their society, to paint, as they say, their spiritual qualities in vivid colours; but this is very difficult for the author. On the one hand he is deterred by his unbounded respect for the spouses of dignitaries, and on the other hand ... on the other hand—it is simply very difficult. The ladies of the town of N were ... no, I am quite unable to proceed: I am filled with absolute timidity. What was most remarkable about the ladies of the town of N was their... It is quite strange, I simply cannot lift my pen, it is exactly as if it were filled with lead. Let it be, therefore: we shall have to leave the painting of their characters to him whose colours are more vivid and who has more of them on his palette, whilst we shall confine ourselves to a word or two about their appearance and about more superficial aspects. The ladies of the town of N were what is known as presentable, and in this respect they could boldly be held up as an example to all others. In such matters as comportment, *bon ton*, etiquette, and many other extreme nuances of decorum, in particular the observance of fashion in the minutest detail, here they surpassed even the ladies of St Petersburg and Moscow. They dressed with great taste, drove about the town in barouches, as the latest fashion dictated, with a lackey bobbing about behind, impressive in gold-braided livery. The visiting card, even had it been printed on the back of a two of clubs or an ace of diamonds, was also a most sacred accoutrement. It was over such a card that two of the greatest of friends and even relatives fell out with one another irreconcilably because one of them had somehow neglected to return a courtesy call. And no matter how hard their husbands and relations tried to reconcile them, the outcome was negative: everything in the world is possible, except to reconcile two ladies who have quarrelled over an omitted visit. Thus, the two ladies remained ill-disposed to one another, to borrow the expression of local society. The matter of precedence also prompted a great many rather strong scenes, which sometimes inspired in their menfolk really chivalrous, magnanimous notions of intercession on their ladies' behalf. There were of course no duels between them, because they were all civilians, but instead one husband would endeavour to do the dirty on another wherever possible, which, as we all know, can be much more wounding than any duel. On questions of morality the ladies of the town of N were strict, filled with righteous indignation against any manifestation of vice and all temptations, and they castigated all weaknesses quite without mercy. If anything *like that* happened in their midst, it was done so covertly that no one was the wiser; all dignity was maintained and the husband himself was so well trained that even if he did see that something *like that* was going on or got to hear of it he would respond succinctly and sensibly with the proverb: "Whose business is it, if Auntie has tea with Uncle?" We should also remark that the ladies of the town of N, like many ladies of St Petersburg, were noteworthily circumspect and decorous in their choice of words and expressions. They would never say: "I blew my nose", "I got sweaty", or "I spat", but would say: "I relieved my nose", "I had need of my handkerchief." Under no circumstances could a lady say: "This glass or that plate stinks", or even anything which might hint at this, but instead they said: "This glass is behaving badly", or something on those lines. In order still further to ennoble the Russian language, almost half of the vocabulary was simply jettisoned from their conversation, and they were therefore frequently compelled to have recourse to the French language, because there, in French, words that were far more stridulous than those already mentioned were permitted. So, this is what we can say about the ladies of the town of N, from a more superficial point of view. But if we look a little deeper, then of course much else will be revealed; but it is a most perilous occupation to gaze too deeply into the hearts of ladies. Therefore, we shall confine ourselves to the surface and proceed further. Until now the ladies had not spoken much about Chichikov, whilst according him his rightful due for his savoir-faire and manners; but the moment the rumours about his being a millionaire became rampant, other qualities were uncovered. The ladies were not, however, after his money; the fault lay entirely with the word "millionaire"—not the millionaire himself, but the actual word alone; for the very sound of this word contains, beside the clinking of gold coins, something which equally affects people of a rascally disposition and people who are not one thing nor the other, and also good people— in a word, it affects everyone. A millionaire has the advantage that he is able to see baseness clearly, pure disinterested baseness, not founded on any considerations of gain: many people know only too well that they will get nothing out of him, and have no right to expect anything, but they will still run ahead of him to catch his eye, they will still grin or doff their hats, they will still try to get themselves invited to a dinner to which the millionaire has been asked. It would be wrong to say that this tender predilection for baseness was shared by our ladies; however, one did start hearing in many drawing rooms that whilst Chichikov was not, of course, the most handsome of men, he was such as a man should be, but that if he were a little more portly it would not have done at all. In the process, certain, even rather unflattering, opinions were expressed of thin men: that they were really more like toothpicks, and not men at all. The ladies' toilets started to acquire a variety of embellishments. The shopping arcade was so crowded, there was almost a crush, and so many carriages congregated outside that the place became a sort of promenade. The merchants were amazed to see that certain lengths of material which they had brought from the fair and been unable to dispose of, due to their allegedly high price, suddenly became fashionable and sold like hot cakes. During Sunday morning service one of the ladies was observed to be wearing a dress with the hem so stiffened that it spread halfway across the church, so much so that the police inspector, who happened to be standing nearby, had to order the congregation to stand back, that is, closer to the churchporch, lest they crush the toilet of her ladyship. At times even Chichikov was not insensible to the extraordinary interest he aroused. Once, on returning home, he found a letter on his table; whence it came and who brought it was impossible to ascertain; the inn servant would only vouchsafe that it had been brought and those that brought it ordered him not to tell who it came from. The letter began with these very resolute words: "Yes, I must write to you!" It then went on to say that there is a secret sympathy between souls; this truth was reinforced with a series of dots, occupying nearly half a line; then followed several sentiments, so remarkable for their veracity that we cannot abstain from including them here: "What is our life?—a vale where sorrows dwell. What is the world?—a crowd of people without feelings." Then the lady writer remarked that she bathed these lines in tears, tears shed for a tender mother, who had departed this life twenty-five years previously; Chichikov was invited into the wilderness, to leave for ever the walled city, where people have no air to breathe; the letter was concluded on a distinct note of despair and closed with the verses:

> *Two turtle-doves will show you*
> *My cold remains.*
> *With languid coos they'll tell you*
> *She died in tears.*

The last line did not rhyme, but this, however, was of no consequence: the letter was composed in the spirit of those times. Neither was there any signature: no name, nor surname, not even the month and day. There was a postscript which merely added that his own heart must tell him the identity of the writer and that she herself would be present at the governor's ball, scheduled for the morrow.

This greatly intrigued him. This anonymous letter contained so much that was enigmatic and that spurred his curiosity that he re-read it a second and a third time and finally declared: "It would be curious to know who wrote it!" In a word, matters were clearly taking a serious turn; for more than an hour he pondered this problem, before finally saying, with outspread hands and lowered head: "A most florid style! Most florid!" Then, it goes without saying, the letter was folded and stowed away in his box, where a theatre notice and an invitation to a wedding had been lying for seven years in the very same position and place. Sure enough, a little later he was brought an invitation to the governor's ball—a highly customary occasion in the life of provincial capitals: where you find a governor there, too, you will find a ball, otherwise he would never win the appropriate love and respect of the local gentry.

All extraneous business was at once set aside and abandoned and all efforts were directed towards preparations for the ball; for there were indeed a great many persuasive and provocative reasons. It is quite possible that so much time has never, in all the history of the world, been spent on a person's toilet. An entire hour was devoted to a mere inspection of his face in the mirror. A multiplicity of diverse expressions was essayed: the grave and dignified, the deferential, but with a slight smile, then the simply deferential without a smile; several bows were made in the direction of the mirror to the accompaniment of indistinct utterances, in parts resembling French, although Chichikov was totally ignorant of the French language. He even gave himself a number of pleasant surprises, raising an eyebrow and twitching his lips and even performing some manoeuvre with his tongue; in other words, there is no end to the things a man might do when he finds himself alone, and he is aware moreover of his own attractiveness, and is, furthermore, quite certain that no one is peeping through the keyhole. Finally he patted himself lightly on the chin and said: "You handsome rogue, you!" and began to dress. He remained in a mood of the utmost contentment throughout his toilet: as he pulled on his braces or knotted his tie he scraped his foot and described the most adroit of bows and, though not a dancer, he performed an entrechat. This entrechat had one slight, innocent consequence: the chest of drawers shook and a hairbrush fell from the table.

His arrival at the ball had an extraordinary effect. All the people present turned to face him, some clutching cards, others intercepted at a most interesting juncture in their conversation, having just said: "So the lower court*

---

*Lower Court—a district court, the lowest administrative body established in 1775.

said in reply—", but what exactly the lower court said in reply was immediately discarded as the speaker hurried to greet our hero. "Pavel Ivanovich! Heavens above, Pavel Ivanovich! My dear Pavel Ivanovich! My most respected Pavel Ivanovich! My dear, dear, dearest Pavel Ivanovich! So there you are, Pavel Ivanovich! There he is, our Pavel Ivanovich! Allow me to embrace you, Pavel Ivanovich! Just bring him here, so I can give him a big hug, my dear Pavel Ivanovich!" Chichikov felt himself simultaneously held in several embraces. He had no sooner wriggled quite free from the president's embrace than he found himself in the arms of the chief of police; the chief of police surrendered him to the inspector of the medical board, the inspector of the medical board to the monopolist, the monopolist to the architect... The governor, who at this time was standing beside the ladies, holding a dance card in one hand and a lap-dog in the other, on seeing him at once dropped both the card and the lap-dog on the floor, which brought a yelp from the lap-dog; in a word, his arrival disseminated general happiness and good cheer. There was not a face that did not wear an expression of pleasure, or, at least, a reflection of the general pleasure. Such an expression is worn on the faces of officials when a superior charged with the supervision of their offices arrives to inspect them: after the first spasms of fear have passed they observe that he is pleased with much that he sees, and he himself finally deigns to drop a little *bon mot*, that is, to deliver himself of a few words with a pleasant little smile. The officials gathered close round him respond to this by laughing twice as loudly; roars of laughter are emitted by those who, in point of fact, have not been able to hear his words properly, and finally, some police officer standing far away by the doors next to the exit, a man who has never laughed in his life before and who has just prior to this been shaking his fist at the crowd, he too is forced by the immutable laws of contagion to arrange his features into a semblance of a smile, although this smile is more akin to the grimace of someone about to sneeze after an inhalation of potent snuff. Our hero returned the compliments of all and sundry and felt beautifully at ease: he bowed to right and to left, inclining in his customary manner somewhat to one side, but with total freedom, in a way that entranced everyone present.

The ladies at once gathered round him in a dazzling garland, bearing with them veritable clouds of fragrance of
every kind: from one wafted the scent of roses, from another spring and violets, a third was drenched in the smell
of mignonette: Chichikov had only to lift his nose in the
air and sniff. Their gowns displayed no end of taste: there
were muslins, satins, chiffons in such fashionable pastel
shades that there was no naming the colours (such was the
refinement of their taste). Bright ribbons and sprays of
flowers were scattered about their dresses in the most picturesque disorder, although much careful thought had
gone into the creation of this very disorder. A light head-
dress rested precariously on the tips of their ears, and
appeared to say: "Ah, I would fly away, if only I could
take this beauty with me!" The bodices were close-fitting
and their contours were firm and most pleasing to the eye
(we should note that in general the ladies of the town of N
were a little on the plump side, but they laced themselves
so skilfully and possessed such agreeable manners that
their corpulence was quite unnoticeable). Every detail of
their toilet had been thought out with the most studied
care; the neck and shoulders were uncovered just as far as
was necessary and no further; each lady exposed her
charms to the point where more would spell a man's ruin;
the rest was concealed from view with exceptional taste:
either some thistledown ribbon, or a scarf, lighter than a
meringue, commonly known as a "kiss", ethereally embraced the neck, or little jagged ruffs of fine lawn, known
by the name of "modesties", edged the neckline. These
"modesties" concealed areas in front and behind which were
in fact quite unable to ruin a man, but they still gave rise
to the suspicion that ruination did indeed lurk there. Their
long gloves were drawn up not quite as far as their sleeves,
but deliberately left provocative sections of arm exposed
above the elbow, alluringly plump in many of the ladies;
some had actually split their kid gloves when attempting to
pull them up further; in a word, written across everything
seemed to be the words: no, this is not the provinces, this is
the capital, this is Paris itself! Only in places there suddenly
hove into sight an outlandish lace bonnet or even a peacock
feather in violation of all fashion, but in accordance with the
wearer's own taste. But this cannot be avoided for such is

the nature of the provincial capital: somewhere it is bound
to fall badly short. Chichikov, as he stood before the ladies,
thought: "Which one, I wonder, wrote that letter?"— and
he made to prod the air with his nose, but past his very nose
swished countless elbows, cuffs, sleeves, ends of ribbons,
aromatic chemisettes and gowns. The gallopade was in full
swing: the postmaster's wife, the captain of police, a lady
with a blue feather, a lady with a white feather, the Georgian prince Chipkhaikhilidzev, an official from St Petersburg,
an official from Moscow, the Frenchman Monsieur Coucou,
Perkhunovsky, Berebendovsky—all rushed past him.

"Goodness! Off they go!" muttered Chichikov to himself, stepping backwards, and as soon as the ladies had
resumed their seats he began to study them again, wondering if he could identify the letter-writer by the expression
on her face and in her eyes; but it was quite impossible to
tell, either from the expression on their faces or from the
expression in their eyes, who the writer was. In every face
he could read the tiniest hint of something, the most elusive nuance, oh so very, very subtle! "No," said Chichikov
to himself, "women are a thing..." Here he gave up the
effort: "Words fail me! Just try and recount or describe all
that flits across their faces, all those little twitches, those
hints—and you will never convey a thing. Their eyes alone
are a boundless kingdom into which, once a man strays,
he's lost for ever! You will never pull him out again, not
with a hook or any other thing. Just try, for example, to
describe their sparkle: it's moist, velvety, sugary—and the
Lord only knows what else besides! It's harsh and soft and
even quite languorous, or, as some would say, voluptuous,
or not voluptuous, but worse than voluptuous, once it
hooks onto your heart your soul will feel as if a violin
bow had been passed over it. No, there are no words for
it: it's the flossy half of the human race and nothing
more!"

I beg forgiveness! It would seem that a word normally
associated with the street has escaped the lips of our hero.
But what can one do? Such is the lot of the writer in Russia! Furthermore, if a word from the street occurs in a
book it is not the writer who is guilty, but the readers, and
primarily the readers from the upper classes: it is from
them, above all, that you will not hear a single decent Rus-

sian word; their speech is so abundantly stuffed with every manner of French, German and English words that you would not even want to hear it, and these words are employed, furthermore, with the retention of every possible type of pronunciation: the French spoken through the nose and the "r" gargled, the English spoken as befits a bird, with the adoption even of an avian physiognomy, and they would even make fun of those who cannot assume this bird-like expression; while only Russian is lacking, though they may perhaps out of patriotism build themselves a cottage in the Russian style at their summer residence. Such are the readers from high society, and they are followed by all those who would assign themselves to high society... And yet they are so exacting! They absolutely insist that everything should be written in the strictest language, purified and noble—in a word, they want the Russian language to descend suddenly from the clouds of its own accord, properly processed, and to alight right on their tongues, so that they need do no more than open their mouths to utter it. Of course, the female half of the human race is unfathomable, but our respected readers, you must agree, are sometimes more unfathomable still.

Meanwhile Chichikov had reached a complete impasse in his endeavours to identify the authoress of his letter. When he fixed his gaze with closer attention on one or another of the ladies he observed that this was met on their part by something provocative both of hope, and of sweet torments in the heart of a wretched mortal, so that he finally said: "No, I shall never guess!" This did not, however, in any way detract from his good spirits. He exchanged pleasantries with some of the ladies in an easy and relaxed way, stepped up to kiss their hands with small, staccato steps, or, as the expression goes, with a mincing gait, like that affected by foppish little old men strutting around on high heels, the type called pint-sized stallions, who prance most adroitly around the ladies. After doing some mincing and rather dexterous turns to right and left, he would describe a little bow, raising his foot behind him like a little tail, or a comma. The ladies were delighted, and not only discovered in him a wealth of charm, but began to discern a majestic expression in his face, something martial and warlike, which, as we all know, is very attractive to women. They even started to quarrel a little over him: noticing that he tended to stand by the doors some of them hurried to occupy the chairs closer to these doors, and when one of them was fortunate enough to get there first, a most unpleasant incident almost occurred, and many others, who had wished to do the same themselves, now thought such audacity quite abominable.

Chichikov was so immersed in conversation with the ladies, or rather, the ladies had so engrossed and dizzied him with their conversation, spicing it with a mass of the most convoluted and refined allegories, all of which had to be deciphered and which caused a sweat to break out on his brow, that he quite forgot to observe the rules of decorum and to pay his respects first of all to his hostess. He realized this lapse only when he heard the voice of the governor's wife, who had already been standing before him for some minutes. The governor's wife announced in a rather caressing and sly voice with a gentle shake of her head, "Ah, Pavel Ivanovich, aren't you naughty!" I cannot reproduce this lady's words exactly, but she gave utterance to something very gracious in the style in which the ladies and their cavaliers express themselves in the tales of our fashionable writers, who are so fond of describing drawing-rooms and showing off their understanding of the best tone, in phrases such as: "Surely they have not so taken possession of your heart that there remains in it no place, not even the tiniest corner, for those so pitilessly forgotten by you." Our hero at once turned to face the governor's wife, and was on the point of delivering his reply, no doubt every whit as gallant as those delivered in fashionable stories by the Zvonskys, Linskys, Lidins, Gryomins and all those other smart military men, when, raising his eyes, he froze in his tracks, as if suddenly struck dumb.

The governor's wife was not alone: she held the arm of a pretty girl of sixteen or so, a sweet blonde, with fine and well-proportioned features, a pointed little chin, a face rounded into an enchanting oval shape, such as an artist would use as his model for the Madonna and which is all too rare in Russia, where everything likes to manifest itself on the grand scale, everything without exception, mountains and forests and steppes, and faces and lips and feet. This was the very same blonde he had encountered on the road coming from Nozdryov's estate, when, whether through the coachman's or the horses' stupidity, their carriages had collided so strangely in a tangle of harnesses, and Uncle Mityai and Uncle Minyai had set about untangling them. Chichikov was so abashed that he could not utter a single coherent word, muttering instead the devil knows what, and certainly nothing that would ever be said by Gryomin, or Zvonsky, or Lidin.

"You have not met my daughter yet, have you?" asked the governor's wife. "She has just finished school."

He replied that he had already had the good fortune to meet her by chance; he tried to add something to this but nothing came out at all. The governor's wife, saying a few more words, moved off with her daughter to join the guests at the other end of the room, leaving Chichikov rooted to the spot, like a man who has gaily stepped outside to take a stroll, his eyes dancing about, looking at everything around him, and who suddenly freezes, realising that he has forgotten something, and cuts a figure that could not be more comic: in an instant the carefree expression vanishes from his face; he strains to recall what it is he has forgotten—was it perhaps a handkerchief? But his handkerchief is in his pocket; his money, then? But the money is also in his pocket, he has everything on him, it seems, and yet some mysterious spirit whispers in his ear that he has forgotten something. Now he gazes distractedly and in confusion at the moving crowd before him, at the carriages flying past, at the shakos and rifles of the regiment marching by, at the signboard—and he sees nothing properly. Thus, too, did Chichikov suddenly become remote from everything going on around him, while there floated to him from the fragrant lips of the ladies a swarm of enquiries, all of them, imbued with refinement and courtesy. "Might we, wretched inhabitants of this earth, make so bold as to venture to enquire whither your fancy has borne you?" "Where are those happy regions over which your thoughts are hovering?" "Might we seek to know the name of her who has plunged you into this sweet vale of reverie?" But he was deaf to all this and the pretty phrases vanished like stones in water. He was even so inconsiderate as to walk away from them to the other side of the room, wishing to establish whither the governor's wife had taken her daughter. But the ladies, it seemed, were not prepared to let him go so soon; each resolved inwardly to use all her available weapons, so perilous for our hearts, and set to work all that was best in her. We should note that some ladies—I am speaking here of some only, not of all—have a slight weakness: if they notice something particularly attractive about themselves—be it their brow, or mouth, or hands—they at once assume that their best feature will be at once evident to everyone, and that all will say as one man: "Just look, just look, what a lovely Greek nose she has!" or "What a charming, clear brow!" A lady who has beautiful shoulders is convinced beforehand that all the young men will be quite enthralled and will repeat to one another whenever she walks past: "My, what gorgeous shoulders that one has,"—and will not even glance at her face, hair, nose, forehead, or if they glance at them, then as if at something unconnected. Some ladies do think like that. Each lady vowed inwardly to be as fascinating as possible on the dance floor and to display in all its glory the pre-eminence of that feature of hers that was pre-eminent. The postmaster's wife, as she waltzed, inclined her head to the side with such langour, that one could indeed sense something out of this world about her. One most charming lady—who had come to the ball with no intention to dance because of a small "incommodité", as she put it herself, in the form of a bunion on the right foot, which compelled her to wear velveteen boots—felt so challenged that she danced a few waltz tours in her velveteen boots, just to take the postmaster's wife down a peg or two.

But all this totally failed to have the desired effect on Chichikov. He did not even look at the waltzing ladies, but continuously rose on tip-toe, craning his neck over the heads of the others looking for his captivating blonde; he crouched down too, to peer between people's shoulders and arms, and at last he spotted her, sitting next to her mother, whose head was crowned with a magnificent, plumed Oriental turban. It was as if Chichikov meant to take them by storm; he thrust his way decisively forward, regardless of anything in his path; whether because he was spurred on by his vernal disposition, or whether because someone bumped into him from behind, the monopolist

received such a shove from him that he recoiled and barely remained standing on one foot, otherwise he would
most certainly have brought down with him an entire row;
the postmaster also stepped back and regarded him with
amazement, tempered with a rather subtle irony, but Chichikov did not look at them; he had eyes only for the
blonde who was drawing on a long glove and was doubtless
burning with desire to soar off across the parquet floor.
Four couples were already doing a dashing mazurka; heels
pounded the floor and the army staff captain, putting body
and soul, as well as arms and legs, into the dance was cutting such *pas* as no one had ever cut before even in a
dream. Chichikov slipped past the mazurka, practically
stepping on the heels of the dancers, and went straight to
where the governor's wife sat with her daughter. He approached them, however, with great diffidence, not mincing in such a nimble and dashing way any more and even
stumbling, for all his movements had become strangely stiff.
It is hard to say for sure whether this marked the awakening in our hero of a feeling of love—it is even doubtful whether gentlemen of his ilk, that is to say, not exactly fat, and yet not really thin either, are even capable of
love; all the same there was something strange about him
now, something which he could not explain to himself: it
seemed to him then, as he was to realise subsequently, that
the entire ball, with all its hubbub and chatter, had somehow receded into the distance for the space of several minutes; the violins and trumpets scraped and tooted away
somewhere far off, and all was cloaked in a mist, like a
carelessly painted field in a picture. Out of this murky,
crudely sketched field there emerged with clarity and defi-
nition only the fine features of the enticing blonde: her
delightfully oval face, her so very slender figure, such as
girls keep for the first few months after leaving school, her
white, almost plain gown, which so softly and nimbly
embraced every part of her slender, youthful limbs, clearly
showing the purity of their lines. In every way she seemed
to resemble some toy, minutely carved from ivory; in her
whiteness and translucence she alone radiated light from
amidst the turbid and opaque throng about her.
Apparently, such things do happen in the world; even
the Chichikovs become poets for a few minutes; but

perhaps the word "poet" would be excessive here. At least
he felt almost a young man, almost a Hussar. Espying an
empty chair beside them he at once occupied it. At first
the conversation was halting, but then things warmed up,
and he even started to get into his stride, but ... here, to
our immense regret, we must remark that gentlemen of a
staid disposition who hold important offices tend to be
somewhat ponderous in their conversation with ladies; the
experts in these matters are lieutenants—never those
whose rank is higher than captain. How they do it God
alone knows: it seems they do not say such intriguing
things, and yet the girl positively sways on her chair with
mirth; your state councilor, however, will tell her the Lord
knows what: either he will embark on a disquisition about
the immensity of the Russian state, or he will deliver himself of a compliment, which has, of course, been conceived
not without esprit, yet has something dreadfully bookish
about it; and if he does permit himself a *bon mot*, he
laughs immeasurably louder and longer than she for whose
delectation it is intended. This has been pointed out here
so that the reader might see why the blonde started to
yawn during the declamations of our hero. Our hero, however, remaining quite oblivious of this, recounted a great
many agreeable things which he had already had occasion
to recount in similar circumstances in different places, to
wit: in Simbirsk Province at the house of Sofron Ivanovich Bespechny, in the presence of the latter's daughter
Adelaida Sofronovna and her three sisters-in-law: Maria
Gavrilovna, Alexandra Gavrilovna and Adelaida Gavrilovna; at the house of Fyodor Fyodorovich Perekroyev in
Ryazan Province; at Frol Vasilievich Pobedonosny's in
Penza Province, and at his brother Pyotr Vasilievich's in
the company of his sister-in-law Katerina Mikhailovna and
her second cousins Rosa Fyodorovna and Emilia Fyodorovna; in Vyatka Province at the house of Pyotr Varsono-
fyevich, in the company of his daughter-in-law's sister Pelageya Yegorovna and her niece Sofia Rostislavna and her
two step-sisters Sofia Alexandrovna and Maklatura Alexandrovna.

    This conduct of Chichikov's was most displeasing to all
the ladies present. One of them deliberately walked past
him to indicate her displeasure, and even rather carelessly

bumped into the blonde with the large bustle of her dress, and so manoeuvred the scarf which fluttered lightly across her shoulders, that the tip flicked the blonde right in the face; at the very same moment a pronouncedly caustic and sarcastic observation wafted across on a cloud of violets from the lips of a lady standing behind him. Either Chichikov really did not hear it, or at least he pretended not to have, but this was a mistake on his part, for the good opinion of ladies must be treasured: he repented of this lapse, but only afterwards, when it was too late.

Indignation, justified in all respects, was written across many faces. However mighty the weight assumed by Chichikov in their society, be he even a millionaire, with majesty in his bearing and a martial and warlike mien, there are certain things which ladies will forgive no man, whosoever he might be, and then all is up with him! There are cases when a woman, however frail and feeble she might be in character in comparison to a man, will suddenly grow stronger not only than any man, but than anything in the world. The disregard evinced almost inadvertently by Chichikov had the effect of re-establishing amongst the ladies a unanimity, which had been on the point of total collapse over the incident of the occupation of the chair. The few dry and commonplace remarks he heedlessly let slip were now found to contain acerbic innuendos. To cap all these disasters, one of the young men composed some impromptu satirical verses about the assembled dancers of the sort that are, as everyone knows, almost inevitably composed at all provincial balls. These verses were at once attributed to Chichikov. Indignation increased, and the ladies gathered in the corners of the room to discuss him in most ungenerous terms; the poor blonde girl was totally annihilated, and her sentence signed and sealed.

In the meantime a surprise of the most unpleasant kind was being prepared for our hero: while his blonde was yawning and he was narrating to her his various *petites histoires* that had taken place at different times, and had even touched upon the Greek philosopher Diogenes, there appeared from the end room the figure of Nozdryov. Whether he had emerged from the buffet, or from the small green drawing-room, where a game of whist with rather higher stakes than ordinary was in progress, and whether he emerged of his own free will or had been thrown out we cannot say; we know only that he emerged joyful, in high spirits, clutching the prosecutor by the arm, in which position he had evidently held him for some time, for the wretched prosecutor was turning his beetling eye-brows in all directions, as if seeking a means of escape from this companionable guided tour. For indeed, his position was intolerable. Nozdryov, who had mustered Dutch courage with two mugs of tea liberally laced with rum, was talking terrible nonsense. Spotting him from afar, Chichikov even resolved to make a sacrifice, that is, to surrender his enviable seat and beat as hasty a retreat as possible: this encounter boded no good for him at all. But, as ill-luck would have it, the governor popped up at this very moment, declaring his indescribable joy at having found Pavel Ivanovich, and stopped him in his tracks, pleading that he adjudicate in an argument he was having with two ladies about whether a woman's love is a lasting thing or not; and in the meantime Nozdryov had already seen him and was making straight for him.

"Aha, the Kherson landowner, the Kherson landowner!" he shouted advancing on Chichikov and roaring with laughter, which made his cheeks, fresh and ruddy as a spring rose, turn ruddier still. "Well? Did you bag a lot of dead 'uns? For I am sure you were unaware, Your Excellency," he at once vociferated, turning to the governor, "that he deals in dead souls! As God's my witness! Listen, Chichikov! Do you know—and I tell you this as a friend, for we're all your friends here, and His Excellency too—I would string you up, honest to God, I would!"

Chichikov was petrified.

"Would you credit it, Your Excellency," continued Nozdryov, "this is what he says to me: 'Sell me your dead souls', and I split my sides laughing. So I drive into town and people tell me that he's bought up three million rubles' worth of peasants for re-settlement: for re-settlement, I ask you! And it was dead ones he was trying to buy off me. Listen, Chichikov, you're a real swine, just ask His Excellency here, isn't that so, prosecutor?"

But the prosecutor, and Chichikov, and the governor himself, were in a state of such bewilderment by now that they were quite at a loss for a reply; meanwhile Nozdryov, totally undeterred, continued his tipsy diatribe: "Now, brother, I know you... I shan't leave you in peace until I find out why you were buying dead souls. Listen, Chichikov, you should be ashamed, you know, you have no better friend anywhere than me, just ask His Excellency here, isn't that so, prosecutor? You simply would not believe it, Your Excellency, how attached we are to one another, I mean, if you were to say: 'Nozdryov! Tell me in all conscience, who is dearer to you, your own father or Chichikov?' I would say: 'Chichikov', as God's my witness... Allow me, my dear chap, let me give you a buss, just one smacker. Please will you permit me, Your Excellency, to give him a kiss. Yes Chichikov, there's no point in resisting, just let me plant one *petit baiser* on that snow-white cheek!"

Nozdryov and his *petit baiser* were so haftily repulsed that he almost went flying: the others all drew away from him and stopped listening; all the same, his words about the buying of dead souls were uttered with such stridency and accompanied with such loud laughter that they even attracted the notice of those in the furthest corners of the room. This news struck them all as so extraordinary that they remained motionless with wooden expressions of idiotic wonder on their faces. Chichikov noticed many of the ladies exchanging winks with a sort of malicious, sarcastic sneer, and the expression on some faces held something so ambiguous that it only increased the general bewilderment further. That Nozdryov was an inveterate liar was something they all knew, and it was nothing unusual to hear him talk the most outrageous nonsense; but it really is hard to understand the way the mortal mind works: however vulgar an item of news, it matters only that it should be news and he will at once communicate it to the next mortal, if only to be able to say: "Just imagine the lies some people tell!", and the next mortal will lend him his ear with pleasure, after which he will say himself: "What a shocking lie, no one should pay the least attention to it!" and immediately will set off in search of a third mortal to whom to impart it, so that they may then exclaim together in righteous indignation: "What a shocking lie!" The news will most certainly make the rounds of the entire town, and all the mortals, as many of them as there are, will most certainly discuss it *ad nauseam* and then declare that no one should pay the slightest attention to it and that it is not even worth discussing.

This apparently trivial incident visibly discomfited our hero. However stupid the words of a fool may be, they are sometimes sufficient utterly to confuse a clever man. He felt ill-at-ease and uncomfortable: exactly as if he had inadvertently put a beautifully polished boot into a filthy, stinking puddle; in a word, things were bad, very bad indeed! He tried not to think about this and, hoping to distract himself with other pursuits, to amuse himself, sat down to whist, but everything went like a crooked wheel: twice he led the opponents' suit and, forgetting that the third hand does not trump, slapped down his trump with all his might and made a fool of himself by taking his partner's card. The president simply could not understand how Pavel Ivanovich who played so well, and had, one might say, a refined mastery of the game, could make such gaffes, losing him his king of spades, the card on which, to borrow his own phrase, he relied as he relied on the Lord Himself. Naturally enough, the postmaster and the president, and even the chief of police himself, poked gentle fun at our hero, as was customary, wondering whether he might perhaps have fallen in love and saying that they knew that Pavel Ivanovich's poor heart had sustained a wound, and they knew, too, from whose bow the arrow had been released; but none of this could in any way console him, however much he tried to smile and laugh off their suggestions. At supper he was still quite unable to recover his composure, despite the fact that the company at table was pleasant and that Nozdryov had been escorted out long before, for even the ladies themselves had finally observed that his behaviour had become a little *trop scandaleuse*. In the middle of the cotillion Nozdryov sat on the floor and lunged at the skirts of the dancers, which was, in the ladies' expression, really too much. The supper was very gay, and all the faces Chichikov glimpsed between the triple candelabrae, the flowers, sweets and bottles, were radiant with the most natural contentment. Officers, ladies, tail-coats—everything exuded such courtesy, that it was rather cloying. The gentlemen leapt from their chairs and ran to take the dishes from the footmen and themselves served them to the ladies with most extraordinary agility. One colonel proffered a lady a sauce-boat balanced on the end of his unsheathed sword. The middle-aged men amongst whom Chichikov was sitting, argued noisily, following each pithy word with a mouthful of fish or beef, which had been ruthlessly dunked in mustard, and they argued on subjects he would normally join in discussing; but he was like a man wearied by a long journey, who can take nothing in and lacks the energy to join in anything. He could not even wait till the end of the meal and made his departure far earlier than was his wont.

There, in that little room, so familiar to the reader, with one door blocked by the chest of drawers, and the cock-roaches peeking occasionally from the corners, his state of mind and spirit was as unsteady as the armchair in which he sat. His mind was unpleasantly troubled, and in his heart there was an emptiness. "The devil take the lot of you for devising these confounded balls!" he was thinking angrily. "What have they got to celebrate, the fools? The harvests have failed, prices are soaring in the province, so they throw a ball! What a farce: dressing up in all their silly finery! Incredible, some of them must be wearing a thousand rubles' worth of stuff! And to think all that is paid for by the peasants' quit rents, or, even worse, by their dear husbands' consciences. We all know why they take bribes, and play the hypocrite: to buy the wife a shawl or some other fritteries and fal-de-lals, may they all roast in hell! And for what? So that some nagging old Sidorovna will not start moaning that the postmaster's wife has a better gown than her—and it's bye-bye to a thousand rubles. They all shout: 'A ball, a ball, what fun!'—but a ball is a lot of nonsense, it's not in the Russian spirit, not in the Russian nature; the devil only knows what nonsense: a big, grown-up man, pinched and squeezed tight into his black evening coat like a puppet-show imp, suddenly leaps up, and starts capering around. There are some who will even discuss a business matter with another man, dancing near him, while their feet continue hopping now to the right, now to the left... It's all aping and parroting. Just because a Frenchman at the age of forty is still as much of a child as he was at fifteen we have to be the same! No, honestly... After every ball I feel as if I've committed some sin; I don't even want to think about it. In your head there is a total emptiness, like after a conversation with a man of society: he talks and talks, touches lightly on everything, tells you everything he has been able to dredge out of books, speaking colourfully, eloquently, but somehow not a thing remains in your mind from all this, and afterwards you realise that even a conversation with a simple merchant, who knows only his own business, but knows it well and from experience, is better than all his prattling. So what can you squeeze out of it, out of this ball? Just let us suppose that some writer were to decide to describe this whole scene exactly as it is? Put it in a book and it would be just as meaningless as in real life. What is it after all: moral? Immoral? The devil only knows! You will say: 'To hell with it!' and clap the book shut.''

Such were Chichikov's disapproving thoughts on balls in general; but it seems that there was another reason for his indignation. His main annoyance was not directed at the ball, but at the fact that he had come a cropper, so to say, that he had suddenly appeared before all and sundry in God knows what light, that he found himself playing such a strange, ambiguous role. Of course, viewing all this with the eye of a sensible man, he could see that it was all nonsense, that a stupid remark meant nothing, particularly now, when the main business had already been properly concluded. But man is a strange animal: Chichikov was most distressed by the disfavour of those very people whom he despised and about whom he expressed such harsh views, vilifying their vanity and their finery. This was all the more vexatious to him as, once he properly analysed the situation, he could see that he himself was partially to blame. He did not, however, get angry with himself, and in this he was of course right. We all share the small foible of wishing to spare ourselves, and trying to find someone else near us on whom we can take out our irritation, for example, a servant, or a subordinate who happens to be at hand at that moment, or a wife, or, failing all else, a chair which is sent flying through the air, landing right by the door and parting company with its arms and back: take that! you say, letting it feel your anger. Thus, too, did Chichikov soon find a victim nearby who bore the brunt of all his irritation. This victim was Nozdryov, and sure enough, he received as thorough a lashing as perhaps only some swindling village elder or coachman is given by a much-travelled, experienced army captain, or sometimes even a general who, in addition to the many objurgations, which have by now become classic, would add many unfamiliar ones, belonging exclusively to himself. Nozdryov's entire genealogy was investigated, and many members of his family in the ascendant line suffered badly in the process.

But as he sat in his hard armchair, troubled by his thoughts and afflicted with insomnia, heaping further abuse on Nozdryov and all his kith and kin, with the tallow candle, guttering and dripping black grease all over the holder, and threatening at any moment to go out; with the impenetrable, dark night staring in at him through the window, shortly to lighten with the blueness of approaching dawn; with the cocks crowing in the distance, while through the slumbering town there perhaps wandered a frieze greatcoat, a miserable wretch of unknown class and rank, who knew only that one path in life (alas!) trodden by the hapless drunks of Russia—at this time an event took place at the other end of town which was to intensify the unpleasantness of our hero's situation. To be precise, in the distant streets and alleys of the town there rattled along a most extraordinary equipage, a name for which it would be hard to select. It was unlike either a tarantass, or a brougham, or a chaise, but was much more like a bulging, fat-cheeked watermelon on wheels. The cheeks of this watermelon, that is to say, the doors, which bore traces of yellow paint, were very difficult to close properly because of the dilapidation of the handles and catches, which were just held together with string. The melon was crammed full of cotton cushions in the shape of tobacco-pouches, bolsters and ordinary cushions, and stuffed with sacks full of bread loaves, buns and rolls. From the top there peeped a chicken pie and a sour-cabbage pie. On the back board stood a character of flunkeyish provenance, clad in a shortcoat made of homespun dimity, unshaven, his hair lightly streaked with grey: the sort of character who goes by the sobriquet "laddie". The clatter and squealing from all the iron catches and rusty bolts awakened the town gate-keeper, and he, brandishing his halberd, still befuddled with sleep, shouted at the top of his voice: "Who goes there?", but seeing that

13*

no one was going there, and that the clatter came from afar, caught some bug on his collar and, stepping up to the lamp, summarily executed it there and then on his fingernail. Whereupon, setting aside his halberd, he resumed his slumbers, in accordance with the code of his warriorship. Every now and again the horses stumbled on their front legs, because they were not shod, and furthermore, as was evident, the quiet town highroad was not very familiar to them. This juggernaut, after describing a number of turns from one street into another, finally turned into a dark side-street next to the small parish church of St Nicholas of the Eternal Spring and halted before the gates of the archpriest's house. A wench climbed down from the carriage, wearing a scarf on her head, and a padded jacket, and banged on the gate with her two fists as powerfully as any man (the "laddie" in the dimity shortcoat later had to be dragged only by his feet, for he was sleeping the sleep of the dead). The dogs started to bark, and the gates finally opened their jaws and swallowed up, albeit with great difficulty, this lumbering contraption. The carriage drove into the cramped courtyard, cluttered with stacks of firewood, chicken coops and all manner of little sheds; a gentlewoman alighted from the carriage: this gentlewoman was Mrs. Korobochka, widow of a Collegiate Secretary. Soon after the departure of our hero the old lady had been thrown into such a state of agitation at the thought that she may have been swindled by Chichikov, that, unable to sleep for three nights in succession, she resolved to travel into town, though the horses were unshod, to ascertain for herself the going price on dead souls and whether, God forbid, she had not slipped up by selling them for next to nothing. As to what the consequences of her arrival were, the reader will learn from a certain conversation which took place between two ladies. This conversation ... but let us rather leave this conversation to the next chapter.

CHAPTER NINE

In the morning, even earlier than the hour appointed in the town of N for calls, the doors of an orange wooden house with an attic and blue columns opened and a lady flitted out, clad in a fashionable check cloak and accompanied by a flunkey in a greatcoat with several collars and a shiny round hat adorned with gold galloon. The next instant and with unusual haste the lady flitted up the steps, lowered in readiness, into the barouche standing at the entrance. The flunkey at once slammed the door after the lady, threw back the steps and, seizing the straps behind the carriage, shouted to the coachman: "Let her go!" The lady was in possession of a freshly garnered news and felt an insuppressible compulsion to pass it on as swiftly as possible. Every second she looked out of the window only to see, to her unutterable vexation, that half the journey still remained. Every building seemed longer than usual, the white stone almshouse with its narrow windows stretched past for an intolerably long time, until she could bear it no longer and exclaimed: "Cursed building, is there no end to it?" The coachman had already been instructed twice: "Faster, faster, Andryushka! You're driving intolerably slowly today!" Finally the destination was reached. The barouche drew up before a dark-grey single-storeyed house, also of wood, with little white bas-reliefs above the windows, a tall wooden fence right in front of the windows and a narrow little garden in which grew spindly little trees, caked white by accretions of the everlasting town dust. Seen in the windows were flower pots, a parrot in its cage swinging from a ring by its hooked beak, and two little dogs, dozing in the sun. In this house lived the dear friend of the lady who had just arrived. The author is completely at a loss to name these two ladies so that he does not once again incur the general wrath, as had happened in times gone by. To use an invented surname would be dangerous. Whatever name you think up you will most certainly find that somewhere, in some corner of our Empire, for all its vastness, there is someone with precisely that name, and that someone will most certainly become a mortal enemy of the author, and will say that the author came for the express purpose to snoop everything out: what he was himself, what sort of a sheepskin coat he wore, which Agrafena Ivanovna he called on, and what his favourite dishes were. Call them by their rank? Heaven forbid, that is even more dangerous. Nowadays all those of rank or class are so irritable that everything they find in a

printed book they take as a personal affront: such, it
seems is the current attitude. Suffice it to say that there is
a stupid person in a certain town, and that is already a
personal slight; suddenly a gentleman of the most respectable appearance will pop up and shriek: "Well, I'm a person
too, so I suppose that means I'm also stupid!"—in other
words he will instantly put two and two together. For that
reason, to avoid all this, we shall refer to the lady on whom
the visitor has called exactly as she was referred to by
practically everyone in the town of N: to wit, a lady
pleasant in all respects. This designation she had acquired
quite legitimately, for it was true that she spared no effort
in her anxiety to make herself agreeable to the ultimate
degree, although, of course, through this amiability there
occasionally slipped that ... oh so impish agility of the
feminine character! And sometimes her every pleasant
utterance would carry ... oh so envenomed a dart! And
God have mercy on the woman who should rouse her fury
by getting ahead of her in anything. However, all this
would be cloaked in the most refined genteelness, found
only in provincial capitals. Her every movement was
performed with the utmost taste, she even liked poetry,
she was sometimes even able to incline her head at a
dreamy angle—and all were unanimous that she was indeed
a lady pleasant in all respects. The other lady, that is to say
the caller, did not have such versatility in her character,
and therefore we shall call her the merely pleasant lady.
The arrival of the visitor awoke the dogs dozing in the sun:
the shaggy Adèle, who was forever getting entangled in her
own fur and the little Pot-pourri with his skinny legs. Both
Adèle and Pot-pourri rushed barking into the hall, where
the guest was divesting herself of her cloak and revealing
beneath it a dress of fashionable design and colour and a
long fur scarf round her neck; the fragrance of jasmine
filled the entire room. No sooner had the lady pleasant in
all respects learnt of the arrival of the merely pleasant lady,
than she dashed into the hall. The ladies grasped each other's
hands, kissed and shrieked just as boarding school
girls shriek when they see each other again after the holidays, before their mammas have had an opportunity to
explain to them that the father of the one is poorer and
lower in rank than that of the other. The kisses were exe-

cuted loudly, because the little dogs had resumed their
barking, for which they were slapped with a handkerchief,
and both the ladies, repaired to the drawing-room, pastel
blue, of course, with a sofa, an oval table and even little
screens entwined with ivy; after them the shaggy Adèle
and tall Pot-pourri on his thin legs came running in. "Come
over here, into this little corner!" said the hostess, seating
her guest in a corner of the sofa. "That's right! That's right!
Here's a cushion for you!" As she said this she thrust
behind her guest's back a cushion on which a knight was
embroidered in wool in the manner in which knights are
always embroidered in cross-stitch: his nose went like a
staircase and the mouth was a perfect rectangle. "How
delighted I am that you... I heard someone driving up and I
wondered who it could be, so early. Parasha says: 'the
Vice-governor's wife! and I said: 'Oh no, not that crashing
old bore again', and I was just going to say that I was not
at home..."

The visitor was anxious to get down to business and
impart her intelligence, but an exclamation voiced by her
hostess suddenly turned the conversation in a different
direction.

"What a jolly print!" exclaimed the lady pleasant in
all respects, gazing at the dress of the merely pleasant lady.

"Yes, isn't it. Praskovya Fyodorovna finds, however,
that it would be better if the little checks were a bit smaller and the dots pale blue and not brown. Her sister has
just received a piece of material: it's so sweet, just too lovely for words; just picture it to yourself: teeny-weeny little
stripes, as small as the human mind could imagine, a pale
blue ground and along every second stripe little tiny eyes
and paws, eyes and paws, eyes and paws... It's really beautiful! One can say quite positively that there's never been
anything like it in the world."

"My dear, that's specky."

"Oh no, it's not specky at all!"

"Oh but it is!"

We should note that the lady pleasant in all respects
was to a certain extent a materialist, inclined towards nega-
tion and doubt and there was much she rejected in life.

Hereupon the merely pleasant lady explained that it was
by no means specky and shrieked:

"Oh, congratulations: flounces are out."

"What do you mean they're out?"

"Everyone's wearing scallops now."

"Really that's not very nice, scallops indeed!"

"It's scallops, nothing but scallops: a scalloped pelerine, scallops on the sleeves, teeny scalloped epaulettes, scallops below, scallops everywhere."

"It's not very nice, Sofia Ivanovna, to have scallops everywhere."

"It's unbelievably sweet, Anna Grigorievna. Everything is stitched in two ribs, with very broad arm-holes, and above... And now I'll tell you something that will really astound you, and that's when you'll say... You'll gasp: just imagine, bodices have become even longer, coming down in a point in front, and the front stay has become quite extreme; the skirt is now gathered all round, like the farthingale in the old days, they even put in a bit of padding at the back to give you the look of the true *belle femme*."

"Well that is all simply too, too, I don't know what!" said the lady pleasant in all respects, tossing her head with a sense of dignity.

"Quite so, it's too, too, I don't know what," answered the merely pleasant lady.

"Well, you may say what you like, but I shall not start imitating that, not for anything in the world."

"No, nor shall I... Really, when you think of the lengths to which fashion takes some people ... it's quite awful! I wheedled a pattern just for a laugh from my sister; my Melanya has started making it."

"Do you mean to say you actually have the pattern?" shrieked the lady pleasant in all respects, not without a perceptible emotion.

"Oh yes, my sister brought me it."

"Darling Sofia Ivanovna, in the name of all that is most sacred, give it to me!"

"Oh dear, I've already promised it to Praskovya Fyodorovna. Perhaps you can have it after her."

"And who would want to wear something after Praskovya Fyodorovna? I must say this is just too surprising on your part, to prefer outsiders to your own nearest and dearest."

"But she is also my aunt, once removed."

"She's removed a lot more than once, might I tell you: and on your husband's side, too... No, Sofia Ivanovna, I wish to hear no more, this means only one thing: you want to offend me deeply... Obviously, I have already grown tedious to you, obviously you wish to sever all ties of friendship with me."

Poor Sofia Ivanovna did not know what to do. She suddenly realised she was trapped between the devil and the deep blue sea. Serves you right for bragging! She would gladly have cut out her own tongue for its stupidity.

"Well, and what of our Prince Charming?" asked the lady pleasant in all respects in the pause.

"Merciful God! What am I doing sitting and never... I'm a good one! You can probably guess, Anna Grigorievna, why I've come to see you?" At this point the visitor took a deep breath and the words were ready to come flying forth in pursuit of one another like hawks, and only someone as inhuman as her own dear friend would have had the heartlessness to arrest her.

"I don't care how much you sing his praises," she said with greater animation than usual, "but I will tell you frankly, and I'll say it to his face, that he is a worthless man, worthless, worthless, worthless..."

"But just listen to what I'm about to reveal to you—"

"He's talked of as handsome, but he's not handsome at all, and as for his nose ... it's the most disagreeable nose."

"Please, I beg you, just hear me out... My dear, sweet Anna Grigorievna, I beg you to hear me out! For this is a real story, do you see: a story, *c'qu'on appele histoire*," declared the visitor with a look almost of despair and with a note of real supplication in her voice. It would be apposite to remark here that a great number of foreign words were inserted into both ladies' conversation, and sometimes entire, long sentences in French. But however great the author's veneration for the salutary benefits brought by the French tongue to Russia, however great his veneration for this praiseworthy custom of our high society, which chooses to express itself in this language at all hours of the day, motivated, undoubtedly, by love for their mother country, yet for all this he cannot bring himself to insert a sentence of any alien tongue whatsoever into this his Russian *poem*. Thus, let us proceed in Russian.

"But what story?"

"My dear, dearest Anna Grigorievna, if only you could imagine the position I found myself in, just picture the scene; today the archpriest's wife comes to see me—you know, Father Kiril's wife—and what do you think? Our shrinking violet, our newcomer—what do you think he is?"

"Surely he didn't *fait le court* to the priest's wife, did he?"

"Oh, Anna Grigorievna, if only it were that, it wouldn't be so bad; but just listen to what the archpriest's wife told me: Mrs. Korobochka arrives at her house, she says, scared out of her wits and as pale as death, and she tells her such a story, and what a story! Listen, my dear, it's just like a novel: suddenly, deep in the night, when everyone is fast asleep in the house, she heard someone knocking at the gate, making the most dreadful noise you could possibly imagine, and shouting: 'Open up, open up, or I'll break down the gates!' Now what do you think of that? What do you think of our Prince Charming after that?"

"Tell me about this Korobochka woman, is she young and pretty?"

"Not at all, she's an old crone."

"Lovely! Going after an old crone. I must say, you have to admire the taste of our ladies after that, there's a fine one for them to fall in love with."

"But no, no, Anna Grigorievna, it's not what you're thinking at all. Just picture him to yourself, he comes armed to the teeth, just like Rinaldo Rinaldini, and demands: 'Sell me all your souls who have died,' he says. Korobochka answers very sensibly, she says: 'I cannot sell them, because they're dead.' 'No,' he says, 'they are not dead, that,' he says, 'is for me to decide, whether they're dead or not, they're not dead, not dead,' he shouts, 'not dead.' In a word, he caused a terrible rumpus: the entire village came running to see, the children were crying, everyone shouting, no one could understand anything anyone was saying, it was quite simply *horreur, horreur, horreur...* But you simply cannot imagine, my dear Anna Grigorievna, how deeply alarmed I became when I heard all that. 'My dear madam,' Mashka says to me, 'just take a look in the mirror, you're quite pale.' 'I've no time for mirrors now,' I say, 'I must go and tell this to Anna Grigorievna.'

That very instant I order the carriage: the coachman Andryushka asks me where we are going, but I simply cannot answer, I just stare back at him like an idiot; he must have thought I had gone mad. Oh dear, Anna Grigorievna, if only you could imagine how deeply alarmed I became!"

"This is rather strange, however," said the lady pleasant in all respects, "what exactly might these dead souls mean? I must confess I understand absolutely nothing. This is now the second time I've heard about these dead souls; but my husband assures me that Nozdryov was lying; all the same, it seems there is something in it."

"But just imagine, Anna Grigorienva, the position I was in when I heard all this. 'And now,' says Korobochka, 'I simply do not know,' she says, 'what to do. He forced me,' she says, 'to sign some false document, and threw down fifteen rubles in banknotes; I'm just a helpless, inexperienced widow,' she says. 'I know nothing about these things...' Such goings on, imagine! Ah, if you only knew how very deeply alarmed I was."

"Only if you ask me this is not just dead souls, there's something else behind all this."

"My very own thought," declared the merely pleasant lady with a certain measure of surprise, and she at once felt a powerful urge to discover what precisely could be behind all this. She even enquired in an offhand way: "So what do you suppose there might be behind it?"

"Well, what do you think!"

"What do I think?.. I must confess, I'm completely at a loss."

"All the same I should still like to know what you think with regard to all this?"

But the pleasant lady could think of nothing to say. She was capable only of worrying, while making some clever assumption was quite beyond her, and therefore, more than any other lady, she felt the need for tender friendship and advice.

"Well then, let me tell you what these dead souls are," said the lady pleasant in all respects, and her guest, on hearing this, was at once all attention: her ears pricked up automatically, she half rose from the sofa, and although she was rather on the stout side, she suddenly became much thinner, and as light as a feather, about to be borne away by the first puff of wind.

Thus too the Russian squire, dog-fancier and inveterate huntsman, as he nears the forest from which the hare will dash out at any moment, driven out by the whippersin, is transformed, together with his mount and his raised whip, into a frozen moment of time, into gunpowder, to which a flame is just about to be applied. He stares into the dim air, and you may be sure he will overtake the hare, he will get it, no matter how violently the whole snowy steppe might rise to oppose him, shooting its silvery stars into his mouth, his moustache, his eyes, his eyebrows and his beaver cap.

"The dead souls..." began the lady pleasant in all respects.

"Yes, yes?" her guest urged her, greatly agitated.

"The dead souls..."

"Oh for pity's sake, do go on!"

"All that has merely been concocted as a cover, but the thuth of the matter is: he wants to elope with the governor's daughter."

This conclusion, to be sure, was totally unexpected and in all respects extraordinary. The merely pleasant lady, on hearing this, froze, went pale, as pale as death and was indeed most deeply alarmed.

"Good Lord!" she exclaimed, flinging up her hands. "Now *that* I could never possibly have guessed."

"And I, let me tell you, guessed it the very moment you opened your mouth," answered the lady pleasant in all respects.

"But what does that say for boarding school upbringing, Anna Grigorievna? That's innocence for you!"

"Innocence indeed! I've heard her saying things which, I must confess, I could not bring myself to repeat."

"You know, Anna Grigorievna, does it not simply break one's heart to see how rife immorality has become?"

"And the men are insane about her. Personally, I must confess, I can see nothing in her... She's intolerably affected."

"Oh, but my dear Anna Grigorievna, she's no more alive than a statue, with never the slightest expression in her face."

"Oh she's so affected! So affected! Goodness, so affected! Who taught it to her I do not know, but I have never yet seen a woman with such airs and graces."

"But darling! She's a statue and as pale as death itself."

"Heavens no, Sofia Ivanovna: it's scandalous the way she rouges her cheeks."

"But my dear Anna Grigorievna, what are you saying: she's chalk, the purest, whitest chalk!"

"My dear, I sat right beside her: the rouge was painted on a finger thick and it was flaking off like stucco, in chunks. She learnt it from her mother, who's also a coquette, but the daughter will outdo the dear mama yet."

"I must disagree. You can ask me to swear by whatever you will, I'm prepared to lose my children, my husband, my entire fortune, this very moment, if she has the tiniest little drop, a grain, or even the veriest shadow of colour!"

"Honestly, what are you saying, Sofia Ivanovna!" exclaimed the lady pleasant in all respects, flinging up her hands in exasperation.

"Now really, Anna Grigorievna, how can you! You really amaze me!" said the pleasant lady and also flung up her hands.

Now let it not seem strange to the reader that the two ladies should fail to agree on something they had both seen at almost the same time. There really are things in the world which have this remarkable property: when one lady looks at them they will appear completely white, but let another look and they will be quite, quite red, like bilberries.

"Well, here's further proof for you that she has no colour," continued the pleasant lady, "I can remember, as if it had happened this very minute, that I was sitting next to Manilov and I said to him: 'Just look how pale she is!' I must admit, it just shows how dull-witted all our menfolk are that they should admire her so. And as for our Prince Charming... Ugh, what a nasty man! You simply cannot imagine, Anna Grigorievna, how nasty I thought him."

"Indeed, nevertheless there were certain ladies who lost their hearts to him."

"Do you mean me, Anna Grigorievna? No, that you cannot say of me, never, never!"

"Oh but I am not speaking of you, there are plenty of others."

"Never, never, Anna Grigorievna! Allow me to inform you that I happen to know my own mind very well; this might be true of certain other ladies who make themselves out to be unapproachable."

"Oh no, Sofia Ivanonva! Allow *me* to inform *you* now that I have never been guilty of anything so shocking. Others have, perhaps: but not I, please allow me to point this out to you."

"But why do you mind so much? After all, there were other ladies there too, there were even some who rushed to grab the chairs by the door, that they might sit closer to him."

Well, after these words uttered by the pleasant lady, a storm should have inevitably broken out, but surprisingly both ladies suddenly cooled off and absolutely nothing ensued. The lady pleasant in all respects recollected that the pattern for the fashionable dress was not yet in her hands, and the merely pleasant lady realised that she still had not ascertained any details of the discovery made by her dear friend, and thus a cease-fire followed very soon. However, it cannot be said that either of the ladies felt an inner compulsion to cause any upleasantness, and on the whole they were not malicious by nature, it was simply that in the course of conversation a tiny urge arose in each quite spontaneously to needle the other; and simply for the small satisfaction it gave them, they missed no chance to slip in a sharp little jibe now and then: as if to say, there, take that! Varied are the urges that move the male and the female hearts.

"However, there is still one thing I cannot quite understand," said the merely pleasant lady, "and that is, how Chichikov, a visitor in our midst, could allow himself such an audacious *passage*. It's quite unthinkable that he had no accomplices."

"You surely do not think he had none?"

"But who, do you think, might have assisted him?"

"Well, Nozdryov might, if anyone."

"Surely not Nozdryov?"

"Why not? He certainly has it in him. Do you know, he wanted to sell his very own father or, worse still, to stake him at cards."

"Goodness me, what exciting news I learn from you! I should never have guessed that Nozdryov could be mixed up in this affair!"

"But I have always thought it."

"When you come to think of it, it's astonishing the things that go on in the world! I mean, who would have supposed, when Chichikov first arrived in the town, that he would cause such an extraordinary *démarche* in society. Oh, Anna Grigorievna, if only you knew how deeply alarmed I was! If it were not for your kindness and friendship ... there I was, I assure you, on the very brink of perdition ... where was I to turn? My Mashka could see I was as pale as death. 'My dear madam,' she says to me, 'you're as pale as death.' 'Mashka,' say I, 'I haven't the time to worry about that now.' What a turn of events! So Nozdryov's in it too, I ask you!"

The pleasant lady was most anxious to ascertain further details concerning the abduction, to wit, at what time it was set and so forth, but she wanted too much. The lady pleasant in all respects swore complete ignorance. She could not tell a lie: making a surmise, yes, that was a different matter, but even then one only did it when the surmise rested on inner conviction; if, indeed, she felt such inner conviction then she could stand up for herself, and let some lawyer, famed for his gift for changing people's minds for them, try his skills here,—he would soon see what inner conviction means.

The fact that both ladies finally believed beyond any doubt that which they had first only surmised is not at all unusual. We, intelligent people that we call ourselves, behave almost identically as witness our scholarly deliberations. At first the scholar feels himself terribly unworthy, and begins cautiously, starting with the humblest of questions: is it not perhaps from there? could not such-and-such a country perhaps derive its name from that corner? or: does this document perhaps not belong to another, later period? or: should we not perhaps understand by this people this other people? He immediately cites various writers of antiquity and the moment he detects any hint of something or imagines such a hint he breaks into a trot and, feeling emboldened, he now chats as an equal with the writers of antiquity, asking them questions, and even answering on their behalf, entirely forgetting how he began with a timid surmise; it already seems to him that he can see it, the truth, that it is clear—and his deliberation is concluded with the words: "So that is how it was, that is how such-and-such a people should be classified, that is the angle from which the subject should be viewed!" This is then publicly declaimed *ex cathedra* for all to hear—and the newly-discovered truth sets off on its travels round the world, gathering followers and admirers as it goes.

While the two ladies were so successfully and astutely untangling this most involved set of circumstances, the prosecutor himself entered the drawing room, his face, with his bushy eyebrows and blinking eye, wearing its usual impassive expression. The ladies began to talk together eager to impart all these events to him, recounting the story of the buying of dead souls, the planned abduction of the governor's daughter, and confusing him so completely that he stood rooted to the spot, batting his left eyelid and flicking snuff out of his beard with his handkerchief, quite unable to understand what it could all mean. That was how the ladies left him, setting off on their various ways to incite the town to mutiny. They succeeded in accomplishing this undertaking in little over half an hour. The town was decidedly aroused but no one had the least idea what was going on. The ladies were so adept at spreading rumours, that everyone, and most particularly the officials, remained stunned for quite some time. In the first moments their position was like that of a schoolboy, who, while still asleep, has had a "hussar"—that is, a paper cone filled with snuff—inserted in his nostril by his school-fellows, who have risen earlier. Inhaling the entire twist of snuff with all his sleeper's zeal, he awakes, leaps out of bed, staring about him like an idiot, the eyes popping out of his head, and is quite unable to understand where he is or what has happened to him. In a little while he is able to make out the walls, illuminated by the oblique rays of the morning sun, then he becomes aware of the laughter of his fellows, hiding in corners, and the dawning day peeping through the window, with the awakened forest, ringing with the chorus of a thousand birds, and with the glistening river, disappearing from view as it twists and turns between the slender reeds, a river teeming with naked boys, urging others into the water, and now at last he feels the hussar lodged in his nose. Exactly such was the situation in which the inhabitants and officials of the town found themselves in the first moments. Everyone stood befuddled, his eyes popping. Dead souls, the governor's daughter and Chichikov were all mixed together in the most extraordinary fashion; and only after the first wave of stupefaction had passed, did they begin to distinguish them one from the other, wanting an explanation and growing angry when they realised that the matter simply refused to explain itself. What was the meaning of all this, in point of fact, what were these dead souls anyway? There was no logic in dead souls, how could one buy dead souls? Was anyone fool enough to do so? And who had all that money to burn? And what earthly use could he make of these dead souls? And why was the governor's daughter mixed up in all this? If he was planning to abduct her, then why was he buying up dead souls? And if he was buying up dead souls, then why abduct the governor's daughter? Did he intend these dead souls as a present for her, then? What was all this nonsense that was being spread round town anyway? What a turn things had taken, that no matter which way you looked another story was being put about, without a scrap of sense in it... All the same, they say there's no smoke without a fire. But where was the fire here, what reason could there be for these dead souls? No reason at all. The answer was simple: a lot of twaddle, flap-doodle, bumkum and hard-boiled boots! The devil knows what! In a word, the tongues flapped away and soon the whole town was talking about the dead souls and the governor's daughter, about Chichikov and the dead souls, about the governor's daughter and Chichikov, and there was the most unholy commotion. This hitherto slumbering town was wide awake and in a whirl! All the sloths and lie-abeds came crawling out of their lairs, all those types who had loafed at home for several years in their dressing-gowns, putting the blame for not going out now on the boot-maker for making their boots too tight, now on the tailor, now on that drunkard of a coachman. All those who had long since ceased all acquaintance and only kept company, as the saying goes, with Polezhayev and Zavalishin (well-known terms, derived from the verbs for lying down and lolling about, which are as widely used here in Russia as the phrase: to call on Sopikov—old Wheezer—or Khrapovitsky—the Snorer, signifying any sort of log-like sleep on the back, the side and in every other imaginable position, accompanied by snorts, nasal whistling and other such musical accompaniment to sleep); all those who could not be enticed from their houses even with an invitation to share a five-hundred-ruble tureen of fish soup with five-foot-long sterlets and every kind of mouth-watering pastry; in a word, it transpired that the town was large and adequately populated. Some fellow called Sysoi Pafnutievich popped up, and so did a Macdonald Karlovich, who had never been heard of before; there appeared in the drawing-rooms an immensely tall character, with a bullet in his arm, a man of a height such as had never been seen here before. The streets became thronged with covered droshkies, brakes of an unknown origin, rattle-traps and shandrydans—and the fat was in the fire. At another time and in other circumstances such rumours might perhaps have attracted no interest; but the town of N had for so long had no news of any kind. For three whole months there had not even been a single occurrence of the kind termed a *commérage* in our capital cities, which, as we all know, has the same importance for a town as the timely arrival of fresh provisions. Suddenly two opposing trends of thought emerged and two opposing schools were formed: the male and the female. The male school, which was extremely dull-witted, concentrated on the dead souls. The female dealt exclusively with the abduction of the governor's daughter. This latter school, we should note to the credit of the ladies, was characterised by an incomparably greater orderliness and circumspection. For such indeed, evidently, is their very purpose, to be good housekeepers and manageresses. With them everything swiftly acquired a vivid and definite aspect, was clothed in clear and manifest forms, was explained, cleansed of clutter, and a finished picture emerged. It transpired that Chichikov had long since been in love, and that they had held trysts by moonlight in the gardens, that the governor would have given his daughter in marriage to him since Chichikov was as rich as a Jew if there had not been the problem of the wife whom he had abandoned (from where they learnt that Chichikov was married was something no one knew), and that his wife, whose hopeless love caused her much suffering, had written a most moving letter to the governor, and that Chichikov, seeing that the governor and his wife would never give their consent now, had resolved to abduct their daughter. In other houses a slightly different version was told: that Chichikov had no wife at all, but that, being a man of subtle ways and no scruples, had commenced his undertaking, with the eventual aim of winning the hand of the daughter, by wooing the mother, and had established a secret liaison with her, and then asked for the hand of the daughter; but the mother, alarmed lest a crime against religion be committed here, and suffering the pangs of conscience in her own soul, gave a flat refusal, and that that was why Chichikov decided in favour of abduction. This was amplified by many elucidations and amendments as the rumours trickled into the more remote back-streets. For Russian folk of the lower classes have a great fondness for discussing scandal that originates in the upper classes, and therefore tongues started to wag about all this in the sort of houses where Chichikov had never been seen and was not even known, the story further embroidered and elucidated. The story became more fascinating by the minute, acquiring more definite shape every day, until finally, exactly as it was, in all its definitiveness, it was delivered into the ears of the governor's wife herself. The governor's wife, as a materfamilias, as the first lady of the town, and as a lady who had never suspected anything like that, was mortally offended by these stories and was quite justifiably infuriated. The poor blonde was subjected to the most unpleasant *tête-à-tête* ever endured by a sixteen-year-old girl. There was a veritable torrent of questions, interrogations, reprimands, threats, reproaches, admonitions, with the result that the girl burst into floods of tears, sobbing and unable to understand a word that was said; the doorman was given the strictest instructions not to admit Chichikov at any time nor in any disguise.

Having done with the governor's wife, the ladies now addressed themselves to the men's camp, attempting to win them over to their side and maintaining that the dead souls were an invention and were used only to deflect any possible suspicion and to increase the chances of a successful abduction. Quite a number of the men were thus seduced into the ranks of the ladies, despite the violent disapprobation of their comrades, who called them old women and sheep, names which, as we all know, are most offensive to the male sex.

But however strongly the men armed themselves, however valiantly they resisted, their camp completely lacked the orderliness of the women's camp. Everything about them was somehow uncouth, awkward, inept, sloppy and ugly, their thoughts were muddled, untidy and contradictory—in short, in every respect they manifested their worthless male nature, coarse and ponderous, incapable either of home-building or of heartfelt convictions, incredulous, indolent, filled with continuous doubts and constant fear. They said that all this was rubbish, that the abduction of the governor's daughter was rather a hussar's undertaking than a civilian's, that Chichikov would not do such a thing, that the women were lying, that a woman is like a sack: whatever anyone puts in her she will carry; that the main thing on which they should focus their attention was the dead souls, which, however, signified the devil knows what, but that, nonetheless, there was clearly something bad and wicked behind them. Why the men should have thought there was something bad and wicked behind them we shall ascertain directly: a new governor-general had been appointed to the town, an event which naturally throws officials into a state of alarm: there will be enquiries, dressings down, shake-ups and all those other official dishes to which a superior treats his subordinates. "Just supposing, he finds out that certan foolish rumours are circulating in our town," thought the officials. "Why, for that alone he might drag us over the coals." The inspector of the medical board suddenly paled, struck by the most awful thought: did the words "dead souls" imply patients who had died in considerable numbers in infirmaries and other places from the epidemic of fever against which proper measures had not been taken, and might Chichikov not be an official sent from the governor-general's chancellory to carry out a secret investigation? He confided his fears to the president of Chambers. The president retorted that this was poppycock, and then himself turned pale, as he asked himself the question: but what if the souls, which Chichikov had bought, really were dead? For did he not allow a purchase deed to be drawn up for them and even act as Plyushkin's attorney, and what if this came to the ears of the governor-general, what then? He did no more about this than to inform one or two others, and these others suddenly paled too; fear is more contagious than the plague itself and is passed on instantly. All of them discovered in themselves sins that they had not even committed. The words "dead souls" had such an indeterminate ring that they even began to suspect that there might be a hint here at these too hastily buried bodies, in consequence of two fairly recent incidents.

The first incident occurred with some merchants from Solvychegodsk, who came to town for the fair and after trading threw a little feast for their friends the merchants of Ustsysolsk, a feast in the true Russian style with German embellishments: orgeats, punches, balsams, and so forth. The feast, as is customary, ended with a fight. The Solvychegodsk contingent beat the men of Ustsysolsk to death, although they themselves received a good few punches in the ribs and under the belt, bearing witness to the formidable size of the fists with which their deceased adversaries were equipped. One of the victors had his nose punched in, as the warriors put it, which is to say completely pulped, so that it hardly protruded from his face. The merchants pleaded guilty, admitting that the party had been a bit wild. It was rumoured that each guilty member of the group had had to shell out four big, five-hundred-ruble notes; however, the case was too shady; from the official inquiries and investigations it transpired that the Ustsysolsk fellows had died from poison by charcoal fumes, and so they were buried as victims of fumes.

The other incident, more recent, was as follows: the state peasants of the little village of Vshivaya-Spes joined forces with other state peasants from the village of Borovka, Zadirailovo-Tozh and, allegedly, simply wiped the district police force from the face of the earth, in the person of a certain deputy Drobyazhkin, because this district police force, that is deputy Drobyazhkin, had taken to coming too often to their village, a bane worse than the plague, and the reason for these comings was that the district police force, which suffered from a certain weakness of an amorous nature, eyed the village wives and wenches. Nothing, however, was established for certain, although in their testimony the peasants stated that the district police force was as lecherous as an old goat, and that they had warned him time and again, and once had even chased him naked out of some cottage which he had sneaked into. Of course, the district police force was deserving of punishment for this amorous weakness, but the peasants of both Vshivaya-Spes and Zadirailovo-Tozh could not be excused for taking the law into their own hands, if indeed they really did participate in the murder. It was an obscure matter: the district police force was found in the road, the uniform or tunic on him was in a mess, and his face was hard to recognize. The case went through the courts and finally reached the Chambers, where at first and behind closed doors it was reasoned that since it was unknown exactly which of the peasants took part, and there were many of them, and Drobyazhkin was dead anyway, so it would do him little good even if he did win the case, while the peasants were still alive, and therefore a decision in their favour was extremely important to them; it was decided, that deputy Drobyazhkin was himself the cause of it all, by unjustly oppressing the peasants of Vshivaya-Spes and Zadirailovo-Tozh, and that he in fact died from a stroke in his sleigh on the way home. With that the case seemed to be wrapped up nicely, but the officials, for some unknown reason, began to think that it was these dead souls that were now in question. As ill-luck would have it, at the very time when the officials were in a difficult position anyway, the governor simultaneously received two letters. The first was to inform the governor that according to evidence received and the testimony of informers there was a forger of banknotes at large in their province, hiding under various aliases, and to instruct him to mount a most thorough hunt immediately. The second was addressed to him by the governor of the neighbouring province saying that a criminal had escaped from prison, and warning him that should any suspicious character appear in their province, lacking any documents or a passport, he had to be detained forthwith. These two letters left everyone stunned. All their previous conclusions and conjectures were totally bedevilled. Of course, it could not possibly be surmised that any of this might refer to Chichikov; nevertheless, all of them, thinking it over, realised that they still did not know who in fact Chichikov was, that he had always been extremely vague about his own self, saying, it is true, that he had suffered in his service for the truth, but still it was rather vague, and when they remembered that he had even admitted to having many enemies who had made attempts on his life, then they started to think even more seriously: so, his life was in peril, so, he was being hunted, so, he must have done something which... But who exactly was he? Of course, no one believed he could be a forger, and even less a brigand: he had such a respectable appearance; but despite all this the question remained: just who the devil was he, anyway? And thus the officials finally asked themselves the question which should have been asked right at the beginning, that is, in the first chapter of our poem. It was decided to put certain questions to those from whom the souls were bought, to elucidate what sort of purchases these were, and what exactly was to be understood by these dead souls, and to find out if he confided to someone, or explained if only inadvertently, or at least mentioned in passing what his actual intentions were, and if he told someone who he was. First of all they addressed themselves to Korobochka, but they did not get much out of her: they were told he had bought souls for fifteen rubles, and he would also buy feathers, and had promised to buy much else besides, he also procured lard for the government and was for that reason most probably a rogue, for once before she had had dealings with a man who bought feathers and procured lard for the government, but he had deceived everybody and swindled over a hundred rubles out of the archpriest's wife. After this all she did was to repeat what she had already said, and all that the officials discovered was that Korobochka was simply a stupid old woman. Manilov replied that he was always prepared to vouch for Pavel Ivanovich, as he would for himself, that he would gladly exchange his entire estate for a mere fraction of Pavel Ivanovich's qualities, and in general spoke of him in the most flattering terms, and then, closing his eyes dreamily, added several observations on the nature of friendship. These observations did, of course, satisfactorily explain the tender motions of his heart, but failed to explain the case in hand to the officials. Sobakevich replied that in his opinion Chichikov was a good man and that he had sold him first-class peasants and in every respect very much alive, but that he would not vouch for what would happen subsequently, that if they were to die off on the road as they were re-settled it would not be his fault, that was all in God's hands, and as for fevers and other mortal illnesses there were plenty in the world, and there were cases when entire villages were wiped out. The officials then resorted to a means which though not entirely reputable is, nonetheless, employed on occasion: and that is, clandestinely, through various servant-class contacts, to find out from Chichikov's servants, whether perhaps they knew any details about the earlier life and circumstances of their master, but this left them little the wiser. From Petrushka they got only a shock from his smell of a long-unaired bedroom, and from Selifan the information that Chichikov had been in government service and had previously served in the customs and nothing more. This class of people has an extremely strange tradition. If you ask them directly about something they will never remember anything, they won't take in the question properly and will answer flatly that they do not know; but if you ask about something else, they will bring in that other matter and will tell you all about it, with all sorts of details that you do not even wish to know. From all the inquiries conducted by the officials they discovered only that they positively did not know what Chichikov was, but that, nonetheless, Chichikov had to be something. They resolved finally to thrash the matter out soundly and decide, at least, exactly what they were to do and how, and which measures were to be taken, and what exactly he was: the sort of person who should be seized and detained as untrustworthy, or was he the sort of person who could seize and detain all of them as untrustworthy? To this end it was suggested that they gather for the purpose in the house of the chief of police, a figure already familiar to the reader as the father and benefactor of the town.

CHAPTER TEN

Gathering at the house of the chief of police, already familiar to the reader as the father and benefactor of the town, the officials had occasion to remark to one another that they had even lost weight as a result of these troubles and worries. And in truth, the appointment of a new governor-general, the receipt of those two letters with such grave contents, and these rumours of God knows what—this had all left perceptible traces in their faces, and the tailcoats on many of them had become noticeably looser. They had all suffered: the president had lost weight, the inspector of the medical board had lost weight and the prosecutor had lost weight, and a certain Semyon Ivanovich, who was never called by his surname and who wore on his index finger a signet ring which he used to show to the ladies, even he had lost weight. Of course, as would happen anywhere, there were some intrepid men among them, who still had not lost their presence of mind, but they were very few indeed. The postmaster was one such. He alone remained unchanging in his permanently equable temperament and in such cases was always wont to say: "We know you, you governor-generals! They might replace you three or four times, but I've been here a good thirty years, my good sir, and I'm sitting tight." To this the other officials would usually retort: "It's all right for you, you deal with the post, receiving and dispatching the mail, all you might do occasionally is pull a fast one by closing your office an hour early to charge a late-arriving merchant extra for accepting a letter after hours, or you might slip up by sending some parcel which should not be sent—in your job, of course, anyone could be a saint. I'd like to see you if you had the devil turning up every day to tempt you, you'd honestly refuse to take the money but he'd keep thrusting it in your hand. It's easy for you, of course, you only have one son, but take me and my Praskovya Fyodorovna: God has blessed her so bountifully that she has a baby a year: one year a Praskushka, the next a Petrushka; you'd sing a different tune then, brother." Thus did the officials talk, and whether or not the devil's temptation could be resisted it is not for the author to judge. In the council which met on this occasion one essential thing was most palpably lacking: what amongst simple folk is called horse sense. In general we, Russians, are not really made for official meetings. All our meetings, from the humblest gathering of villagers to every kind of scholarly and other committee, unless there is one person who has full control of everyone, are characterized by the utmost chaos and disorder. There is really no telling why this should be so; apparently, we are simply that kind of people who only make a success of those meetings which are called for the purpose of feasting and dining, for example: social clubs and pleasure-gardens in the German manner. But we are ready to undertake anything at all this very minute. According to how the wind blows we will suddenly set up benevolent societies, societies for the encouragement of something or other, and every other manner of society. The aim will be admirable, but nothing will be achieved. Maybe because we feel contented with the very idea and imagine that everything has been done. For example, if we set up a charity society to aid the needy, contributing considerable sums to it, we begin by giving a dinner to mark this praiseworthy undertaking for all the senior dignitaries of the town, naturally consuming half the monies contributed; with what remains we rent a magnificent suite of offices for the committee, with heating and watchmen, and when all that is left for the needy is about five and a half rubles, the question of how to distribute this sum, causes discord among the committee members, each one claiming it for some relative of his own. The meeting called here was of quite a different kind, however; it came about as a result of necessity. No one was concerned here with any needy folk or other outsiders; this matter concerned each official personally, it concerned a disaster that threatened them all equally and one would expect them to have shown a greater unanimity, a closing of the ranks, so to speak. But for all that the result was a mess. To say nothing of the disagreements which are characteristic of all councils, the opinions of those gathered together disclosed a quite unaccountable indecisiveness: one said that Chichikov was a forger of banknotes and in the next breath added, "or perhaps he's not a forger," another insisted that he was an official from the governor-general's chancellory, and at once qualified this assertion: "but then, the devil only knows if he really is. After all, it's not written on his face". The surmise that he might be a brigand in disguise met with universal opposition; they found that besides his appearance, which was of the most respectable kind, there was nothing in his conversation to indicate a man of a violent disposition. Suddenly the postmaster, who had remained sunk in some sort or reverie for several minutes, whether struck by a momentary flash of inspiration or by something else, exclaimed to everyone's surprise:

"Do you know who he is, gentlemen?"

There was something shattering about the way he said this, which caused all the officials to cry out in one voice:

"Who?"

"He, my good sirs, is none other than Captain Kopeikin!"

And when they all asked in one voice: "And just who is this Captain Kopeikin?" the postmaster said:

"You mean to say you do not know who Captain Kopeikin is?"

They all replied that, indeed, they did not have the slightest idea who Captain Kopeikin was.

"Captain Kopeikin," said the postmaster and opened his snuff box only halfway, fearing that one of his neighbours might thrust in his fingers, in the cleanliness of which he had little faith, and even saying rudely: "Who knows where you go visiting with your fingers, and snuff is something which requires cleanliness"; "Captain Kopeikin," repeated the postmaster, taking a pinch of snuff, "well, you know, if that story were to be told some writer chappie could make something most entertaining out of it; it might make a whole poem."

All those present declared their desire to hear this story, or as the postmaster put it, something most entertaining for a writer chappie, maybe a whole poem, and he began as follows:

The Tale of Captain Kopeikin

"After the campaign of 1812, my good sir," began the postmaster, although there were no less than six good sirs in the room, "after the campaign of 1812 a certain Captain Kopeikin was sent back amongst the wounded. It was either at Krasny, or perhaps Leipzig, but imagine, he lost an arm and a leg. Well, in those days, you know, there were no special arrangements for the wounded; this invalid pension fund was only started one way or another, as you can imagine, some time later. Captain Kopeikin saw that he would have to work for a living, only the arm he lost happened to be the right one. He goes home to see his father and his father says: 'I've got nothing to feed you'—can you credit it—'I've got hardly enough bread for myself.' So my Captain Kopeikin decides to set off, my good sir, for St. Petersburg, to petition the Tsar for monarchic grace, saying to him: 'That's how it is, you see, this and that, in a manner of speaking, so to say, I sacrificed my life, spilt my blood...' Well, somehow or other, you know how it is, on carts and official wagon trains, he eventually gets himself to St. Petersburg. Well, you can imagine the scene: there you have some fellow or other, that is Captain Kopeikin, and there he is suddenly in the capital city, like which there is no other in the world! Suddenly he sees the great world before him, so to say, a certain sphere of life, the fabled Sheherezade. Suddenly there's this something or other, you can just imagine, this Nevsky Prospekt, or, you know, some Gorokhovaya Street or other, damn it all! Or some sort of Liteinaya Street or other; over there is some spire sticking up somewhere in the air; bridges hanging over the river somehow or other, the devil knows how, you can just imagine, without even any supports that is—in a word, my good sir, Semiramis pure and simple! He's about to set about renting some digs, but they sting you something terrible for everything: curtains, blinds, the devil knows what nonsense, carpets—it's just like Persia; your feet, so to speak, are trampling on money. You walk along the street and your nose veritably twitches because you smell money, thousands, in the air; now my Captain Kopeikin's store of banknotes, you understand, amounted to about a dozen blue fivers. Well, somehow or other he gets himself lodgings in an inn—the Revel—for a ruble a day; dinner is cabbage soup and a lump of beef. He looks around: his money won't last long here. He asks where he should go. They tell him that there is, in a manner of speaking, a certain supreme commission, some sort of board, you understand, and the chairman is General-en-chef such-and-such. Now the Tsar, I should tell you, was not yet back in the capital; the army, you see, still hadn't returned from Paris, they were all still abroad. My Kopeikin gets up good and early, shaves off his beard with his left hand, because having to pay a barber will, in a certain sense, be an expense, pulls on his old uniform and clomping along, as you can imagine, on his wooden stump, heads off to see the chairman, the big man himself. He asks for the address. There it is, they tell him, pointing to a house on the Palace Embankment. It's a fair old hovel, let me tell you: glass in the windows, mirrors the height of two men, so that the vases and everything else in the rooms inside looks as though it's outside—just stick your hand in and help yourself, you would think; the walls faced with precious marble, fancy metal doo-dahs, and the kind of door handles that will make you clash off to the nearest smallgoods shop, buy a kopek's worth of soap, and then spend a good two hours scrubbing your hands, before you dare grab hold of those handles—in a word: the polish and varnish on everything— in a certain sense it's enough to make the mind boggle. Even the doorman looks like a generalissimus: with a gilt mace, a micn like a duke's, like some sleek, overfed, pugdog; and little lawn collars, confound it all... My Kopeikin somehow manages to drag himself on his wooden peg up into the reception room, squeezes himself into a corner, lest he knocks his elbow into some Amcrica or India—one of those gilded porcelain vases, you understand. Well, sure enough he has his fair share of waiting because, you can imagine, he arrived at an hour when the general had barely risen from his bed in a manner of speaking, and his valet was only just bringing him some silver basin or other for his various ablutions and so forth. My Kopeikin waits about four hours before finally some adjutant or other duty officer arrives. 'The General,' he says, 'will shortly come out into the reception room.' By this stage the crowd in the reception room is as dense as beans on a plate. And these are not the likes of us simple folk either, these are all personages of the fourth and fifth class, colonels, and on some of them there's a big wad of silver macaroni gleaming on their epaulettes—in other words, grandees. Suddenly there's ever such a slight commotion in the room, like some fine ethereal breeze. Here and there people say: 'Shh, shh!' and finally the most fearful silence settles over the room. The great man enters. Well... You can imagine: a man of state! The look on his face, so to speak ... well, in conformity with his title, you understand ... with his high rank ... the same sort of expression, you understand. Everyone in that room, naturally enough, is at once as taut as a bowstring, hoping, trembling, waiting for a decision about his fate, in a manner of speaking. The minister, or grandee, goes up to one, then to another: 'Why are you here? Why are you here? What do you want? What's your business?' And finally, my good sir, he arrives at Kopeikin. Kopeikin plucks up his courage: 'It's like this and that, Your Excellency: I spilt my blood, lost, in a manner of speaking, an arm and a leg, cannot work, and make so bold as to seek monarchic grace.' The minister can see: the man has a wooden leg and his right sleeve is pinned empty to his uniform: 'Good,' he says, 'call in again in a few days' time.' My Kopeikin leaves almost in a state of rapture: first—he has gained an audience with a dignitary of the highest order; and second—at long last a decision will be reached, in a manner of speaking, about his pension. He is in such high spirits, you understand, that he fair jumps for joy on the pavement. He calls into the Palkin Inn to drink a glass of vodka, he dines, my good sir, at the London, orders a cutlet with capers, a roast chicken with all sorts of trimmings, and a bottle of wine, and later in the evening he goes to the theatre—in short, you understand, he goes on a real spree. And then he sees her, walking along the pavement, this slender English miss, as graceful as a swan, can you just imagine it, a real swan. Now my Kopeikin—the blood really boiling in him, you know—starts to run in hot pursuit on his stump, clip-clop, clip-clop... 'But no,' he thinks, 'better wait till later, when I get my pension, I've blown rather a lot already.' So, my good sir, my Kopeikin pitches up at the Minister's reception room three or four days later and waits for him to appear. 'It's like this,' he says, 'I've come,' he says, 'to hear what Your Excellency has decreed on the matter of the illnesses I am suffering and the wounds sustained...' and so on and so forth, you know, all in the right jargon. The grandee, imagine this, recognized him at once: 'Ha,' he says, 'excellent,' he says, 'but right now I have nothing more to say, except that you shall have to await the arrival of His Majesty; then, you can be quite sure, certain instructions will be issued regarding the wounded, but,' he says, 'without His monarchic approval there's nothing I can do.' A bow, you know the sort of thing, and farewell. Kopeikin, you can imagine, left in a state of great uncertainty. He had thought that they would give him his money the very next day: 'There you are, my good fellow, get drunk and make merry', but instead he's

instructed to wait and not even told when to come back. So
here he is, walking down the steps miserable as a dog, you
know, when the cook has thrown a bucket of water over it;
his tail between his legs and his ears flat against his head.
'No, no,' he is thinking, 'I'll go again and explain that I'm
eating my last scrap of food, and if you don't help, I shall
starve to death, in a manner of speaking.' And so my good
sir, he goes back to the Palace Embankment; there they
tell him: 'No, he's not receiving anyone, come back tomorrow.' The next day it's the same story; and the doorman
hardly deigns to look at him. Meanwhile of those blue notes
he had there's now only one left in his pocket. Instead of
the cabbage soup, and a big lump of beef for dinner, he
now goes to a stall and buys a piece of herring or a pickled
cucumber and a heel of bread for two kopeks—in short,
the poor fellow is starving and, to make things worse, he
has an appetite like a wolf. He goes past some fancy restau
rant, and the chef, of course, is some sort of foreigner: a
Frenchman or something with a big smile, wearing Dutch
linen, an apron white as the driven snow, preparing some
sort of *fines herbes*, or veal cutlets with truffles—I mean
the sort of mouth-watering delicacies that give you such an
appetite that you could quite simply, so to speak, eat
yourself alive. He goes past the Milyutin shops, and there
he sees this big salmon staring out of the window, cherries
at five rubles apiece, a monster watermelon, the size of a
carriage, poking out of the window, so to speak and looking for some idiot to come along and pay a hundred rubles
for it—in a word, at every turn there's such temptation
that his mouth waters, and all the while he keeps hearing
the word: 'tomorrow'. So you can well imagine his position:
on the one hand, so to speak, there's salmon and watermelon, and on the other the one and only dish he gets served
is this 'tomorrow'. Finally it's more than the poor fellow
can stand, and he decides to take the place by storm, in a
manner of speaking, whatever the cost. He waits at the
entrance until some other petitioner arrives, and then slips
past, you understand, with some general or other, and
clamps into the reception room on his peg leg. In accordance with his custom the grandee emerges: 'What do you
want? What do you want? Ha!' he exclaims, seeing Kopeikin, 'but have I not already explained to you that you

will have to await a decision?' 'But I beg you, Your Excellency, I do not have a crust of bread to eat.' 'But what can I do? I cannot do a thing for you; for the time being try to do something for yourself, look for a way to earn some money.' 'But, Your Excellency, you can judge for yourself, what money can I earn, when I am missing an arm and a leg?' 'But,' says the dignitary, 'you must agree: I cannot be expected to maintain you at my own expense, can I? I have many wounded petitioners, they all have an equal right... Arm yourself with patience. I can give you my word of honour, that when His Majesty returns, his monarchial kindness will not be denied you.' 'But, Your Excellency, I cannot wait,' says Kopeikin, and he says it quite rudely, you might say. The great man, you understand, is already vexed. And to be sure, when you think that there are generals all round awaiting decisions, instructions; that there are matters of importance, so to speak, affairs of state, requiring the promptest possible action—a moment's delay might be crucial, and here some importunate devil comes along to pester him. 'I am sorry,' he says, 'I have no time... I have more important matters to attend to than yours.' He thus reminds him in this subtle manner, shall I say, that it is time at last for Kopeikin to leave. But my Kopeikin—it's the hunger, you know, spurring him on, says: 'As you will, Your Excellency. I shall not leave this place until you give me your decision.' Well! You can imagine: talking back like that to a grandee who has only to say the word and you'll be sent flying so far the devil himself would never find you again. If an official only one rank below us spoke like that, we would already count it as insolence. But look at the difference here, what a divide: a General-en-chef, and some Captain Kopeikin or other! Ninety rubles and nought! The General only glares in answer, but his glare shoots fire no worse than a rifle! Anyone would be scorched senseless. But my Kopeikin, imagine it, he doesn't budge, not an inch. 'How dare you!' says the general and grabs him, so to speak, by the scruff of his neck. However, to tell the truth, he still treated him fairly mildly; another in his place would have so blown his top that the entire street would have been topsy-turvy for the next three days, but he only says: 'Very well,' he says, 'if you cannot afford to live here in the capital and you cannot

wait quietly for your fate to be decided then I shall have
to deport you at the state's expense. Call the courier! Take
him to his place of residence!' Next thing the army courier,
you understand, is standing there: seven foot tall in
his stockinged feet, massive great fists, you can imagine,
designed by nature herself for teaching coachmen—I mean,
a real knocker-out of teeth... So they grab him, poor soul,
and bundle him into a cart, with the army courier. 'Well,'
thinks Kopeikin, 'at least I shan't have to pay my own
travelling expenses, there's that to be grateful for.' So there
he is, my god sir, riding at the courier's expense, and there,
as he rides with his courier, he reasons to himself: 'So the
general tells me I must find the means to help myself: very
well,' he says, 'I'll find the means!' Well, how eventually
they got him to where they were taking him, and where
precisely they took him, no one has any idea. So, you see,
all news of Captain Kopeikin finally sank in the river of
oblivion, in some Lethe or other, as the poets call it. But
this, gentlemen, this is only the beginning, so to speak, of the
thread, the start of the story. We do not know where Kopeikin had got to; but less than two months later a band of robbers appears in the Ryazan forests, and who do you think,
my good sir, is the robber chief? Why, none other than..."

"Forgive me for interrupting, Ivan Andreyevich," the
chief of police broke in suddenly, "but surely Captain
Kopeikin, as you said yourself, is missing an arm and a leg,
while Chichikov..."

Here the postmaster gasped and struck his forehead with
the full force of his hand, calling himself an ox, in the full
hearing of all. He could not understand how this circumstance had not struck him at the very commencement of his
tale, and confessed that there was much truth in the proverb: "The Russian is wisest after the event." The very
next minute, however, he recovered his cunning and tried
to get off the hook by pointing out that in England great
progress had been made in mechanics, as could be seen
from the newspapers, and someone had invented wooden
legs that were so fashioned that the wearer needed only
touch a hidden spring and these legs would carry him off
to heaven only knows where.

But everyone was highly sceptical that Chichikov might
be Captain Kopeikin, and they agreed that the postmaster's

guess was too wide of the mark. However, not to be out-shone, and inspired by the astute deduction of the post-master, they made suggestions that were perhaps even more far-fetched. Out of the many ingenious-enough surmi-ses, one in particular was even strange to relate: might Chi-chikov not perhaps be Napoleon in disguise? For the English had always envied Russia her vastness, and there had been cartoons depicting a Russian speaking with an Englishman. The Englishman stands holding a dog behind him on a lead, and the dog is meant to be Napoleon: "You look out," says the Englishman, "if you step out of line I'll let this dog loose on you!"—and so now, perhaps, they had indeed released him from the island of St Helena and he had made his way to Russia, pretending to be Chichikov, but in fact not being Chichikov at all.

Not that the officials believed this to be true, but just the same they thought about it, and when each of them reviewed the matter for himself, he found that Chichikov's face, if he were to turn and stand sideways, was very like Napoleon's portrait. The chief of police, who had fought in the campaign of 1812 and had seen Napoleon in the flesh, had to admit that in height he was no taller than Chi-chikov, and that in the shape of his figure Napoleon was also not what you could call overfat, nor yet was he exact-ly thin. Perhaps some readers will regard all this as impro-bable; the author would also be prepared to gratify them by dismissing it all; but, whether we like it or not, every-thing took place precisely as we have recounted, and it is all the more astonishing since this town was not in the backwoods but, on the contrary, not far from both capi-tals. We should remember, however, that all this happened shortly after the glorious expulsion of the French. At that time all our landowners, officials, merchants, shop-assis-tants, and every other class of literate and even illiterate persons became, at least for the space of eight years, pas-sionate politicians. The *Moscow Gazette* and the *Son of the Motherland* were avidly devoured and reached their last reader in pieces, no longer good for anything. Instead of the questions: "How much did you get for your oats, old chap?" or "What use did you make of yesterday's fall of snow?" they would ask: "What's new in the papers, they haven't let Napoleon off his island again, have they?"

The merchants greatly feared such an eventuality, for they implicitly believed the prediction of a certain prophet, who had been incarcerated for the last three years; the prophet arrived from heaven knows where clad in bast shoes and an uncured sheepskin coat, that stank dreadfully of rotten fish, and proclaimed that Napoleon was the Antichrist and was being held by a stone chain, behind six walls and seven seas, but that eventually he would break his chains and take possession of the entire world. The prophet was duly put in gaol for his prophecy, but the deed was done and the merchants were now totally disturbed. For a long time thereafter, even after the most profitable transactions, when the merchants went to the inn to finalise the deal over a glass of tea, they would discuss the Antichrist. Many officials and even the landed gentry involuntarily found themselves thinking about it, and, infected by the mysticism which, as everyone knows, was then greatly in vogue, ascribed some special significance to each letter of the word "Napoleon"; many even discovered the apocalyptic numbers* in them. Small wonder then that the officials should automatically have pondered this point; they soon came to their senses, however, realising that their imaginations had run away with them and that all this was too wide of the mark. They thought and thought, talked and talked, and finally decided that it would not be a bad idea to question Nozdryov thoroughly. Since he had been the first to bring up the story of the dead souls and was, as the saying goes, thick as thieves with Chichikov, it would seem that he must surely know something of the circumstances of his life, and it was worth trying again, therefore, to see what Nozdryov had to say.

They are strange folk, these officials, and so are all other professions: after all, they knew only too well that Nozdryov was a liar, that you could not believe a word he said, not even in trifling matters, and yet he was the very one to whom they resorted. What a strange creature man is! He does not believe in God, but he does believe that if the

---

Apocalyptic numbers—during the war of 1812 when Napoleon's armies invaded Russia, some mystically-inclined Russian patriots translated Napoleon's name into numerals and arrived at 666 the number of the Beast (*Revelation*, Chapter. 13, verse 18).

bridge of his nose itches he is definitely going to die; he
disdains to read the creation of a poet, as clear as day and
imbued with harmony and the lofty wisdom of simplicity,
yet he pounces eagerly on a book in which some wiseacre
has hashed everything up, spun a lot of nonsense, bent and
twisted nature inside out. He will love this book and will
shout from the rooftops: "This is it, here is true knowledge of the mysteries of the heart!" All his life long he de-
spises doctors, and he ends up going to some old crone
who cures by whispering spells and spitting curses or, better still, devises some concoction of his own out of all sorts
of rubbish, which, God knows why, he imagines to be the
very treatment he needs for his illness. Of course, to some
extent the officials can be excused because of their truly
difficult position. A drowning man, as the saying goes, will
even clutch at a straw, and he does not have the presence
of mind at such a moment to realise that whilst a fly might
just be able to ride along on the straw, he weighs almost
four poods, if not five; but he does not reason clearly at
such moments and he clutches at his straw. Thus, too, did
our gentlemen now clutch at Nozdryov. The chief of police at once wrote him a note, inviting him to a soirée that
evening, and the constable, a handsome, ruddy-cheeked fellow in jack-boots, promptly ran off at full gallop, steady-
ing his sword with his hand, to Nozdryov's lodgings. Nozdryov was occupied with a most important matter; for four
days he had remained closeted in his room, admitting no
one and receiving his meals through the hatch; he had even
lost weight and gone a greenish colour. The matter he was
occupied with demanded the closest attention: he had
to select from hundreds of decks of cards, two decks on
which he could depend as on the most loyal of friends.
There was still enough work to keep him busy for another
two weeks; throughout this period Porfiry was under instructions to groom the mastiff puppy by brushing his
tummy with a special brush and washing him with soap
three times a day. Nozdryov was extremely angry that his
privacy had been invaded; his first reaction was to send the
constable to the devil, but when he read in the governor's
note that there might be some profit in the evening,
because they were expecting some greenhorn at the gathering, he at once relented, briskly locked up his room, dressed

in the first clothes that came to hand, and set off as summoned. The evidence, depositions and hypotheses furnished by Nozdryov were so drastically opposite to those arrived at by the officials, that even their latest surmises were confounded. This was most decidedly a man who did not even admit the possibility of doubt; all the shakiness and timidity of their own surmises were matched by the firmness and certainty of his. He responded to all the points without a moment's hesitation, declaring that Chichikov had bought up dead souls to the value of several thousand rubles and that he had sold him some himself, seeing no reason not to; to the question whether Chichikov might be a spy after some piece of intelligence, Nozdryov replied that he _was_ a spy, that even while they were still at school together, he had been called a tell-tale and had been given a hiding by his school-fellows, of whom Nozdryov had been one, so that afterwards they had to apply two hundred and forty leeches to his temples alone— actually, he had meant to say forty, but the two hundred somehow came out by itself. To the question whether he might be a forger of banknotes Nozdryov replied that he was, and took the opportunity to recount an anecdote about Chichikov's extraordinary dexterity: how, when it was discovered that there were counterfeit notes to the value of two million in his house, the house was sealed off and a guard was set on it, with two soldiers at each door, and how Chichikov substituted them all overnight so that the very next day, when they unsealed the house, they found that all the notes were genuine. In the question whether it was true that Chichikov was plotting to abduct the governor's daughter and whether it was true that he himself had undertaken to help and participate in the plot, Nozdryov replied that he had helped, and that if it had not been for him nothing would have come of it, but here he suddenly realised that he was lying quite without purpose and that he could easily land himself in serious trouble, but he was by now quite unable to stay his tongue. This was difficult anyway, because such interesting details were suggesting themselves, quite spontaneously, which it was utterly impossible to resist: he even named the village where the wedding was to take place, namely the village of Trukhmachovka; the priest, Father Sidor, was to be paid seventy-five rubles for the service, but even for that much he would never have agreed if Nozdryov had not put the wind up him, threatening to denounce him for having married the corn-chandler Mikhail to his own cousin, and if he had not offered Chichikov the use of his own carriage and arranged fresh horses at all the posting stations. He went into such detail that he started giving the coachmen's names. The officials hinted at the Napoleon version, but were sorry they did, because Nozdryov spun such a cock-and-bull story, which did not sound like anything at all, let alone the truth, that the officials merely sighed and drew away. Only the chief of police persevered, and sat on for a long time listening in the hope that there might be something later, but at last he too shrugged and said: "What the devil is all this!" And everyone agreed that however hard you work at your bull you still won't get any milk out of him. So the officials were left in an even worse position than before, and ended up by agreeing that there was absolutely no way of finding out what exactly Chichikov was. One thing was clear, and that concerned human nature: a person might be prudent, sagacious and sensible in all matters concerning other people, but not himself, how judicious, how decisive the advice he gives others in difficulties! "What a quick thinker!" cries the crowd. "What a strong character!" But let some disaster befall this quick thinker and may he find himself in difficulties, and you will wonder what happened to his character, the pillar of strength is gone completely and instead there is a wretched little coward, a small, weak child, or simply a nannygoat, as Nozdryov would say.

For some unknown reason all these discussions, theories and rumours had the strongest effect on the poor prosecutor. They had such an effect on him that when he arrived home he started to think and think and suddenly, for no earthly reason, he went and died. Perhaps it was a stroke or some other seizure, but suddenly, as he was sitting in his chair, he just keeled over. After some wringing of hands and cries of "Oh my God!", the doctor was sent for to let his blood, but it was now obvious to all that the prosecutor was no more than a soulless cadaver. Only then did people realise with condolence that the dead man had indeed had a soul, although in his modesty he had never displayed it. And yet the appearance of death is just as awesome in a little man as it is in a great one: someone who so recently was walking around, moving, playing whist, signing various documents and was so frequently seen amongst the officials with his bushy eyebrows and twitching eye, was now laid out on a table, and the tic was quite gone from his left eye, although one eyebrow still remained raised somewhat interrogatively. Exactly what the deceased was asking, whether it was why he had died or why he had lived, God alone knows.

But still all this is absurd! This is quite at odds with everything! It is impossible that the officials could have so frightened themselves; that they should have dreamt up so much nonsense, strayed so far from the truth when even a child could have seen what was going on! This will be the reaction of many readers, who will reproach the author for his absurdities or call the poor officials fools, for man is generous with the word "fool" and is happy to oblige his neighbour twenty times a day with the appellation. If, out of ten aspects of your character, there is but one that is stupid you will be recognised for a fool despite the nine good ones. It is easy for readers to pass judgement, as they gaze from their untroubled height commanding a full view of everything happening below, where man can only see the object immediately before him. And in all the history of mankind there are many entire centuries which, one would think, could be struck out and eradicate as unnecessary. Many have been the errors made in the world, which, it seems, even a child would not make today. How crooked, dark, narrow, impassable, and misleading have been the paths followed by mankind in its striving after the eternal truth, when the straight road lay open before it, like the road leading to the splendid temple, appointed as a palace for the Tsar! It is broader and more luxurious than all the other roads, bathed in sunlight by day and illuminated by torches all night, yet people streamed past in the Stygian dark. And however often they have had the way pointed out to them by the good sense that descends from heaven, still they managed to fall by the wayside and wander from the true path, to stray once again in broad daylight into the impassable thicket, to confuse one another, and, dragging themselves in pursuit of will-o'-the-wisps, succeeded in reaching the edge of the abyss, to ask each other in horror: where is the way out, where is the road? The current generation sees everything clearly and marvels at the errors, ridicules the folly of its ancestors, failing to observe that this chronicle is illuminated by heavenly fire, that every letter in it cries out, that from every direction a piercing finger is pointed towards it, towards the current generation; but the current generation merely laughs and with self-satisfaction and proudly embarks on a series of new errors, over which future generations will one day laugh in their turn.

Chichikov knew absolutely nothing about all this. As if by ill-design at this very time he had developed a slight cold—accompanied by toothache and a sore throat—of the sort so liberally dispensed by the climate of many of our provincial capitals. Lest his life might be ended somehow, God forbid, without leaving heirs, he decided it would be best to stay indoors for about three days. During this confinement he repeatedly gargled with milk and figs, afterwards eating the figs, and keeping a little bolster of camomile and camphor tied to his cheek. To pass the time he compiled several new and detailed lists of all the peasants he had bought, read the novel *La Duchesse de la Vallière* which he found in his suitcase, re-examined the various objects and notes in his casket, ran through some of them once more, and was immensely bored. He simply could not understand what it might portend that not one of the town officials had called on him, not even once, to ask after his health, when so recently their droshkies had frequently stood outside the hotel—either the postmaster's or the prosecutor's or the president's. He merely shrugged his shoulders as he paced about the room. At last he began to feel better and was delighted beyond words at the possibility of stepping out into the fresh air. Without further delay he set about his toilet: opening his little box, he poured some hot water into a glass, took out his brush and soap and arranged his face for shaving, an operation which, to be sure, was long overdue, because, as he tested his beard with his fingers and stared into the mirror he exclaimed: "Phew, what thickets we have growing here!" Indeed, his cheeks and chin were covered by a fairly dense growth. After shaving, he dressed himself swiftly and briskly, all but jumping out of his pants in his haste. At last he was dressed and, dousing himself in eau de Cologne and wrapping himself up warmly, he ventured forth into the street, with a scarf prudently tied around his face. His emergence, like that of any person who has recovered from an illness, was in the nature of a true celebration. Everything his eye lit upon seemed to smile back at him: the houses, and the passing peasants, who were, truth to tell, rather glum, and some of whom had already had fights with their fellows. Chichikov decided to pay his first call on the governor. All sorts of ideas came into his head as he made his way there; the blonde hovered in his memory, his imagination started to play mild pranks and he then began once more to joke and poke gentle fun at himself. It was in this sort of mood that he found himself before the governor's house. He was on the point of shrugging off his overcoat in the entrance hall, when the doorman astonished him with a most unexpected statement:

"I've instructions not to admit you!"

"What, what do you mean, you clearly do not recognise me! Take a close look at my face!" said Chichikov.

"How can I not recognise you, it's not the first time I've seen you," said the doorman. "But you're the very one I'm ordered not to admit, all the others can come in."

"You don't say! Why? Why on earth?"

"That's the orders, so, I suppose, there's a reason," said the doorman. After this he adopted a free and easy pose before Chichikov, dropping that attentive air with which he used to hasten forward to take his coat. He seemed to be thinking as he looked at Chichikov: "Uh-huh! Seeing as you're to be chased off this porch you must be just riff-raff!"

"I can't understand it!" said Chichikov to himself, and promptly set off to the house of the president, but this latter was so embarrassed on seeing him that he was unable to string two words together, and he babbled such a lot of rubbish that they both felt quite awkward. Chichikov took his leave, but however much he racked his brains on the way back in an effort to grasp what the president may have meant and to what his words may have referred, he remained quite baffled. He then called on the others: the chief of police, the vice-governor, the postmaster, but they all either would not receive him or did so very strangely, speaking in such a stilted and incomprehensible manner, becoming so embarrassed and prattling such senseless drivel, that he began to doubt their very sanity. He attempted to make a few more calls if only to ascertain the reason for all this, but no reason was forthcoming. Like one in a trance he roamed aimlessly about the town, quite unable to decide whether he had lost his mind, or the officials had lost theirs, whether all this was a dream, or whether reality had concocted these ravings which were worse than any nightmare. It was already late, almost dusk, when he returned to his room which he had left in such excellent spirits, and out of sheer boredom he called for some tea. Musing in an incoherent fashion about the strangeness of his position, he started to pour the tea when the door was suddenly flung open, and there to his astonishment stood Nozdryov.

"As the proverb says: to a true friend seven versts is only a stone's throw!" he said, taking off his cap. "I was walking past and saw the light in the window, so I said to myself I'll just pop in, he's probably not asleep. Aha! We're drinking tea, are we? Excellent! I'll gladly have a cup: I ate so much rubbish for dinner today I can feel a riot beginning in my stomach. Be a good fellow and order a pipe for me! Where's your pipe?"

"But you know I do not smoke a pipe," answered Chichikov drily.

"Nonsense, you think I don't know that you smoke like a chimney? Hey! Tell me again, what's your man called? Hey, Vakhramey, listen!"

"He's not Vakhramey, he's Petrushka."

"What? But how come you had a Vakhramey before?"

"I have never had a Vakhramey."

"But of course, it's Deryobin who has a Vakhramey. Just imagine how lucky Deryobin is: his aunt fell out with her son because he married a serf, and so she's now made her entire estate over to him. I keep thinking how nice it would be to have an aunt like that for the future! But tell me, brother, why are you being so stand-offish and not calling on anyone? Of course, I know you are sometimes busy with various learned pursuits, you like to read—" (but why Nozdryov should have concluded that our hero was busy with various learned pursuits and liked to read, I must confess, we have no idea, and Chichikov even less). "Why, Chichikov, brother, if you could only have seen ... now that would most definitely have been food for your satirical mind—" (why Chichikov should have had a satirical mind is also unknown). "Just imagine, brother, we were playing cards at Likhachov, the merchant, and what a laugh we had! That old Perependev, who was playing with me says, 'If only Chichikov were here, I'd really show him...'" (yet Chichikov did not know Perependev from a bar of soap). "But you must admit, brother, that you did play a very dirty trick on me that time, do you remember, when we were playing draughts, because I'd won, you know... Yes, brother, you quite simply bamboozled me. But I'm like that, dammit, I really can't nurse a grudge. The other day at the president's house... Oh yes! Of course, I must tell you, everyone in the town has turned against you; they think that you make counterfeit money, they started pestering me, but I stood by you, firm as a rock, I told them that we were at school together and I knew your father; well, I have to admit it, I spun them one hell of a yarn."

"I— making counterfeit money?" exclaimed Chichikov, rising from his chair.

"But why did you have to give them such a fright, all the same?" continued Nozdryov. "The devil knows, they are beside themselves with terror; they have you down as a brigand and a spy... The prosecutor has died of fright, his funeral's tomorrow. Won't you be there? To tell you the truth, they're all scared of the new governor-general, in case there may be trouble because of you; but I'm of the opinion that if the new governor-general starts looking down his nose and giving himself airs and graces he won't be able to do a blind thing with the gentry. Gentlefolk require a cordial approach, isn't that so? Of course, he can always shut himself away in his office and never throw a single ball, but what's the good of that? He'll gain nothing that way. But all the same, Chichikov, truth be told, that's a dicy plan you've hatched."

"What dicy plan?" asked Chichikov uneasily.

"Why, abducting the governor's daughter. I must admit, I was expecting it, honest to God, I was! The very first time I saw the two of you together at the ball, well, I said to myself, old Chichikov's up to something, all right... But I don't think much of your choice, I must say, I can't see anything special about her. But there's this one girl, a relation of Bikusov's, his sister's daughter, now there's a pretty girl for you! You might even say: a card from a different deck!"

"But what is all this, what are you talking about? Abducting the governor's daughter, what on earth?" said Chichikov, his eyes starting from his head.

"Now come on, brother, you are a dark horse! I must confess that's the real reason I called on you: if you wish I'm prepared to assist you. If you like, I'll be your best man, I'll provide the carriage and change of horses, only on one condition: you'll have to lend me three thousand. Brother, I need the money desperately!"

Throughout Nozdryov's blather Chichikov repeatedly rubbed his eyes, wanting to ensure that he was not dreaming. Forging of banknotes, abduction of the governor's daughter, death of the prosecutor, for which it seemed he was responsible, arrival of the new governor-general—all this threw him into a state of great alarm. "Well, seeing this is the turn events have taken," he thought, "there's no point in hanging about any longer, it's time to get out of here without further delay."

He got rid of Nozdryov as soon as he could, and at once summoned Selifan and ordered him to be ready at dawn, so that they could make their departure from the town no later than six in the morning, and that everything should be prepared: the chaise greased, and so on and so forth. Selifan declared: "Yessir, Pavel Ivanovich!" but still remained standing by the door for several minutes, as if rooted to the spot. The master then ordered Petrushka to pull his suitcase out from under the bed, where it had already gathered a considerable layer of dust, and together they stuffed in everything that came to hand: shirts, clean and dirty linen, boot trees, a calendar... All this was thrown in any old how: he was determined to be packed that every evening, so that nothing might delay them in the morning. Selifan, having stood for a couple of minutes by the door, withdrew from the room very slowly. Slowly, unimaginably slowly, he descended the stairs, leaving footprints with his wet boots on the battered steps and scratching the back of his head. What did this scratching mean? And what does scratching mean in general? Could it have been regret that he would not now have that drink at the pub with his new friend in the unsightly sheepskin coat, belted with a sash, or had he already found himself a sweetheart in this new place and there would be no more standing at her gate and discreetly holding her dainty white hands at an hour when the town was pulling the mantle of night over its weary shoulders, when a hefty chap in a red tunic was strumming his balalaika before the assembled household servants and a mixed crowd of working folk engaged in quiet gossip at the end of the day's labours? Or was it merely regret at leaving his nice warm spot in the bustling kitchen, where he slept wrapped in his sheepskin, next to the stove, with his cabbage soup and a nice fresh, townbaked pie, in order to drive once more in the rain, and the slush, to face all the adversities of the road? God knows, we can never guess. Many and various are the things that are meant when the Russian peasant scratches the back of his head.

CHAPTER ELEVEN

However, nothing worked out the way Chichikov had planned. To begin with, he awoke later than he had intended—that was the first unpleasantness. He at once sent to inquire if the chaise was harnessed up and everything was ready; but it turned out that the chaise was not yet harnessed and that nothing was ready. This was the second unpleasantness. He lost his temper, he wanted to administer something in the nature of a thrashing to our friend Selifan, and only waited impatiently to hear what excuse the man would give him. Soon Selifan appeared in the doorway and his master had the pleasure of listening to those very same speeches which are customarily heard from servants when a hasty departure has to be made.

"Well, you see, Pavel Ivanovich, the horses will have to be shod."

"Ah, you dolt! You dunderhead! Why didn't you mention it before? I suppose you didn't have time?"

"Well, yes, there was time... And there's also the wheel.

See, Pavel Ivanovich, the rim will have to be pulled good and tight, because the road's so bumpy now, and you find such big potholes everywhere... And also, if I may say so, the front of the chaise is all rickety, so it probably won't make two stages now."

"You scoundrel!" screamed Chichikov, flinging up his hands in vexation, and stepping up so close to Selifan that the coachman recoiled somewhat and stood aside, afraid he might receive a box on the ears from his master. "Are you trying to kill me? Speak up, are you? Trying to cut my throat? Planning to cut my throat somewhere on the highway, you brigand, you confounded dunderhead, you sea monster! Are you? Are you? You've been sitting here on your backside for three whole weeks, haven't you? And never a peep, you dissolute wretch, and now at the last moment you come out with it! When everything else is almost ready: we only have to get in and drive away. So you have to play your dirty trick, do you? Because you knew it before, didn't you? Answer me! You knew, didn't you?"

"I did," answered Selifan, hanging his head.

"So why didn't you say so then?"

To this question Selifan found no answer, but merely hung his head still lower and seemed to be saying to himself: "Now, how did this come about: I did know, but I never said!"

"And now you can go and fetch the smith, and make sure everything's ready in two hours. Do you hear? In two hours, and no more, or else I'll ... I'll ... I'll bend you in a hoop and tie you in a knot!" Our hero was fearfully enraged.

Selifan was on the point of turning to go and carry out his master's order, but he stopped and said: "There's one other thing, sir, it's that dappled stallion, it'd be better to sell him, you know, sir, because, Pavel Ivanovich, he's a complete rogue: a terrible horse that one, he just gets in the way."

"Fine! So I'll run straight to the market this very minute and sell him!"

"As God is my witness, Pavel Ivanovich, he only looks useful, but in truth he's a most cunning horse; with a horse like that you'll never..."

"Fool! When I want to sell it, I'll sell it. Who's asking you? Just you listen to me: if you don't bring me the blacksmiths right now and if everything is not ready in two hours, I'll give you such a thrashing... You won't be able to see the nose on your face... Off with you! Go!" Selifan departed.

Chichikov was by now in a terrible mood and threw down the sabre which he carried with him on his travels to instil the proper fear into the right quarters. For a little over a quarter of an hour he did battle with the blacksmiths before coming to an agreement, because the blacksmiths, as is customary, were thorough scoundrels and, once they had caught on that the work was urgent, stuck out for exactly six times the normal rate. No matter how Chichikov fumed and seethed, calling them swindlers, brigands, highway robbers, even hinting at the Day of Judgement, the smiths were adamant: they stood as firm as a rock—and not only did they stick to their price they spent not two hours on the job, but no less than five and a half. All this time he had the pleasure of savouring those delightful moments, familiar to any traveller, when everything is packed away in the suitcase and all that is left in the room are bits of string, scraps of paper and other assorted rubbish, when a man is neither travelling already, nor staying put, when he looks out of the window at the people plodding along, discussing their paltry affairs and rising their eyes with a sort of silly curiosity to glance at him before continuing on their way, and all this only further exacerbates the discomfiture of the poor, marooned traveller. Everything around him, everything he sees: the little stall opposite his window, and the head of the old woman living in the house across the road who comes up to her window with its short little curtains—everything is loathsome to him; yet he cannot tear himself away from the window. He remains standing there, either lost in reverie or once again turning his numbed attention to all that moves and does not move before him, and with vexation he squashes some fly which buzzes and pounds its wings against the window as his finger descends upon it. But all things come to an end, and at last the long awaited moment was at hand: everything was ready, the front of the chaise had been fixed, the wheel fitted with a new rim, the horses watered, the robber blacksmiths had departed, having counted their rubles and wished the travellers God speed. The chaise was at last harnessed up, two hot loaves were put in with the luggage, Selifan stowed something away in the pocket attached to his coachbox, and finally the hero himself, seen off by the cap-waving waiter, the flunkeys and coachmen from the inn and elsewhere, who had gathered to gape at someone else's master making his departure, and actually never missing a departure, seated himself in the carriage— and the chaise, of the sort travelled in by bachelors, which had stood in the town for so long, and which, quite possibly, has by now sorely tired the reader, finally drove out of the inn gates. "Thank the Lord!" thought Chichikov and crossed himself. Selifan cracked his whip; Petrushka, who had been standing on the step for some time, now climbed up next to him, and our hero making himself more comfortable on his Georgian rug, placing a leather cushion behind his back, squashing the two hot loaves as he did so, the carriage went lurching and bouncing on the cobblestones. It was with a certan indefinable feeling that he beheld the houses, walls, fences and streets, which in turn also seemed to move slowly away, lurching up and down, and which God only knows if he would ever be destined to see again in the course of his life. At the turning into one of the streets the chaise was forced to come to a stop, because the entire length of the street was occupied by an endless funeral procession. Thrusting his head out of the window Chichikov ordered Petrushka to ask who was being buried, and learnt that it was the prosecutor. Filled with disagreeable sensations, he at once hid from view in the corner, pulling up the leather lap-robe and drew the curtains together. While the carriage was thus delayed, Selifan and Petrushka piously doffed their caps and studied the scene with interest to see who was there, driving in what, counting the people on foot and in conveyances, while their master, who had ordered them not to acknowledge or greet any of the lackeys they might know, also started to peek cautiously through the small panes fitted into the leather curtains: walking behind the coffin, bareheaded, were all the town's officials. He was afraid they might recognize his carriage, but their minds were on other things. They did not even engage in small talk as mourners walking behind the hearse usually do. All their thoughts were turned in on themselves: they wondered what the new

Governor-General would be like, how he would get down to business and how he would receive them. The officials were followed by carriages in which rode the ladies in mourning bonnets. From the movement of their lips and hands it was apparent that they were engaged in lively conversation; perhaps they were also talking about the arrival of the new Governor-General and were making surmises about the balls he would give, and were fussing as ever about their scallops and falbalas. The rear of the procession was brought up by several empty droshkies, proceeding in single file, and after them at last there was nothing and our hero was able to proceed. Opening his leather curtains he sighed, and declared from the bottom of his heart: "So there you go, prosecutor! You lived and lived, and then you died! Now they'll print in the papers that he passed away to the grief of his subordinates and of all mankind; a respected citizen, an unparalleled father, an exemplary husband, and they will write all sorts of nonsense; probably adding that he was accompanied to the grave by the weeping of widows and orphans; but to be quite honest, the only remarkable thing about you were your bushy eyebrows." At that he ordered Selifan to go faster and in the meantime thought: "Still, it's a good omen meeting a funeral procession: it's supposed to bring good luck."

By now the chaise had turned on to more deserted streets; soon only the long wooden fences stretched on both sides, presaging the end of the town. Then the cobbled road ended too; the turnpike and the town were behind them, and nothing ahead of them: and on they went. Once again along both sides of the highroad they passed verst poles, they saw station masters, wells, strings of carts, dreary villages with their samovars, womenfolk and a spry bearded inn-keeper, running to the coachyard with oats; a pedestrian who has come from eight hundred versts away in his worn-out bast shoes, small wretched towns with the houses arranged haphazardly, with their little shops, flour barrels, bast shoes, bread loaves and other trifling wares; striped turnpikes; bridges under repair; fields stretching as far as the eye can see on both sides of the road; landowners' broughams; a mounted soldier carrying a green box of lead shot bearing the legend: "such-and-such an artillery battery"; green, yellow and freshly-ploughed black stripes running across the steppes; a song borne from afar; the tops of pine trees in the mist; the ringing of bells fading in the distance; crows as numerous as flies, and an endless horizon... Russia! Russia! I see you, I see you from my wonderful, beautiful far away: how wretched, scattered and uncomfortable is your life, there are no startling marvels of nature, crowned by startling marvels of art to delight or alarm the eye, no cities with lofty, many-windowed palaces, growing out of cliffs, no picturesque trees and ivy, creeping over the houses, none of the roar and eternal spray of waterfalls; the neck is not craned for a look at stone piles, towering massively to an infinite height above; through dark archways set one above the other, and choked with vines, ivy and millions of wild roses, no glimpse is to be had of the eternal contours of radiant mountains in the distance, soaring up into the silvery skies above. Everything in you is open, desolate and level; your squat towns barely protrude in the midst of the plains like dots, like counters; there is nothing to tempt or enchant the onlooker's gaze. But what is this inscrutable, mysterious force that draws me to you? Why do my ears ring unceasingly with your plaintive song, that carries through all your length and breadth, from ocean to ocean? What is in it, in that song? Why does it so beckon, and sob, and tug at the heart? What are those sounds that caress so painfully, steal into my soul and hover about my heart? Russia! What is it you want of me? What is the hidden, inscrutable tie that binds us? Why do you gaze like that, and why is it that everything in you has turned to gaze at me with eyes full of expectation? And yet I stand here motionless, full of bewilderment, and my head is already overshadowed by thunderclouds, heavy with imminent rains, and my mind is numb before your vast spaces. What does this immense expanse portend? Is not here, in you that thought without end should be born, since you yourself are without end? Is not here that the giant of legend is to appear, where there is space for him to launch out and stride about? Terrible is the embrace in which this mighty expanse holds me, terrible the force with which it strikes me to the very core; supernatural the power with which it lights up my vision: Ah! What a sparkling, wondrous expanse, vaster than any there is on earth! Russia!..

"Whoa, whoa! You fool!" Chichikov shouted at Selifan. "You wait, I'll give you a taste of my broadsword!" shouted an army courier with moustaches two feet across who had come galloping up. "Have you no eyes in your head, the devil flay your soul: this is an official carriage!" and like a mirage, the troika vanished in a cloud of dust.

What a strange, enticing, enthralling, marvellous sound there is to the word: the road! And how marvellous it is itself, this road: a bright day, autumn leaves, a nip in the air... Pull your travelling coat tighter about you, your cap down on your ears, and huddle more snugly in your corner! One last time your limbs will convulse with a fit of cold shivers before a delightful warmth envelops you. The horses gallop on... How irresistibly drowsiness creeps over you and your eyelids droop, and you are already dozing when you hear the coachman singing "White the snows", and the wheezing of the horses and the rattle of the wheels, but you are already snoring, as you squash your fellow traveller into his corner. You awake: five stages have passed; the moon, an unfamiliar town, churches with ancient wooden cupolas and black spires, dark timbered and white stone houses. Here and there shafts of moonlight: it is as if white linen kerchiefs have been hung about the walls, along the highroad, and laid down in the streets; they are criss-crossed by the oblique, coal-black shadows; the wooden roofs, illuminated at an angle, gleam like shining metal, and nowhere is there a soul to be seen, all is asleep. Perhaps somewhere, in one little window, a solitary light glimmers: perhaps it is the local cobbler stitching a pair of boots or a baker busy in his bakery—who cares? But the night! Merciful heavens! What a night is being enacted high above! The air, and the sky, far away, high above, in its inaccessible profundity, is so boundless, harmonious and clear. But the cold of the night breathes its freshness right into your eyes and lulls you to sleep, and you are soon dozing and lost in your slumbers, and snoring, and the poor fellow traveller you have squashed into his corner writhes in annoyance, feeling your weight against his body. You awake—and now once again before you there are only fields and the steppe, and nothing more: on all sides there is wasteland, open vistas. A milestone with a number on it flashes by; morning is breaking; a pale golden swathe stretches across the cold white horizon; the wind grows fresher and harsher: wrap that greatcoat more tightly about you! What glorious cold! What marvellous sleep embraces you again! A jolt—and you awake once more. The sun stands high in the sky. "Easy now, easy now!" shouts a voice, the carriage makes its way down a steep incline: below is a broad dam and a wide, clear pond, gleaming like a copper plate in the sun; a village, cottages scattered across the hillside; the cross of the village church sparkling like a star; the chatter of peasants and unbearable pangs of hunger in your belly... O Lord! How marvellous you sometimes are, long, long road! How often, like a drowning, dying man, have I clutched at you, and every time you have magnanimously borne me to safety and rescued me! And how many wonderful designs, poetic fancies have been born in you, how many wonderful impressions experienced!

But our friend Chichikov was also at this time enjoying fancies that were not without poetry. Let us have a look at what he was in fact feeling. At first he did not feel anything at all, and merely kept looking back, anxious to convince himself that he had finally left the town behind him; but when he saw that the town had long since been lost from sight, that no smithies, no mills nor any of those things that are found around towns were visible, and that even the white spires of the stone churches had long since vanished from sight, he turned his attention wholly to the road, looking only to right and to left, and the town of N might not have been in his memory, as if he had travelled through it long ago, in childhood. Finally even the road ceased to hold his attention and he started to close his eyes a little and to drop his head on the cushion. The author must confess that he is quite glad of this, as it gives him an opportunity to say a few things about his hero; for hitherto, as the reader has seen, he has constantly been hindered either by Nozdryov, or by balls, or by ladies, or by the town gossip, or by thousands of those trifles which only reveal themselves as trifles when you put them in a book, but while they happen in the world are regarded as matters of great importance. But let us now set all this completely aside and get right down to business.

It is most doubtful whether the hero we have selected will please our readers. He will not please the ladies, that we can state with certainty, for ladies require a hero to be absolute perfection, and if he has the smallest spiritual or physical blemish, then woe to him! However deeply the author may pry into his soul, however well reflect his image, more clearly than any mirror—and they will still reject him as quite worthless. The very fullness of Chichikov's figure, the very maturity of his years were already greatly to his disadvantage: fullness of figure can never be forgiven a hero, not in any circumstances, and a great many ladies will turn aside, exclaiming: "Pooh, how nasty!" Alas! The author knows all this well, and for all that he still cannot choose as his hero a virtuous man, although ... it may be that in this very story different strings may sound, ones which have not yet been touched, the incalculable wealth of the Russian spirit may yet be displayed, there may appear a man endowed with godlike virtues or else a wondrous Russian maiden, such as cannot be found anywhere else in the world, with all the miraculous beauty of the female soul, woven of magnanimous impulses and selflessness. Then all the virtuous members of other tribes will seem as dead men beside them, just as a book is dead beside the living word! Russian emotions will stir ... and it will be seen how deeply rooted in the Slav nature are those qualities which have merely skated over the surface of the nature of other peoples... But why and to what purpose should we talk about what is to come? It is unseemly for the author, who has long since entered manhood, who has been trained by a stern inner life and the invigorating sobriety of solitude, to forget himself like a callow youth. Everything has its proper turn, and place, and time! All the same, we have not taken a virtuous man as our hero. And we can even say why not. Because it is time, at last, that we give the poor virtuous man a rest; because the words "virtuous man" have lost all meaning on our lips; because the virtuous man has been turned into a horse, and there is no writer who would not ride him, urging him forward with his whip or anything else that comes to hand; because the virtuous man has been worn so thin that he no longer retains even a shadow of his virtue, and of his body there remain only skin and bones, because the appeal to the virtuous man is sheer hypocrisy; because the virtuous man is not respected. No, it is time at last to put the rogue in harness too.

So, let us put the rogue in harness! Modest and obscure are the origins of our hero. His parents were gentlefolk, but whether they were noblemen of hereditary lineage or through personal merit, God only knows. He did not look at all like them: at least, a female relative who was present at his birth, a short, squat woman of the type usually called puddle ducks, took the child in her arms and exclaimed: "Hasn't come out at all as I expected! He should have taken after his granny on the mother's side, that would have been better, but this one's just like the saying: 'not like father, not like mother, from a family another'." At first life looked on him in a sour and unwelcoming way, as through a blind, snow-encrusted window: no friend or playmate in childhood! A poky room with little windows, opened neither in winter nor in summer, a father who was in poor health and always went about in a long dressing gown with a lambskin lining and knitted slippers worn on bare feet, who was forever sighing as he walked about the room, and spitting into a sand-box standing in the corner; the boy having to sit for hours on end at the writing table, quill in hand, ink on his fingers and even on his lips, the copybook forever before him, with texts such as: "Do not lie, be obedient unto your elders and foster virtue in your heart"; the interminable scraping and shuffling of the slippers around the room, the familiar and invariably stern voice saying: "Playing the fool again!" every time the boy, bored by the monotony of his task, added a little hook or tail to a letter; and that eternally familiar, always unpleasant sensation when these words were followed by long fingers reaching out from behind and tweaking the malcreant's ear very painfully. Such is the wretched picture of his earliest childhood, of which he barely retained the vaguest of memories. But everything changes swiftly and briskly in life: and one day, in the first rays of spring sunshine, when the rivers burst their banks, the father took his son off in a cart, pulled by a skewbald mare, of the kind known by horse traders as magpie; the driver was a small hunchback coachman, father of the one and only serf family that belonged to the Chichikovs who performed practically all the duties in the house. They trundled along for something over a day and a half, they slept by the roadside, forded a river, fed on cold pie and roast mutton, and only reached town on the morning of the third day. The boy was dazzled by the unexpected magnificence of the streets, which caused him to gape, openmouthed for several minutes. Then together with the cart the magpie plunged straight into a large pothole, which marked the beginning of a narrow alley, running steeply downhill and deep in mud; here she toiled away lengthily with all her might and main, wading through the mud, whipped on by the hunchback and by the master himself, until finally she hauled them up the side of a hill into a small courtyard before an old cottage, with two blossoming apple-trees in front, and a little garden at the back, a tiny, wretched plot, boasting only a rowan, and some elder bushes. At the back of this garden was a little wooden shack, with one narrow, dark window, and roofed with shingle. Here lived a relative of theirs, a decrepit old woman, who still walked to market every day and then spread her stockings before the samovar to dry; she patted the boy on the cheek and admired his chubbiness. Here he was to remain and to go every day to the local school. The father stopped only the night and in the morning set off on his homeward journey. On their parting no tears were shed by the parental eyes; a fifty-kopek coin was given the boy for expenses and sweetmeats and, which is far more important, a wise admonition: "Mind you learn your lessons, Pavlusha, don't play the fool and don't get into scrapes, but above all please your teachers and superiors. So long as you please your superiors it does not matter if you are no good at learning and God has not endowed you with talent, you will still go far and outstrip all the others. Do not associate with your schoolfellows; they will teach you no good; but if you must, then associate with those that are richer so that when the occasion arises they may be useful to you. Do not treat or give freely to anyone, but rather conduct yourself in such a manner that others will treat you, and, most important, be careful with your money and save every kopek: money is the most reliable thing in the world. A playmate or friend will lead you a merry dance and will be the first to betray you in times of trouble, but a kopek will never betray you, whatever trouble you might be in. With that kopek you can do everything and achieve everything in this world." After delivering this admonition, the father took his leave of the son and trailed homewards in the cart behind his magpie, and Chichikov never saw him again, but his words and admonitions remained deeply engraved in his soul.

The very next day Pavlusha started attending classes. He did not reveal any particular aptitude for any subject; he was distinguished mostly by his assiduity and neatness; but, on the other hand, he did display great intelligence in another respect, in matters practical. He quickly saw the lie of the land and his conduct towards his fellows was precisely such that they would give him treats, whilst he not only never treated them, but sometimes, after concealing the delicacies in question, would even sell them back to them afterwards. While still a child he developed the ability to deny himself everything. Of the fifty kopeks given him by his father he did not spend a single kopek; on the contrary, that very same year he even added to it, demonstrating an almost uncanny resoursefulness: he moulded a bullfinch out of wax, painted it and sold it for a very good price. For some time thereafter he embarked on other speculative ventures, to wit: he would buy various comestibles at the market and choose a seat in class near the richer boys, and then as soon as he observed that a classmate was becoming uneasy—the first sign of approaching hunger— he would as it were accidentally pull out from under his desk the corner of a honey cake or a bun and, having thus excited his neighbour's desires, would name a price in proportion to his appetite. For two months he toiled away tirelessly in his room with a mouse, which he had confined to a small wooden cage, and he finally succeeded in getting the mouse to stand on its hind legs, to lie down and get up again on command, and then he sold it for a nice sum. When he had amassed a total of five rubles he sewed them up in a little bag and started to fill another bag. With respect to his superiors he behaved even more astutely. No one could sit in class more quietly than he. We should note that his teacher was a great lover of silence and good behaviour and could not abide pert and clever boys; he always suspected them of making fun of him. It was sufficient for any boy, who had suffered a reprimand for sharpness of wit, to make the slightest movement or even accidentally to twitch an eyebrow, suddenly to receive the full brunt of his rage. He would persecute and punish him mercilessly. "I shall thrash the arrogance and disobedience out of you, my young friend!" the teacher would say, "I know you through and through, better than you know yourself. I'll have you kneeling in the corner! I'll have you going without dinner!" And the poor innocent would rub his sore knees and go hungry until supper. "Talents and gifts? That's all a lot of poppy-cock," the teacher would say, "I look only at behaviour. I will give full marks in all subjects to someone who doesn't know a thing but behaves himself commendably; but if I detect a rebellious or mocking attitude in a boy I shall give him nought, even if he makes Solon look like a dunce!" Such were the words of their teacher, who passionately hated the fabulist Krylov for saying: "You can have your fill of drink, just so long as you can think", and he loved to tell, with a look of relish on his face and in his eyes, how in the school where he had taught previously, there had been such silence that you could hear the beating of a fly's wings; that not one of his pupils ever once, throughout the entire years, coughed or blew his nose in class and that it was impossible to tell, until the bell went, whether there was anybody in the class or not. Chichikov swiftly caught on to the spirit of this teacher and realised what his conduct must be. He never moved an eye or twitched an eyebrow throughout the entire lesson, however much the boys behind pinched him; as soon as the bell rang he would dash forward to give the teacher his cap before anyone else could get there (the teacher wore one of those warm caps with ear-flaps); having given him his cap he would be the first to leave the classroom and would endeavour to meet his teacher at least three times on his way home, never failing to doff his cap. His scheme was an unqualified success. Throughout his time at the school he was regarded as an exemplary pupil, and when he left he was given full marks in every subject, a certificate and a book prize with the words "For Exemplary Application and Good Conduct" engraved in gold letters. Once out of the school he turned into a rather attractive youth, with a chin that already needed shaving. At this time his father died. His inheritance consisted of four irreparably worn-out vests, two old frock-coats lined with lambskin and a small sum of money. His father, it seemed, was only good at advising others to save their kopeks, but had not saved many himself. Chichikov at once sold the dilapidated old house with its miserable patch of land for a thousand rubles, and moved his family of serfs to the town, planning to establish himself there and enter the civil service. At this same time their poor teacher, that lover of silence and commendable behaviour, was sacked from the school for stupidity or some other failing. From grief the teacher took to the bottle; finally he no longer even had the money to buy drink; sick and helpless he was starving somewhere in an abandoned, unheated hovel. His former pupils, the pert and clever lads, whom he always suspected of disobedience and arrogance, when they learnt of his plight, at once made a collection for him, even selling many of their own essentials. The sole exception was Pavlusha Chichikov, who pleaded poverty and offered a five-kopek piece which his schoolfellows at once threw back at him, saying: "You lickpenny!" The poor teacher hid his face in his hands when he heard about his former pupils' kindness; the tears flowed from his dimmed eyes as from those of a helpless child. "The good Lord has brought me to tears on my death-bed," he said in a feeble voice and sighed deeply, and when he was told about Chichikov, he added: "For shame, Pavlusha! See how a person can change! To think what a well-behaved boy he was, nothing wild about him, as smooth as silk! He took me in, he really took me in!"

We cannot, however, say that our hero was by nature so harsh and severe, and that his feelings were so blunted that he knew neither pity nor compassion; he felt them both, he would even have liked to help, but not with a large sum and so that he would not have to touch the money which was not intended to be touched; in a word, his father's admonition, save the kopeks, had fallen on fertile soil. But he did not love money for its own sake; he was not possessed by miserliness and stinginess. No, it was not these that spurred him on: he nursed the dream of a life of pleasure, a life with all the comforts; carriages, an excellently appointed house, delicious dinners—such was the constant substance of this dream. It was in order that eventually, in the fulness of time, he might savour all this in reality that he saved the kopeks so carefully, stingily denying them both to himself and others until that time should come. When a rich man flew past him in a splendid droshky, pulled by richly harnessed trotters, he would stand rooted to the spot and then, coming to his senses as if after a long sleep, he would say: "To think he was a mere copy-clerk, wearing his hair in a pudding-basin cut!" Everything redolent of wealth and ease made an impression on him which he himself could not understand. On leaving school he did not rest for a moment: so anxious was he to enter service and to get down to work. Nevertheless, despite his laudatory reports, he had great difficulty finding a place in the civil service. Even in remote back-waters influence is required! He managed to get only the most paltry job, at a salary of some thirty or forty rubles a year. But he re-solved to throw himself zealously into his work, overcoming and surmounting all obstacles. And to be sure, his zeal, patience and self-denial were quite without parallel. He remained at his desk from early morning to late at night, suffering neither physical nor mental fatigue, copying away, buried deep in his official papers, not even bother-ing to go home, but sleeping on the tables in the office, often taking his dinner with the night watchman and yet still managing to preserve his neat appearance, dressing tidily, giving his face a pleasant expression and even dis-playing something noble in his movements. We should point out that clerks of this department were especially noted for their unprepossessing and unattractive appearance. Some had faces that were exactly like loaves of badly baked bread: a bloated cheek protruding on one side, the chin pointing askew on the other, the upper lip swollen and to make matters worse, cracked; a far from pretty sight. They always spoke glumly, as if threatening to beat someone up; they often worshipped at the altar of Bacchus, thereby demonstrating that the Slav nature still retains many traces of paganism; sometimes they even came to work pickled, as they say, making things in the office distinctly nasty and filling the air with a miasma that was anything but aro-matic. Amongst such clerks it was impossible that Chichi-kov would not stand out and be noticed, representing in all respects the exact opposite of his colleagues, with his pre-possessing mien, his cordial voice, and his total abstention from any strong liquor. But for all that his road was a hard one; his head clerk was a dotard, the very personification of stony insensibility and imperturbability: never changing, inaccessible, his face never crossed by even the shadow of a smile, never once greeting anyone even with an enquiry after their health. No one had ever seen him any other than he always was, whether outside or at home; never once had he displayed any concern for anything, or got drunk and laughed in his drunkenness; or at least abandoned himself to that wild gaiety which a ruffian knows when in his cups; but no, there was not even a shadow of any of this in him. There was quite simply nothing in him at all: neither good nor bad, and there was something terrible in this total absence of anything. His dry, marble features, void of any sharp irregularity, suggested no resemblance to anything; they were remarkable only for the harsh congruity between them. Only the abundant pits and pock-marks that riddled his face made him like other people, those about whom country folk say that the devil had been threshing peas on their faces by night. It seemed as though human powers alone were insufficient to gain access to such a man and win his favour, but Chichikov undertook to do just that. At first he set about obliging him in all sorts of imperceptible trifles: he carefully noted how his superior liked his quills to be sharpened and, having prepared several like them always placed them by his hand; he swept and blew the dust and snuff from his desk; he provided new rags for his ink-well; he always placed his cap, the most revolting cap the world has ever seen, beside him one minute before the office closed; he dusted down his back, if his superior had brushed against a chalky wall—but all this passed entirely without acknowledgement, as if he had done nothing at all. Finally he nosed out everything about his private, domestic life, ascertaining that he had a grown-up daughter whose face also looked as though it had served as a floor for the nocturnal threshing of peas. It was from this flank that he planned to launch his assault. He found out which church she attended on Sundays and always took up a position where she could see him, immaculately dressed with a stiffly starched shirt front—and his ploy proved successful: the severe autocrat capitulated and invited him to tea! And before the clerks in the office could blink, things had been so arranged that Chichikov had moved into his superior's house, making himself useful and indispensable, buying the flour and sugar, treating the daughter like his betrothed, calling the autocrat "dear papa" and kissing his hand; in the office it was generally assumed that the wedding would take place at the end of February, before the beginning of Lent. The stern head clerk even solicited for a promotion for Chichikov, and before long Chichikov was appointed head clerk to fill a recently vacated position in another office. This appeared to be the primary purpose of his liaison with the old head clerk because without further ado he secretly dispatched his trunk home and the next day established himself in new quarters. He ceased to call the old head clerk "dear papa" and no longer kissed his hand, while all talk of a wedding stopped as abruptly as if nothing had ever happened. Nevertheless, whenever they chanced to meet, he always warmly shook the older man's hand and invited him to tea, which made the old head clerk, despite his eternal impassivity and harsh indifference, shake his head and mutter to himself: "He took me in, he took me in, the devil's spawn!"

That was the hardest threshold Chichikov had to cross. Thereafter things progressed more easily and successfully. He became a man of prominence. He proved to have all the qualities necessary for this world: a pleasant manner in his speech and actions and a facility in his business dealings. By this means he managed to achieve in a short time what is called a lucrative position, and he made excellent use of it. We should point out that at that very time the harshest measures were introduced against bribery; he was not intimidated by these measures and at once turned them to his own advantage, thereby demonstrating that purely Russian ingenuity which only comes to the fore when the squeeze is on. Matters were arranged thus: as soon as a petitioner entered his office and put his hand in his pocket in order to bring out those well-known "Prince Khovansky's letters of recommendation",* as we say in Russia, he would exclaim: "No, no," smiling and staying the petitioner's hand. "You surely do not think that I... No, no.

Prince Khovansky—was the director of the State Bank and his signature was on all the banknotes issued.

It is our duty, our obligation, to assist without any recompense! In this regard you may put your mind at rest: by tomorrow all shall be done. Be so good as to give me your address and there will be no need for you to trouble yourself further, everything will be brought directly to your house." The enchanted petitioner returned home almost in a state of rapture, thinking: "Now that's the sort of man we need more of, a gem, a real gem!" But the petitioner waited a day, then another, and nothing was brought to his house. On the third day, he called at the office: the matter had not even been started. Then he went to see the "gem". "Ah, forgive me!" Chichikov said with great civility, taking him by both hands, "we were so terribly busy; but tomorrow everything will be done, tomorrow, without fail, I am really quite ashamed!" And all this was accompanied by enchanting gestures. But neither tomorrow nor the day after, nor the day after that were the papers brought to the petitioner's house. The petitioner, now put his mind to it and wondered if there wasn't something behind it? He made enquiries; and learnt that he must grease the clerks' palms. "Well, why not? I'm quite willing to give them a quarter ruble or two." "No, not twenty-five kopeks, twenty-five rubles." "Twenty-five rubles each, to the clerks!" gasps the petitioner. "But why are you so shocked? That's how it will work out; twenty-five kopeks each for the clerks and the rest goes to their superiors." The slow-witted petitioner slaps himself on the forehead and curses the new order of things for all it is worth, with its campaign against bribe-taking and with the courtesy of the officials. In the old days you at least knew what had to be done: you slipped the head clerk a ten-ruble note and that was that; now you hand over twenty-five rubles, having already wasted a whole week before you have tumbled to it, the devil take all incorruptible and noble officials! The petitioner is right, of course, but then there are no bribe-takers nowadays: all head clerks and higher-ups are the most honest and noble-minded of people, and only the secretaries and scribes are rogues. Soon a much wider field was opened up to Chichikov: a commission was set up for the erection of some very prestigious government building. He managed to get himself on this commission and proved to be one of its most energetic members.

The commission set to work without delay. For six years it busied itself with the building; but either the climate or something hindered progress, or perhaps the materials were faulty, but whatever the reason the government building rose no higher than its foundations. And in the meantime each member of the commission acquired a handsome new house at different ends of the town: clearly the ground there was rather firmer. The members now began to prosper and to start families. It was only at this juncture that Chichikov began to extricate himself from his strict rules of abstinence and his implacable self-denial. Only now did he allow himself to break his dragging fast, and it transpired that he had at no time been insensible to the various pleasures he had been able to deny himself in the years of ardent youth, when no man has complete power over himself. One or two excesses were committed: he engaged a rather good cook, and took to wearing fine linen shirts. For his suits he now bought the sort of stuff that no one wore in the whole of the province, and from then on he favoured brown and reddish-brown shades of shot silk; he acquired an excellent pair and held one rein himself, forcing the trace horse to dance as he wanted it around in circles; he was already in the habit of sponging himself down with a mixture of water and cologne; he now took to buying a certain brand of soap at most considerable expense in order to impart a smoothness to his skin, he now...

But suddenly the old fogy he was working under was replaced by a new director, a military man, stern and authoritarian, the enemy of bribe-takers and of all foul practices. The very next day he put the fear of God in the entire commission, demanding reports, spotting deficits and missing sums of money at every step, at once noticing the handsome houses, and the fat was in the fire. Commission members were removed from office; the handsome houses were confiscated by the state and converted into various charitable institutions and schools for the sons of soldiers, everyone was put to rout, and Chichikov more than the others. For some reason the new director took a dislike to his face, despite its agreeable aspect, and what exactly displeased him so only God would know—such things do happen for no reason—and he conceived a mortal loathing of him. A holy terror he was to them all, this implacable new director. But since he was a military man after all, and therefore not familiar with all the nuances of civilian machinations, in due course other officials wormed their way into his favour thanks to their righteous appearance and adept ability and he soon found himself in the hands of even greater rogues whom he regarded as thoroughly honest men; he was really pleased that he had at last chosen the right men, and quite seriously boasted of his fine skills of discernment. The new officials quickly became wise to him. All his subordinates became the most fearful persecutors of improbity; they hunted it out everywhere, in all dealings, just as a fisherman hunts out a plump beluga with his spear, and they hunted it out with such success that within a short time all of them accumulated several thousand rubles each. During this time many of the previous officials turned to the paths of righteousness and were reinstated. But Chichikov was quite unable to worm his way back, for all the efforts of the general's first secretary, prompted by "missives from Prince Khovansky". This man had fully mastered the art of leading his general by the nose, but even he was quite unable to do a thing here. The general was one of those people who, for all that they are led by the nose (unbeknown to them), are adamant once some idea gets stuck in their head, and it is like an iron nail lodged in their brain: nothing on earth can wrench it out. All that the artful secretary could achieve was the destruction of Chichikov's sullied service record, which he did by appealing to the director's compassion, with a colourful description of the lamentable plight of Chichikov's family, a family which, fortunately, he did not have.

"Ah, well!" said Chichikov. "I hooked it, played it a bit and then my line broke—ours not to reason why. There's no point in crying over spilt milk, I must get down to work." And he resolved then and there to begin a new career, again to arm himself with patience, again to limit himself in all things, however freely and enjoyably he had indulged himself before. He had to move to another town and there make a new name for himself. Somehow nothing seemed to go right. He was forced to change his job two or three times in a very short space of time. The positions he held were somehow filthy and demeaning. It should be borne in mind that Chichikov was the most decorous man that had ever existed in this world. Although at first he was indeed compelled to endure a filthy company, in his heart he remained a great lover of cleanliness, he liked there to be polished writing tables in the offices and everything to be proper. In his speech he never permitted himself to use an indecorous word, and felt offended if he marked in the words of others a lack of due respect for rank or position. The reader will, I believe, be pleased to learn that he changed his linen every two days, and in summer during the hot weather even daily: any smell that was ever so slightly unpleasant was offensive to him. For this reason, whenever Petrushka came to undress him and to pull off his boots he would insert a clove in his nostril, and in many respects his nerves were as sensitive as a young lady's; and that is why it was so hard for him to return once more to those walks of life where everything reeks of vodka and behaviour is indecorous. However much he rallied in spirit, he nonetheless grew thin and his face paled to a greenish hue during these times of adversity. And yet he had already begun to grow stout and acquire those goodly, rounded contours in which the reader found him at the time they became acquainted, and, as he gazed into the mirror, he had already begun to muse on many pleasant things: a little woman, a children's room, and such thoughts would be followed by a smile. And now, when he accidentally caught sight of himself in the mirror, he could not forbear to cry out: "Holy Mother of God! How revolting I have become!" And for a long time thereafter he could not bring himself to have another look. But our hero endured it all, endured it stoically, patiently, and— at last he was given a position in the customs service. We should remark here that this service had long formed the secret object of his ambitions. He saw what foppish foreign articles the customs officers came by, what porcelains and cambrics they sent to their cousins, aunts and sisters. He had often said to himself with a sigh: "Now that's where I should like to work: the frontier is close by, the people are enlightened, and to think what fine Dutch linen shirts one might have!" We should add here that his thoughts touched also on a particular sort of French soap, which promised to impart

an extraordinary whiteness to the skin and a freshness to
the cheeks; never mind what it was called, but he assumed
that it was most certainly to be had at the border. Thus, he
would have long since sought a post in the customs, but he
was deterred by various current advantages accruing from
the construction commission, and he correctly reasoned
that the customs, for all its merits, was still only two birds
in the bush whilst the commission was already a bird in the
hand. But now he had resolved at whatever cost to get into
the customs, and get in he did. He took up his duties with
an extraordinary zeal. It appeared that fate itself had decreed he should be a customs officer. Such promptness,
perspicacity and intuition had not only never been seen
before, they had never been heard of. In the space of three
or four weeks he had become so adept in the customs business that he knew absolutely everything: he did not even
weigh or measure anything, he could tell just from the tex-
ture how many arshins of cloth or other material there
were in each bolt; merely by picking up a parcel in his
hands he could tell at once how many pounds it weighed.
And when it came to searches, here, as even his colleagues
themselves put it, he had quite simply a nose like a blood-
hound: it was amazing what resources of patience he had
to feel every little button, and to carry out all this with a
self-possession that was incredibly polite and yet killing.
And while the travellers who were being searched lost
their temper, and felt a malevolent urge to beat up his
pleasant face, Chichikov would merely repeat, without the
slightest change of expression or deviation from his courteous manner: "Might I request that you trouble yourself
somewhat to stand up?" Or: "Might I request, Madam,
that you repair to the next room? There the wife of one of
our officers will explain matters to you." Or: "Pray allow
me to make a little slit in the lining of your coat with my
little knife." And, as he said this, he would be pulling out
from there shawls and scarves as nonchalantly as if from
his own trunk. Even his superiors declared that this was a
devil and no human being: he would poke around and find
smuggled goods inside wheels, carriage shafts, horses' ears
and God knows where else, in the sort of places where no
author would dream of venturing and in which only customs officers are permitted to look. The poor traveller,

after crossing the border, could not come to his senses for
several minutes and, mopping the sweat from his brow,
could only cross himself and repeat: "Dear, oh dear, oh
dear!" His frame of mind was very like that of a schoolboy emerging from the secret room to which the headmaster had summoned him for a verbal admonition, but where,
to his great surprise, he had been caned instead. Before
long he made life quite impossible for smugglers. He was
the scourge and despair of all the Jews in Poland. His
integrity and incorruptibility were unassailable, almost
preternatural. He did not even accumulate a little nest-egg
from various confiscated goods and personal possessions
which had not gone into the exchequer to avoid too much
paper-work. Such zealous and selfless service could not fail
to evoke general amazement and to come finally to the
notice of his superiors. Chichikov was promoted in rank
and thereupon submitted a plan for the capture of all
smugglers, requesting only that he be granted the funds to
carry this out himself. He was at once put in command of
the project and given unlimited rights to carry out any
searches he liked. This was exactly what he wanted. At
this time a powerful company of smugglers had been
formed in a carefully planned manner; their daring enterprise held the promise of millions in profit. He had long
had information about this company, and had refused the
bribes offered by its emissaries, commenting drily: "The
time has not yet come." The minute he received full authority he sent word: "The time has now come." His calculations were very sound. Now in a single year he could
make more than he could in twenty years of the most
zealous service. Until now he had not wished to enter into
any relations with these smugglers, because being no more
than a pawn he would have received too little, but now...
Now it was quite a different story: he could impose whatever conditions he wished. To ensure that things went as
smoothly as possible he enlisted the connivance of a fellow officer, who proved unable to resist the blandishments
offered, although he was already grey-haired and ought to
have known better. The terms were agreed on and the
company went to work. Matters proceeded splendidly at
first: the reader must surely have heard the oft-repeated
story of the cunning ploy by which Merino sheep were

sent across the border in false coats under which they carried a million rubles worth of Brabant lace. And it was during Chichikov's service in the customs that this took place. No Jew in the world could have carried out such an undertaking, if Chichikov acted as a customs officer and not an accomplice. After three or four such ovine border crossings both officers found their capital increased by some four hundred thousand rubles. It is said that Chichikov even hit the half-million mark, because he was rather more dexterous. God only knows to what astronomical figure these already copious sums would have grown had not matters been fouled up by the intervention of the imp of discord or some such evil beast. This imp confounded the two officers; to put it simply, they quarrelled over nothing. Once, in a heated discussion, and perhaps when in his cups, Chichikov called the other officer the son of a priest, and the latter, although he was in fact a priest's son, for some obscure reason took mortal offence and at once hit back in strong and uncommonly sharp words: "No, you lie, I am a state councillor and not the son of a priest, it's you who are the son of a priest!" And then to add insult to injury, continued: "That's what you are!" Although in this manner he had soundly rebuffed Chichikov, by throwing his own insult back at him, and although the taunt "That's what you are!" might have been forceful enough, he was not content with that and wrote a secret denunciation of Chichikov. It is rumoured, besides, that apart from this exchange they were anyway at loggerheads over some young wench, fresh and lusty as a juicy apple, in the words of the customs officers themselves; the story even goes that men had been hired to give our hero a beating under cover of night in some dark alley; but that both officers were made fools of by some staff-captain, Shamsharyov, who took his pleasure with the pretty wench. How things actually were no one knows; the eager reader would be best advised to complete the story himself. The main point is that their secret relations with the smugglers were now revealed. The state councillor lost out, but at least he cooked Chichikov's goose. The officers were arraigned, all their ill-gotten gains were confiscated and distrained, and all this burst over their heads like a bolt from the blue. They came to their senses like men awakening from a stupor and realised with horror what they had done. The state councillor followed the Russian custom and took to drink for consolation, but Chichikov, the collegiate councillor, stood firm. He managed to hide some of his money despite the keen scent of the top officials who arrived to conduct the inquiry. He used all the guile, all the wiles of a man of experience, who knows his fellow men only too well; with some he relied on his agreeable turn of phrase, with others he pleaded for compassion; he knew where to employ flattery, which never hurts, and when to grease a palm—in short, he so managed things that at least he was not left in such dire straits as his comrade, and he wriggled free from criminal proceedings. But he was now left without capital, without any fancy articles of foreign manufacture, without anything; everything had found eager new owners. He retained a paltry ten thousand or so, put aside against a rainy day, a dozen or two fine linen shirts, a smallish chaise of the kind bachelors drive, and two serfs, his coachman, Selifan, and his valet, Petrushka. The customs officers, out of the kindness of their hearts, let him have five or six bars of soap for him to maintain the freshness of his cheeks—and that was all. Such was the position in which our hero again found himself! Such was the torrent of misfortune that had befallen him! This is what he referred to when he spoke of suffering in the service for the truth. Now one might conclude that after such tempests, such ordeals, such vicissitudes of fate and tribulations in life, he would withdraw with his hard-preserved ten thousand to the tranquil backwater of some little provincial town, there to fritter away his remaining days sitting in a cotton-print dressing gown by the window of a squat little cottage, act as intermediary in the fights that flared up on Sundays between the peasants outside his window, or stepping out for a breath of fresh air to his chicken run and personally squeezing the hen selected to go into his soup, and in this way live out an uneventful, but in its own way not unrewarding, life. But this did not happen. We must give due credit to the insuppressible resilience of his character. After all this, which would have been sufficient if not to kill a man then at least to subdue him and cool his ardour forever, his incredible passion remained unquelled. He was vexed and aggrieved, he railed against the entire world, raged at the injustice of fate, berated the injustice of his fellow men, and yet was unable to resist new undertakings. In a word, he demonstrated an endurance against which the wooden endurance of the German, already innate in the slow, sluggish circulation of his blood, is as nothing. Chichikov's blood, on the contrary, coursed strongly through his veins and he had to use all his will power and common sense to curb the energy that longed to leap out and range freely abroad. He reasoned, and there was a certain justification in his reasoning: "Why me? Why should this calamity have befallen me? Does anyone miss his chance in the service these days? Everyone grabs his. I made no one unhappy: I neither robbed the widow nor did I cause anyone's ruination; I helped myself to the surpluses, I took where every man would have taken; had I not helped myself, others would have helped themselves. So why should others prosper, and why should I be the one to be crushed like a worm? What am I now? What am I good for? How can I now look any respected husband and father in the face? How can I not suffer the pangs of conscience, knowing that I am a worthless encumbrance on this earth, and what will my children say when they find out? 'What a swine our father was,' they'll say, 'he never left us a bean!' "

We already know how concerned Chichikov was about his heirs. What a sensitive subject this was! Another man might not, perchance, have thrust his hand in so deep, had it not been for this question, which, in some obscure manner, arises of its own volition: what will the children say? And there you see the future paterfamilias, squinting like the cautious tom-cat, lest the master is watching from somewhere, swiftly snatching up whatever is within his reach, soap, candles, pork fat, or even a canary, should he get his hands on it—he misses nothing. Thus did our hero weep and lament his fate, yet in the meantime the activity of his brain did not cease for a moment; the ideas were ready to form and all that was needed was a plan. Once again he drew in his horns, once again he braved a life of hardship, once again he denied himself everything, once again he descended from a position of cleanliness and decency into the filth of lowly life. And in the hope of better things to come he was even forced to take up the calling of solicitor, a calling that has not yet gained its citizenship with us, that is jostled on all sides, reviled by the most contemptible clerks, and even by people who engage his services, condemned to grovelling in waiting rooms, to rude treatment and the like, but need forced him to try anything. Of his commissions there was, however, one that suited him: he was to solicit the mortgaging of several hundred peasants to the Board of Trustees.* The estate had been utterly and totally ruined. It had been ruined by cattle murrains, by scoundrelly bailiffs, by crop failures, by epidemic fevers that carried off the best workers and finally, by the incompetence of the landowner himself, who had furnished himself a house in Moscow in the latest fashion and had squandered his entire fortune, to the very last kopek, on this luxury. Starvation stared him in the face, and so he was obliged to mortgage his last remaining estate. Mortgaging was a new idea in those days, one which people ventured on to not without trepidation. Acting in his capacity as solicitor, Chichikov first gained everyone's favour (for without such preliminary gaining of favour it is, as we all know, quite impossible to get even a simple form or document, it is always necessary to lubricate every throat with at least a bottle of Madeira), and, having gained the favour of all those necessary, he explained that there was, however, one circumstance: half the peasants had died, so in order that there would be no complications afterwards...

"But they do still figure on the census list, don't they?" said the secretary.

"They do," said Chichikov.

"So what are you afraid of then?" said the secretary. "One dies, but then again, another's born, it's all in the day's work."

While speaking with the secretary, the most inspired thought that has ever entered the portals of the human mind had dawned upon our hero. "My, what a village idiot I am," he said to himself. "I'm hunting for my mittens when all the time they're stuck in my belt. Now if I

*Board of Trustees—a body which ran the Foundling Home in Moscow, where asylum was given to orphans and widows mainly of noble birth. The Board maintained its own bank where money could be deposited for safekeeping and loans could be obtained against estates, serfs and other property.

were to buy all the peasants that have died before they
take a new census, let's suppose I buy a thousand of them,
and let's suppose the Board of Trustees gives me two hundred per soul: why, that'll give me a capital of two hundred
thousand rubles! And now's a good time, there was an
epidemic recently, and the numbers of peasants that peg-
ged out, thank God, are considerable. The landowners have
been losing money at cards, carousing and clearing themselves out good and proper; then they scurry to St. Petersburg to get jobs in the government; their estates are abandoned, they're managed any old how, every year it gets
harder to find money to pay the dues, so they'll all be only
too glad to let me have them, if only so that they no
longer need to pay the poll-tax on them; who knows, it
might well be that I can squeeze the odd kopek out of
some of them for that too. It'll be hard, of course, a great
deal of bother, there's the danger that I may get into more
trouble. But then man was not given his brains for nothing.
The best thing about it is that the idea will seem so incredible, no one will believe it. Admittedly, without land one
can neither buy nor mortgage. But then I shall be buying
them for transfer, for transfer: these days land in Tavrida
and Kherson provinces is being given away, just so long as
you come and settle it. I'll take them all there. Off to
Kherson with them. Let them live there. The re-settlement
can be done quite legally, according to the rules. If they
should wish to inspect the peasants, with pleasure, I shall
have no objection to that either, why should I? I shall present a certificate of inspection signed by the captain of
police himself. I can call my village Chichikov Hamlet, or
after my christian name: the village of Pavlovskoye." Thus
this strange design took shape in the mind of our hero, for
which I do not know whether the readers will thank him,
yet for which the author is more grateful than words can
express. For, say what you will, had this idea not entered
Chichikov's head, this *poem* would not have seen the light
of day.

Crossing himself in the Russian manner he set about
implementing his design. Under the pretext of selecting a
place to settle in and under other such pretexts he undertook a journey to various corners of our land, and primarily to those which had suffered most from calamities, crop

failure, high mortality and so on and so forth—in short, where it would be easiest and cheapest to buy up the requisite peasants. He did not approach all the landowners indiscriminately, but selected people who were more to his taste or those with whom he could strike such deals with the least difficulty, endeavouring first to make their acquaintance, to gain their favour, in order, if possible, to acquire peasants through friendship rather than by purchase. Thus the reader must not be indignant with the author if the characters who have appeared until now have not been to his taste: this is the fault of Chichikov, for here he rules supreme, and whither he decides to go, there we, too, must follow. For our own part, if, indeed, accusations are made that the characters are insipid and nondescript, we shall only rejoin that it is never possible at the outset to see the full course and extent of any matter.

The entry into any town, be it even a capital, is always somehow insipid; initially everything is grey and monotonous: endless lines of soot-blackened factories stretch past us, and only afterwards do you see the corners of six-storeyed buildings, shops, signboards, wide streets, abounding in bell-towers, columns, statues, towers, with the brilliance, the noise and the clatter of the city and every other wonder produced by the hand and mind of man. How the first purchases were made the reader has already seen; how things shall go on from here, what success and failure awaits our hero, how he will face and surmount still higher obstacles, what colossal figures shall arise before him, how this tale shall be moved forward by its hidden levers, as its horizons extend into the distance and it takes on a majestic, lyrical flow, that he shall see in due course. A long way still has to be travelled by this equipage, consisting of a gentleman of middle years, a chaise, of the kind used by bachelors, a valet, Petrushka, a coachman, Selifan and a threesome of horses, already familiar to us by name, from Assessor to the rascally dappled grey. So there we have our hero before us, as large as life. To complete the portrait, however, one final detail might be required: what sort of a person is he with regard to moral qualities? That he is not a hero filled with every perfection and virtue is manifest. So what is he then? A rogue? But why a rogue, why be so hard on one's fellows? There are no real rogues amongst us nowadays, there are well-intentioned people, agreeable people, whilst of those who would be prepared to disgrace themselves by sticking their faces out to be publicly slapped you would be hard put to find more than two or three specimens, and even those are now starting to talk about virtue. It would be fairest of all to call him an *acquirer*. The acquisitive instinct is the root of all evil: because of it things have been done to which the world has given the name *not very clean*. True there is already something repulsive about such a character, and that same reader who in his own life will be friendly with such a man, exchange visits and enjoy his company, will start to look askance at him if he pops up as the hero of a play or a poem. But wise is the man who does not disdain any character, and instead, examining him with a searching look, plumbs him to the very main-springs of his being. Swift are the transformations in man; before you can bat an eye a terrible worm has grown up inside him and is tyranically sucking up all his vital juices. Only too often have some paltry little foible, let alone a grand passion taken root and grown in a man destined for the finest achievements, and forced him to forget his great and sacred duties and instead to see something great and sacred in worthless baubles. Numberless as grains of sand are the passions of man, and no one of them is like another, while all of them, base and noble, are initially subordinate to man and only afterwards become terrible tyrants over him. Lucky is the man who from all their multitude has selected the noblest passion; his immeasurable bliss grows and increases tenfold by the hour and minute as he penetrates ever more deeply into the infinite paradise of his soul. But there are passions which are not of man's choosing. For they are born with him when he comes into the world, and he is not given the strength to reject them. They are directed by some higher design, and there is in them something eternally beckoning, something which never falls silent all the days of his life. They are destined to achieve great things here on earth: it matters not whether this be in a shadowy form or in a blaze of light that flashes by to delight the world,—in equal measure are they summoned forth for some good unknown to man. And perhaps it is so with our very own Chichikov, perhaps the passion that

draws him on is not of his choosing, and his own cold existence already contains within it that which will one day
destroy him and bring man to his knees before the wisdom
of Providence. It remains a mystery why this particular
image should have taken shape in the *poem* now being
presented to the world.

What is hard to bear, however, is not that people will
be displeased with the hero but the irresistible certainty
that, on the contrary, readers might have been pleased
with this same hero, with this very same Chichikov. Had
the author not peered so deeply into his soul, had he not
raked up from its lower depths all those things which slip
away and shun the light, had he not revealed those inner-
most thoughts which man will entrust to no other, but had
he instead shown him as he appeared to the whole town,
to Manilov and the others, they would all have been
delighted with him and would have regarded him as an
interesting man. No matter that his face and his entire
person would not have haunted the reader's mind, and,
having finished reading, his soul would not have been
in any way troubled and he could have gone back to the
card-table—the solace of all Russia. Yes, my good readers,
you would prefer not to see the wretchedness of man in all
its nakedness. Why, you ask, what's the use of this? Do we
not already know that there is much in life that is despicable and stupid? In the normal course of events we often
see things that are far from comforting. You should rather
present us with something sublime and alluring. Let us forget ourselves for a while! "Listen, brother, why do you tell
me that business is going badly?" says the landowner to his
bailiff. "I know that without your telling me, brother, so
haven't you got anything else to say? Just let me forget
about that for a little while, let me not know it, and then
I'm happy." And so that same money that could to some
extent have set matters to right is directed towards various
means of procuring such oblivion. Thus sleeps a mind
which might otherwise have discovered a hidden source of
great wealth; and meanwhile the estate crashes beneath the
auctioneer's hammer and the landowner sets off into the
world in search of oblivion, his soul in extremity quite
ready now to plumb such depths of baseness before which
in earlier times he would have recoiled in horror.

Reproaches will also be hurled at the author by those so-called patriots, who quietly sit in their corners busying themselves with quite extraneous matters, amassing small fortunes, and lining their own nests at the expense of others; but as soon as something happens which to their mind is injurious to the mother country, should some book appear which dares to state the occasional bitter truth, they come scurrying out of their corners like spiders when they see a fly caught in their web, and they all start shouting together: "Is it a good thing to bring all this to light, to proclaim it from the rooftops? After all, everything described here is all ours—is that such a good thing? What will the foreigners say? Do *you* think it's fun to hear a bad opinion of oneself? Do *you* think it doesn't hurt? Do *you* think we are not patriots?" In answer to such wise remarks, particularly with regard to the opinions of foreigners, I must confess that nothing comes to mind. Unless perhaps this: in a distant corner of Russia there lived two men. One was a husband and father, by name Kifa Mokievich, a meek and mild man who lived his life in an easy-going way. He did not attend to his family's needs; his existence was directed more towards meditative pursuits and taken up with the following, as he termed it, philosophical question: "Take for example a beast," he would say, striding up and down the room, "a beast is born naked into the world. But why should it be naked? Why not like a bird, why is it not hatched out of an egg? It's a funny thing: you simply cannot understand nature, the deeper you delve into it!" Thus did the one inhabitant, Kifa Mokievich, ruminate. But this is still not the main point. The other inhabitant was Mokiy Kifovich, his own son. He was cast in the mould of a *bogatyr*, the hero of legend, and while his father was investigating the genesis of beasts, this broad-shouldered, twenty-year-old youth feverishly sought breadth and scope for his natural energies. He was quite incapable of touching lightly on anything: somebody's arm would be sure to crack or a bump would spring up on another's nose. In the house and neighbourhood everyone, from the backyard wench to the backyard dog fled at the sight of him; he even broke his own bed in his bedroom into smithereens. Such was Mokiy Kifovich, but he was really a good soul. But this is not the main point either, the main point is this: "Begging

your pardon, master, Kifa Mokievich," the servants—both
his own and others'—would say to the father, "but what
sort of lad is your Mokiy Kifovich? Nobody's safe from
him, he's such a bone-crusher!" "Yes, he's a playful lad, a
playful lad," the father would usually reply, "but what can
I do? It's too late to thrash him, and then everyone would
accuse me of cruelty; but he's an ambitious fellow, and if I
told him off in the presence of two or three others he
would quieten down, but it would get out—that's the
trouble! The whole town would hear about it and call him
a real dog. Do they think I don't feel the pain of it? Am I
not his father? Just because I practise philosophy and on
the odd occasion I may have no time, does that mean I'm
no longer a father? Oh no, indeed it does not! I'm a father
all right, a father, damn them all, a father! This is where I
have Mokiy Kifovich, right in my heart!" At this Kifa
Mokievich would pound himself violently on the chest
with his fist and get quite carried away. "And if he does
choose to remain a dog, then I shan't be the one to spread
it abroad, let me not be the one to give him away." And
having thus demonstrated his paternal concern he would
leave Mokiy Kifovich to continue his heroic endeavours,
whilst he himself returned to his favourite pursuit, suddenly
posing himself some such question as: "Now let's suppose
that an elephant was born in an egg, the shell, surely,
would be mighty thick, a cannon ball wouldn't break it;
some new sort of fire-arm would have to be invented."
Such were the lives led by these two inhabitants of a peaceful corner, who have so unexpectedly peeped out in
order to furnish a modest reply to the accusation of certain ardent patriots, who hitherto have been quietly occupied with some philosophical pursuit or the amassing of
wealth at the expense of their dearly beloved country, who
are concerned not that they should do no wrong, but only
that no one should say they are doing wrong. But no, it is
not patriotism which lies behind these accusations, there is
something else concealed there. And why should we not
admit it? If not the author, who then is to pronounce the
sacred truth? You fear the deeply searching stare, you are
terrified to direct your own penetrating look at anything,
you like to skim over everything with unthinking eyes.
You will even laugh heartily at Chichikov, perhaps you will

even praise the author, saying: "You have to hand it to him, he's got something there, the fellow must be a jolly sort!" And after these words you will turn to yourself with redoubled pride, a complacent smile will play on your lips, and you will add: "There's no getting away from it: you do find some mighty strange and funny customers in some provinces, and the damnedest scoundrels to boot!" And which of you, full of Christian humility, will direct this weighty question, not aloud, but in silence, alone, at moments of solitary self-examination, deep into his own soul: "But might there not be some little bit of Chichikov in me too?" No fear, none of you will! But let some acquaintance happen by at this moment, a man of rank, not too great nor too small, and he will at once nudge his neighbour's arm and say, almost snorting with laughter: "Look, look, it's Chichikov, there goes Chichikov!" And then, like a child, forgetting all the decorum consonant with his age and calling, he will set off in pursuit of him, taunting him from behind, and parroting: "Chichikov! Chichikov! Chichikov!"

But we have started to speak rather loudly, forgetting that our hero, who has been asleep throughout the narration of his story, has already awakened and might easily hear his name being repeated so often. For he is quick to take offence and does not like to be spoken about in a disrespectful way. It is all one to the reader whether or not Chichikov is angry with him, but as for the author, he must not under any circumstances quarrel with his hero: there still remains a long road for them to journey together hand in hand; two big parts still lie ahead, and that is no trifling consideration.

"Hey! What are you doing!" shouted Chichikov to Selifan, "Hey, you!"

"What?" said Selifan in a slow drawl.

"What d'you mean—what? You goose! Look how you're driving this thing! Come on now, get a move on!"

And indeed, for quite some time Selifan had been driving with his eyes shut tight, only now and then giving the reins a slight shake against the flanks of the likewise dozing horses; as for Petrushka, his cap had flown off long ago heaven knows where, and he himself was reclining with his head firmly on Chichikov's knee, so that the latter was forced to give him a thump. Selifan perked up and, giving the dappled horse a few lashes across the back, after which he broke into a trot, and cracking his whip above them all, called out in a thin ringing voice: "Don't you worry!" The nags bestirred themselves and surged forward, pulling the light chaise along like a piece of fluff. Selifan merely waved his whip and emitted shouts of: "Hey! Hey! Hey!" bouncing smoothly on the box, while the troika flew up and plunged down the humps and dips of the highroad, which ran imperceptibly downhill. Chichikov only smiled as he jigged gently on his leather cushion, for he loved to drive fast. For what Russian does not love to drive fast? How can his soul, which longs to whirl and revel, to say at times: "The devil take it all!"—how can his soul help loving it? How can it help loving it when something rapturous, something wondrous is heard in it? It is as though some unseen force has picked you up onto its wing, and you are flying, and everything is flying: the versts are flying, the merchants on the coachman's seats of their kibitkas are flying towards you, the forest with its dark rows of firs and pines, with its chopping of axes and cawing of crows, is flying past on both sides, the road itself is flying away who knows where into the unknown, fading distance and there is something terrible in this swift evanescence, where objects fade before they are properly seen—and only the sky above your head, and the light clouds, and the moon showing through them, appear motionless. Ah, troika, you bird of a troika, who dreamed you up? Surely you could only have been born among a spirited people, in that land where things are not done by halves, in a land which has spread in a smooth, level plain over half the earth, and you may count the verst-poles until your eyes begin to smart. This would not seem to be a crafty conveyance, it is not secured by an iron bolt, but carelessly knocked together with an axe and a chisel by a bright Yaroslavl peasant. No German topboots for the coachman: a beard, a pair of mittens and something to perch on; but let him rise a little, let him crack that whip, let him break into song— and the horses surge forward like a whirlwind, the wheel-spokes melt into a single smooth disc, the road quakes, and a terrified pedestrian cries out, stopping in his tracks—and it's off and away! It's off and away! It's off and away!..

And in no time at all you only see something raising clouds of dust in the distance and thrusting into the horizon.

And do you not dash forward too, Russia, like some eager, matchless troika? The road wreathes beneath you in a trail of smoke, the bridges rattle, everything falls back and is left behind. Struck by this miracle of God the onlooker stops short: is this not a bolt of lightning cast from the heavens? What does this terrifying motion mean? And what unearthly force lies hidden in these unearthly horses? What horses, what horses! Are there whirlwinds caught in your manes? Is there some alert, sensitive ear straining through your every vein? You have heard the familiar song ring out above you, in one concerted surge you have set your bronze chests to the harness, and, your hooves barely touching the ground, you have turned into mere taut lines, flying through the air, and the entire troika hurtles forward, inspired by God!.. Russia, where are you flying? Give an answer! No answer. With a wondrous peal the little bells ring out; torn into shreds, the air rumbles and turns into wind; everything on earth flies past, and, with a wary look, other nations and states step aside and give way to the flying troika.

VOLUME TWO

CHAPTER ONE*

Why indeed should we expose to view the poverty and
sad imperfection of our life, digging up people from the
backwoods, from the remote nooks and crannies of our
state? What can we do, if this is that kind of author who
is so sick at heart with his own imperfection, that he can
no longer portray anything but the poverty of our life,
digging people up from the backwoods, from the remote
nooks and crannies of our state! So here once again we
have wound up in the backwoods, once again we are stuck
in some remote cranny.

But then what backwoods and what a cranny!

For a thousand versts and more a range of hills stretched
like the gigantic rampart of some endless fortress, towering
majestically over the plain, now in a sheer clayey-lime wall,
slashed with ruts and gulleys, now as a green rounded
bulge, swathed, as in lamb's wool, in young undergrowth
springing from the felled trees, or a stretch of dark forest
which had as yet escaped the axe. A river, now true to its
banks, described with them the same swerves and bends,
now flowed off into the meadows, there to meander in a
series of loops, flashing like fire in the sun, before hiding in
a copse of birch, aspen and alder and emerging therefrom
in triumph with an entourage of bridges, mills and weirs,
which seemed to pursue it round every turn.

*In this edition the text of the early edition of Volume Two of *Dead Souls*
is followed, as the fullest version.

In one place the sheer wall towered higher than else-where and was covered from top to bottom with the foli-age of densely clustered trees. They were all together here: the maple, the pear, the squat broom, the yellow acacia, the birch, the fir, the rowan, enmeshed with hops (*two words erased from ms. here*). On the hilltops, amid the green crowns of the trees you could see the red roofs of the farm-buildings, the ridge-trees of peasant cottages behind them, and the upper storey of the manor house itself. And above all this confusion of trees and roofs an ancient church raised aloft its five gilded cupolas. Each of them was crowned by a golden filigree cross, fastened to the cupola by golden filigree chains, so that from afar you saw the glitter of gold apparently suspended in the air and attached to nothing. And all these trees, roofs, the church and the crosses, were reflected upside down in the river, where the ugly old willows, some standing on the bank, others right in the water, into which they dipped their drooping branches, appeared to be examining this wond-rous reflection, which they had gazed at with unsatiated admiration through all the many years of their lives.

The view was very beautiful, but the view from above, from the upper storey of the house down over the plain and into the distance was better still. No guest or visitor stand-ing on the balcony could remain unmoved. His breath caught from amazement, and he would only exclaim: "Lord, how wide open it is here!" Endless vistas stretched away before him. Beyond the meadows, dotted with groves and watermills, there stretched dark blue and green forests, like oceans or a far-spreading mist. Beyond these forests the yellow of sands showed through the hazy air. Beyond these sands there rose like a crest on the distant horizon, a line of chalk hills, which sparkled a brilliant white even in the foulest weather, as if illuminated by an eternal sun. In the foothills, misty-grey dots stood out against the dazzling whiteness. These were distant villages, too far away for the human eye to make out. Only a gold church cupola flashing in the sun betrayed that these were large, populous settle-ments. All this was enveloped in an imperturbable stillness, unruffled even by the barely audible cries of the airborne songsters thronging the sky. In a word, no guest or visitor contemplating the scene from the balcony for two solid hours could remain unmoved and would exclaim, just as he had on first beholding it: "Lord, how wide open it is here!"

Who was the resident and owner of this village, which, like some impregnable fortress could not be even approached from the hilly side and had to be reached across pastures and wheat fields and, finally, through a grove of oak-trees scattered picturesquely across the sward and coming right to the cottages and manor-house themselves? Who was the inhabitant, master and owner of this village? To which lucky man did this lost cranny belong?

To none other than Andrei Ivanovich Tentetnikov of Tremalakhansk district, a young gentleman of thirty-three, Collegiate Secretary, and as yet unmarried.

But what manner of man, of what disposition, qualities and character was this landowner Andrei Ivanovich Tentetnikov?

Naturally, this question must be put to his neighbours. That neighbour who came from the now disappearing line of retired fire-breathing staff-officers, delivered himself of the following succinct verdict: "The most consummate swine!" The general who lived ten versts away declared: "A young man, far from stupid, but much too conceited. I could be useful to him, because I have connections in St. Petersburg, and even at..." The general did not complete his sentence. The local captain of police remarked: "But then he only has a measly rank; in fact I shall be calling on him tomorrow to collect his tax arrears!" A peasant from his village, when asked what their master was like, would give no answer. In short, public opinion of him was sooner unfavourable than favourable.

Speaking impartially though, Andrei Ivanovich was neither a good nor a bad man, he simply idled his life away. When there are already so many people in this world who do that, why should Tentetnikov not idle his life away? Here, however, in a few words is a full journal of his day, and let the reader judge for himself what his character was like.

In the morning he awakened very late, and propping himself up, remained for a long time sitting on his bed, rubbing his eyes. These eyes, as ill-luck would have it, were small, and therefore this rubbing operation continued for an uncommonly long time. Throughout this procedure his manservant Mikhailo stood at the door holding a wash-basin and a towel. This poor wretch would stand there an hour, even two, and then go away to the kitchen and on return find his master still rubbing his eyes and sitting on the bed. Finally he rose from the bed, washed his face, put on a dressing-gown and proceeded to the drawing room to drink tea, coffee, cocoa and even milk fresh from the cow, taking a little of everything, scattering breadcrumbs carelessly and dropping pipe ash over everything. For two whole hours he sat over his breakfast; as if this were not enough he took a cup of tea, quite cold by now, and moved over to the window that faced the yard. The following scene was invariably enacted in front of the window.

First of all the unshaven footman Grigori would roar, addressing himself to Perfilyevna, the housekeeper, in the following terms:

"You jumped-up nobody, what fine estate did you come from?! You ought to shut your mouth, silly woman, and keep it shut."

"Don't think I'll listen to you, you loudmouth!" shouted back the nobody, or Perfilyevna.

"No one can get along with you, you'll even get into a fight with the bailiff, you granary chaff!" bellowed Grigori.

"Anyway the bailiff's just as big a thief as you!" shrieked the nobody for all the village to hear. "You're both drunkards, pilferers, bottomless barrels! Do you think the master doesn't know about you? Here he is, he can hear you himself."

"Where's the master?"

"There he is, sitting by the window; he can see everything."

True enough, the master was sitting by the window and could see everything.

To complete the mayhem, some servant's kid, cuffed by his mother, started bawling at the top of his voice; a borzoi was howling squatting on his hindquarters, scalded by some boiling water dashed at him by the cook as he stuck his head out of the kitchen. In a word, there was the most intolerable screeching and wailing. The master saw and heard everything. And only when the din became so unbearable that it interfered with the master's idleness did he send to tell them to shout more quietly.

Two hours before dinner Andrei Ivanovich withdrew to his study to get down to some real, serious work. This work was indeed serious. It consisted in the contemplation of a composition, which he had been long and constantly contemplating. This composition was to embrace the whole of Russia from all aspects: the civic, the political, the religious, and the philosophical, it was to solve the most complex tasks and problems posed by the age, and it was to determine with clarity its great future: in short, its scope was extensive. But for the time being things went no further than contemplation; the pen was chewed, doodles appeared on the paper, and then all this was pushed to one side, a book was taken up instead and it remained in his hands right until dinner time. The reading of the book went together with the eating of the soup, the roast and even the dessert, so that some dishes grew cold while others remained quite untouched. After dinner he sipped a cup of coffee while smoking a pipe, and then had a game of chess against himself. As for what he did until supper time, we must confess, it is hard to say. It seems, quite simply nothing.

And that is how he spent his time, quite alone in the whole world, this young man of thirty-two years, a stay-at-home, in a dressing-gown, without a necktie. He did not feel like going for a stroll or a walk, he did not even want to climb the stairs to gaze out into the distance and admire the views, he did not even wish to throw open the windows to let in some fresh air, and the beautiful sight of the village, which did not seem to exist for the owner, although there was not a visitor who did not go into raptures over it.

From this journal the reader can see that Andrei Ivanovich Tentetnikov was a member of that tribe who are legion in Russia, and who go by the names of marmots, lie-abeds, lazybones, and the like.

Whether such characters are born such or are formed afterwards it is hard to say. I believe that instead of answering we should recount the story of the childhood and upbringing of Andrei Ivanovich.

In his childhood he was a keen-witted, talented boy, by turns lively and pensive. Whether by good or ill fortune, he wound up in a school whose headmaster was an extraordinary man in his own way, despite certain vagaries. Alexander Petrovich had the gift of understanding the nature of his fellow Russian and knew in what language to talk to him. None of the boys, when summoned to the headmaster's room, ever came out in tears; on the contrary, even after the most severe dressing-down a boy would feel sort of buoyed up and anxious to make amends for his misdeed. His young charges appeared at first sight so naughty, disorderly and frisky that you might easily have mistaken them for a riotous, unruly crowd. But you would have been mistaken: the crowd was very strongly influenced by the power of that one man. There was no mischief-maker or malefactor who did not come to the headmaster of his own free will and confess all his pranks. He knew the slightest movement of their minds. He acted unusually in all matters. He said that first of all you must arouse ambition in a person—he called ambition a force which propelled man forward—without which it would be impossible to stir him to any activity. There were many kinds of pranks and horse-play he did not discourage at all: in those early childhood pranks he saw the beginning of the development of a person's spiritual properties. They were therefore necessary to tell him what exactly lay concealed within the child. Thus does the wise doctor watch with equanimity the various temporary attacks and rashes that break out on the skin, doing nothing to cure them, but studying them attentively in order to ascertain what exactly is going on inside the patient.

He engaged few teachers: most of the subjects he taught himself. And we must point out that he did this without any of those pedantic terms, orotund opinions and views, with which young professors love to show off, he was able in a few words to convey the quintessence of a science, so that even the youngest pupil could grasp precisely why he needed it, this science. He maintained that the thing man needed most was the science of life, and that, once having mastered this, he would then discover for himself what should be his principal object of study.

He made this same science of life the object of a special course of training to which only the most outstanding pupils were admitted. Those of little ability he released to join the government service after their first course, asserting that they need not be subjected to unnecessary suffering: for them it was enough if they had learnt to be patient, hard-working executives, free of arrogance and any sort of grand ideas. "But with the bright ones, with the gifted ones I have to work long and hard," he used to say. In this course they met a quite different Alexander Petrovich, who declared right from the start that where hitherto he had demanded their mere wit, now he would demand the highest intelligence, not the intelligence which can make fun of a fool and hold him up to ridicule, but that which can suffer any insult, can suffer a fool—and feel no irritation. Now he started to demand of them what others demand from children. It was this that he called intelligence of the highest order. To be able to preserve in the face of every possible disappointments the sublime calm in which man should remain in perpetuity—that is what he called intelligence! In this course Alexander Petrovich showed that he knew the science of life perfectly. Of the sciences he selected only those which could shape a person into a responsible citizen of his country. In most of his lectures he told them what lay in store for a man in all the professions and at all levels of government service and private careers. He set out before them all the disappointments and obstacles that could possibly lie in a man's path, all the temptations and blandishments which faced him, and showed them in their nakedness, concealing nothing. He knew it all, just as if he himself had served in all professions and offices. In a word, he traced out before them a future that was far from roseate. And how strange! Whether because their ambition had already been so strongly awakened; whether because there was something in the very eyes of this extraordinary tutor that exhorted a youth: "Forward!"—a word that works such miracles in a Russian— or for whatever other reason, but that youth from the very beginning would seek out only difficulties, eager to act only where things were difficult, where he had to display greater strength of spirit. There was something sobering in their lives. Alexander Petrovich carried out all sorts of tests and experiments with them, subjecting them to the most wounding insults, delivered either by himself or by their own comrades, but, once they had fathomed his schooling they became even more circumspect. Very few completed this course, but these few were tough ones, men who had been properly tempered. In the service they were able to hold the most precarious positions where many others, far cleverer than they, either quit their jobs altogether because of some trifling personal unpleasantnesses, or unaware of it themselves wound up in the clutches of bribe-takers and knaves. But Alexander Petrovich's alumni not only did not stumble, but, made wiser by their knowledge of man and his soul, were able to exercise a strong moral influence even on bribe-takers and corrupt men.

But poor Andrei Ivanovich was not destined to take this training. He had just been transferred to this higher course as one of the very best students when disaster struck: their extraordinary tutor, whose one word of encouragement would cause his heart to flutter deliciously, died suddenly. Everything changed in the school: Alexander Petrovich's place was taken by a certain Fyodor Ivanovich, a good man and diligent, but with quite a different view of things. He fancied he saw something unbridled in the free and easy manner of the advanced course students. He began by enforcing certain rules of behaviour demanding that the young men should maintain a state of total silence, that on no account were they to walk other than in pairs. He even started measuring the distance between the pairs with a yardstick. At table, for the sake of better symmetry, he seated them according to height, and not intelligence, so that the dunces received the choicest pieces and the bright boys the leftovers. All this created murmurs, especially when the new headmaster, as if deliberately contrarying his predecessor, declared that to him intelligence and success in their studies meant nothing, that he was concerned only with their conduct, that if a boy was a poor learner but conducted himself well he would prefer him to a wiseacre. But it was precisely this, the very thing he sought, that Fyodor Ivanovich failed to achieve. Secret mischief became the order of the day, and this, as we all know, is far worse than open pranks. In the daytime all was stiff and prim, but at night there were wild binges.

In teaching itself he turned everything upside down. With the very best of intentions he brought in all sorts of innovations—and all of them misfired. He engaged new teachers, with new attitudes and new points of view. They taught in a learned way, tossing out to their listeners a mass of new words and terms. The logical connection could be seen, and the pursuit of new discoveries, but alas! there simply was no life in the study itself. All this seemed so much dead matter to students who had already begun to use their intelligence under Alexander Petrovich. Everything went topsy-turvy. But the worst thing was that all respect for authority and power was lost: students mocked the tutors and masters, they started to call the headmaster Fedka, old Bun-face and various other names; things came to such a pass that it was necessary to suspend and expel many boys.

Andrei Ivanovich was of a quiet disposition. He did not participate in the nocturnal orgies organized by his fellow students, who, despite the strictest supervision, had secretly recruited a mistress—one to serve eight of them—nor in the other pranks, which went to such extremes as blasphemy and mockery of religion itself for the mere reason that the headmaster demanded that they attend church frequently and that their new priest was no good. But he lost heart. His ambition had been strongly aroused, but he was offered no vocation or chosen activity. It would have been better not to have aroused his ambition at all! He listened to the new professors ranting on their rostrums, but he thought of their previous tutor, who had been able to talk intelligibly, without ranting. He heard lectures in chemistry, and the philosophy of law, he listened to the professor's abstruse investigations of the finer points of political science, and an investigation into the universal history of mankind on such an enormous scale that in three years the professor only got through his introduction and the development of the "Gemcinde" in certain towns; and all this formed an ugly jumble in his head. Thanks to his native wit he was at least able to see that this was no way to be taught, but what the right way was he did not know. He often recalled Alexander Petrovich, and such sadness overcame him that he did not know what to do in his misery.

But youth has a future. As the students came nearer to graduation his heartbeat started to quicken. He would say to himself: "After all this isn't life yet, this is only the preparation for life: real life begins in the service. That's where you can achieve great things." And without so much as a glance at the beautiful view which so astounded every guest and visitor, without even paying his last respects at his parents' graves, the went, like all ambitious men, careering off to St. Petersburg, which draws our ardent young men like a magnet from all four corners of Russia—thither they flock to serve, to shine, to seek promotion or merely to scrape the surface of that deceptive society education, pallid and cold as ice. Any stirrings of ambition in Andrei Ivanovich were, however, arrested at the very outset by his uncle, full state counsellor Onufry Ivanovich. He declared that the most important thing was a good hand, and nothing else, that without this you would never become a minister, nor even a state counsellor, whereas Tentetnikov had the sort of handwriting of which they say "a magpie scrawled that with its claw".

With great difficulty and with the assistance of his uncle's contacts, having devoted two months to lessons in calligraphy, Andrei Ivanovich finally secured a position as a copy-clerk in some government department. When he set foot in the brightly lit hall, where all around gentlemen sat scribbling at varnished desks, scratching away with their quills their heads inclined to one side, and when he himself was thus seated and instructed to copy some document then and there, he was overwhelmed by a most singular feeling. For a moment it seemed to him that he had found his way into some primary school to learn his alphabet all over again, that, as punishment for some misdeed, he had been transferred from the top class to the very lowest. The gentlemen sitting around him looked so like schoolboys to him. Some of them were reading novels, which they had concealed between the large sheets of the file they were supposedly working on, and they would give a start every time their superior appeared. He suddenly remembered his schooldays like an irretrievably lost paradise, so elevated did the study of the sciences seem when compared to this wretched clerking. How superior that scholarly preparation for service was to the service itself! The image of his incomparable, marvellous tutor, the irreplaceable Alexander Petrovich rose before him so vividly that the tears suddenly came flooding from his eyes. The room started to spin, the desks swam about him, the officials melted together, and he almost fell off his chair from a sudden dizziness. "No," he said to himself, coming to his senses, "I shall get down to work, however pettifogging it might at first seem." Thus, with a heavy heart and spirit he resolved to serve after the example of others.

Is there any place where no pleasures are to be found? They exist even in St. Petersburg, notwithstanding its severe, gloomy aspect. An angry, thirty-degree frost may chase pedestrians off the streets, the snowstorm may wail like a despairing demon, flinging up the collars of fur-coats and greatcoats over their wearers' heads, powdering the moustaches of men and the muzzles of beasts, but somewhere high up a little window will shine welcomingly, even if it is on the fourth floor; in a cosy little room, lit by thin stearine candles, to the hissing of a samovar, a conversation will be held, warming the heart and the soul, or someone will be reading a beautiful page of some inspired Russian poet, of the kind God has bestowed upon His Russia, and the youthful heart will palpitate with an exalted ardour, that is unknown anywhere in any other lands, not even under the brilliant southern sun.

Soon Tentetnikov grew accustomed to the service, only it did not become the main activity and purpose of his life, as he had originally supposed it would, but something of secondary importance. It served to divide up his time, causing him to cherish the remaining minutes more dearly. His uncle, the full state counsellor, was already beginning to think that some good might come of the nephew after all, when the nephew suddenly messed it all up. It has to be said that Andrei Ivanovich's circle of friends included two men who were what one would describe as embittered people. They were examples of that strange, restless type who not only cannot bear injustice with equanimity, they cannot bear anything at all that appears to them as unjust. Initially kind men, but disordered in their own actions, they are filled with intolerance of others. Their fiery speeches and the noble image of indignation they projected had a most pronounced effect on the young man. Arousing his impatience and irritability, they made him notice all those trifles to which previously he had paid no heed. He suddenly took a dislike to Fyodor Fyodorovich Lenitsyn, the chief of the department in which he worked, a man of the most pleasing appearance. He discovered in him a countless mass of faults and hated him for putting on too sweet an expression when he spoke to his superiors, and then, as he addressed a subordinate, immediately becoming sour as vinegar. "I would forgive him," said Tentetnikov, "if only this facial metamorphosis didn't take place so rapidly; but how can he be sweet and sour at one and the same time, right there before my very eyes!" From this time forth he started to notice his chief's every move. It seemed to him that Fyodor Fyodorovich was putting on airs, that he had all the foibles of petty bosses, such as making a note of those subordinates who did not come to him with their congratulations on his feast-days, and even avenging himself on all those whose names did not figure on his porter's list of callers, and a great number of other venal failings, of which no man, good or bad, is altogether free. He felt a nervous repulsion for him. Some evil spirit urged him to do Fyodor Fyodorovich a disservice. He sought this opportunity with a particular relish and he managed it. One day he spoke to him in such strong language that he was ordered by his superiors: either to apologize or to resign from the service. He handed in his resignation. His uncle, the full state counsellor, called on him in a state of alarm and pleaded with him.

"In the name of all that's holy, Andrei Ivanovich! What are you doing? To resign from a career in which you have made such a good start just because your chief wasn't quite... So what of it? After all, if such things mattered no one would remain in the service. Think again, my boy, think again. There is still time! Curb your pride, go and make your apologies to him!"

"That is not the point, Uncle," said the nephew. "It's not hard for me to ask his pardon, particularly as I really am in the wrong. He is my superior and on no account should I have spoken to him thus. But the point is this: you have forgotten that I have another service; I have three hundred souls, an estate in complete disorder and a manager who's a fool. It is small loss to the state if, instead of me, someone else sits in the chancellery copying out papers, but it is a great loss if three hundred men do not pay their taxes. I am a landowner: and that is not an idle calling either. If I can improve the lot of the peasants in my charge, looking after them and preserving them, and can give the state three hundred of the fittest, soberest and most hard-working subjects—will my service be less worthy than that of some department chief by the name of Lenit-syn?"

The full state counsellor stood there gaping in astonishment. He had not expected such an oration. After a few moments' thought he ventured as follows:

"But all the same ... but all the same... How can you bury yourself in the country? What sort of society will you find amongst peasants? Here at least as you walk down the street you may encounter a general or a prince. If you wish you may stroll past some fine public buildings, you may go and have a look at the Neva, but down there all you will encounter will be village men or village wives. Why do you wish to condemn yourself to ignorance for the rest of your life?"

Thus did the uncle, the full state counsellor, reason. He himself had never, in all the days of his life, walked along any other street than that which led to his place of service, where there were no fine public buildings; he noticed none of the people he encountered, whether generals or princes; he knew none of the temptations which in the capitals entice men wanting in abstinence and had never in his life been to the theatre. He said all this with the sole purpose of reawakening the young man's ambition and exciting his imagination. However, he failed: Tentetnikov obstinately stood his ground. Government departments and the capital had grown tedious to him. He now saw his village as a carefree refuge, inspiring thought and reflections, and the sole arena of purposeful activity. A week or two after this conversation he was already approaching those places where he had spent his childhood. How well he began to remember everything, how his heartbeat quickened when he sensed the nearness of his home country! Many places he had forgotten altogether, and he beheld them with curiosity, like a stranger gazing on fine views. When the road ran through a narrow ravine into the thick of a huge, overgrown forest and he saw above and below, towering over him and growing beneath him all those trees: three-hundred-year-old oaks, with a girth it would take three men to reach round, silver-firs, elms and black poplar, and when to his question "Whose forest is this?" the answer came: "Tentetnikov's"; when, as they emerged from the forest, the road led through meadows, past aspen groves, young and old willows and osiers, with a view of high ground stretching away in the distance, then bridged one and the same river in various places, leaving it now to the left now to the right, and to his question "Whose pastures and water-meadows are these?" the answer came: "Tentetnikov's"; when then the road went uphill and ran across a plateau with on the one side unharvested grain-fields of wheat, rye and barley, and on the other all those places they had already driven through, which were now seen at a picturesque distance, and when the road, gradually darkening, entered and then ran along beneath the shade of spreading trees, scattered here and there over the green carpet right up to the village itself, and the peasant cottages and the red-roofed farm buildings flashed before them; when his ardently beating heart knew even without asking whither they had arrived, the sensations which had been mounting up all the time within him finally burst from him in these words: "Well, have I not been a fool until now? Fate appointed me the proprietor of an earthly paradise, a Prince among men, and I went and enslaved myself as a clerk in an office! After studying, acquiring education and enlightenment, amassing a respectable store of the very knowledge which is necessary for the administration of people, for the improvement of an entire region, for the performance of the many varied duties of a landowner, who is at one and the same time judge, and ruler, and guardian of the peace—to entrust this place to some ignoramus of a bailiff! And to prefer this to what?—To the copying of papers, something a schoolboy who has never studied anything can do much better!" And once again Andrei Ivanovich Tentetnikov bestowed upon himself the title of fool.

In the meantime another spectacle awaited him. When they learnt about the arrival of their master, the population of the entire village gathered by the porch. Bright headscarves, kerchiefs, homespun coats, beards of every kind: spade beards, forked beards and goatees, red, brown and silvery white, filled the entire courtyard. The men roared: "Father and benefactor, you've come at last!" The women wailed: "You are the gold, the silver of our hearts!" Some people standing further off even came to blows in their anxiety to push forward. A decrepit old woman, as shrunken as a dried pear, slipped between the legs of the others, stepped up to the master and shrieked: "Oh, you poor little dear, how scrawny you are! Those cursed German heathens have starved you to death!" "Let him be, you fool woman!" the spade, forked and goatee beards shouted at her. "Pushing yourself at him like that, you pockmarked old hag!" To this someone appended the sort of word which only a Russian peasant can hear without laughing. The master also laughed, but nonetheless he was deeply moved. "So much love! And for what?" he asked himself. "For having never seen them, having never attended to their needs! From now on I solemnly pledge to share your toil and your activity! I shall do all in my power to make you what you should be, what you are destined to be by that good nature concealed within each and every one of you, so that your love for me shall be deserved, so that I shall indeed be your father and benefactor!"

And true enough, Tentetnikov took up the reins of his estate in all earnest. Now that he was on the spot he could see that the bailiff was an old woman and a fool with all the qualities of a useless manager, which is to say that he kept an accurate count of the chickens and eggs, of the wool yarn and linen which the peasant women brought in, but he did not know the first thing about sowing and harvesting, and to make matters still worse he suspected the peasants of plotting against his life. He sacked this fool of a bailiff, and appointed a quick-witted man in his place. Tentetnikov ignored trifles and concentrated on the main problems, reduced the corvee, lessened the number of days the peasants had to work for him and gave them more time to work for themselves, and believed that matters would now proceed in the best possible manner. He took an interest in everything himself, he could be seen in the fields, on the threshing floor, in the barns, at the mills, on the jetty, and at the loading and casting off of the barges and wherries.

"Just look at him, fleet-footed, isn't he now!" the peasants began to say, wondering what to do, because after long years of slipshod management they had all grown decidedly slothful. But their bafflement did not last long. The Russian peasants are shrewd and resourceful: they quickly caught on that although their master might be sharp and eager to take on as much as he could, he still had not worked out where to start or how to do it, and he spoke in too highbrow and confusing a fashion, quite above the peasants' heads and teaching them nothing. The upshot was that while master and peasant did not exactly fail to understand each other, they were simply unable to get attuned, they simply could not hit one and the same note. Tentetnikov noticed that on the estate lands the crops did not do as well as on the peasants' own: they were sown earlier and ripened later. And yet the serfs seemed to be working well: he supervised them in person and even gave orders that they each receive a mug of vodka for their hard work. The peasants' rye had long been in ear, their oats were knee-high, their millet clustering while in his fields the stalks of the wheat were only beginning to thicken. In a word, the master started to notice that the peasants were quite simply cheating him, despite all the new privileges. He tried to reproach them, but he received the following reply: "But, your honour, how could we not care for our master's good? You yourself saw how hard we worked when we were ploughing and sowing: and you gave us a mug of vodka each." How could he argue against this? "But why then has it turned out so badly?" pressed the master. "Heaven knows! Maybe the worm got at the roots, and then, it's been that sort of summer: no rains at all." But the master could see that on the peasants' plots the worm had not gotten at the roots and even the rain seemed to be falling in a strangely biased manner: plenty for the peasants and nary a drop on the master's fields. He had an even harder job sorting things out with the women. They kept asking to be excused from field work, complaining that the corvee was too much for them. How very strange! They no longer had to bring in any linens, berries, mushrooms or nuts, he had cut their other labours by half, thinking that the women would put this time to good purpose in house work, making clothes for their menfolk and tending their vegetable plots, but nothing of the sort happened! Idleness bred such brawls, scandal-mongering and quarrelling amongst the fair sex that their husbands often came to him to plead: "Master, make that she-devil pull her horns in! She'll be the death of me!" On several occasions, with great reluctance, he steeled himself to take severe measures. But how could he be severe? The woman would come looking such a sight, whimpering and wailing, too ill for words, and wrapped in such wretched, filthy rags, God knows where she had found them. "Go away, go away, just get out of my sight, for God's sake!" poor Tentetnikov would say, and immediately would have the pleasure to see the sick woman, once outside the gates, grappling with a neighbour over some turnip or other and pummelling her sides with heftier blows than many a strong man could deliver. He had the idea of setting up a sort of school for them, but this was such a flop that he was quite disheartened—he wished he had never even thought of it! All this considerably dampened his ardour both for managing the estate and for matters of judicial arbitration, and in general for any sort of activity. He now supervised the farmwork all but absently: his thoughts were far away, his eyes sought other objects. During the haymaking he no longer watched the swish of sixty scythes swinging in unison and the rhythmic fall of the rows of long grass, sinking to the ground with a gentle rustle; instead he gazed at a bend in the river, along the banks of which strutted a red-billed, red-legged wader—a bird, of course, not a man: he watched this wader catch a fish and hold it crossways in his bill, as if debating whether or not to swallow it, all the while staring fixedly a little way down the river where another wader could be seen, as yet with no prey, but staring back just as fixedly at the wader which had caught the fish. During the harvesting he did not care if the sheafs were laid crosswise in ricks or simply anyhow. It mattered not to him whether the work was done briskly or lazily. Screwing his eyes shut and lifting his head a little, he left it to his sense of smell to inhale the fragrance of the fields and to his hearing to marvel at the voices of that airborne, singing populace, when from all sides, from the skies above and the earth below, it blends into a single mellifluous choir, not one note clashing with another. The quail twits, the corncrake crakes in the grass, the soaring linnet twitters and chatters, the trilling of skylarks comes cascading down an unseen heavenly scale, and the crying of the cranes sweeping past in a long line—just like the call of silver trumpets—rings in the echoing emptiness of the vault of the sky. If work was in progress nearby, he would stand far away from it; if it was in the distance, his eyes would search for something near at hand. He was like the absent-minded schoolboy who stares at his book but sees the fico his classmate is showing him. Finally, he gave up going to watch the work, and also completely forsook his judicial pursuits and all his arbitrations. He stayed indoors all the time and even stopped receiving reports from his bailiff.

Occasionally a neighbour called on him, perhaps the retired lieutenant of Hussars, an inveterate pipe-smoker who was smoke-cured to the bone, or the fire-breathing colonel, a great adept and enthusiast of conversations on all topics. But this, too, began to bore him. He thought their conversation superficial; the lively, witty remarks, the slaps on the knee and other marks of familiarity now seemed to him too bold and in rather bad taste. He resolved to break off his acquaintance with them, and did so in a fairly abrupt manner. To be precise, when Varvar Nikolaich Vishnepokromov, the representative of all the fire-breathing colonels, the most pleasant conversationalist about nothing, called on him for the express purpose of talking to his heart's content about everything under the sun, touching on politics, and philosophy, and literature, and morality, and even the state of the economy in England, he sent word that he was not at home, and at the same time was careless enough to show himself at a window. The eyes of guest and host met. The one, naturally enough, muttered through his teeth: "Swine!", the other also responded with some similar epithet. And there the acquaintance ended. From that day no one called on him again. Total solitude reigned in the house. The owner donned his dressing-gown once and for all, surrendered his body to inactivity and his mind to the consideration of a great composition on Russia. The reader has already had occasion to see the manner in which this composition proceeded. The days came and went, each one as monotonous and colourless as the one before. It would not, however, be true to say that there were no moments when he seemed to bestir himself from his slumbers. When the post brought newspapers, new books and journals, and he saw in print the name of some acquaintance or former comrade, who had already gained advancement in a prominent area of the state service or had contributed splendidly to the cause of science and universal education, a quiet, secret sadness crept upon his heart and an unspoken, sad, silent complaint against his own inactivity disrupted his peace of mind. Then his life seemed repellent and foul to him. With remarkable vividness his schooldays re-appeared before him, and he suddenly saw Alexander Petrovich as in real life... The tears burst from his eyes and he continued to sob all day.

What did this sobbing mean? Was this how his ailing soul manifested the mournful secret of its ailment; that the high-minded, inner man that had begun to form within him had not managed to develop and grow strong; that, untested in his youth by struggle against adversity, he had not attained that higher state where he could rise and gain strength through the surmounting of barriers and obstacles; that, by melting like heated metal, his rich store of lofty feelings had not been properly tempered and hardened, and now, without that resilient firmness, his will was powerless; that the remarkable tutor had died too early for him and there was now no one in this world capable of rousing and stirring to action his forces, shattered by incessant vacillation, and his weak will, bereft of its resilience; that there was no one to call out in a loud, rousing voice: "*Forward!*"—the command that the Russian longs for everywhere, at every level of life, whatever his rank or estate or ambition?

Where is that man who in the native tongue of our Russian soul would say to us that all-powerful word: *Forward*; who, knowing all the resources and properties and the full depth of our nature, with one magical wave of his hand could direct his fellow Russians to a higher life? With what words of appreciation, with what love would the grateful Russian repay him! But one century succeeds another; half a million stay-at-homes, lie-abeds and marmots slumber on oblivious, and but rarely does Russia witness the birth of a man capable of uttering it, this all-powerful word.

There was, however, one circumstance that nearly roused Tentetnikov and nearly wrought a complete transformation of his character. What happened was something not unlike love, but here, too, things somehow came to nothing. In the vicinity, some ten versts from his village, lived

a general, who, as we have seen, expressed a less than totally favourable opinion of Tentetnikov. The general lived
like a general, entertaining on a grand scale, always pleased
when the neighbours called to pay their respects, whilst he
himself, of course, did not pay visits, spoke in a hoarse
voice, read books and had a daughter, a strange, lovely creature, more like some fantastical vision than a woman.
Sometimes a dream like this appears to a man, and from
then on he is haunted all the days of his life by this vision;
reality fades away altogether for him and he becomes quite
incapable of any useful work. Her name was Ulinka. The
upbringing she had had was rather strange. She was brought
up by an English governess, who knew no word of Russian.
She lost her mother while still a child. Her father had no
time to spend with her. However, this was just as well,
because loving his daughter to distraction, he might only
have spoilt her. It is uncommonly difficult to paint her
portrait. She was like life itself. She was more pretty than
beautiful, more kind than clever; more graceful, more ethereal than any classical beauty. It was quite impossible to
say which country had made its imprint on her, because it
would be hard to find a profile like hers anywhere, except
perhaps on the cameos of antiquity. A child reared at liber-
ty, she was the very embodiment of wilfulness. If anyone
had seen how she knitted her fair brow in sudden anger or
how hotly she argued with her father, he would have
thought her the most capricious creature alive. However,
her anger was aroused only when she heard about someone
being treated unfairly or cruelly. But this anger would pass
at once if she saw that the person against whom it was
directed was himself suffering, and she would quickly throw
him her purse if he was poor, no matter if this were wise or
stupid, and she would tear a strip from her own dress for a
bandage, if he was wounded! She was so impulsive that
when she spoke, everything in her seemed to fly after her
thoughts; her face, the tone of her voice, the movements
of her hands, and the very folds of her dress, and it was as
though she herself would suddenly fly off in the wake of
her own words. There was nothing secretive about her. She
would have no fear of speaking her mind before anyone,
and when she wanted to speak no power on earth could
stop her. She had such a free and fearless walk, unique to

her alone, that everyone involuntarily stepped aside to let her pass. The malevolent became diffident in her company, and held their peace, while the kind people, even the shyest, became loquacious as they had never been with anyone else before, and—strange illusion!—from the first minutes of conversation they felt that they had known her somewhere some time, perhaps in their childhood, at home, on a cheerful evening, happily playing with a crowd of children, after which, and for a long time to come, the sensible talk of grownups seemed so dull!

Andrei Ivanovich Tentetnikov would have been quite at a loss to say how it happened that from their very first meeting he felt as if he had known her always. A new inexplicable feeling entered his soul. His dull life was brightened for a moment. His dressing-gown was cast aside. It did not take him so long now to get out of bed, Mikhailo did not have to stand for hours with the basin in his hands. The windows in the rooms were thrown open and the owner of this picturesque estate often strolled down the dark, winding paths of his park and paused for hours at a time to admire the captivating views in the distance.

At first, the general received Tentetnikov fairly well, and with courtesy; but they were quite unable to get along with each other. Their conversations always ended in an argument that left an unpleasant feeling on both sides. The general did not like to be contradicted and opposed, although at the same time he was fond of discussing even things of which he was totally ignorant. Tentetnikov, for his part, was also a touchy man. But for the sake of the daughter he forgave the father much, and peace was maintained between them until two female relations came on a visit to the general, the Countess Boldyryova and the Princess Yuzyakina: the one a widow, the other an old maid, both erstwhile ladies-in-waiting, both gossips and scandal-mongers, not excessively enchanting in their amiability, but nonetheless ladies with considerable connections in St. Petersburg, before whom the general actually grovelled a bit. Tentetnikov thought that from the very day of their arrival the general's attitude towards him became somehow colder, he hardly noticed him and treated him as if he were a nobody, the paltriest of copy clerks. He called him by turns "young chap", and "my good fellow" and once even said "tu" to him as to a menial instead of "vous". Andrei Ivanovich was incensed; he could feel his blood boil. Gritting his teeth and with great reluctance he held himself in hand and said in a most respectful and soft voice, while angry blotches appeared on his face and everything within him seethed with rage:

"I must express my gratitude to you, General, for the favour you bestow on me. By saying 'tu' to me you invite me into the most intimate friendship, obliging me to address you with equal familiarity. But permit me to observe that I cannot ignore the difference between our ages, which totally prohibits such familiar intercourse between us."

The General was embarrassed. Gathering his thoughts and words, he started to say, albeit in rather an incoherent way, that Andrei Ivanovich had misunderstood him, that surely an old man could sometimes be permitted to address a young man thus familiarly (he did not say a word about his own rank).

Naturally enough, their acquaintance ended there and then, and the romance was nipped in the bud. The light which had flashed before Andrei Ivanovich for a moment grew dim and the twilight which set in its place became gloomier than ever. The marmot crept back into his dressing-gown. Once more his life was reduced to utter inactivity and lying abed. Disorder and filth reigned in his house. The floor brush lay for a whole day in the middle of the room together with the sweepings. His underpants found their way into the drawing-room. On the fancy table before the settee lay a grimy pair of braces, and his life became so insignificant and somnolent that not only did his house servants lose all respect for him, but even his chickens all but pecked at him. He would spend hours on end listlessly drawing little twiggles, little houses, huts, carts, troikas on a piece of paper, or copying out the words "My dear Sir!" complete with exclamation mark, in every possible hand and style of lettering. Sometimes, in moments of total oblivion, his pen would of its own will, without the owner's knowledge, draw a woman with delicate features, fluffy upswept hair escaping the comb in a cascade of long ring-lets, and with young, bare arms—a woman that seemed to be flying. To his astonishment he would see a portrait emerge of that creature whose portrait could be painted by no living artist. Then his heart would grow still sadder, and confirmed in his belief that there was no happiness on this earth, he would remain taciturn and out of sorts for the rest of the day.

Such were the circumstances of Andrei Ivanovich Tentetnikov's life. Suddenly one day, as he sauntered up to the window in his customary manner, with a pipe and a cup of tea, he noticed a certain commotion and activity in the yard outside. The kitchen boy and the scullery maid ran to open the gates, and in the gateway there appeared an equine ensemble exactly like those sculpted or painted on triumphal arches: a muzzle to the right, a muzzle to the left, and a muzzle in the middle. Above these on the coach-box, sat a coachman and a lackey in a loose frockcoat, fastened round the waist with a sash. Behind them sat a gentleman in a peaked cap and greatcoat, with a rainbow-coloured muffler round his neck. When the carriage turned before the porch it transpired that it was nothing other than a light sprung chaise. A gentleman of an extraordinarily agreeable mien leapt on to the porch with quite the alacrity and agility of an officer.

Andrei Ivanovich was frightened. He took the visitor for an official from the government. We should say here that in his youth he had been implicated in a certain imprudent affair. A group of philosophically inclined hussars, together with a student who had dropped off his studies and a bankrupt gambler founded a certain philanthropic society, under the administration of an old rogue, both a freemason and a card-player, a drunkard and the most silver-tongued of orators. The society was formed with the purpose of securing lasting happiness for the whole of mankind, from the banks of the Thames to Kamchatka. An enormous fund of money was required for this, and the donations forthcoming from their generous members were incredible. The final destination of all this money was known only to the head administrator. Andrei Ivanovich was drawn into this society by two friends belonging to the genus of discouraged men; they were kind people but they had so often had to drink toasts to science, enlightenment and progress, that they became inveterate drunkards. Tentetnikov soon regretted joining and removed himself from this circle. But the society had already become entangled in certain other activities, of a kind not altogether becoming to a member of the landed gentry, so that subsequently the interest of the police was aroused... It is therefore small wonder that although he had broken off all ties with the great benefactors of humankind, Tentetnikov still could not quite recover his peace of mind. His conscience was not entirely comfortable. So it was not without alarm that he now stared at the opening door.

His fear subsided at once, however, when the guest gave him an incredibly nimble bow, preserving a respectful attitude with his head slightly inclined. He explained in a few short but definite words that he had been travelling about Russia for a long time now, urged on both by his needs and by his curiosity; that our nation abounded in remarkable objects, not to mention the beauty of its scenery, the abundance of crafts and the variety of soils; that he had been attracted by the picturesque setting of Tentetnikov's village; that, notwithstanding, however, the picturesque setting he still would not have presumed to disturb his host with his untimely visit had there not been a slight accident with his chaise, necessitating a helping hand from blacksmiths and craftsmen; that despite all this, however, even if there had been no accident with his chaise, he still would not have been able to deny himself the pleasure of calling in person to pay his respects.

When he finished his speech, the guest scraped his foot in a most charming manner and, despite his corpulence, at once skipped backwards a little way with the lightness of a small India-rubber ball.

Andrei Ivanovich decided that this must be some scholarly professor of enquiring mind, travelling the length and breadth of Russia in search of some plants or even minerals. He announced his willingness to assist him in every possible way; he offered the services of his craftsmen, wheelwrights and blacksmiths to repair the chaise; he asked him to make himself comfortable and to feel quite at home; he seated his courteous guest in a large Voltaire chair and prepared to listen to his discourse, no doubt on matters scholarly and scientific.

The guest, however, touched more on events of the inner world. He spoke of the vicissitudes of fate; he likened his life to a barque tossed on the seas and buffeted everywhither by the winds; he mentioned that he had often been forced to change his position and duties, that he had suffered much for the truth, that even his very life had more than once been in danger from his enemies and he recounted much else in the same vein, from which Tentetnikov could see that his guest was more of a practical man. By way of concluding his account he blew his nose into a white lawn handkerchief more loudly than Andrei Ivanovich had ever heard before. Sometimes there is a rogue of a trumpet like that in an orchestra, and when it lets out its blast you think something has burst inside your own ear. It was precisely such a sound that rang out through the newly awakened rooms of the slumbering house, and this was followed by the fragrant whiff of eau de Cologne, invisibly diffused by an adroit flick of the lawn handkerchief.

The reader has perhaps already guessed that the guest was none other than our honoured friend Pavel Ivanovich Chichikov, whom we abandoned so long ago. He had aged a little: obviously the time since we last saw him had not passed without its storms and anxieties for him. Even the very coat on his back appeared to have aged somewhat, and the chaise, the coachman, the manservant, the horses, the harness were all somehow a little battered and worn. It seemed that his finances, too, were in an unenviable state. But the expression on his face, his decorum and courtesy all remained unaltered. He had grown even more agreeable in his gestures and turns of phrase, he tucked one leg even more adroitly behind the other leg when he sat in an armchair, there was still greater softness in the delivery of his speeches, more circumspection in his words and expressions, more skill in the way he held himself and more tact in all things. His collars and shirtfronts were purer and whiter than the driven snow and, although he had just been on the road, no speck of dust had alighted on his frockcoat: he could have been dressed for a birthday dinner! His cheeks and chin were so smoothly shaved that only perhaps a blind man could have failed to marvel at their agreeable plumpness and roundness.

A transformation took place in the house. That half of it which hitherto had languished in a state of blindness behind shuttered windows suddenly regained its sight and was filled with light. Servants set about unloading the chaise. The things were taken to the newly lighted rooms and soon everything was arranged as follows: the room that was to be the guest's bedroom accommodated the things essential for his night toilet; the room that was to be his study... But first it should be known that this room contained three tables; one writing table, before the settee; the second a card table between the windows, up against the wall; the third a corner-table, in the corner, standing between the door to the bedroom and the door to an unlived-in room used for storing broken furniture. It was on to this table that the clothes had been unpacked from the suitcase, to wit: a pair of trousers to go with his tailcoat, a pair of trousers to go with his frockcoat, a pair of grey trousers, two velvet waistcoats and two satin waistcoats, a frockcoat and two tailcoats. (The white piqué waistcoats and the summer trousers were placed with the linen in the chest of drawers). All this was piled into a pyramid and covered with a silk kerchief. In another corner, between the door and a window, his boots were set out in a row: boots that were not brand-new, boots that were brand-new, boots with new uppers, and patent leather ankle boots. These were also bashfully screened with a silk kerchief—just as if there were no boots there at all. On the table between the two windows stood a casket. Placed on the writing table in front of the settee was the guest's briefcase, also a jar of eau de Cologne, sealing-wax, tooth-brushes, a new calendar and two novels, both volume two. The clean linen was put away in the chest of drawers there was in the bedroom; but the linen that needed laundering was tied into a bundle and stuffed under the bed. The suitcase, once it had been emptied, was also shoved under the bed. The guest's sabre was likewise taken into the bedroom, and there it hung on a nail within reach of the bed. Both rooms now looked extraordinarily clean and tidy. Nowhere was there a scrap of paper, or a feather, or a speck of dust to be seen. The very air seemed to have been ennobled. It was filled with the pleasant odour of a healthy, fresh man, who does not wear his linen too long, goes to the bath-house regularly and rubs himself down with a wet sponge on Sundays. An attempt had been made by the manservant Petrushka's smell to establish itself in the vestibule, but

Petrushka was promptly removed to the kitchen, as was right and fitting.

For the first few days Andrei Ivanovich feared for his independence, lest his guest should somehow or other encumber him, inhibit him by some changes to the manner of his life, and lest the happily established routine of his day be disrupted—but his fears were unfounded. Our Pavel Ivanovich displayed remarkable flexibility in his capacity to adapt to everything. He expressed approval of his host's philosophical leisureliness, declaring that it would ensure him a very long life. On the question of seclusion he acquitted himself most felicitously, averring that it nourished great ideas in a man. Casting a look at the library and expressing his praise of books in general, he went on to observe that they saved man from indolence. In a word, he spoke little, but always significantly. As far as his actions were concerned, he conducted himself still more appositely. His appearances were timely and so were his departures. He did not weary his host with questions when the latter was in an uncommunicative mood; he played chess with pleasure, he sat in silence with pleasure. When the host sprawled blowing clouds of pipe smoke, the guest, who did not smoke a pipe, devised a corresponding pastime for himself: he would, for example, take out his black and silver snuff-box and, holding it firmly between the thumb and finger of his left hand, spin it round with a finger of his right hand, just like the earth spinning on its axis, or he would simply drum on its lid with his fingers, whistling something noncommittal. In short, he did not impose on his host in any way. "This is the first time I have met a man," Tentetnikov would say to himself, "with whom it is possible to live. It is an art sadly lacking amongst us. There is amongst us a sufficiency of clever men, well educated men, good men, but as for men who are constantly agreeable, constantly equable in character, men with whom one can live one's entire life and never quarrel—I very much doubt you would find any like that among us!" Such was Tentetnikov's assessment of his guest.

Chichikov for his own part was delighted to sojourn for a while with so serene and peaceable a host. He had grown weary of the gypsy life. To have a little rest, if only for a month, in a lovely village, with a view of fields and the

approaching spring, was of benefit even from the haemorrhoidal point of view. A better haven of rest would be
hard to find. The oncoming spring adorned this haven with
fabulous beauty. What brightness there was in the greenery!
What freshness in the air! What melodious birdsong in the
orchards! The paradise, joy and exultation of all things!
The countryside hummed and sang as if it were new born.

Chichikov took many walks. Sometimes he directed his
steps along the flat plateau that overlooked the valleys
stretching beneath, in which there still remained great
lakes from the flood-waters; at other times he entered the
ravines, where the trees, only just beginning to don new
foliage, were weighed down with birds' nests, and here he
was deafened by the cawing of crows, the chattering of daws
and the crunking of rooks, which flew hither and thither
in great flocks, darkening the sky; or else he went down to
the water-meadows and the burst dams, to watch the water
crashing down on the mill wheels with a deafening roar; or
he strolled as far as the quayside, from which the first
boats were embarking on the spring waters, laden with
peas, oats, barley and wheat; or he set out for the fields to
watch the first spring labours, to see the first furrows being
cut in a black swathe through the green sward, or to admire
the skilful sower casting his handfuls of seeds evenly and
precisely, without a single seed falling to one side or the
other. He chatted with the bailiff, the peasants and the
miller—discussing this and that, what sort of harvests might
be expected, how the ploughing was proceeding, what price
wheat was fetching, what they charged in the spring and
autumn for grinding the flour, and asking the name of each
peasant, and who was related to whom, and where he
bought his cow, and what he fed his pig—in a word, everything. He also found out how many peasants had died. It
transpired that not many had. Being a man of intelligence
he at once noticed that Andrei Ivanovich's management of
affairs was far from perfect. There was neglect, careless-
ness, thieving and also widespread drunkenness. And he
said to himself: "What a swine that Tentetnikov is, honestly! Letting his estate go to rack and ruin like that, when it
could bring in at least fifty thousand a year!" And then,
quite unable to suppress his righteous indignation, he
repeated: "What a perfect swine!" Often, during these

walks, he wondered whether he himself might not one day—
that is, not now, of course, but later, when his great undertaking was completed and he was in funds—whether he
himself might not become a peace-loving proprietor of
just such an estate. At this point he usually pictured a young
wife, a healthy, fair-faced wench, perhaps even from the
merchant class, but educated and brought up like a gentlewoman—with an understanding of music, too, although,
of course, music was not really the most important thing,
but, if that was the custom, why go against the general
opinion? He also saw the younger generation, destined to
perpetuate the name of Chichikov: a sprightly scamp of a
boy and a beautiful little daughter, or even two boys, two
or even three little girls, so that everyone would know that
he really had lived and existed, that he had not merely
passed across the earth like a shadow or phantom—so that
he would have no cause for shame before his country either.
It also occurred to him that it would be no bad thing to
gain a certain promotion in rank: to state counsellor, for
instance, an honourable and respected rank... Thus, he
indulged in the sort of thoughts that carry a man away
from the dreary reality of his present life, teasing and stirring him up, and welcomed by him even when he knows
perfectly well that none of it will ever come true.

Pavel Ivanovich's servants also found the village much
to their liking. Like him, they also grew quite at home
there. Petrushka quickly made friends with the butler Grigory, although at first they both put on airs and showed
off insufferably to each other. Petrushka bragged to Grigory
that he had been to Kostroma, Yaroslavl, Nizhny and even
Moscow; Grigory promptly countered with St. Petersburg,
which Petrushka had never visited. The latter now attempted to regain the upper hand by vaunting the great dis-
tances he had travelled; but Grigory named a town which
you would find on no existing map and cited a distance of
some thirty thousand versts or more, so that Petrushka
could only goggle owl-like and gape in astonishment, to
the immediate derision of all the assembled household
staff. However, this rivalry ended in the most intimate
friendship: one of the peasants, old "Baldy" Pimen, kept
a much-celebrated pothouse at the end of the village
named "Akulina" after some woman or other and it was

here that they were to be seen at all hours of the day. Here they became fast friends, or what the peasants call pothouse regulars.

Selifan found another kind of lure. Never an evening passed in the village without the singing of songs, and the winding and unwinding of spring round-dances. The village girls, comely and statuesque, of a beauty hard to find anywhere else, would make him stand and gape for hours on end. It was hard to tell which of them was the fairest: they were all full-breasted, all with eyes as round as saucers, all with eyes that beckoned, with plaits reaching to their waists, and strutting about like peacocks. When he took their white hands in his own, and moved slowly with them in a round-dance or stood in a line facing them with the other lads, as the fiery sunset faded and dusk settled over the surrounding fields, and the echo of the unchangingly sad refrain was wafted back to them from far beyond the river—he himself no longer knew what was happening to him. For a long time thereafter, in his sleeping and his waking hours, in the morning and at dusk, he would continue to imagine that he held those white hands in his own and that he was moving with them in the round-dance. With a wave of his hand he would say: "Cursed wenches!"

Chichikov's horses also found their new habitat to their liking. The shaft-horse, and Assessor, the brown trace horse, as well as the dapple grey himself, whom Selifan used to curse as a "scoundrel-horse", all found their stay on Tentetnikov's estate anything but tedious; the oats excellent and the stables extraordinarily well-appointed. They each had their own stall, and though they were separated from one another it was still possible to see the other horses over the partitions, so that if any of them, even the one standing furthest off, took a sudden notion to neigh, he could be answered immediately in like manner.

In a word, they all felt perfectly at home. The reader might be surprised that so far Chichikov had not said a word on the well-known subject of souls. He knew better now. Pavel Ivanovich had grown very circumspect in this respect. Even if he had found himself dealing with utter fools he still would not have broached the subject right away. But Tentetnikov, for all his faults, read books, philosophized, endeavoured to discover all sorts of reasons for everything—the whys and the wherefores... "No, damn it all!" thought Chichikov, "Perhaps I should start from the other end?" In his frequent chats with the household servants he found out, amongst other things, that their master used to make fairly frequent visits to his neighbour the general, that the general had a daughter, that the master seemed to like the young lady, and the young lady seemed to like the master too... But then they fell out suddenly over something and parted company. He himself noticed that Andrei Ivanovich was always drawing women's profiles with pen or pencil, and all exactly alike. One day after luncheon, as he pursued his customary pastime of spinning his silver snuff-box round its axis, he ventured to remark:

"You have everything, Andrei Ivanovich, except for only one thing."

"What's that?" asked his host, emitting a spiral of smoke.

"A wife," said Chichikov.

Andrei Ivanovich made no reply. There the conversation ended.

Chichikov was not discouraged, he merely chose another moment, this time just before supper, and, in the course of a general conversation, suddenly said: "But you know, Andrei Ivanovich, you really ought to marry."

Not a word did Tentetnikov say in reply to this, just as if the very mention of the subject was disagreeable to him.

Chichikov was not put off. A third time he chose his moment, now after supper, and spoke as follows:

"All the same, whichever way I look at your circumstances I still see that you must get married: otherwise you will succumb to hypochondria."

Either Chichikov's words on this occasion were especially convincing, or perhaps Andrei Ivanovich's mood was particularly disposed towards candour, but he sighed and said, blowing a cloud of pipe smoke towards the ceiling: "In all things you have to be born a fortunate man, Pavel Ivanovich," and he told him all that had happened, the entire story of his acquaintance with the general and their rift.

When Chichikov heard the full story and learnt that such a debacle could have been caused by the word "tu" instead of "vous", he was dumbfounded. For several minutes he stared fixedly into Tentetnikov's eyes and concluded to himself: "But the man's quite simply a complete fool!"

"But Andrei Ivanovich, my dear fellow," he said, taking hold of both his hands. "What is so insulting about that? What is insulting about the word 'tu'?"

"There's nothing insulting in the word itself," said Tentetnikov, "but the tone of voice in which it is said, contains the insult. It implies: 'Don't you forget that you're worthless rubbish; I've only been receiving you because there was no one better around, but the moment some Princess Yuzyakina or other arrives, make sure you know your place, stand by the door.' That's what it implies."

As he said this the meek and humble Andrei Ivanovich's eyes flashed with fire and his voice rang with outraged feeling.

"Well, even if it was in that sense—so what?" asked Chichikov.

"So what?" said Tentetnikov, staring at Chichikov in amazement. "You want me to continue calling on him after such an action?"

"After what action? It wasn't even an action!" said Chichikov.

"This Chichikov's a strange chap!" said Tentetnikov to himself.

"This Tentetnikov's a strange chap!" said Chichikov to himself.

"That is no action, Andrei Ivanovich. It is no more than a habit with generals: they say 'tu' to everyone. And after all, why shouldn't that be permitted a distinguished, high ranking man?"

"That's a different matter," said Tentetnikov. "If he had been an old man, a poor man, not proud or haughty, not a general, then I should have permitted him to say 'tu' to me and should even have taken it with deference."

"He's a complete fool," thought Chichikov. "He'd permit a poor wretch but not a general!" And after this deliberation he objected aloud: "Very well; let us suppose that he did insult you, but then you are now quits with him: he slighted you and you slighted him. But as for falling out forever over some trifle—forgive me, but what sort of tomfoolery is that? How can you give up something which has only just started? Once you have chosen your goal you must stop at nothing. Why pay attention to somebody's slight? People will always slight others; you will not find a single man anywhere in this wide world who does not slight anyone."

Tentetnikov was quite nonplussed by these words, and stared dumbfounded into Pavel Ivanovich's eyes, thinking: "But what a most peculiar man this Chichikov is!"

"All the same, what an odd customer this Tentetnikov is!" thought Chichikov at the same time.

"Allow me to try to sort this matter out somehow," he said aloud. "I can call on His Excellency and I shall explain that this came about through a misunderstanding on your part, by reason of your youth and your ignorance of people and the ways of the world."

"I do not intend to grovel before him," said Tentetnikov firmly.

"The Lord forbid that you should grovel!" said Chichikov, crossing himself. "I intended to remonstrate with him, as a fair-minded intermediary, but as for grovelling... Forgive me, Andrei Ivanovich, for my good intentions and devotion, I never thought you'd take my words in such a wrong sense!"

"Forgive me, Pavel Ivanovich, I am in the wrong!" exclaimed Tentetnikov, deeply moved, and he gratefully seized hold of both Chichikov's hands. "Your kind concern is most dear to me, I swear it! But do let us leave this matter, let us never talk of it again."

"In that case I shall simply call on the general without a pretext," said Chichikov.

"But whatever for?" asked Tentetnikov, staring at Chichikov in bewilderment.

"To pay my respects," said Chichikov.

"What a strange fellow this Chichikov is!" thought Tentetnikov.

"What a strange fellow this Tentetnikov is!" thought Chichikov.

"Since my chaise is not yet in a fit state," said Chichikov, "permit me to take one of your carriages. I should like to call on him tomorrow, without further ado, at about ten o'clock."

"My dear fellow, what a request! My house is *your*

house, take whichever carriage you wish. Everything is at your disposal."

They said their good-nights and went their separate ways to bed, but not without reflecting upon each other's strangenesses.

A strange thing now occurred, however: the next day, when the horses were harnessed up and Chichikov sprang into the carriage with quite the agility of an officer, clad in his new tailcoat, white cravat and waistcoat, and rattled off to pay his respects to the general, Tentetnikov was thrown into such a state of excitement as he had not experienced for a very long time. The entire rusty and somnolent course of his thoughts was galvanised into a frenzy of activity. A nervous fret suddenly afflicted all the emotions of this sluggard, who had hitherto languished in a state of carefree torpor. He sat down on the settee, then jumped up and went to the window, then he took up a book, tried to think—it was all futile! Thought simply refused to come into his head. Then he tried to think of nothing at all—wasted endeavour! Snatches of something akin to thought, scraps and tails of uninvited thoughts thronged his mind and got stuck there. "What a strange condition!" he said and stepped closer to the window to stare at the road which cut through the oak grove, at the end of which the cloud of dust thrown up by the departing carriage still lingered. But let us now leave Tentetnikov and hasten in pursuit of Chichikov.

CHAPTER TWO

In a little more than half an hour the horses had transported Chichikov a distance of some ten versts—first through the oak grove, then through wheatfields where the young crop was starting to show green against the freshly ploughed earth, then along the crest of a hill, from which each successive minute brought new distant vistas, and at last they carried him down a broad avenue of spreading lime trees into the general's village. The avenue of limes turned into an avenue of poplars, protected at their base with wicker cages, and led to wrought-iron gates through which could be seen the magnificent rococo facade of the general's house, supported by eight columns with Corinthian capitals. There was an all-pervading smell of the paint with which all parts of the house were constantly being freshened up before they could grow shabby. The courtyard was as clean as a dance floor. As they drove up to the entrance Chichikov alighted with dignity on to the porch, asked to be announced and was conducted directly into the general's study.

The general impressed him with his majestic appearance. He was clad at that time of day in a raspberry-red satin dressing-gown. He had an open look, a manly face, sideburns and a large greying moustache, cropped hair, a thick neck, with the so-called three storeys, or three folds, with a vertical crease, a deep, slightly hoarse voice, and the gestures of a true general. General Betrishchev, like all of us sinners, was endowed with many virtues and many shortcomings. Former and latter, as is customary with the Russian character, were mixed together in him in picturesque disarray. A capacity for self-sacrifice, for magnanimity at decisive moments, courage, intelligence—and added to all this a generous admixture of vanity, ambition, egotism, a petty testiness in matters personal and many other foibles of the sort that no man is altogether free of. He loathed all those who had gone ahead of him in service, and spoke splenetically of them, in sardonic, biting epigrams. The one who got the worst tongue-lashing was his former friend and colleague whom he considered inferior to him both in intelligence and abilities, and yet who had gone ahead of him and was already the governor-general of two provinces. To make matters worse, these were precisely the provinces in which the general's own estates were situated, so that he found himself in some way under his jurisdiction. By way of revenge, he vilified him at every opportunity, criticized his every administrative disposition and thought his every measure and act as the very last word in ineptitude. Despite his kind heart the general was a scornful man. Generally speaking he loved to be in command, loved adulation, loved to dazzle and impress with his intelligence, loved to know things others did not know, and did not like people who knew something he did not know. Having received a half-foreign education he wished at the same time to play the role of the Russian squire. With such an inequitable character, he was inevitably bound to come up against all sorts of unpleasantnesses in his service, and this did, in fact, precipitate his retirement. He blamed it on some hostile conspiracy against him, and lacked the good grace to take on any of the blame himself. In retirement he preserved his same picturesque, magisterial bearing. Whether wearing a frockcoat, a tailcoat or a dressing-gown, he would be just the same. Everything about him, from his voice to the slightest movement of his hands, spoke of authority, imperiousness, and instilled in members of the lower orders if not respect, then at least timidity.

Chichikov experienced both sensations—respect and timidity. Inclining his head deferentially to one side, he began as follows:

"I deemed it my duty to present myself to Your Excellency. Feeling a profound esteem for the valour of those men who defended our fatherland on the battlefield, I thought it my duty to present myself in person to Your Excellency."

This overture was not, as could be seen, altogether displeasing to the general. Making a markedly gracious motion with his head he said:

"Delighted to make your acquaintance. Please be seated. Where did you serve?"

"The route of my service," said Chichikov, sitting down not in the middle of the chair, but perched on the edge and clutching its arm with one hand, "commenced in the Treasury, Your Excellency; its path then led through various offices: I served in the civil court, on a construction commission and in the customs. My life may be likened to a barque tossed on the waves, Your Excellency. I was reared, you might say, on patience—I was suckled on patience, was swaddled in patience, and am myself, so to speak, the very embodiment of patience. I have suffered more at the hands of my enemies than it is within the power of words or paints to convey. Now, however, in the evening, so to speak, of my life, I go in search of a little haven in which to live out my remaining days. For the time being I am sojourning with a close neighbour of Your Excellency."

"Who is that?"

"Tentetnikov, Your Excellency."

The general frowned.

"He, Your Excellency, is most repentant for having failed to show due respect—"

"To what?"

"To the merits of Your Excellency. Words fail him. He says 'if only there were some way in which I could ... because, to be sure,' he says, 'I know how to value men who have saved our fatherland,' he says."

"Heavens above, what does he mean!.. But I'm not angry with him," said the mollified general. "In my heart I formed a most sincere liking for him and I am convinced that in time he will become a thoroughly useful man."

"Perfectly right, Your Excellency. Yes, a thoroughly useful man, who has a flair for speaking and writing as well."

"But I expect he writes a lot of rubbish, verses or something?"

"Oh no, Your Excellency, not rubbish at all—"

"Well, what then?"

"He is writing ... a history, Your Excellency."

"A history! A history of what?"

"A history..." Here Chichikov paused, and whether because a general sat before him or because he wished to impart a greater significance to the topic, he continued: "A history of generals, Your Excellency."

"What do you mean: of generals? What generals?"

"Of generals in general, Your Excellency, as a generality ... that is, properly speaking, of Russian generals," said Chichikov, whilst thinking: "What rubbish I'm talking!"

"I'm sorry, but I do not quite understand... Does that mean a history of some period or other, or individual biographies, and then is it of all generals, or merely those who participated in the 1812 campaign?"

"Exactly so, Your Excellency, those that participated in the 1812 campaign." As he said this, Chichikov thought: "I'll be hanged if I know what I'm on about!"

"Why doesn't he come to see me then? I could collect a lot of interesting material for him."

"He does not dare, Your Excellency."

"Stuff and nonsense! All because of some trifling thing... And I'm not that sort of man at all. I think I'll go and see him myself."

"He will not let you take the trouble, he'll come himself," said Chichikov, and thought at the same time: "All that stuff about generals did the trick after all; and to think my tongue blurted it out in all ignorance."

A whisper of a sound was heard. The carved walnut door swung open of its own accord, and on the other side there appeared a living statuette, her lovely hand grasping the door handle. If a translucent tableau had suddenly lit up the room, illuminated by a lamp from behind, it would not have so amazed the onlooker as did this figure, who positively radiated vitality, who seemed to have appeared before them with the express purpose of filling the room with radiance. It was as if with her arrival the rays of the sun flew into the room, suddenly lighting up the ceiling, the cornices and the dark corners. She seemed to be of a dazzling height. That was an illusion, caused by her extraordinarily slender form and the harmonious proportion of all the parts of her body, from her head to toe. Her dress of one colour was made with such perfect taste that surely the dressmakers of the world's capitals must have conferred how best to adorn her. This, too, was illusory. She had pinned an uncut piece of cloth in two or three places and it draped itself around her in such graceful clinging folds that a sculptor would have immediately done her in marble, and all the young ladies dressed in the latest fashion would look like so many strutting popinjays next to her. Although Chichikov knew her face from Andrei Ivanovich's drawings he gazed at her like one struck dumb, and only afterwards, when he had come to his senses, did he notice that she did have a substantial fault, namely a lack of plumpness.

"Allow me to present my darling daughter," said the general, turning to Chichikov. "Forgive me, I still don't know your name and patronymic."

"Is there really any need to know the name and patronymic of a man who has not distinguished himself with deeds of valour?" said Chichikov.

"Well, nevertheless, one should know..."

"It's Pavel Ivanovich, Your Excellency," announced Chichikov, with a slight sideways motion of his head.

"Ulinka! Pavel Ivanovich has just told me a most interesting piece of news. Our neighbour Tentetnikov is not such a stupid man as we supposed. He has embarked upon a project of considerable importance: the history of the generals of the 1812 campaign."

Ulinka suddenly blushed, and objected quickly:

"But who thought he was a stupid man, anyway? Only that Vishnepokromov could have thought that, and you go and believe him, Papa, such an empty-headed and base man!"

"Why do you say base? He is rather empty-headed, of course," admitted the general.

"He's mean and revolting, and not just rather empty-headed," Ulinka quickly interjected. "Anyone who could so offend his brothers and banish his own sister from his house must be a base man..."

"But those are only stories told about him."

"There's no smoke without fire. You have the kindest of souls and an uncommonly soft heart, Father, but from the way you act a person might form quite a different opinion of you. Must you receive a man knowing full well that he is a good-for-nothing, simply because he has a glib tongue and is adept at fawning on you?"

"My dear pet! How can I turn him away?" said the general.

"You don't have to turn him away, but neither do you have to love him!"

"Oh no, Your Excellency," said Chichikov to Ulinka, with a slight bow of his head and an agreeable smile. "According to Christian teaching it is precisely such men that we must love."

And at this point he turned to the general and said with a smile, this time slightly roguish:

"Might I ask whether Your Excellency has heard the little story about 'Try and love us when we're dirty; anyone can love us when we're clean'?"

"No, I've not heard it."

"Well, this is a most appropriate anecdote," said Chichikov still with his roguish smile. "Now, on the estate of Prince Gukzovsky, with whom Your Excellency is undoubtedly acquainted—"

"Don't know him."

"There was a manager, a young man of German stock. On the matter of recruits and other business he had to go to town and there, naturally, to grease the palms of the law officers." Here Chichikov, screwing up his eyes, showed by the expression on his face how palms were greased. "They also took a liking to him, and wined and dined him. And so one day at dinner with them he said: 'Well now, gentlemen, you must come and visit me some time, on the Prince's estate.' They promised to visit him. Shortly after this assizes were held there on a case concerning the estates of Count Trekhmetyov, whom Your Excellency is also certain to know."

"Don't know him."

"As things happened the assizers did not carry out the investigation at all, but the lot of them turned off to the house of the Count's old steward and stayed there for three days and three nights playing cards the whole time. The samovar and grog, naturally enough, never left the table. In the end the old man grew tired of them, and to get rid of them suggested: 'Gentlemen, you should call on the Prince's German manager: he lives near here and is expecting you.' 'Why not, indeed,' they agreed, and just as they were, half drunk, unshaven and groggy with sleep, they climbed on their carts and repaired to the German's house. Now I should tell you, Your Excellency, that the German had only just got married. He had married a young lady fresh from finishing school, a young, fragile thing" (here Chichikov's facial expression demonstrated fragility). "The two of them were sitting together having tea, with never a care in the world, when suddenly the doors opened and in burst this ugly mob—"

"I can just imagine them—a splendid sight!" exclaimed the general with a laugh.

"The manager was totally dumbfounded and said: 'What do you want?' 'Aha,' they cried, 'it's like that, is it?' And suddenly changed completely... 'We want to make a check up! How much vodka do you distil on the estate? Let's see your records.' The German rushed to and fro in a panic. 'Let's have some witnesses!' They grabbed hold of him, bound him and the German spent the next year and a half in gaol."

"Well I never!" said the general.

Ulinka clasped her hands.

"The wife petitioned, of course," continued Chichikov. "But what could a young, inexperienced woman do? Luckily she happened upon some kind people who advised her to make a deal with those assizers. The German got off with two thousand and the cost of a dinner for them. At this dinner, when they were already feeling gay, and the German himself too, they said to him: 'Aren't you ashamed of the rotten welcome you gave us that time? You only want to see us smart and clean-shaven and in our best bib and tucker. No, you must try and love us dirty, anyone can love us clean.' "

The general guffawed heartily; Ulinka sighed.

"Papa, I do not understand how you can laugh!" she said angrily, her fair brow shadowed... "That was the most dishonourable act, for which they should all have been banished to I don't know where."

"My dear, I am not condoning them at all," said the general. "But what can we do if it's funny? How docs it go: 'try and love us clean...'?"

"Dirty, Your Excellency," corrected Chichikov.

" 'Try and love us dirty, anyone can love us clean.' Ha, ha, ha, ha!"

And the general's body started to rock with laughter. Those shoulders that had once worn heavy epaulettes shook, just as if they were still wearing heavy epaulettes.

Chichikov also permitted himself an interjection of laughter, but out of respect to the general, he articulated it not as "Ha, ha" but as "He, he, he, he, he!" and his body also started to rock with laughter, although his shoulders did not shake, because they had never worn heavy epaulettes.

"I can imagine, those unshaven assizers must have been a fine sight!" said the general, continuing to laugh.

"Indeed, Your Excellency, whichever way one looks at it ... after ... a three day vigil, playing cards and drinking, actually fasting too: they must have been pretty worn out!" said Chichikov, continuing to laugh.

Ulinka lowered herself into an armchair and placed a hand over her lovely eyes; as if annoyed that there was no one with whom she could share her indignation, she said: "I don't know, I find the whole story extremely vexatious."

Indeed, the feelings aroused in the hearts of the three persons assembled here in conversation were most oddly contradictory. One of them found the German's slowness and unresourcefulness funny. Another found it funny because rogues had played a funny trick on someone. The third was sad because injustice had been allowed to go unpunished. There only lacked a fourth, who could have mused over these very words, which had occasioned laughter in one and sadness in another. What does it mean, however, that even in his fall a sullied, degraded man should demand that he be loved? Is this some animal instinct? Or the feeble cry of a soul, choked by the oppressive weight of base passions, a voice that can still be heard through the hardening crust of loathsomeness, crying out: "Brother, save me!" There was no fourth person, to whom the degraded soul of his brother would have seemed the most distressing thing of all.

"I don't know," said Ulinka, removing her hand from her face, "the whole story only vexes me."

"Only, I beg you, don't be vexed with us," said the general. "We are not to blame in any way for this. Give me a kiss and go to your room, because I am now going to dress for dinner. I hope," said the general turning to Chichikov, "you are going to dine with us?"

"If Your Excellency—"

"No ceremonies please. There's plenty of cabbage soup!"

Chichikov bowed his head in an agreeable fashion and when again he raised it he could no longer see Ulinka. She had disappeared. In her place there stood a giant of a valet, with a bushy moustache and whiskers, holding a silver basin and pitcher in his hands.

"Would you permit me to dress in your presence?" asked the general, throwing off his dressing gown and rolling up the shirt sleeves on his massive arms.

"Why of course, and not only to dress, but in my presence Your Excellency may do anything you see fit," said Chichikov.

The general started to wash, splashing and spluttering like a duck. Water and suds flew in all directions.

"How does it go?" he asked, rubbing his fat neck all round, "try and love us clean...?"

"Dirty, Your Excellency."

"Try and love us dirty, for anyone can love us clean. Very good, very good!"

Chichikov was in an uncommonly fine mettle; he felt himself inspired.

"Your Excellency!" he said.

"What?" said the general.

"There's another story too."

"What story?"

"Also a funny story, but it's not really funny for me. I would even say that, if Your Excellency—"

"Say what?"

"Well, Your Excellency, it's like this..." Here Chichikov glanced about him and, seeing that the valet with the basin had left, he began thus: "I have an uncle, a dotard. He has three hundred souls and, besides myself, not a single heir. In his senility he's unable to manage his estate himself, neither will he hand it over to me. And he gives such a strange reason. 'I don't know my nephew,' he says; 'maybe he's a spendthrift. Let him prove to me that he's a reliable man, let him first acquire three hundred souls of his own, and then I shall give him my three hundred.'"

"What a fool!"

"Your Excellency is quite right. But just picture to yourself my own position..." Here Chichikov, lowering his voice as if confiding a secret: "In his house, Your Excellency, he has a housekeeper, and this housekeeper has children. Before I know it, he'll bequeath the lot to them."

"The old fool has clearly gone ga-ga, that's all there is to it," said the general. "Only I do not see in what way I can be of assistance."

"I've thought of something. At the moment, before the new census lists are submitted, landowners with big estates have, besides their living souls, accumulated a goodly number of fugitive and dead ones... So if, for example, Your Excellency were to make these over to me just as if they were alive, by drawing up a deed of purchase, I could then present this deed to the old man and he, whether he likes it or not, will have to hand over his estate to me."

At this the general laughed so heartily as probably no man has ever laughed before. He collapsed into his armchair; he threw back his head, and all but choked on his guffaws. The entire house was thrown into commotion. The valet appeared. The daughter came rushing in, alarmed.

"Papa, what's happened to you?"

"Nothing my dear. Ha, ha, ha! Run along to your room, we shall be coming to dinner directly. Ha, ha, ha!"

Speaking made him gasp for breath, and then his guffaws rang out with renewed vigour, resounding through the high-ceilinged chambers from the vestibule to the most remote room in the house.

Chichikov anxiously waited for this extraordinary fit of laughter to end.

"I say, brother, do forgive me: the devil himself must have put you up to that joke. Ha, ha, ha! What a treat for the old man, slipping him a lot of dead ones! Ha, ha, ha! Poor old uncle! What a fool you'd make of him! Ha, ha, ha, ha!"

Chichikov's situation was awkward in the extreme: before them stood the valet, his mouth hanging open and his eyes starting from his head.

"But Your Excellency, this laughter arises from another's lamentable predicament," he said.

"Forgive me, brother! Goodness, you'll be the death of me! I'd give five hundred thousand only to see your uncle's face when you bring him a deed of purchase for dead souls. But is he so very old? How old is he?

"Eighty, Your Excellency. But this is rather confidential, I would rather we..." Chichikov gave the general a significant look and at the same time glanced sideways at the valet.

"Go away, now. You can come in later," the general told the valet.

"Yes—well now—Your Excellency... This, Your Excellency, is the sort of matter I would rather keep secret..."

"Of course, I understand perfectly. What an old fool! Imagine getting such foolhardy notions in your head at the age of eighty! But what is he like to look at? Sprightly? Still on his pins?"

"Still on his pins, but only just."

"What a fool! Still got his teeth?"

"Only two left, Your Excellency."

"What an ass! Don't take it to heart, my dear chap... But he really is an ass!"

"Exactly, Your Excellency. Although he is my relative and it pains me to admit it, but he really is an ass."

This as the reader may have grasped for himself, was not at all difficult for Chichikov to admit, all the more so because he had probably never had an uncle in his life.

"So, if Your Excellency would be so kind—"

"As to let you have some dead souls? Why for an idea like that I'll let you have them complete with land and dwellings! You can take the entire graveyard! Ha, ha, ha, ha! The poor old boy! Ha, ha, ha, ha! What a fool! Ha, ha, ha, ha!"

And the general's laughter again reverberated through the rooms.

(The end of the chapter is missing. The first edition of the second volume of *Dead Souls* [1855] contains the note: "Missing here is the reconciliation between General Betrishchev and Tentetnikov; dinner at the general's and their conversation about the 1812 campaign; Ulinka's betrothal to Tentetnikov; her praying and weeping at her mother's graveside; the conversation of the engaged couple in the garden. Chichikov departs on a commission from General Betrishchev to his relatives, to give news of the daughter's betrothal, and he calls on one of these relatives, Colonel Koshkaryov.")

CHAPTER THREE

"No, no," said Chichikov, finding himself once more surrounded by open fields and spaces, "no, I shall not arrange my life like that. As soon as I finish everything successfully, God willing, and become a real man of property, a wealthy man, I shall proceed quite differently: I shall have a cook, and a house full of plenty, and the farming side will also be in good order. Not only will I make ends meet, I shall also put away a little sum each year for my descendants, if the good Lord should bestow fertility upon my wife... Hey you, blockhead!"

Selifan and Petrushka both looked round from the coach-box.

"Where do you think you're going?"

"Just as you ordered, Pavel Ivanovich, to Colonel Koshkaryov's," said Selifan.

"And did you ask the way?"

"But, Pavel Ivanovich, sir, seeing as how I was busy the whole time with the carriage, and so... I only saw the general's stableman... But Petrushka asked the coachman."

"You stupid fool! I've told you before, not to rely on Petrushka: Petrushka's a dolt."

"But it doesn't take brains to remember," said Petrushka, looking askance at him, "after coming down the hill you've got to go straight, that's all."

"I suppose you've been guzzling all this time? And I suppose you're soused now too?"

Seeing the direction in which this discussion was leading, Petrushka became fidgety. He wanted to swear that he hadn't even sampled the stuff, but this was too shameless a lie.

"Nice carriage this, sir, to travel in," said Selifan, turning round.

"What?"

"I was saying, Pavel Ivanovich, sir, that your honour's carriage is nice to travel in, sir, better, sir, than the chaise, it doesn't jolt."

"Drive on! No one's asking for your opinion."

Selifan lightly brushed the rounded haunches of the horses with his whip and addressed Petrushka:

"You know, they say old Koshkaryov got his peasants dressed up just like Germans; from a distance you wouldn't have known them, strutting around stork-fashion, just like Germans. And as for the women, he wouldn't let them wear their usual head-scarf or fancy head-dress, but made them don those German bonnets, just like the German women wear, those bonnet things, you know. One of those German bonnets."

"I'd just like to see you dressed up like a German with a bonnet on!" said Petrushka, grinning gleefully at Selifan's expense. Heavens, how ugly he was with that grin! He did not appear to be smiling at all, but rather looked like a man who had caught cold and was trying to sneeze with a stuffed nose, but no sneeze came and the grimace of someone on the point of sneezing remained frozen on his face.

Chichikov looked up at this mug from below, curious to know what was going on, and said: "What a sight! And he fancies he's good-looking!" We should say here that Pavel Ivanovich was seriously convinced that Petrushka was obsessed with his own good looks, when in point of fact his manservant often forgot that he had any sort of mug at all.

"And here," Selifan said, turning round from the box, "what a pity we didn't think of asking Andrei Ivanovich for another horse, in exchange for the dapple-grey; he's that friendly disposed towards you, like, he wouldn't have refused, but the horse here is nothing but a rascal and a hindrance."

"Drive on and stop nattering!" said Chichikov, thinking: "It's quite true; a pity I didn't think of it."

In the meantime the swift carriage was careering forward. It swept lightly up the hills, although the road was often uneven; it flew lightly downhill, although the descent on those country roads was also rough. They came down a hill. The road led through meadows across bends in a meandering river, past mills. In the distance sandy banks glittered, and aspen groves followed one another in picturesque succession; they flew swiftly past the clumps of osier, slender alders and silvery willows, whose twigs slapped the faces of Selifan and Petrushka sitting up on the coachbox. They were forever knocking the cap off Petrushka's head. He would leap down from the box, abuse the stupid tree and the farmer who had planted it, but it never occurred to him to tie his cap down or even to hold it on with his hand, always trusting his luck that it would not happen again. The trees, however, were becoming denser: the ranks of aspen and alder were swelled by birch, and soon the travellers found themselves in the thick of a forest. The sun's light was hidden. The pines and firs loomed dark above them. The impenetrable gloom of an endless forest thickened and seemed to be about to turn day into night. Then suddenly amidst the trees there were glints of light—here and there between the branches and stumps, like streams of silver, or so many mirrors. The forest started to brighten, the trees grew thinner, shouts could be heard—and suddenly they saw a lake before them. It was a watery glade, some four versts across, surrounded by trees and with cottages beyond them. About twenty men, waist-deep, shoulder-deep and neck-deep in water, were dragging a net across to the opposite shore. In their midst, swimming busily, shouting and issuing orders, was a man who measured no more in height than in girth, as perfectly rounded he was as a great water-melon. Because of his fatness it was quite impossible for him to drown, and however hard he might try to dive under, the water would only have borne him up to the surface again; if two men had sat on his back he would still have remained afloat with them, like a huge, stubborn bladder, only grunting a little beneath their weight and emitting bubbles from his nose and mouth.

"Now that, Pavel Ivanovich," said Selifan, turning from the box, "must be the master, Colonel Koshkaryov."

"How do you know?"

"Because, if you'd like to take a look, sir, his body is whiter than the others, and he has more flesh on him, like a master should."

In the meantime the shouts had become clearer. The water-melon-master was shouting rapid instructions in a ringing voice:

"Denis, pass it to Kozma! Kozma, take the end from Denis! Big Foma, go where Little Foma is! Pull in on the right, pull in on the right! Stop, stop, the devil take you both! Now you've gone and tangled me in the net! You've tangled up my belly, do you hear, you confounded idiots!"

The net-pullers on the right flank stopped, seeing that an unforeseen accident had indeed taken place: the master had got entangled in the net.

"Just look at that," said Selifan to Petrushka, "they've netted their master, just like a fish."

The master floundered about, and in an effort to free himself turned on his back, belly uppermost, only to get further enmeshed in the net. For fear of tearing the net, he swam along together with the caught fish, ordering only that the men tie a rope around him. When this had been done, the end of the rope was thrown on to the shore. About twenty fishermen, standing there, caught hold of the rope and started to pull it in carefully. When he reached shallower waters the master stood up, covered by the criss-cross mesh of the net, like a lady's hand in summertime in its lace glove; at this point he looked up and espied the visitor, who had driven up to the dam in his carriage. He gave him a nod. Chichikov doffed his cap and respectfully bowed from the carriage.

"Have you had luncheon?" shouted the master, wading up to the shore with the netted fish, shading his eyes from the sun with one hand, and holding the other a little lower— à la Venus de Medicis emerging from the bath.

"No," said Chichikov.

"Then thank the Lord!"

"What for?" asked Chichikov with curiosity, holding his cap over his head.

"For this!" said the squire, arriving on the shore together with all the carp and bream, flailing around his legs and leaping two feet into the air. "That's nothing, don't look at that; but I've got something, you'll see!.. Hey, Big Foma, show him the sturgeon." Two hefty peasants hauled some monstrous creature out of the tub. "What a prince! He strayed in from the river!"

"That's a prince indeed!" said Chichikov.

"It is that all right. Now you drive on ahead, and I'll follow. Coachman, take the lower road, there's a good fellow, through the vegetable garden. Little Foma, you dolt, run ahead and raise the barrier. And I'll follow, I'll be there in a brace of shakes."

"The Colonel's a bit of a rum card," thought Chichikov, as they finally left the endless dam behind them and drove up to the cottages, some of which were scattered along the slope of a hill, like a flock of ducks, while others stood below on piles, like herons. Everywhere hung nets of various shapes and sizes. Little Foma lifted the barrier, the carriage drove through the vegetable garden and arrived in a square before an antiquated wooden church. Further off, beyond the church, they could see the roofs of the manor house and farm buildings.

"Look, here I am!" announced a voice from the left. Chichikov looked round. The squire was now driving along beside him on a droshky—he wore a grass-green nankeen frock-coat, yellow trousers, a shirt with an open collar and no necktie, just like a cupid! He sat sideways on his droshky, filling all the available space. Chichikov was about to say something to him, but the fat man had disappeared. He glimpsed the droshky for a moment and heard the master's voice: "Take the pike and the seven carp to that dolt of a cook, but bring the sturgeon here: I'll take it with me on the droshky." More voices rang out: "Big Foma and Little Foma! Kozma and Denis!" But when Chichikov drove up to the porch of the house, to his great astonishment the fat master was already standing there and received him into his embraces. How on earth he had managed to fly ahead like that was quite beyond comprehension. They exchanged three kisses, first on one cheek, then on the other.

"I bring you regards from His Excellency," said Chichikov.

"From which Excellency?"

"From your relation, General Alexander Dmitrievich."

"Who's this Alexander Dmitrievich?"

"General Betrishchev," answered Chichikov, somewhat surprised.

"Don't know him, not acquainted."

Chichikov's surprise increased.

"But how can that be?.. I do trust, at least, that I have the pleasure of addressing Colonel Koshkaryov?"

"Pyotr Petrovich Petukh, Petukh Pyotr Petrovich!" said his host.

Chichikov was stunned.

"My goodness! Hear that, you fools!" he said, turning to Selifan and Petrushka, who gawked and goggled back, one sitting on the coach-box, the other standing by the doors of the carriage. "See what you've done, you fools? Didn't I tell you—to Colonel Koshkaryov's... But this is Pyotr Petrovich Petukh..."

"The lads have done splendidly!" said Pyotr Petrovich. "For that you can have a mug of vodka each and a meat pie into the bargain. Unharness the horses and go at once to the servants' quarters!"

"I am so terribly sorry," said Chichikov, with a bow, "such an unexpected mistake..."

"No mistake," gaily interjected Pyotr Petrovich, "no mistake. First sample the lunch, then tell me whether it's a mistake. Please, be my guest," he said, taking Chichikov's arm and leading him into the house.

Chichikov, with his usual genteelness, negotiated the doorway sideways, to permit his host to pass through together with him; but to no avail: his host would not have fitted, and anyway he was no longer there. Instead his voice could be heard shouting in the yard: "What's with that Big Foma? Why isn't he here yet? Yemelian, you dunderhead, run along to that dolt of a cook and tell him to gut the sturgeon as fast as he can. The milt, roe, innards and bream can go into the soup and the carp can be used for the sauce.

And crayfish, crayfish! Little Foma, you dunderhead, where's the crayfish, I said, crayfish!" And for a long time yet the words rang out: crayfish, crayfish.

"The good master is certainly going to great trouble," said Chichikov, sitting down in an armchair and surveying the walls and corners of the room.

"Well, here I am," said the master, coming into the room followed by two youths clad in summer frockcoats. As skinny as willow saplings, they towered a foot and more above Pyotr Petrovich.

"My sons, grammar school boys. Here for the holidays. Nikolasha, you stay with our guest and you, Alexasha, come along with me."

And once again Pyotr Petrovich Petukh vanished.

Chichikov was left with Nikolasha who turned out to be a talkative lad. He told the guest that the teaching was none too good in their school, that favour was shown to those boys whose mamas sent bigger presents, that the Ingermanland Hussar regiment was stationed in the town; that Captain Vetvitsky had a better horse than his own colonel, although Lieutenant Vyazemtsev was a far finer horseman.

"Now tell me, what condition is your father's estate in?" asked Chichikov.

"Mortgaged," replied the father himself, having reappeared in the drawing room, "mortgaged."

Chichikov could only respond with that motion of the lips that a man makes when matters come to nought.

"But why did you mortgage it?" he asked.

"I just did. Everyone's mortgaging these days, so why should I lag behind? They say it pays to mortgage. And besides, I've always lived here, now I'll see what it's like living in Moscow."

"The fool, the fool!" thought Chichikov, "he'll squander everything and even turn his boys into wastrels. You should stay where you belong, you meatloaf, in the country."

"I bet I know what you're thinking," said Petukh.

"What?" asked Chichikov, in some embarrassment.

"You're thinking: 'What a fool, what a fool this Petukh is! He invites me to lunch, but there's still no lunch.' It'll be ready soon, my most respected sir. It'll be served sooner than a crop-haired wench can plait her braids."

"Daddy, Platon Mikhailovich is coming!" said Alexasha, looking through the window.

"Riding his bay!" said Nikolasha, leaning across to the window. "What do you reckon, Alexasha, is our dark grey worse than that?"

"No worse, maybe, but he hasn't got a stride like that."

An argument flared up between them about the bay and the dark grey. In the mean-time a most handsome man entered the room: tall and slender, with lustrous fair curls and dark eyes. He was followed into the room by a fearsome monster of a hound, the brass collar rattling under its massive jaws.

"Have you lunched?" asked Pyotr Petrovich Petukh.

"I have," said the visitor.

"So why have you come then, to mock me?" asked Petukh crossly. "What use are you to me after lunch?"

"By the way, Pyotr Petrovich," said the visitor, laughing, "I can console you by saying that I did not eat a bite at lunch: I have no appetite at all."

"What a catch I had, if only you had seen it! What a sturgeon swam into our nets! And there was no counting the carp."

"It makes me envious just to listen to you," said the visitor. "Teach me how to escape boredom and be as cheerful as you."

"But why should I be bored? No reason at all!" said their host.

"Why be bored? Because life's boring."

"You don't eat enough, that's why. Just try and eat a good lunch. All this boredom has only been invented recently, you know. In the old days no one was bored."

"That's boasting! You're not trying to tell us you've never been bored?"

"Never! Anyway, I wouldn't have the time to be bored. You wake up in the morning—and you have to drink your tea, and then there's the bailiff, and then you go fishing, and then it's time for lunch. After lunch you hardly have time to get up a good snore and it's supper time, and after supper along comes the cook—you have to order the lunch for the next day. When's there time to be bored?"

Throughout this conversation Chichikov studied the visitor. Platon Mikhailovich Platonov was Achilles and Paris rolled into one: a good slender build, a picturesque height, a clear skin—everything was combined in him. His pleasant grin with its slight suggestion of irony seemed only to increase his good looks. But, despite all this, there was something lethargic and torpid in him. No violent passions, sorrows or ordeals had etched any wrinkles on his fresh, virginal face, but then neither had they lent it any vitality.

"I must confess," declared Chichikov, "I cannot understand it either, if you pardon my saying so, how anyone with looks like yours could be bored. Of course, there may be other reasons: lack of money, persecutions by some illwishers or other, one does come across such wicked people who are prepared to make an attempt on your very life."

"But that's the whole point, that there's none of that," said Platonov. "Would you believe it, at times I honestly wish there were, so that there'd be some worry and excitement in my life. If only someone would just make me angry! But no! Boredom, that's all there is."

"I don't understand. But, perhaps your estate is insufficient, with too few souls?"

"Not at all, my brother and I have twenty-five thousand acres and a thousand souls to go with them."

"And, with all this, you're bored. Incomprehensible! But, perhaps the estate is in disarray? The crops have failed, many peasants have died?"

"On the contrary, everything is in perfect order and my brother is a most excellent manager."

"I fail to understand!" said Chichikov, and shrugged his shoulders.

"Well now, we shall drive away that boredom," said their host. "Alexasha, run to the kitchen and tell the cook to send in those little fish pies double quick. Now where's that dunderhead Yemelian and that thief Antoshka? Why are they not serving the appetisers?"

The door opened. The dunderhead Yemelian and the thief Antoshka appeared with napkins, they laid the table, and brought in a tray with six decanters filled with homemade brandies of different colours. Soon a garland of plates was set around the trays and decanters with caviare, cheeses, and salted mushrooms, and then hot delicacies were brought from the kitchen in covered dishes, under which the butter could be heard sizzling. The dunderhead

Yemelian and the thief Antoshka were good and efficient men. Their master only bestowed these names on them because without nicknames everything seemed somehow flat, and he did not like flat things; he himself had a good soul, but he liked his speech spicy. Moreover, his peasants did not hold this against him.

The appetisers were followed by lunch. Here their good-hearted host became a holy terror. The moment he noticed that a guest had only one piece of something on his plate, he instantly helped him to another, declaring: "No man nor bird can live in the world without a mate." If the guests ate the two helpings he would heap on a third one, declaring "What sort of number is two? God loves a trinity." Should the guest eat three—he would say: "Show me a cart with three wheels! Who ever builds a house with three corners?" For four he would have another saying, and for five yet another. Chichikov consumed something like twelve helpings and thought: "Well now, my host cannot possibly put anything more on my plate." But not so: his host, without saying a word, deposited on his plate a rib of veal, spit-roasted, the very best part, complete with kidneys, and from such a fine calf too!

"I reared it for two years on milk," said their host, "I nursed it like my own son!"

"No more!" said Chichikov.

"Just try it first, and then say: no more!"

"It won't go in. There's no room."

"Why, there was no room in the church either. In came the mayor—and room was found. Yet there had been such a crush there wasn't room for an apple to drop. You just try: that piece is your mayor."

Chichikov tried—and indeed, the piece was like the mayor. Room was found for it, even though it had seemed that nothing more could go in.

It was the same thing with the wine. Having received the mortgage money Pyotr Petrovich had stocked up with provisions for ten years ahead. He kept topping up and topping up their glasses; what the guests did not finish he handed over to Alexasha and Nikolasha, who knocked back glass after glass but when they stood up from table they were as steady as rocks, as if they had been drinking water. It was not so with the guests: with difficulty, with great difficulty they dragged themselves to the balcony, and with great difficulty they lowered themselves into armchairs. No sooner had their host seated himself in his, some sort of four-seater, than he fell fast asleep. His fleshy person was transformed into a blacksmith's bellows. Through the open mouth and nostrils it started to emit noises such as are not even heard in modern music. It had everything: a drum, a flute, and a sort of staccato sound, much like a dog's bark.

"Listen to him whistling and wheezing!" said Platonov. Chichikov laughed heartily.

"Of course, if one lunches like that," said Platonov, "how can boredom set in? Sleep sets in."

"Yes," said Chichikov indolently. His little eyes became even smaller. "You know, all the same, and forgive me for saying so, but I cannot understand how one can be bored. There are so many remedies for boredom."

"Such as?"

"Well, especially for a young man! You can dance, play some instrument or other ... or else—get married."

"To whom? Tell me."

"Do you mean to say there are no nice and wealthy young girls in the area?"

"There aren't."

"Well then, seek them elsewhere, travel around." Here a fertile thought flashed through Chichikov's head, and his eyes grew a little bigger. "Now there's an excellent remedy!" he said, staring into Platonov's eyes.

"What?"

"Travel."

"But where can one go?"

"Well, if you are free, come with me," said Chichikov, and said to himself as he looked at Platonov: "That wouldn't be bad: we could share the expenses and repairs to the carriage could be entirely to his account."

"Where are you going?"

"Now how can I say where? I travel, for the time being, not so much on my own business as on behalf of someone else. General Betrishchev, a close friend, and, I might say, benefactor, has asked me to visit his relations... Of course, relations are all very well, but in a sense, so to speak, it's also for myself; for, to see the world, the circumfluence of people—say what you will, it's like a living book, a second science."

Platonov grew thoughtful.

Meanwhile Chichikov's thoughts went as follows: "A really good idea! He might pay the expenses. It might even be arranged that we use his horses and leave mine to fatten up on his estate. To save money I could leave my carriage in his village and travel in his."

"Indeed? Why not do a bit of travelling?" thought Platonov in the meantime. "You never know, it might be less boring. There's nothing for me to do at home, after all, the business is all taken care of by my brother as it is, and so nothing would be upset. Yes, why not do some travelling?"

"But would you agree," he said aloud, "to spend a day or two at my brother's house? Otherwise he would never let me go."

"With great pleasure! Even three."

"Well, in that case, let's shake on it! Travel we will!" said Platonov, livening up.

"Bravo!" said Chichikov, slapping the other's hand, "We'll travel!"

"Where? Where?" exclaimed their host, waking up and goggling at them in amazement. "No, my good sirs, I have ordered the wheels to be removed from your carriage, and your stallion, Platon Mikhailovich, is fully fifteen versts from here by now. No, you shall stop the night here, and tomorrow after an early luncheon you can set off on your travels."

"How d'you like that!" thought Chichikov. Platonov made no reply, knowing that Petukh was a man of fixed habits. They had to stay.

They were rewarded, though, with a remarkable spring evening. Their host organized an outing on the river. Twelve rowers, wielding twenty-four oars, bore them with songs across the mirror-like surface of the lake. From the lake they sped along a vast river, with gently sloping banks on both sides. Not so much as a ripple disturbed the water. They drank tea and ate hot buns, as the boat slid beneath a succession of ropes stretched across the river to secure the nets. Before tea, their host undressed and dove into the river, where he splashed about yelling at the fishermen for

half an hour or so, shouting orders to Big Foma and Koz
ma, and, when he had had his fill of shouting and fussing
and of getting chilled through in the water, he reappeared
in the launch with a keen appetite and drank his tea with
enviable gusto. In the meantime the sun had set. A glow
remained in the skies. The shouts rang out more sono-
rously. The place of the fishermen was taken all along the
banks by groups of bathing boys, and the air rang with
their merry splashing and laughter. The rowers, rhythmi-
cally plying their four and twenty oars, suddenly raised
them all aloft and the boat glided like a light bird over the
mirror-like surface of the water. A well-built red-cheeked
young lad sitting third from the stern, started a song in a
pure voice; five others took up the melody, and then the
last six joined in—and freely flowed the song, as infinite as
Russia herself. Feeling pleasantly stirred Chichikov thought:
"Yes, really I must get my own little village one day!"
"Now, what's so good about this plaintive singing?"
thought Platonov. "It only spreads a greater gloom over
the soul."

Dusk had already fallen as they returned home. In the
dark the oars slapped on water that no longer reflected the
sky. The lights on the shore were barely visible. The moon
was rising when they moored at the quay. Here and there
fishermen were bent over their tripods, boiling up fish
soup from ruffs and other twitching-fresh fish. All creatures
were already at home. The geese, cows and goats had long
since been penned, even the dust they raised had long since
settled, and the shepherds who had brought them in now
stood by the gates, awaiting their jugs of milk and invita-
tions to share the fish soup. Here and there could be heard
the chatter and hubbub of voices, and loud barking of
local dogs and the distant barking from other villages far
away. The moon rose and the darkness began to recede
before its radiance; finally everything was illuminated:
the lake and the cottages; the fires grew dimmer; the smoke
from the chimneys became visible, silvery in the moonlight. Nikolasha and Alexasha galloped past on two spirited colts, racing each other; the dust rose behind them as
from a herd of rams. "Yes, really I must get my own little
village one day!" said Chichikov. Again he started to
see the comely wife and the little Chichiks in his mind's

ye. Who could fail to be stirred by such an evening?

And at dinner they gorged themselves once more. When Pavel Ivanovich had retired to the guest bedroom he lay on the bed and prodded his belly: "Taut as a drum!" he said, "No mayor would squeeze in there!" As ill-luck would have it, however, his host's study was on the other side of the wall. The wall was thin, and everything that was said next door could be heard. The host was giving his cook instructions for a huge dinner to be served under the guise of an early breakfast the following day. And what an order he gave! A dead man's mouth would have watered. The words rang out: "Fry it well and let it simmer for a good long time!" And the cook replied in a piping falsetto: "Yes, sir. Can do, sir. Can do that too, sir."

"And bake us a four-cornered fish pie. In one corner I want you to put the sturgeon cheeks and the gristle cooked soft, in another throw in some buckwheat, and then some mushrooms and onions, and some sweet milt, and the brains, and whatever else, you'll know what..."

"Will do, sir. Can do that too."

"And make sure that on the one side it's, you know, a nice golden brown, but not so much on the other side. And the pastry, do you see, make sure it's baked through, till it just crumbles away, so that the juices soak right through, do you see, so that you don't even feel it in your mouth—it melts like snow."

"Dammit!" grumbled Chichikov. "He simply won't let me sleep!"

"And make me a stuffed pig stomach-bag. Put a piece of ice in the middle, so it swells up nicely. And mind that the garnish for the sturgeon is nice and rich! Surround it with crayfish and small grilled fishes, and garnish it with a sparling stuffing, and add some chopped vegetables, some horse-radish and mushrooms, and turnips, and carrots, and beans, and haven't we got anything else?"

"We could decorate it with swedes or beetroot cut in little stars," said the cook.

"Do that both swedes and beetroot. And here is the garnish I want for the roast..."

"Sleep's gone now!" said Chichikov, turning on to his other side, burying his face in the pillows and pulling the blanket right over his head, so as not to hear any more.

But through the blanket he still could hear his host speaking. "And fry it well and bake it well and let it simmer a good long time." He finally fell asleep at a roast turkey.

The next day the guests so gorged themselves that Platonov could no longer ride horse-back; the stallion was dispatched home with Petukh's stable-boy. They took their seats in the carriage. The big-jowled hound followed sluggishly behind: he had also gorged himself.

"No, that's really too much," said Chichikov, once they had driven out of the yard. "That is simply making a pig of oneself. Are you not uncomfortable, Platon Mikhailich? The carriage was extremely comfortable before, and now suddenly it's uncomfortable. Petrushka, I suppose in your stupidity you went and re-packed everything? What are all these boxes sticking out everywhere?"

Platonov chuckled.

"That I can explain," he said. "Pyotr Petrovich sent it in for us to eat on the road."

"Yes sir," said Petrushka, turning round from the box, "orders was given to put it all in the carriage—liver pasties and pies and that."

"That's right, Pavel Ivanovich, sir," said Selifan, turning round from the box and beaming. "A very decent gentleman. A hospitable landowner! He sent us each a glass of champagne! He did, I swear it, and he sent us down some dish from the table—a very good dish it was too, it tasted delicate-like. Such a decent gentleman as there's never been before."

"Do you see? He has made us all content," said Platonov. "Please, tell me frankly: could you spare the time to turn into a village about ten versts from here? I'd like to say goodbye to my sister and brother-in-law."

"With great pleasure," said Chichikov.

"I'm sure you won't regret it: my brother-in-law is a most remarkable man."

"In what respect?" asked Chichikov.

"He runs the best estate Russia has ever seen. In ten years or so he has brought this estate, which was so run down when he bought it that it hardly yielded twenty thousand a year, to the point where it now brings in two hundred thousand."

"Ah, an estimable man! The life of a man like that should

be held up as an example to others! I would be most, most pleased to make his acquaintance. What is his name?"

"Kostanzhoglo."

"And his first name and patronymic?"

"Konstantin Fyodorovich."

"Konstantin Fyodorovich Kostanzhoglo. I shall be delighted to make his acquaintance. It will be most instructive to get to know such a man." And Chichikov set about asking questions about Kostanzhoglo, and everything he learnt about him from Platonov, was, indeed, astonishing.

"Look over there, that's where his lands begin," said Platonov, pointing to some fields. "You'll notice at once how they differ from the others. Coachman, here you take the road to the left. Can you see that sapling forest? He planted it. With anyone else it wouldn't have grown so tall in fifteen years but he grew it in eight. Look, that's the end of the forest. Now the wheatfields start; and after another hundred acres or so there will be more forest, also planted, and then fields again. Look at the wheat, see how much thicker it is than the previous lot."

"I see. But how does he do it?"

"Well, just you ask him and you'll see ... (*the next four words are indecipherable in the ms.*) "He is a font of wisdom, such a font of wisdom, you won't find another like him. Not only does he know what soil is best for what crop, he even knows what should be grown next to what, which grain should be planted next to which trees. With all the rest of us the land is cracking from droughts, but not with him. He works out exactly how much moisture is needed, and he plants the right number of trees; everything performs two or three functions for him: the forest provides timber, fertilizes the fields with the rotting leaves, and keeps out the heat. That's his way with everything."

"An astonishing man!" said Chichikov and gazed with great interest at the fields.

Everything was in extraordinarily good order. The forests were fenced off; everywhere they saw animal pens, also laid out with careful thought and enviably well-maintained; the corn was heaped in gigantic ricks. All was abundance and plenty. It was immediately apparent that the owner was nobody's fool. Ascending a small hillock, they saw a large village, scattered over three hills. Everything here looked prosperous: the smooth roads, the solid cottages; the carts they saw were sturdy and shining new; the horses well-fed and healthy; the cattle—all choice specimens. Even the peasants' pigs looked like noblemen. Thus it was apparent that the peasants living here were precisely the ones who, in the words of the song, dug up silver by the spadeful. There were no *jardins anglais* here, no gazebos, bridges, follies, or landscaped views before the house. Work-yards stretched from the peasant cottages to the manor house. Mounted on the roof was a large lantern, not for admiring the view, but for inspecting what work was being done, where and how.

They drove up to the house. The owner was not in; they were met by his wife, Platonov's sister, a beauty fair of face and hair, with an essentially Russian expression, just as good-looking and just as listless as her brother. It seemed she was little concerned about the concerns of others, either because the all-consuming industry of her husband left nothing for her to do, or because she belonged, by her very character, to that philosophical category of people who, possessed of feelings, and thoughts, and intelligence, somehow live only half-heartedly, looking at life with only half an eye, and when they see any distressing conflicts that greatly trouble everyone they say: "Let them rave, the fools! It's their funeral."

"Goodday, sister!" said Platonov. "And where's Konstantin?"

"I don't know. He should have been here long ago. Something must be keeping him."

Chichikov paid scant attention to his hostess. He wanted to examine the dwelling of this remarkable man. He hoped to discover in it the qualities of its occupant—just as you can judge from a shell what sort of oyster or snail lived in it. But he was disappointed. The rooms were utterly without character—spacious and nothing more. No murals, no pictures on the walls, no bronzes on the tables, no what-nots with porcelain figurines or pretty cups, no vases, no flowers, no statuettes—in a word, it was somehow bare. Simple, ordinary furniture, a piano, and even that was covered with dust: apparently the lady of the house rarely sat down to play. From the drawing-room [the door into their host's study stood] * open; but there, too, it was the same: simple and bare. It was clear that the master came to the house only to rest, and not to live in it; that for the elaboration of his plans and ideas he did not need a study with sprung armchairs and all sorts of quiet comforts, and that his life consisted not in daydreaming beside a glowing fireplace, but in forthright action. His ideas arose spontaneously out of circumstances, at the moment when these circumstances occurred, and were immediately acted upon, without any need to be written down.

"Aha! There he is! He's coming," said Platonov.

Chichikov also hastened to the window. Walking up to the porch was a man of some forty years, lively, and swarthy in appearance. He wore a velveteen peaked cap. Two men of a lower class, their caps doffed, walked along beside him, deep in conversation, discussing something with him. One seemed to be a simple peasant; the other, in a dark blue caftan, looked like a visiting kulak and knave.

"Give your order then to accept it!" said the peasant with a bow.

"No, no, brother, I've already told you twenty times not to bring any more. I've got so much material piled up there's nowhere to put it."

"But with you, Konstantin Fyodorovich, sir, everything is put to use. There isn't another master as clever as you anywhere in the world. You find a place for everything. So please give orders to accept."

"Brother, what I need are hands; supply me with workers, not material."

"That's one thing you'll have no shortage of. Whole villages will come to work: we're that poor in grain, we can't remember a year like it. What's real bad is that you don't want to take us for good, because we'd serve you in good faith, honest to God we would. With you there's all sorts of clever things to be learnt, Konstantin Fyodorovich. So please give orders to accept just this once."

"But that's what you said last time too: and you've gone and brought some more."

---

*Sentence left incomplete in the ms. The words in square brackets were added by P. Kulish in the edition: *Works and Letters of N. V. Gogol,* St Petersburg, 1857.

"This really is the last time, Konstantin Fyodorovich. If you don't take it no one will take it off me. So please, Your Honour, give orders to accept."

"Now listen, I'll take it this time, and that's only out of pity for you going to all this trouble for nothing. But if you bring any more you can stand and whine at me for three weeks—I won't take it."

"Yes, sir, Konstantin Fyodorovich; you can take my word for it, I swear I won't bring any more, I thank you most humbly." The peasant departed, satisfied. He was lying, of course; he would bring some more: he'd take a chance.

"How about it, Konstantin Fyodorovich, be so kind ... bring down your prince a little," said the visiting kulak in the blue caftan walking on his other side.

"But didn't I tell you right at the beginning? I don't like to haggle. Let me tell you again: I'm not your usual landowner on whom you descend on the very day he has to pay interest to the bank. Look, I know the lot of you. You people have lists of all the landlords, you know exactly who has to pay what and when. There's no great mystery to it. He's hard-pressed, and so he lets you have what you want at half-price. But what's your money to me? I can leave things lying around for three years if I like! I don't have to pay off any mortgages..."

"Quite true, Konstantin Fyodorovich. But then I'm just ... it's only so as to do business with you in the future, and not for any personal gain. Won't you accept three thousand in advance?"

The kulak took out a wad of greasy banknotes from inside his caftan. Kostanzhoglo accepted the money very coolly and, without bothering to count it, stuffed the wad in the back pocket of his frock-coat.

"Hm!" thought Chichikov. "Just as if it were a handkerchief!"

A moment later Kostanzhoglo appeared in the doorway of the drawing-room.

"Goodness, brother, you here?" he said, seeing Platonov. They embraced and kissed. Platonov introduced Chichikov. Chichikov reverentially stepped up to his host, kissed him on the cheek and received the impression of a kiss in return.

Kostanzhoglo's face was most remarkable. It betrayed

his southern origins. The hair on his head and his eyebrows was dark and thick, his eyes glowed with an intense brightness. Every expression of his face was eloquent of intelligence, and there was no trace of lethargy in it. There was, however, a noticeable admixture of something splenetic and embittered. What, in point of fact, was his nationality? In Russia there are many Russians of non-Russian stock, who are yet true Russians. Kostanzhoglo did not delve into his origin, considering such activity pointless and irrelevant to running an estate. And, besides, he knew no language other than Russian.

"You know what I've thought of doing, Konstantin?" said Platonov.

"No, what?"

"I've thought of travelling around various provinces in the hope that it might cure me of my spleen."

"Why not? It might at that."

"I'll travel with Pavel Ivanovich."

"Excellent! To which places," asked Kostanzhoglo, turning affably to Chichikov, "do you now propose to travel?"

"I must confess," said Chichikov, inclining his head to one side and gripping the arm of his chair with one hand, "I travel, for the moment, not so much on my own behalf, as on that of another. General Betrishchev, a close friend, and, I might say, benefactor, has asked me to visit his relations. Relations, of course, are all very well, but it is partly, so to speak, for myself too; because, to be sure, not to mention the benefit that can be derived in the haemorrhoidal sense, it is already something to see the world, the circumfluence of people ... say what you will, it is, so to speak, a living book, a science in itself."

"Yes, some corners are worth peeping into."

"You do put it most excellently," remarked Chichikov, "it is, indeed, just so. You see things you would not have seen otherwise; you meet people you would never have met. Conversation with them is its own reward. Teach me, my most esteemed Konstantin Fyodorovich, teach me, I appeal to your wisdom! I await your sweet words like manna from heaven."

Kostanzhoglo became embarrassed.

"But what, though?.. Teach you what? My own education was paid for with brass coins."

"Wisdom, my most esteemed sir, wisdom! The wisdom to manage an estate like you; to be able, like you, to derive a reliable income; to acquire, like you, property that is not imaginary but substantial, and thereby to fulfil my duty as a citizen, to earn the respect of my fellow countrymen."

"Do you know what?" said Kostanzhoglo, "just spend the day with me. I'll show you all my management and tell you about everything. There's no wisdom here, as you'll see, none at all."

"Brother, do stop the day here," said his wife, turning to Platonov.

"Why not? It's all the same to me," replied this latter indifferently. "It's up to Pavel Ivanovich."

"I too, with great pleasure... But there's one small cicumstance—I have to call on a relation of General Betrishchev. There's a certain Colonel Koshkaryov—"

"But he's... Don't you know? He's a fool and a lunatic."

"I've already heard that. I have no business with him. But since General Betrishchev is a close friend, and even, so to speak, a benefactor ... it wouldn't seem right, somehow."

"In that case, you know what," said Kostanzhoglo, "call on him right away. My trap is standing ready. He's less than ten versts away, so you'll be there in no time. You'll even be back here in time for supper."

Chichikov availed himself of the offer with delight. The trap was brought up and he at once drove off to the colonel's, who caused him more amazement than it had ever before been his lot to experience. Everything about the colonel was extraordinary. His whole village was in a jumble: new buildings going up, old ones being rebuilt, heaps of lime, bricks and logs all over the streets. Some buildings had been put up in the style of government offices. Written in gold letters on one of them was: "Agricultural Implements Depot", on another: "Chief Paymaster's Department", then "Committee for Rural Affairs" and "School for Normal Enlightenment of the Villagers"—in a word, the devil only knows what! Chichikov wondered if perhaps he had strayed into some provincial capital. The colonel himself was stiff and prim. There was a prudish arrogance in his triangular face. The sideburns ran down his cheeks in a thin string; his hair, coiffure, nose, lips, chin—everything

looked as if it had just come out of a press. However, when
he started to speak, he seemed a sensible sort of fellow.
He began by complaining to Chichikov about the lack of
education in the surrounding landowners, and about the
great labours awaiting him. He received Chichikov with the
utmost courtesy and cordiality, taking him entirely into
his confidence and recounting with considerable self-
gratification exactly how much effort it had cost him to
bring his estate to its present prosperity; how difficult it
had been to convince the simple peasant that there are
higher joys which a man derives from enlightened splendour
and the arts; how hard he had had to struggle against the
ignorance of the Russian peasant, to get him to wear
German trousers and to make him experience, if only ever
so slightly, the higher dignity of man; that notwithstanding
all his efforts he had still been unable to persuade the
womenfolk to wear corsets, whereas in Germany, where he
had been stationed in 1814, the miller's daughter had even
been able to play the piano, had spoken French and
dropped curtseys. With genuine compassion he described
the depths of his neighbours' ignorance; how little they
thought about their subjects; how they laughed when he
tried to convince them that it was imperative to set up on
an estate an inventorial office, offices for commissions and
even committees, as a safeguard against all kinds of theft,
and to have every item recorded, and for the clerks, stew-
ards and bookkeepers to be properly educated people
with university degrees; how, despite all his powers of per-
suasion, he had been unable to convince the other landowners what benefit it would bring their estates if each peasant
was so well educated that, as he walked behind the plough,
he could at the same time be reading a book about lightning conductors.

At this Chichikov thought: "He'd hardly have the time.
I learnt to read and write, but I still haven't been able to
finish *La Duchesse de la Vallière*."

"Such terrible ignorance!" exclaimed Colonel Koshkaryov in conclusion. "The obscurity of the Middle Ages,
and there are no ways of helping... None at all! And yet
I could help everything; I know one remedy, a most infall-
lible remedy."

"What's that?"

"To make every man, woman and child in Russia dress as they do in Germany. No more than that, and I give you my word that everything will work like clockwork: the sciences will scale new heights, trade will soar, a golden age will dawn in Russia."

Chichikov stared at him and thought: "Why not? No point in standing on ceremony with this one." And postponing matters no further he at once explained to the colonel how things stood: there was a need for certain souls and for the effecting of certain purchases.

"As far as I can tell from your words," said the colonel, not in the least surprised, "you're making a request; am I correct?"

"You are indeed."

"In that case put it in writing. It will go before the General Requests Commission. The General Requests Commission will record it and send it on to me. From me it will proceed to the Committee for Rural Affairs, and the various inquiries and recommendations will be made with regard to this matter. The Managing Director will reach his decision in consultation with the office in no time at all, and the matter will be settled."

Chichikov was confused.

"But that way the matter will drag on."

"Ha!" said the colonel with a smile, "now that is precisely the advantage of paper work! It does rather drag on, of course, but then nothing will be overlooked: every little detail will be visible."

"But then... How can this be dealt with in writing? After all this is the sort of matter... The souls, you see, are in a certain sense ... dead ones."

"And a very good thing too. Write it down like that, that the souls are in a certain sense dead ones."

"But how can I? That cannot be written down. They may be dead, but they must seem alive."

"Fine. Just write it like that: 'but it is necessary, or required, that they should seem alive.' "

What was to be done with the colonel? Chichikov decided to go and see for himself what sort of commissions and committees he had set up; and what he found there was not merely astounding, it quite surpassed all comprehension. The General Requests Commission existed only on the sign outside the building. Its chairman, previously a valet, had been transferred to the newly established Rural Construction Committee. His place had been taken by the counting clerk Timoshka, who had been sent off to settle a dispute between the drunkard of a bailiff and the village elder—a swindler and rogue. And so there was no official available.

"But how do we... How can one get anything done?" said Chichikov to his companion, the Commissioner for Special Assignments, whom the colonel had sent to accompany him.

"Oh no, you won't get anything done," said his escort. "We don't know if we're coming or going. You see, the Construction Commission rules the roost here; it takes all the men away from their work, and sends them here, there and everywhere. That's the best place to be, on that Commission, I mean." It was clear he was displeased with the Construction Commission. "The system with us is that everyone leads the master by the nose. He thinks that everything's in its place, but it only exists in name."

"All the same, someone should tell him all that," thought Chichikov, and, on his return to the house, told the colonel that his affairs were a total hodge-podge, that it was impossible to get anything done, and that the Construction Commission was robbing him right and left.

The colonel boiled up with righteous indignation. Without further ado, he reached for pen and paper, and wrote down eight questions of the utmost severity: by what right did the Construction Commission order officials from other departments about? How could the Managing Director have permitted the Chairman to depart on an inquiry without first appointing someone in his place? And how could the Committee for Rural Affairs remain unconcerned knowing that a Requests Commission did not even exist?

"I can see the fuss there's going to be," thought Chichikov and started to make his farewells.

"No, I shall not let you go. In two hours, no more, everything will be settled to your satisfaction. I shall now entrust your business to a very special man, who has only just graduated from the university. Just sit a while in my library. You will find all that you need there: books, paper, pens, pencils—everything. Please make use of it all—feel quite at home."

Such were Koshkaryov's words as he led Chichikov to his book repository. This was an enormous chamber, lined with books from floor to ceiling. There were some stuffed animals too. Collected here were books on all subjects—on arboriculture, cattle-breeding, pig-breeding, horticulture, thousands of journals of every kind, manuals and journals dealing with the very latest developments and improvements in stud farming and in the natural sciences. There were such titles as: *Pig-breeding As a Science*. Seeing that there was nothing here for whiling away the time pleasantly, he turned to another bookcase. From the frying-pan into the fire! Here there were only books of philosphy. One had the title: *Philosophy As a Science*; six tomes stood in a row with the title: *Propaedeutics to the Theory of Thought in Their Communality, Totality, and Essentiality and in Application to the Comprehension of the Organic Principles of the Reciprocal Bifurcation of Social Productivity*. Whichever book Chichikov leafed through, on every page he would read "manifestation", "development", "abstract", "exclusivity", "compactness", "coherence", and the devil knows what else besides. "No, I'm not up to any of this," said Chichikov, and turned to a third case, which held books all about the arts. Here he pulled out a large, fat volume at random: there were immodest mythological illustrations in it and he started to peruse these. This was more to his liking. Pictures of this kind are pleasing to middle-aged bachelors. It is said that in recent years this predilection has even infected old men, who have cultivated this taste at balletic performances. Whether we like it or not, the people of this world and age are fond of spicy delicacies. When he had finished examining this book Chichikov was on the point of pulling down another in the same vein, when Colonel Koshkaryov suddenly entered, beaming radiantly and carrying a piece of paper.

"All has been done and done most excellently. This man most definitely knows his job to perfection. For that I shall promote him above all the others: I shall institute a special, higher managerial department and appoint him its president. This is what he writes..."

"Well, the Lord be praised," thought Chichikov and prepared to listen. The Colonel started to read:

"Embarking upon the deliberation of the commission assigned to me by Your Honour, I have to report thereupon as follows:

1) The actual petition submitted by Collegiate Counsellor and Cavalier Pavel Ivanovich Chichikov Esq. contains a certain misconception: in elucidation of his requirement for registered souls overtaken by various calamities, the word dead has been put in. Hereunder, it is presumed, that what the aforesaid gentleman had in mind were those close to death, and not those already dead; for dead ones cannot be acquired. How, indeed, can they be acquired when there is nothing there? Logic itself refutes this. Indeed, it would seem the gentleman has received but a limited instruction in the verbal sciences..." Here Koshkaryov paused for a moment and said: "At this point the rogue ... he's had a bit of a jab at you. But you can't deny he has a great agility with words—the style of a Secretary of State; but to think he only spent three years in the university and didn't even finish his course." Koshkaryov read on: "... limited instruction ... the verbal sciences ... for he called the souls *dead*, whereas any person who has taken a course of study in the human sciences, knows that the soul is immortal. 2) Of the aforementioned registered souls, whether newly arrived or, as the gentleman incorrectly saw fit to describe them, dead, there are none on hand which are not already mortgaged, for not only have they all been mortgaged in their totality and without exception, but they have even been re-mortgaged, with the addition of one hundred and fifty roubles per soul, except for the small village of Gurmailovka, which is in a disputatious position owing to our litigation with the landowner Predishchev, and which cannot therefore be entered into either sale or mortgage."

"Now why on earth did you not tell me all this before? Why waste my time with all this nonsense?" said Chichikov heatedly.

"But don't you see—how could I have known all that before? That's the beauty of paper work: now you can see everything as clearly as your own hand."

"You fool, you stupid ass!" thought Chichikov angrily.

"All that digging about in books and what have you learnt."

Disregarding all courtesies and proprieties he grabbed his cap and stormed out of the house. The coachman was standing there, the trap was ready and the horses were still in harness: a request for fodder would have had to be made in writing and the order to supply oats to the horses would only have been issued the following day. Notwithstanding all Chichikov's abruptness and rudeness, Koshkaryov remained the very soul of courtesy and tact with him. He squeezed his hand hard and pressed it to his heart, thanking him for giving him the opportunity to see his system of production in operation; that he would have to issue a few drubbings and dressings-down, because the pall of lethargy could settle over everything and the springs of rural management would rust and weaken; that as a result of this incident he had had a happy thought: to set up a new commission which would be called the Commission for the Supervision of the Construction Commission so that then no one would dare steal a thing.

"Ass! Fool!" thought Chichikov, fuming throughout the journey. The stars were already out. Night was in the sky. Lights twinkled in the villages. As they drove up to the porch he could see through the windows the table set for supper.

"What kept you so late?" asked Kostanzhoglo, when he appeared in the doorway.

"What have you been discussing with him for so long?" said Platonov.

"He wore me out!" said Chichikov. "In all my life I've never seen such a fool."

"You've seen nothing yet!" said Kostanzhoglo. "Koshkaryov is a comforting phenomenon. He is necessary because he reflects in caricature and more graphically the foibles of those 'clever' people who've set up offices and chancellories and manufactories and industries and schools and commissions and the devil knows what else besides. Just as if they were a state in themselves! I ask you, how do you like that? There's one landowner who hasn't got enough peasants to plough his own fields, yet he's set up a candle factory and imports skilled candle-makers from London, he's turned himself into a petty tradesman! And there's another fool who's done even better: he's set up a silk factory!"

"But you have factories too, don't you?" observed Platonov.

"But who set them up? They set themselves up: there was a surplus of wool, impossible to get rid of the stuff, so I started to weave cloth, plain, thick cloth; I sell it cheaply right here in the markets. For six years they used to dump the fish-scales on my banks; what else could they do with it, anyway? So I've started to boil it up into glue and it's brought in forty thousand. That's the way everything is with me."

"What a clever devil!" thought Chichikov, staring at him wide-eyed, "what grasping paws!"

"And I don't put up any special premises for all this; you won't find any colonnaded, pedimented buildings on my estate. I don't import any skilled craftsman from abroad. And on no account will I take the peasants away from tilling the fields. Peasants work in my factories only in years of famine, all of them migrants too, looking for a crust of bread. I could have a lot of factories like that. You only have to take a close look about the place and you will see that any old rag can be put to use, any old rubbish can bring in profit, there's so much of it that you can't be bothered any more and you say to yourself: I don't need it."

"That's astounding! But the most astounding thing is that any rubbish can bring in profit!" said Chichikov.

"And not only that!.." Kostanzhoglo had not finished his speech: the bile had risen in him and now he was out to abuse his landowner neighbours. "Now there's one smart fellow—and what do you think he's set up? A charity home, a stone building in the village! A Christian deed! But if you want to help your fellow man, then you should help him to fulfil his own duty and not tear him away from his Christian duty. Help the son nurse his ailing father in his own home, and don't give him the chance to shift the burden onto to someone else's shoulders. Better give him the means to shelter his nearest and dearest in his home, give him the money, help him in every possible way, but don't exempt him, or he will forget all his Christian duties altogether. There are Don Quixotes all over the place! Spending two hundred rubles a year for one person's keep in a charity home! I could keep ten men in my village for that money!" Kostanzhoglo spat in disgust.

Chichikov was not interested in the charity home: he wanted to pursue the subject of how any old rubbish could bring in profit. But Kostanzhoglo was angry now, the bile seethed within him, and the words came pouring out:

"And there's another Don Quixote of enlightenment: he's set up schools! Of course, there's nothing more useful to a man than knowing how to read and write. But what do you think happened? The peasants come to me from his village with this new trouble. They told me: 'Our sons have got quite out of hand, they don't want to help in the fields, they all want to be clerks, but we only need one clerk in the village.' That was the upshot of it!"

Chichikov did not need to hear about schools either, but Platonov took up the subject:

"But the fact that we don't need clerks now is no reason to stop! They'll be needed later. You should work for posterity."

"You at least, brother, should use your brains! What's all this worry about posterity? Everyone imagines himself another Peter the Great or someone. Just look under your own feet and don't worry about posterity; see that you make your peasant contented and rich and that he has the time to study of his own free will and not with you standing over him with a stick in your hand, shouting 'Study!' They start from the wrong end, that's what!.. Just listen to this, I'll let you be the judge of this one yourself..." Here Kostanzhoglo moved closer to Chichikov and in order to get him to look more closely into the matter thrust his finger through the button-hole of his tailcoat. "Well now, what could be clearer? Your peasants are there for you to guide them in their peasant lives. What is the essence of these lives? What is the essence of a peasant's work? Tilling the land? So make sure he's a good tiller. Clear? Oh no, there are these smart alecks who say: 'He must be brought out of this state. He leads too harsh, too plain a life: he must be acquainted with luxury.' Yet it's precisely because of this luxury that they themselves have gone soft, they fall ill with the devil knows what diseases, and you'll no longer find an eighteen-year-old youth amongst them who hasn't tried it all: he has no teeth, no hair either... So now they want to infect the peasants too! But we should thank the Lord that we still have at least one healthy class left, which has not yet acquired a taste for those pursuits! We really should thank the Lord for that. Yes, tillers of the soil are the most respected of men for me. I would to God we were all tillers of the soil!"

"So would you hold that agriculture is the most profitable occupation?" asked Chichikov.

"The most legitimate, not the most profitable. 'In the sweat of thy brow shalt thou till the land.' Those words are said to us all; with good reason are they said. It has already been proven with the experience of centuries that the man who follows the calling of land-tiller is purer in his morals. Where tilling the land has formed the foundation of a social community there will be sufficiency and plenty; there is no poverty and no luxury, but there is sufficiency. Till the land, man is told, work and toil... It's all very simple. I tell my peasant: 'Whoever you're working for, for me, yourself, your neighbour, work properly. In your industry I am your first assistant. If you have no animals, here's a horse, here's a cow, here's a cart for you... I'm prepared to provide all you require, but you must work. I can't stand the sight of disorderliness and poverty in your household. But I will not tolerate idleness. The reason I am here over you is to make sure you work.' Ha! They think they can increase incomes with their charity homes and factories! First think about how to make all your peasants rich, and then you will also be rich, without any factories, or any stupid notions."

"The more one listens to you, my most esteemed Konstantin Fyodorovich," said Chichikov, "the more one wants to listen. But tell me, my venerable sir: if, for example, I should conceive the ambition to become a landowner, let us suppose in this province, to what primarily should I lend my attention? What should I do, how should I act, in order to grow rich in a relatively short time, in order thereby, so to speak, to fulfil my duty as a citizen?"

"What to do in order to get rich? This is what..." said Kostanzhoglo.

"Let's go in to supper!" said the lady of the house, rising from the settee, and wrapping a shawl round her chilled young shoulders.

Chichikov sprang from his chair with the agility of quite an officer, flew across to his hostess with the soft, smiling expression of a sensitive man of the world, held out his arm to her like a yoke and ceremoniously took her through two rooms into the dining-room, the whole time keeping his head agreeably tilted somewhat to one side. The servant removed the lid from the soup tureen; they all moved their chairs closer to the table and the meal began.

Having dispatched his soup and followed it with a glass of home-made brandy (the brandy was excellent) Chichikov turned to Kostanzhoglo:

"Permit me, my most esteemed host, to return once more to the subject of our earlier discussion. I was asking you how to act, what to do, what best to undertake...*

. . . .

"It's such a fine estate that if he were to ask even forty thousand I would pay him on the spot."

"Hm!" Chichikov grew pensive. "But then," he continued with a certain timidity, "why don't you buy it yourself?"

"You have to know where to stop. As it is I have enough bother with my present estates. Besides, the local gentry are already shouting at me for taking advantage of the sorry state of their affairs to buy up land for a song. I'm quite sick of hearing it."

"The gentry is prone to malicious talk!" said Chichikov.

"Quite so, and right here, in our own province... You simply couldn't imagine the things they say about me. They actually call me a moneygrubber and skinflint of the first degree. They won't accept the blame for anything. 'Of course, I frittered it all away,' they say, 'but only because I followed the nobler aspirations of life. I need books, I must live in splendour in order to encourage industry; of course, one needn't go bankrupt till the end of one's days if one lives as swinishly as Kostanzhoglo.' That's what they say!"

"How I should like to live so swinishly!" said Chichikov.

"And it's all because I do not give great dinner parties or lend them money. I do not give dinners because I would find them tedious and anyway I'm not accustomed to

*Two pages are missing here in the ms. The first edition of Volume Two of *Dead Souls* (1855) contains the note: "Here there is a hiatus in Kostanzhoglo's conversation with Chichikov. We must presume that Kostanzhoglo suggests to Chichikov that he purchase the estate of his neighbour, the landowner Khlobuyev."

them. But if you wish to come and take pot-luck with me—I shall be only delighted! To say I do not lend money is nonsense. If you are in real need, come and explain in detail how you are going to dispose of my money. If I see from what you say that you are going to use it wisely and the money will bring you definite profit, I shan't refuse you and I shan't even charge interest. But I am not going to throw money away. The gentleman will have to forgive me. He wants to give a dinner or something for his mistress or furnishes his house in a crazily grand manner, and I'm expected to lend him money!"

At this point Kostanzhoglo spat and very nearly uttered one or two indecent and abusive words in the presence of his wife. The severe shadow of melancholy darkened his lively face. Wrinkles gathered across and down his forehead, betraying the angry upsurge of bile within him.

Chichikov drank a glass of raspberry brandy and spoke thus: "Allow me, my esteemed sir, to return you once again to the subject of our interrupted conversation. If, let us suppose, I were to acquire that same estate which you have mentioned, in how much time and how quickly could I get sufficiently rich to—"

"If you wish," interjected Kostanzhoglo abruptly and in a stern voice, still very much out of sorts, "to get rich quickly, then you will never get rich at all; if, however, you merely wish to get rich, without asking when, you will get rich quickly."

"Oh, really!" said Chichikov.

"Yes," Kostanzhoglo said brusquely, as if he were actually angry with Chichikov himself. "You have to love work; nothing would be achieved without that. Yes, you have to love running your estate. And believe me, it's not in the least bit tedious. It's said that life in the country is a bore... I for one would die of boredom if I had to spend even a single day in the town living like those townsmen. A landowner has no time for boredom. There is no emptiness in his life—everything is fullness. You only have to consider the whole cycle of activities through the year—and what activities! Activities that truly elevate a man's spirit, not to mention their great variety. Here a man walks side-by-side with nature, with the seasons of the year, he is both participant and interlocutor in all the processes of creation.

Spring has not come yet but work already begins: you have to bring in a stock of firewood and everything else to last while the roads are impassable for mud; the seed must be prepared; there is the sorting and weighing of the grain in the barns, and the drying; the levies to be set. When the snows have melted, and the rivers are flowing, there are countless new jobs: there are the barges to be loaded, forests to be cleared, orchards to be replanted, and the ground has to be dug up everywhere. In the vegetable gardens the spade is hard at work and in the fields—the plough and harrow. Then the sowing starts. A small matter? Sowing the future harvest! Next it's summer—haymaking, the farmer's jolliest time. A small matter? And then one harvest follows the other: rye followed by wheat, barley by oats, and here the hemp has to be pulled. Hayricks are built, sheaves laid in. Now August is half over—everything has to be brought into the barns. Autumn is here—the ploughing and sowing of winter crops, repairing the barns, the threshing sheds, the animal pens, storing the first yield of threshed grain. Winter comes—and there's work waiting to be done: the first deliveries to town, threshing on all the floors, carting the grain from the threshing sheds to the barns, tree-felling and chopping of firewood in the forests, bringing in bricks and materials for the spring building jobs. In fact, I could not possibly cover it all. What a great variety of jobs! You pop in here and there to take a look: to the mill, to the workyard, to the manufactories, and to the threshing floors! You also take a look at your peasants, to see how they're doing their own work. A small matter? And it's a joy for me to watch a carpenter who really knows how to wield an axe; I can stand watching him for two hours, it's such a delight to see. And then if you also remember to what purpose all this work is done, how everything around you grows and multiplies, bringing forth fruit and profit! Yes, I couldn't even describe the pleasure it gives me. And it's not because the money increases—money's not everything—but because all that is the work of your own hands; because you can see that you are the cause and creator of everything, and that you dispense goodness and plenty as if you were some sort of magician. Where else can you find me pleasure to equal that?" said Kostanzhoglo. His face gazed upwards and all the wrinkles vanished. He was happy as a tsar on the day of his coronation. "No, nowhere in the whole world will you find another such pleasure! It is here, precisely here, that man imitates God: God has reserved to Himself the task of creation as the supreme pleasure, and He likewise demands of man that he be the creator of prosperity and a smooth flow of work. And some people call that boring work!"

Chichikov listened to his host's mellifluous speeches as to the singing of a bird of paradise. His mouth watered. An unctuous look came into his eyes, and he could listen to Kostanzhoglo's discourse forever.

"Konstantin! It's time to get up," said the hostess, rising from her chair. Platonov rose, Kostanzhoglo rose. Chichikov also rose, although he wished only to sit on and listen. Holding out his arm like a yoke he took his hostess back to the drawing-room. But his head was not inclined respectfully to one side, nor was there sufficient adroitness in his movements, because his thoughts were occupied with more down-to-earth speculations and considerations.

"Say what you may, it's boring all the same," said Platonov, walking behind them.

"Our guest, it seems, is a far from stupid man," thought the host, "moderate in his words and not a braggart either." And these reflections made him still more cheerful, just as if he had been warmed by his own words and was, as it were, rejoicing at having found a man willing to listen to wise counsel.

When afterwards they had all taken their seats in a small cosy drawing-room, illuminated by candles, which looked out on to the balcony through a French window, Chichikov felt more content than he had for a very long time. It was as if after long peregrinations he had at last reached home and, to cap it all, had already had all his desires fulfilled and declared, casting aside his wayfarer's staff: "Enough!" This spell of entrancement had been cast on his soul by the sagacious words of his host. For every man there are certain types of discourse which are somehow dearer and closer to him in spirit than any other. And it often happens that in some God-forsaken backwater, in a desert of desolation, you unexpectedly meet a man whose warming conversation makes you forget the foulness of the roads, the ugliness of the night's lodgings, and the modern world, full of follies and delusions. An evening thus spent will remain vividly alive forever after, and you will remember everything that happened and who was present, who sat where, what he held in his hands, you will remember the walls, the corners and every smallest trifle.

Thus too did Chichikov's memory record everything: this small unpretentiously furnished room, the good-natured expression on the face of his host, the pipe with the amber mouthpiece given to Platonov, the smoke which he started to blow into Yarb's fat jowls, Yarb's snorting, and the laughter of their attractive hostess, interrupted with the words: "Enough, don't tease him"; and the cheerful candles, the cricket in the corner, the French window, the spring night, which gazed back in at them, leaning on the tops of the trees, from the dense midst of whose foliage came the warbling of spring nightingales.

"Your words are sweet to me, my esteemed Konstantin Fyodorovich," announced Chichikov. "I can say that in all Russia I have not met a man equal to you in wisdom."

Kostanzhoglo smiled.

"No, Pavel Ivanovich," he said, "if you really wish to meet a wise man, there is one such among us, someone of whom you really can say: 'a wise man,' and whose shoelaces I am not fit to tie."

"Who is that?" asked Chichikov in amazement.

"That's our monopolist, Murazov."

"This is the second time I've heard about him!" exclaimed Chichikov.

"Now that's a man capable of managing not just a landowner's estate, but an entire state. If I had a state of my own I would at once make him minister of finance."

"I've heard of him. They say he is a man whose capabilities surpass all comprehension, he has amassed ten million, they say."

"Ten, nothing! It's way over forty. Soon half of Russia will be in his hands."

"Really!" gasped Chichikov.

"Without a shadow of doubt. His riches should now be increasing at a quite incredible rate. That's obvious. Only the men with a few hundred thousand grow rich slowly; the one with millions, has a larger radius: whatever he lays his hands on will at once increase two- or three-fold. His field, his scope is too extensive. He simply has no competitors. There is no one who can contend with him. Whatever price he fixes for anything stands: there is no one to outbid him."

His eyes popping and his mouth gaping, Chichikov stared into Kostanzhoglo's eyes like a man struck dumb. He was quite breathless with excitement.

"The mind positively boggles!" he said, recovering his composure somewhat. "Thought itself is petrified. People marvel at the wisdom of Providence when they contemplate a little bug; but what I find more astounding is that such immense sums can be handled by a mere mortal! Permit me to put one question to you with regard to a certain circumstance: tell me, surely the first step to acquisition must have been made in a not entirely blameless manner?"

"In the most irreproachable manner and by the most regular means."

"I cannot believe it, my most respected sir, forgive me, I cannot believe it. If it had been thousands, then perhaps, but millions... Forgive me, I cannot believe it."

"On the contrary, with thousands it would be hard to be blameless, but millions are easy to amass. There is no need for a millionaire to have recourse to crooked methods. Just follow the straightest possible road and grab everything lying in your path! No one else can pick it up."

"The mind boggles! But what makes it boggle most is that all this must have started with a single kopek!"

"But it never happens any other way. That is the proper order of things," said Kostanzhoglo. "The man born with thousands, reared on thousands, will never acquire anything: he already has established whims and caprices and whatever else! You have to start from the very beginning, and not from the middle. You must start at the bottom, the rock bottom. Only there will you properly get to know the people and the milieu in which you will later have to make your way. When you have endured this setback and that, when you have learnt that every kopek is held fast by a three-kopek nail, when you have passed through every ordeal, then you will be so well-taught and schooled that you will never again slip up and lose your grip in any enterprise. Believe me, it's the truth. You must begin at the beginning and not in the middle. If a man tells me: 'Give me a hundred thousand, I'll get rich immediately,' I don't believe him: he's banking on good luck and not on certainty. You must start with a kopek!"

"In that case I shall grow rich," said Chichikov, "because I am beginning almost, so to speak, from nothing."

He had in mind the dead souls.

"Konstantin, it's time to let Pavel Ivanovich rest and have a little sleep," said the hostess, "but you keep chattering away."

"You will most definitely grow rich," said Kostanzhoglo, without listening to his wife. "Rivers will flow to you, rivers of gold. You will not know what to do with the profits."

Pavel Ivanovich sat there spell-bound, his thoughts spinning in a golden sphere of blossoming fancies and daydreams.

"Really, Konstantin, it's time for Pavel Ivanovich to retire."

"Why are you fussing? Run along, if you wish!" said the host and stopped short: the loud noise of Platonov's snoring filled the room, and this was followed by the even louder snoring of Yarb. Watchmen had long been making their rounds, and the sound of the metal boards they struck regularly came from faraway. Midnight had come and gone. Kostanzhoglo realised that it was, indeed, time for bed. They all went their various ways, wishing one another a good night's sleep, and wasted no time putting these wishes to good effect.

Chichikov alone was unable to sleep. His thoughts refused to quiesce. He was pondering how to become a landowner like Kostanzhoglo. After his conversation with his host everything had become so clear; the possibility of growing rich seemed so self-evident. The arduous task of managing an estate now seemed so simple and comprehensible, and so suited to his own nature that he started to think in earnest about the acquisition of a real, and not an imaginary, estate; he at once decided to use the money which he would receive by mortgaging chimerical souls to obtain an estate that was anything but chimerical. He could already see himself acting and managing affairs just as Kostanzhoglo had instructed—promptly, circumspectly, introducing nothing new without first learning the old through and through, inspecting everything himself, getting to know all his peasants, renouncing all excessive luxuries for himself, and dedicating himself utterly to his labours and management. He could already savour the pleasure he would experience when a harmonious order had been established and all the mainsprings of his industry moved smoothly, efficiently setting one another in motion. His estate would seethe with activity and, just as the flour is ground swiftly by the spinning stones of a mill so would lucre and more lucre be ground from all sorts of lumber and refuse. The image of his wonderful host stood constantly before his eyes. This was the first man in all Russia towards whom he had felt a personal respect. Hitherto he had respected a man either for his high office, or for his great wealth! There had not been a single man whom he had respected for his mind alone. Kostanzhoglo was the first. Chichikov understood, too, that with such a one as this there was no point in raising the issue of dead souls and that the very subject would be out of place. His mind was now engaged by a new project: to buy Khlobuyev's estate. He had ten thousand: he reckoned to borrow another ten thousand from Kostanzhoglo, since the latter himself declared his willingness to help any man who wished to grow rich and to take up the management of an estate. The remaining ten thousand he could obtain subsequently, by mortgaging his souls. It was still impossible to mortgage all the souls he had bought; because as yet he lacked the lands on which they were to be resettled. Although he averred that he had such lands in Kherson province, these in fact existed mostly in his imagination. He did intend to buy such lands in Kherson province, because they were sold there for a song, and were even assigned gratis to anyone prepared to settle there. His thoughts even turned on the necessity of making haste and buying whatever fugitive and dead souls he could from anyone, for the landowners were racing one another to mortgage their estates, and soon there might not remain a single unmortgaged nook or cranny in all Russia. All these thoughts jostled one another in his mind and kept sleep at bay. Finally the sleep which for the last four hours and more had held the entire house, as the saying goes, in its embrace, at last also enfolded Chichikov. He fell sound asleep.

CHAPTER FOUR

The next day everything turned out in the best way imaginable. Kostanzhoglo was delighted to lend him ten thousand without interest, without security—merely against a signed I. O. U. Thus was he prepared to help any man on his road to the acquisition of property. And that is not all. He undertook to accompany Chichikov to Khlobuyev's himself, in order that they might survey the estate together. After a filling breakfast they all set off, the three of them sitting together in Pavel Ivanovich's carriage: Kostanzhoglo's trap followed them empty. Yarb ran on ahead, chasing birds from the road. In a little over an hour and a half they covered eighteen versts and caught sight of a little village with two manor houses. One was large and new, still unfinished, the building work abandoned some years before, the other was small and dilapidated. They found the owner dishevelled and sleepy, and only just out of bed: there was a patch on his frockcoat and a hole in his boot.

He was delighted beyond all measure at the arrival of his visitors, and welcomed them like long-lost brothers.

"Konstantin Fyodorovich! Platon Mikhailovich!" he exclaimed. "My dear friends! How good of you to visit me! Let me rub my eyes! To be honest, I thought no one would ever visit me again. They all shun me like the plague: they think I'll ask for a loan. Oh, it's hard, it's hard, Konstantin Fyodorovich! I can see I'm to blame for everything! What can I do? A pig living in a pigsty. Forgive me, gentlemen, for receiving you in such attire: my boots, as you see, are full of holes. But what can I offer you, tell me?"

"Please, let's not beat about the bush. We've come to you on business," said Kostanzhoglo. "We've brought you a buyer, Pavel Ivanovich Chichikov."

"Delighted to make your acquaintance. Let me shake your hand." Chichikov held out both hands.

"I should have very much liked, my most esteemed Pavel Ivanovich, to show you an estate that merited your attention... But may I ask you, gentlemen, whether you have eaten?"

"We've eaten, we've eaten," said Kostanzhoglo, wishing to get on. "Let's waste no more time and get going right away."

23*

"In that case let's go."

Khlobuyev picked up his cap. The guests also donned their caps and the party set off on foot to view the village.

"Let's go and inspect my disorder and dissipation," said Khlobuyev. "Of course, you were right to eat first. Would you believe it, Konstantin Fyodorovich, there's not a single chicken in the house—that's what things have come to. I live like a pig, quite simply a pig!"

With a profound sigh, and as if sensing that little sympathy would be forthcoming from Konstantin Fyodorovich who had a rather hard heart, he put his arm through Platonov's and walked ahead with him, pressing him now and then to his chest. Kostanzhoglo and Chichikov were left behind and, walking arm in arm, followed at some distance.

"It's hard, Platon Mikhailovich, it's hard!" said Khlobuyev to Platonov. "You can't imagine how hard it is! No money, no grain, no boots! It would have been small worry if I were young and single, but when all these misfortunes strike as you approach old age, with a wife to support and five children—you do feel sad, you can't help feeling sad..."

Platonov felt sorry for him.

"Well, now if you sell your estate, will that set you right?" he asked.

"How can it set me right!" said Khlobuyev, with a hopeless wave. "It will all go to pay off my most pressing debts and after that I shan't even have a thousand left."

"So what are you going to do?"

"God knows," said Khlobuyev, shrugging his shoulders.

Platonov was amazed.

"But why aren't you trying to do something to get out of this predicament?"

"Like what?"

"Do you mean to say you have no money left?"

"Not a bean."

"Well, look for a post, take up some position or other."

"But my rank is only Gubernia Secretary. What sort of well-paid position could I find? My salary would be miserable and I have a wife and five children."

"Well, some private appointment then. Become manager."

"Who would entrust his estate to me! I've ruined mine."

"But if you're threatened by starvation and death, you

have got to do something. I'll ask my brother-in-law, he may be able to secure an appointment for you through someone or other in town."

"No, Platon Mikhailovich," said Khlobuyev, with a sigh, and squeezing his arm tight, "I'm no longer any good for anything. I have grown old before my time, my back aches from the sins of my youth and I have rheumatism in my shoulder. Where can I go! Why ruin the Treasury! As it is, there are hordes of civil servants looking for lucrative appointments. May God forbid that because of me, because of the need to pay me a salary, the taxes on the poor should be increased: their lot is hard enough with all those leeches bleeding them. No Platon Mikhailovich, forget it."

"What a predicament!" thought Platonov. "That's worse than my lethargy."

In the meantime Kostanzhoglo and Chichikov, following behind them at a considerable distance, were conversing as follows:

"See how he's let everything go to rack and ruin!" said Kostanzhoglo, pointing about him. "Reduced his peasants to such poverty! When the cattle plague struck, he shouldn't have clung to his belongings. He should have sold everything and bought his peasants some cattle, so they wouldn't remain without the means of productive work for a single day. And now you could not put all this right in years: the peasants have grown lazy and taken to drink."

"Does that mean it's not really profitable to buy an estate such as this?" asked Chichikov.

Here Kostanzhoglo gave him a look as if to say: "What an ignoramus! Do we have to go right back to the ABC with you?"

"Not profitable! In three years I'd be getting twenty thousand a year in profit from this estate. That's how unprofitable it is! A mere fifteen versts. A trifle! And the land? Just look at the land! It's all water-meadow. I'd plant flax, and I'd take in a good five thousand from the flax alone: I'd plant turnips, and I guarantee four thousand from the turnips. And look over there: the rye growing along the slope of the hill: it's all self-seeded, you know. He's sown no rye, I know that. No, this estate should be worth a hundred and fifty thousand, and not forty."

Chichikov became apprehensive that Khlobuyev might

hear, and for that reason hung back still further.

"Look over there, how much land he's left fallow!" said Kostanzhoglo, his temper rising. "If he'd only given advance notice he'd have found people willing to work it. And if he's got nothing to plough with he should at least have dug the soil up for vegetables. He'd have made a profit on vegetables. He's made his peasants sit idle for four years. Is that a trifle? I tell you, with that alone you corrupt them and ruin them for ever. They've grown used to slovenliness and vagrancy, it's become their life now." And, saying this, Kostanzhoglo spat, and his brow clouded with rancour...

"I can't remain here any longer! I hate to see all this disorder and neglect! You can now conclude matters with him without me. Take this treasure away from that fool as soon as you can. He is only discrediting a gift from God!"

And, with these words, Kostanzhoglo took his leave of Chichikov and caught up with his host, to whom he also said goodbye.

"But my dear Konstantin Fyodorovich," said his astonished host, "you've only just arrived—and you're off!"

"I can't stay. I have to be at home urgently," said Kostanzhoglo.

He made his adieux, got into his trap and drove off.

Khlobuyev seemed to have understood the reason for his departure.

"Konstantin Fyodorovich couldn't take it," he said. "I can feel how unpleasant it is for a good farmer like him to view such slovenly management. Believe me, I'm at my wits' end, Pavel Ivanovich... I sowed practically no grain at all this year! I give you my word. There was no seed, not to mention horses, ploughs and things. Your brother, Platon Mikhailovich, is reputed to have extraordinary talents as a landowner; and there's no question of it, in his way Konstantin Fyodorovich is a Napoleon. I must admit I often think: 'But why should there be so much intelligence put into a single head? If only a drop of his had fallen into my numbskull, just enough for me to keep my own house in order! I'm good for nothing, I can do nothing. Ah, Pavel Ivanovich, take over my estate! I feel so sorry for my poor peasants. I feel that I have failed to be... (*the next word is obscure in the ms.*), do what you like, but I am quite unable to be exacting and severe. Anyway, how could I teach them to be orderly when I'm so disorderly myself! I would give them their freedom this very second if it weren't that a Russian needs to have someone to drive him on otherwise he'll only fall into sloth and go to pot."

"It really is very strange," said Platonov, "why is it like that with us that if you don't watch your peasants like a hawk they turn into drunkards and scoundrels?"

"From lack of enlightenment," observed Chichikov.

"Oh well, God knows why. Look at us: We're enlightened, and how do we live? I went to the university and heard lectures on all subjects, but not only did I fail to learn the art and system of living, I became even more skilled in the art of squandering as much money as possible on all sorts of new refinements and comforts, and I became more intimately acquainted with those luxuries that require money. Was it because I was a poor student? Far from it. My fellow students were much the same, you know. Perhaps two or three derived some real benefit from our education, but probably that was only because they were clever enough without it, while the rest of us only learned things that ruin our health and wheedle all our money out of us. God's truth! In fact, people came to study only so that they could applaud the professors and hand out awards to them, and not to receive any themselves. So from enlightenment we select only the more worthless aspects: we gladly assume its outward appearance and ignore the essence. No, Pavel Ivanovich, we don't have the art of living because of something else, but what, I honestly, don't know."

"There must be reasons," said Chichikov.

"I must say, that sometimes the Russian seems to me a sort of hopeless case. No will-power, no courage to persevere. You want to do everything, and you can do nothing. You are forever thinking that tomorrow you will start a new life, tomorrow you will start to do everything properly, tomorrow you will go on a diet—and nothing comes of it: by that very same evening you have gorged yourself so full that you sit and stare at everyone like an owl, blinking and unable to utter an articulate word—honestly, everyone's like that."

"One must keep some prudence in store," said Chichikov, "one must confer with prudence every minute, conduct a friendly dialogue with it."

"Come now!" said Khlobuyev. "I must confess, I think that we were not born for prudence at all. I do not believe that any one of us has ever been prudent. If I see someone living in quite a decent manner, making and saving money—I still don't trust him! Even he will be led astray by the devil in his old age—and then he'll blow the lot! And we're all like that: the nobles, and the peasants, the enlightened ones, and the unenlightened. You take some very clever peasant: stárting from nothing he amasses a hundred thousand, and then, when he has his hundred thousand he takes a crazy notion to fill a tub with champagne and bathe himself in it. Well now, I think we've seen everything. There's nothing more. Unless, of course, you want to take a look at the mill? It doesn't have a wheel, by the way, and anyway the building is no good."

"So why bother looking at it!" said Chichikov.

"In that case let's go home." And they all directed their steps towards the house.

On their way back they saw the same sights, all equally untidy and disgraceful. Everything was neglected and overgrown. The only addition was a new puddle in the middle of the road. An angry peasant woman, in a grimy sackcloth dress, was beating a wretched little girl to within an inch of her life and calling her all the ugliest names she knew. Two peasants, standing a little way off, were observing the drunken woman's anger with a stoic indifference. One was scratching himself in the small of his back, the other was yawning. Gaping yawns were visible in all the buildings. The roofs also yawned. Looking at them, Platonov yawned.

"These peasants—they're my future property," thought Chichikov. "Nothing but holes and patches!" Indeed, one cottage had an entire gate on top of it instead of a roof; the sagging windows were propped up by poles pinched from the master's barn. In short, they seemed to have introduced the Trishka's caftan system into their farming methods: you cut off the coat-tails and lapels to make patches for the elbows.

They went inside. Chichikov was somewhat startled by the signs of dire poverty rubbing shoulders with some glittering knick-knacks in the very latest luxurious fashion. Amidst the tattered curtains, rugs and furniture he saw brand new bronzes. A miniature bust of Shakespeare or someone was mounted on the ink-well, and on the table lay a natty ivory back-scratcher. Khlobuyev introduced them to his wife. She was a sight for sore eyes. She would have held her own even in Moscow. Her dress was fashionable and in good taste. She liked to talk more about the town and the theatre which had been opened there. It was obvious that she was even less fond of the country than was her husband, and that she was more bored than Platonov when left on her own. Soon the room filled with children, little girls and boys. There were five of them. A sixth was borne in his nurse's arms. They were all handsome children. The boys and girls were dressed charmingly and with taste, they were playful and spirited. And this only made it all the sadder to look at them. Better they had been dressed poorly, in plain dimity skirts and shirts, running around the yard by themselves and not differing in any way from the simple peasant children! A lady friend of their hostess arrived. The ladies withdrew to their part of the house. The children ran after them. The men were left to themselves.

Chichikov broached the question of the purchase. In accordance with the custom of all buyers he began by heaping criticism on the estate he wished to buy. And having thoroughly run it down, he said:

"Now what would your price be?"

"You know what," said Khlobuyev, "I shall not ask a high price of you, and anyway I would not want to: it would be dishonest of me. Neither shall I attempt to conceal from you that of the hundred souls in my village who figure on the census list, there are less than fifty actually in evidence: the others have either died from the epidemic, or have run away without passports, so that you can count them as good as dead. For that reason I'm only asking you for thirty thousand in all."

"I say—thirty thousand! The estate is neglected, the peasants dead, and thirty thousand! Make it twenty-five."

"Pavel Ivanovich! I could mortgage it for twenty-five thousand, don't you see? Then I would get the twenty-five thousand and the estate would still be mine. The sole reason why I'm selling it is that I need the money urgently, but mortgaging would mean delays, and I'd have to pay the clerks, and I've nothing to pay them with."

"Well, why don't you make it twenty-five thousand, all the same?"

Platonov felt ashamed for Chichikov.

"Buy it, Pavel Ivanovich," he said. "It's well worth the price. If you don't give thirty thousand for it, my brother and I will go halves and buy it."

Chichikov took fright...

"Very well!" he said. "I'll give you thirty thousand. I'll give you an advance of two thousand now, eight thousand in a week's time, and the remaining twenty thousand in a month."

"No, Pavel Ivanovich, only on condition that I get the money as soon as possible. Give me at least fifteen thousand now, and the rest not later than in two weeks' time."

"But I haven't got fifteen thousand! All I have now is ten thousand. I need time to collect the rest."

In fact Chichikov was lying: he had twenty thousand.

"No, please Pavel Ivanovich: I insist that I absolutely must have fifteen thousand."

"Dear me, I'm short of five thousand. I don't know where to get it from."

"I'll lend it to you," offered Platonov.

"Well, if you will!" said Chichikov, thinking: "It suits me very well, that he's giving me a loan: in that case I shall be able to bring the money tomorrow." The box was brought from the carriage, and ten thousand taken out and handed to Khlobuyev then and there: the remaining five thousand, however, were promised for the morrow: that is to say that five were promised but Chichikov meant to bring only three; the rest would come a little later, in two or three days, and if possible later still. Pavel Ivanovich was not overfond of letting money out of his hands. And if it was absolutely essential to do so, then it still seemed better to him to hand over the money tomorrow rather than to-day. In this he was like the rest of us! For do we not all like to lead our petitioners a merry dance? Let him cool his heels a bit in the hall! Why shouldn't he wait? What do we care that every hour may be dear to him and that waiting causes him great inconvenience! "Call in tomorrow, brother, I haven't the time today."

"But where will you live after this?" Platonov asked Khlobuyev. "Do you have another little village?"

"No little village, but I shall move to the town. I'd have to do so anyway, not for my own sake but for the children's. They need tutors in divinity, music, dancing. After all, you can't get those in the country."

"He hasn't a crust of bread, but he wants to teach his children dancing!" thought Chichikov.

"Strange!" thought Platonov.

"Well now, this calls for a little celebration," said Khlobuyev. "Hey, Kiryushka, bring us a bottle of champagne."

"There isn't a crust of bread, but there is champagne!" thought Chichikov.

Platonov did not even know what to think.

The champagne was brought in. They drank three glasses each and grew merry. The wine loosened Khlobuyev's tongue and he became witty and charming. Bons mots and anecdotes simply tumbled from his lips. His words displayed such knowledge of people and the world! He saw so many things so well and so correctly, so succinctly and so adroitly did he sum up his landowner neighbours in a few words, so clearly did he see their errors and shortcomings, so well did he know the history of those local squires who had been ruined—the how, why and wherefore of their ruination, with such originality and accuracy could he imitate their pettiest mannerisms, that both his listeners were totally entranced and ready to declare him quite the wittiest of men.

"Listen," said Platonov, seizing him by the arm, "how is it that you, with all your intelligence, experience and knowledge of life, cannot find the means to extricate yourself from your own predicament?"

"Well, the means are there," said Khlobuyev, and dumped before them a whole heap of projects. These were all so absurd, so weird, so far removed from any knowledge of people and the world, that all the listeners could do was to shrug their shoulders and say to themselves: "Heavens above! What an immense gap there is between _knowledge of the world_ and the ability to make use of this knowledge!" Practically all the projects were based on first obtaining from somewhere or other a hundred or two hundred thousand, after which, so it seemed to him, everything would right itself, the farm would run smoothly, the holes would all be patched up, profits would be quadrupled, and he would bring himself into a position where he could repay all his debts. And he concluded his speech: "But what would you advise me to do? There is no benefactor who would risk a loan of two hundred or even only one hundred thousand! It seems God Himself does not wish it."

"I should think not," thought Chichikov. "Fancy God sending a fool like that two hundred thousand rubles!"

"I do, as a matter or fact, have an aunt worth three million," said Khlobuyev, "a pious old lady: she donates generously to the churches and monasteries, but when it comes to helping her near and dear she keeps a tight fist. But the old girl's quite remarkable. A rare specimen of the old school: it's worth taking a look at her. She has about four hundred canaries alone. Pug-dogs, hangers-on, servants the likes of which you don't see these days. The youngest of the servants must be sixty if he's a day, though she still calls him: 'Young fellow!' If a guest should somehow displease her she'll order the waiter to bypass him at dinner. And bypassed he will be."

Platonov chuckled.

"What's her name and where does she live?" asked Chichikov.

"She lives right here in town—she's Alexandra Ivanovna Khanasarova."

"But why don't you turn to her?" asked Platonov with real concern. "It seems to me that if she were only acquainted a little more closely with the predicament of your family she would not be able to refuse you, however tight-fisted she might be."

"Oh no, she'd be able to refuse all right! My aunt is a tough old bird. That old lady's hard as flint, Platon Mikhailovich! And anyway, apart from me there are all sorts of sycophants hanging around her. There's one amongst them, a chap who aspires to being a governor, claims some sort of kinship with her ... good luck to him! Maybe he'll succeed! Good luck to the lot of them! I never was any good at grovelling, and it's too late to begin now: my back will no longer bend."

"Fool!" thought Chichikov, "I would have cosseted that sort of aunt like a nanny cossets an infant child!"

"Talking parches your throat, doesn't it," said Khlobuyev. "Hey, Kiryushka! Bring us another bottle of champagne!"

"No, no, I shan't drink any more," said Platonov.

"Nor shall I," said Chichikov. And they both were adamant in their refusals.

"Well then at least promise to be my guests in town: on the 8th of June I shall be giving a dinner for our local dignitaries."

"My dear chap!" exclaimed Platonov. "In a state like this, utterly ruined, and you're giving a dinner?"

"What can I do? I've got to. It's my duty," said Khlobuyev. "They have also entertained me."

"What is to be done with him?" thought Platonov. He did not yet know that in Russia, in Moscow and in the other cities, there are people whose life is an inexplicable puzzle. A man seems to have squandered everything, he is up to his ears in debt, and the dinner which he is giving must surely be his last: the diners imagine that the very next day their host will be dragged off to gaol. Ten more years pass, and he is still going strong, he is over his ears in debt and once again giving a dinner, and everyone thinks this must be his last, and they are all convinced that their host will be hauled off to gaol the very next day. Such a one was Khlobuyev. Only in Russia could anyone lead such an existence. Without a kopek to his name, he received and entertained guests, and even set himself up as a patron of the arts, supporting all sorts of painters who flocked into the town, taking them under his own roof. Anyone glancing into his house while he was in town would have been quite unable to establish who the owner was. Today a priest in full vestments would be conducting a thanksgiving service there, tomorrow a troupe of French actors would be rehearsing. The next day some fellow, unknown to practically everyone in the house, would install himself with all his papers in the drawing-room itself and turn it into his study, and this would not disturb or incommode anyone in the house, just as if it were the most natural thing on earth. Sometimes there would not be a crumb in the house, at others a dinner would be served that would satisfy the taste of the most exacting gourmet. The owner would appear in a cheerful, festive mood, with the air of a rich nobleman, and the gait of a man whose life is spent in abundance and contentment. At other times, things looked so hopeless that anyone else would long since have hanged or shot himself. But he was saved by his devoutness which was combined in him in some strange way with the fecklessness of his life. In these bitter, painful moments he would read the lives of martyrs who had trained their spirit to transcend all suffering and adversity. At these times his soul would be quite softened, his spirit deeply moved and his eyes would fill with tears. And—strange to relate!—some unexpected help would almost invariably arrive from somewhere or other. Either one of his old friends would remember about him and send him some money; or some lady travelling through, a stranger to him, would chance to hear someone talking about him, and in the impetuous magnanimity of her female heart would send him a generous gift, or some lawsuit he himself had never even heard of would be settled somewhere or other in his favour. With piety and gratitude he would then acknowledge the unbounded mercy of Providence, would order a thanksgiving service and instantly return to his feckless life.

"I pity him, really I do!" said Platonov to Chichikov when they had taken their leave and driven off.

"The prodigal son!" said Chichikov. "There's nothing to pity in people like that."

And soon they both stopped thinking about him altogether. Platonov did because he observed the predicaments of others just as indolently and sleepily as everything else in the world. The sight of suffering wrung his heart, but somehow no deep impressions were left in his soul. Thus he did not think about Khlobuyev, because he did not think about himself. Chichikov did not think about Khlobuyev because his thoughts were all occupied with the purchase he had just made. He enumerated, calculated and pondered all the advantages of the estate he had bought. And however he looked at it, whichever way he turned the deal, he saw that in every event the purchase was advantageous. He could mortgage the estate. He could mortgage only the dead and fugitive peasants. He could first sell off all the best land in sections, and then mortgage the rest. He could take over the management of the estate himself and became a landowner in Kostanzhoglo's mould, following his advice as his neighbour and benefactor. He could even sell the estate back into private hands (if, of course, he decided not to take on the running of it himself), retaining ownership only of the fugitives and the dead souls. Then he could see another advantage: he could slip away from this part of the country altogether and not pay back the money he had borrowed from Kostanzhoglo. In short, whichever way he turned the matter over in his mind he saw that in every event the purchase was advantageous. He felt gratified because he had now become a landowner, and not an imaginary landowner, but a real one, a landowner who really owned land, and pastures, and peasants—not chimerical peasants, confined to the realm of the imagination, but ones that actually existed. And gradually he started to bounce on his seat, and rub his hands, and hum a little tune, and talk to himself, and trumpet a march through his fist held clenched against his mouth like a bugle, and even to utter aloud a few laudatory words and epithets addressed to himself, such as "Clever Chops" and "Smart Little Birdie". But then, recalling that he was not alone, he suddenly fell silent, endeavoured somehow or other to suppress this immoderate surge of exultation, and when Plàtonov, taking some of these noises to be remarks addressed to him, asked: "What?" he answered: "Nothing."

Only now, as he looked about him, did he notice that they were driving through a splendid grove: a gracious colonnade of birches stretched away to right and left. Among the trees he caught a glimpse of a white stone church. A gentleman appeared at the end of the avenue, walking towards them, wearing a peaked cap, with a knobbly stick in his hand. A sleek long-legged English hound ran before him.

"Stop!" said Platonov to the coachman and sprang down.

Chichikov also alighted from the carriage after him. They walked towards the gentleman. Yarb had already managed to nuzzle up to the English hound, with which he had apparently been long acquainted, because he received with total indifference the lively licking Azor (such was the English hound's name) administered to his own fat jowls. Azor, a frisky dog, finished licking Yarb, ran over to Platonov, licked his hand with his swift tongue, leapt up against Chichikov's chest with the intention of licking his lips, but did not reach them and, repulsed by Chichikov, ran back to Platonov and tried to lick him at least on the ear.

Platonov and the gentleman had by this stage reached each other and embraced.

"My dear brother Platon! What are you doing to me?" asked the gentleman in agitation.

"What do you mean?" answered Platonov calmly.

"Now, really, I ask you: not a word from you for three whole days! The stable-boy brought your stallion across from Petukh's. 'He went off with some gentlemen,' he says. Well, you could at least have left word: where, why, for how long? I ask you, brother, is that kind? I've been worried sick these last few days!"

"I'm sorry, I forgot," said Platonov. "We called on Konstantin Fyodorovich... He sends his greetings, and our sister too. Allow me to introduce Pavel Ivanovich Chichikov. Pavel Ivanovich—my brother Vassili. Be as good to him as you've been to me."

Brother Vassili and Chichikov removed their caps and exchanged kisses.

"Now just who might this Chichikov be?" wondered brother Vassili. "Brother Platon is indiscriminating in his friendships and probably never found out what sort of man he is." He tried to size him up without staring impolitely and saw him standing with his head inclined somewhat to one side, a pleasant expression fixed on his face.

For his part, Chichikov also tried to size up brother Vassili without staring impolitely. Vassili was shorter than Platon, with darker hair and not nearly as good-looking, but his face was full of life and animation. Obviously this brother did not languish in lethargy and drowsiness.

"Do you know, Vassili, what idea I've had?" said brother Platon.

"What?" asked Vassili.

"To travel around holy Russia, together with Pavel Ivanovich here: who knows but that it might shake off and dissipate my spleen."

"How can you have decided so suddenly?.." Vassili began, seriously alarmed at such a decision, and he was on the point of adding: "And you're contemplating travelling with a man you've clapped eyes on for the first time, who may be trash, and the devil knows what!" And, full of mistrust, he started to examine Chichikov askance and saw that he held himself in an extraordinarily decorous manner, still keeping his head inclined somewhat to one side and preserving a respectfully affable facial expression, so that it was quite impossible to tell quite what sort of a fish this Chichikov was.

All three proceeded in silence along the road, with the white stone church winking at them on the left through the trees, and on the right the first signs, also glimpsed through the trees, of the estate buildings. Finally the gates came into view. They entered the yard, in which there was an old-fashioned high-roofed manor house. Two immense limes, growing in the middle of the yard, covered practically half of it in shade. The walls of the house behind were barely visible through their densely foliated, hanging branches. Beneath the limes stood a few long benches. Brother Vassili invited Chichikov to sit down here. Chichikov sat down and so did Platonov. The entire yard was filled with the fragrance of blossoming lilac and bird-cherry. Their branches overlapped into the yard on all sides from the orchard behind the pretty hedge of birches, and were like a chain of blossom or a necklace of pearls adorning the courtyard.

A smart and fleet-footed servant lad of about seventeen in a handsome pink shirt, brought out and set before them carafes of water and kvasses of every sort and colour, which fizzed like carbonated lemonades. After setting out the carafes he walked up to a tree and, picking up the spade which leant against it, went off into the garden. On the Platonov brothers' estate the entire household staff worked in the garden, all the servants were gardeners, or, to be more precise, there were no actual servants, but the gardeners performed their duties in turn. Brother Vassili constantly averred that one could get by without servants. Anyone could serve up food, and it was quite unnecessary to train a special class of people for the purpose. He believed that the Russian peasant was good, efficient, handsome, easy-going, and hard-working, only so long as he wore a shirt and a homespun coat, but that as soon as he donned a German frockcoat he became clumsy, unsightly, inefficient and slothful. He averred that even his cleanliness would be maintained only so long as he went about in his peasant homespun clothes, but once be donned the German frockcoat he would never change his shirt, he would stop going to the bath-house, he would sleep in his frockcoat and become infested beneath his coat by bedbugs and fleas and the devil knows what. In this he may well have been right. In their village the peasants were somehow particularly dashing and neat in their dress, and you would have had to travel far to see such fine shirts and coats.

"Would you not like to refresh yourself?" brother Vassili asked Chichikov, pointing to the carafes. "These kvasses are of our own making: our house has long been famed for them."

Chichikov poured himself a glass from the first carafe—it was just like the *lipec* he had once drunk in Poland: it sparkled like champagne and the gas fizzed in a pleasant commotion from the mouth into the nose.

"Nectar!" said Chichikov. He drank a glass from another carafe—it was even better.

"But in which direction and to which places are you proposing to travel?" asked brother Vassili.

"I travel," said Chichikov, rubbing his knee with his hand, an action he accompanied with a gentle rocking of his entire upper body and a sideways inclination of his head, "not so much for my own needs as for those of another. General Betrishchev, a close friend and, I might say, benefactor, has asked me to visit his relations. Relations, of course, are all very well, but it is partly, so to speak, also for myself, for—not to mention the benefits in the haemorrhoidal respect—to see the world and the circumfluence of people is in itself, so to speak, already a living book and a second science."

Brother Vassili grew pensive. "This man speaks in a rather florid way, but there is truth in his words," he thought. "My brother Platon lacks knowledge of people, the world and life." After a few moments' silence he said aloud:

"I'm beginning to think, Platon, that travel may, indeed,

rouse you. You suffer from spiritual lethargy. You have simply fallen asleep, and fallen asleep not from any surfeit or fatigue, but from a lack of vivid impressions and sensations. Now I am quite the opposite. I would dearly love not to feel everything so keenly and to take everything which happens so close to heart."

"But who's asking you to take everything close to heart?" said Platonov. "You go looking for worries yourself and invent causes for concern."

"Why should I invent them when, as it is, there is some unpleasantness at every step?" said Vassili. "Have you heard what trick Lenitsyn has played on us while you were away? He's seized that waste plot which our people have always used for their St. Thomas week fêtes."

"He doesn't know that, that's why he's seized it," said Platon. "He's a new man, he's only just arrived from St. Petersburg. It must be explained to him so he understands."

"He knows, he knows very well. I sent to tell him but he was just abusive."

"You should have gone to explain to him in person. Have a chat with him yourself."

"No, no. He's putting on too many airs and graces. I shan't go to him. You go, if you wish."

"I would go, but then I don't want to interfere. He'd lie to me too and I'd be taken in."

"Well, if you wish, I shall go," said Chichikov.

Vassili looked at him and thought: "This one certainly likes to travel around!"

"Just give me an idea of what sort of man he is," said Chichikov, "and what's going on."

"I feel ashamed to burden you with such an unpleasant commission, because for me it's unpleasant enough just having to speak with a man like that. I should tell you he comes from a family of small-holding landowners here in our province, he served in St. Petersburg, somehow or other made his way in the world by marrying somebody's natural daughter, and became insufferably conceited, so now he thinks he ought to set the tone here. But here in our province, thank the Lord, people are not stupid: fashion is not an edict for us, and St. Petersburg not the Church."

"Of course," said Chichikov, "but what is the problem?"

"The problem, in point of fact, is a lot of nonsense. He does not have sufficient land, so he went and seized someone else's waste plot, that is, he reckoned that it was not needed and that the owners had forgotten about it, but it just so happens that our peasants have gathered there since time immemorial for celebrating St. Thomas Sunday. I would be prepared to surrender other land, better land, rather than give up this plot. For me custom is sacred."

"Does that mean you would be prepared to let him have some other land?"

"I would, if he had not been so high-handed with me; but it appears he wants to go to court. Very well, let us see who wins. Although it is not all that clear on the map, but there are witnesses—old men are still alive who can remember."

"Hm! stick-in-the-muds both of them, I can see," thought Chichikov. And aloud he said:

"But it seems to me this matter can be resolved peaceably. Everything depends on the mediator. In writing..."

(*There are two pages missing here in the ms*. The first edition of Part II of *Dead Souls* (1855) contains the note: "Here there is a hiatus, which, it can be surmised, contains an account of Chichikov's setting off to visit the landowner Lenitsyn.")

"... that it would be very much in your own interests, for example, if you transferred into my name all the dead souls which figure in the last census lists of your estates, so that I would then pay the tax on them. And to avoid any scandal you will make this transfer with a proper deed of purchase, just as if these souls were alive."

"Just listen to that!" thought Lenitsyn. "This is most peculiar." And he even moved back a little with his chair, because he was so totally confounded.

"I have absolutely no doubt that you will agree to this transaction," said Chichikov, "because it is entirely of the nature we were discussing. It will be concluded confidentially between reliable people and there will be no scandal."

What should he do? Lenitsyn found himself in an

awkward position. He could not have foreseen that the opinion he had so recently voiced would be acted upon so quickly. The proposition was extremely unexpected. Of course, there could not be anything prejudicial for anyone in this course of action: the landowners would have mortgaged these souls along with their living ones in any case, which meant that the Treasury could not suffer any loss: the only difference was that now they would all be in the hands of one person, whereas before they were in various hands. Nevertheless he was at a loss. He was a stickler for the law and a businessman in the best sense of the word: no matter what bribes he was offered, he would never act dishonestly in any deal. But here he hesitated, not knowing what to call this deal: honest or dishonest? If anyone else had come to him with such a proposition he could have said: "What rubbish! What nonsense! I have no wish to play such silly games like a fool." But his guest had already made such a favourable impression on him, they had found so much in common with regard to the progress of enlightenment and the sciences: so how could he refuse him? Lenitsyn was in a most difficult predicament.

But in that very moment, as if to help him out, Lenitsyn's wife entered the room. She was a small pale young woman with a retroussé nose and dressed with taste, like all St. Petersburg ladies. She was followed by the wet-nurse, bearing in her arms their first-born child, fruit of the tender love of this recently wedded pair. Chichikov, of course, stepped up at once to the lady, and not to mention his most agreeable courtesies, greatly earned the favour of his hostess by the mere sideways inclination of his head. Then he skipped across to the child. It started crying, but Chichikov nevertheless managed to entice it into his own arms by crooning: "Coo-coo, sweetikins," snapping his fingers and dangling the cornelian seal of his watch in front of the baby's nose. Having taken it into his arms he began tossing it up in the air and thereby caused the child to chuckle, which greatly delighted both parents.

But whether through pleasure or for some other reason the baby suddenly committed an indiscretion. Lenitsyn's wife shrieked:

"Oh goodness me! He's absolutely ruined your tailcoat!"

Chichikov looked: the sleeve of his nice new tailcoat

was wet. "May Satan take you to hell, you cursed little devil!" he muttered angrily to himself.

The host and the hostess and the wet-nurse all rushed off for eau de Cologne and then set about rubbing at him from all sides.

"It's nothing, it's nothing, it's nothing at all," reiterated Chichikov. "What harm can an innocent child do?" And all the while he was thinking: "He's certainly got a good aim, the nasty little brat!"—"The lovely age of innocence!" he said, when he had been wiped clean and the agreeable expression had returned to his face.

"You know, it's true," said his host, turning to Chichikov, also with a pleasant smile, "what could be more enviable than the age of infancy: no worries, no thoughts of the future..."

"A state for which we would exchange everything this very moment," said Chichikov.

"Without thinking twice," said Lenitsyn.

But, one thought, they were both lying: offer them such an exchange and they would both shoot out of the back door at once. Indeed, what sort of pleasure was it to sit in a wet-nurse's arms and ruin people's tailcoats! The young hostess and the first-born departed with the wet-nurse, because certain repairs had to be carried out on him too: in bestowing his favours on Chichikov he had not neglected himself.

This seemingly insignificant circumstance persuaded Lenitsyn to satisfy Chichikov's request. For, to be sure, how could one refuse a guest who had shown such affection for his child and had so magnanimously paid for it with his own tailcoat? Lenitsyn reasoned thus: "Why indeed should I not grant his request, if such is his desire?"... (*the end of the chapter is missing in the ms.*)

ONE OF THE FINAL CHAPTERS*

At the very time when Chichikov, sprawling on the divan in his new Persian dressing-gown of gold lamé, was haggling with the visiting contraband dealer of Jewish descent and a

---

*Taken from an earlier edition than the other chapters.

German accent, and the merchandise was already lying before them, to wit, a length of the very finest Dutch linen for shirts and two cardboard boxes containing the most excellent soap of top-class quality (this was the very same soap that he himself used to acquire when stationed in the Radziwill customs; it did indeed have the property of imparting a remarkable tenderness and whiteness to the cheeks); at the very time when he, as a true connoisseur, was purchasing these products so essential to the cultured man, the quiet was shattered by the thunderous clatter of a carriage driving up, answered by the slight trembling of the windowpanes and the walls, and His Excellency Alexei Ivanovich Lenitsyn entered.

"Might I ask Your Excellency to judge: what fine linen, what soap, and what a nice litte thing I purchased yesterday!" Saying this Chichikov placed on his head a skull-cap, embroidered with gold thread and beads, and looked at once so full of dignity and majesty that he might be the Shah of Persia!

But His Excellency, without answering the question, said with a worried look:

"I have something serious to discuss with you."

He looked noticeably upset. The esteemed merchant of the German accent was at once despatched and they remained alone.

"Do you know what an unfortunate thing has happened? Another will by the old lady has come to light, drawn up five years ago. Half the estate is to be given to the monastery and the other half to be shared equally between her two wards, and not a bean for anyone else."

Chichikov was dumbfounded.

"But that will is rubbish. It carries no weight, it's countermanded by the second one."

"But there's no mention in the second will that it countermands the first one."

"That goes without saying: the later one countermands the earlier one. The first will is quite invalid. I know exactly what the old lady wanted. I was with her at the time. Who signed it? Who were the witnesses?"

"It was witnessed properly, in court. The witnesses were the former common-law magistrate Burmilov and Khavanov."

"Bad," thought Chichikov. "They say Khavanov is an honest man; Burmilov is an old bigot, he reads the gospels in church on holy days."

"But it's rubbish, rubbish," he said aloud, and at once felt equal to anything. "I know best. I was present at the old lady's last minutes. I know it better than anyone. I am prepared to swear it on oath."

These words and this decisive tone temporarily calmed Lenitsyn. In his agitation he had already begun to suspect that Chichikov might have done some fabricating with regard to the will. Now he reproached himself for harbouring such suspicions. The readiness to swear on oath was unchallenged proof that Chichikov was innocent. We do not know whether Pavel Ivanovich would in fact have had the courage to swear on oath, but he had the courage to say that he would.

"Do not worry, I shall discuss this matter with certain legal consultants. There need not be any involvement on your side; you must keep quite out of it. And now I can live in town as long as I wish."

Chichikov at once called for his carriage and set off to see his legal consultant. This consultant was a man of uncommonly wide experience. He had been under investigation for the past fifteen years and he managed his case with such skill that it had been quite impossible to strip him of office. Everyone knew him, his exploits were such that he should already have been sent into exile six times over. He was under suspicion by one and all, but no convincing and proven evidence could be brought against him. There really was something mysterious about it, and he could have been rightfully called a magician if the story we are recounting had belonged to the dark ages of ignorance.

The legal consultant astounded Chichikov with the coldness of his mien and the griminess of his dressing-gown, presenting such a complete contrast to the fine mahogany furniture, the gold-domed clock, the chandelier, peeping through the muslin cover put on to protect it, and in general to everything around him, which bore the unmistakable stamp of dazzling European enlightenment.

Unabashed, however, by the sceptical air of the legal consultant, Chichikov explained the vexatious points of his case and offered the alluring prospect of the gratitude which would inevitably ensue upon good advice and sympathy.

The legal consultant responded to this by depicting the fickleness of all earthly things and also skilfully indicated that two birds in the bush were worth nothing: the bird in the hand was what he wanted.

There was nothing for it: the bird had to be put into the hand. The sceptical *froideur* of the philosophical legal consultant instantly vanished. It transpired that he was the most affable of men, the most talkative and the most agreeable in conversation, an equal to Chichikov himself in the adroitness of his turns of phrase.

"Allow me to suggest, instead of initiating lengthy legal proceedings, that you have probably not examined the actual will properly: there, I am sure, you will find a little codicil somewhere. Just take it home with you for a while. Although, of course, it's forbidden to take such things home with one, but if you ask certain officials nicely... I shall use my own influence too."

"I understand," thought Chichikov, and said:

"In point of fact it's true, I cannot quite remember whether there is a codicil there or not." As if he did not write the will himself.

"The best thing would be for you to have a good look at it. However," the lawyer continued in the most good-natured tone, "I assure you, you need have no apprehensions, even if the worst possible thing should happen. Never despair of anything: there is no case which cannot be set to rights. Look at me: I am always calm. Whatever the charges raised against me my composure remains unshakable."

The face of the lawyer-philosopher did indeed preserve an aspect of remarkable composure, so that Chichikov was very... (*the sentence is left unfinished in the ms.*)

"Of course, that is the most important thing," he said. "But all the same, you must agree that there can be such matters and cases, such actions and calumnies perpetrated by one's enemies and such complex predicaments that you'll forget what composure means!"

"Believe me, that is simply faint-heartedness," answered the lawyer-philosopher with great calm and affability. "Only try to ensure that every step of your case is backed by written records, and that nothing is left as spoken words. And as soon as you see that things are reaching an issue and that a decision is imminent, make every effort—not to justify and defend yourself—no, merely to confuse matters with new and extraneous issues."

"You mean, in order—"

"To confuse them, confuse them, and nothing more," answered the philosopher, "introduce other extraneous circumstances into your case, which in their turn would involve others, to complicate matters, and nothing more. And then let some St. Petersburg official be called in and try to sort it out. Let him try, just let him try!" he repeated, gazing into Chichikov's eyes with pure delight, just as a teacher gazes at his pupil when explaining to him some alluring point of Russian grammar.

"Yes, it's all very well if you can find circumstances which can throw a veil of obscurity over things," said Chichikov, also looking with delight into the eyes of the philosopher, like a pupil who has understood the alluring point being explained by his teacher.

"The circumstances can be found, they can be found! Believe me: frequent practice teaches the mind to be resourceful. First of all remember that people will help you. Many stand to gain from a complicated case, more officials will be needed and their remuneration will be higher... In a word, draw as many people as possible into the case. It doesn't matter that some will be involved for no reason: after all, it will be easy for them to justify themselves, they will have to answer inquiries, they will have to buy themselves... That's a bit of money coming in already... Believe me, the moment the situation becomes critical, spreading confusion is the first rule. Confuse things, create such a muddle that no one will understand a thing. Why am I so calm? Because I know: just let my affairs get worse and I will involve everyone—the governor, and the deputy governor, and the chief of police, and the government paymaster—I'll enmesh them all. I know all their backgrounds: who is angry with whom, who has fallen out with whom, and who wants to get even with whom. Now let them try to disentangle themselves, and while they are doing so others will be lining their pockets. After all, crayfish can only be caught in muddy water. Everybody is only waiting to spread a little fog." Here the lawyer-philosopher gazed into Chichikov's eyes once again with the pure delight with which a teacher explains to a pupil the most alluring point in Russian grammar.

"No, this chap definitely knows his onions," thought Chichikov, and he took leave of the legal consultant in the very best and most pleasant of spirits.

Completely reassured and mentally fortified he leapt with carefree adroitness into his carriage with the springy cushions, ordered Selifan to throw back the hood (he had driven to the consultant's with the hood drawn over and with the leather flaps closed) and sat back, exactly like a retired Colonel of Hussars or like Vishnepokromov himself—with one leg gracefully turned under the other, his face beneath his new silk hat cocked slightly over one ear, smiling at everyone he met. Selifan was told to make for the arcade. The merchants, visiting and local, who stood by the doors of their shops, respectfully doffed their hats, and Chichikov, not without dignity, slightly lifted his in response. Many of them were already known to him; as for the others, although they were visitors they were so enchanted by the dashing sight of a gentleman with such fine manners that they, too, greeted him like acquaintances. The fair in the town of Tfuslavl was unending. When the horse and agricultural fair was over the textile fair would begin for the enlightened populace. The merchants who arrived in carts counted on staying long enough to go back home in sleighs.

"Step in, good sir, step in!" Chichikov was invited with a respectful flourish by a cloth stall merchant dressed in a German frockcoat, of Muscovite cut, holding his hat in his hand, with two fingers barely touching a clean-shaven, round chin and an expression of refined enlightenment on his face.

Chichikov entered the shop.

"Show me some of your cloth, my good fellow."

The obliging merchant at once raised the hinged top of the counter and, thus creating a passage for himself, slipped into the shop and stood with his back to his wares and his face to his customer.

Standing thus with his back to his wares and his face to the customer, the bare-headed merchant, his hat held in his hand, welcomed Chichikov once again. Then, placing his hat back on his head and bending pleasantly at the waist, he rested both hands on his counter, and said:

"What kind of cloth would the gentleman be wanting? Of English make or our own Russian manufacture?"

"Our own Russian manufacture," said Chichikov. "Only of the very best sort, the one called *anglaise*."

"Which colours would you like to have?" asked the merchant, propping himself on his hands and still rocking in the same pleasant manner.

"Dark colours, olive or bottle green, with a fleck, approaching, in a manner of speaking the colour of cranberries," said Chichikov.

"I may say that you will be getting the very best quality, there's none better in either our capital cities," said the merchant, reaching for a bolt of cloth above him; he threw it smartly on to the counter, unwound it from the farther end and held it up to the light. "See that sheen, sir! It's in the best of taste, the latest fashion!"

The cloth shone like silk. The merchant had sensed with his special flair that this was a connoisseur of fine cloth who stood before him, and thus he had no intention of beginning with ten-ruble rubbish.

"Not bad," said Chichikov, stroking the cloth gently. "But you know what? Show me the stuff you're going to show me later on anyway, and something with a colour that's more ... more sparkly, with more of a sparkle to it."

"I understand, sir! You want the colour which is now coming into fashion in St Petersburg. I have some cloth of the most excellent quality. I warn you that the price is high, but it's well worth it."

"Let's see it."

Not a word about the price.

The bolt tumbled down from above. The merchant unfurled it with even greater skill, catching hold of the other end and revealing a material that was in truth silken, and held it up so close to Chichikov that the latter was able not only to inspect it, but even to sniff it, and merely said:

"This is it, sir! Navarino smoke-grey shot with flame-red."

They agreed on the price. With an iron arshin-rule, like a magician's wand, the merchant quickly measured off enough for a tailcoat and trousers for Chichikov. Making a snick with his scissors he tore the cloth across its entire width, on the completion of which operation he bowed to Chichikov in the most winning manner. The cloth was at once rolled up and wrapped in paper; the package was tied with a piece of thin twine. Just as Chichikov reached into his pocket for the money he felt someone's gentle arm being delicately placed around his waist, and his ears heard:

"What are you buying here, my most esteemed friend?"

"Ah, what a pleasant surprise!" said Chichikov.

"A most pleasant encounter," said the voice of the person whose arm had encircled his waist. This was Vishnepokromov. "I was about to pass by the shop when I suddenly saw a familiar face—so, how could I deny myself the pleasure! I must say that the cloths this year are incomparably better. You must admit, it's disgraceful, outrageous! I was quite unable to find anything... I'm prepared to pay thirty rubles, forty rubles ... take fifty even, but give me something good. To my mind, either you have a thing which is really first class, or not have anything at all. Isn't that so?"

"Ab-solutely!" said Chichikov. "Really, why should one toil if not to have something that is good?"

"Show me your medium-priced cloths," called out a voice behind them, which struck Chichikov as familiar. He turned round: it was Khlobuyev. His frockcoat was so badly frayed that obviously buying the cloth was a necessity and not a whim.

"Ah, Pavel Ivanovich! Allow me to have a few words with you. It's impossible to catch you in. I called several times—but you're never there."

"My most esteemed friend, I was so busy that—dear, dear me, there's just no time." He looked about him, to find some way to evade an explanation, and saw Murazov coming into the shop. "Afanasy Vasilievich! Good heavens!" said Chichikov. "What a pleasant encounter!"

And after him Vishnepokromov repeated:

"Afanasy Vasilievich!"

Khlobuyev repeated:

"Afanasy Vasilievich!"

And the courteous merchant, holding out his hat as far

out as his arm would stretch and leaning right forward also, uttered:

"Our most humble respects to Afanasy Vasilievich!"

Printed on their faces was that canine servility, which is displayed to millionaires by the people, with a currish mentality.

The old man bowed to all and addressed himself directly to Khlobuyev:

"Forgive me: I spotted you entering the shop from a distance and decided to trouble you for a moment. If you should be free afterwards and should be passing my house, be so kind as to call in for a moment. There is something I must discuss with you."

Khlobuyev said:

"I shall indeed, Afanasy Vasilievich."

"What glorious weather we're having, Afanasy Vasilievich," said Chichikov.

"Yes indeed," chimed in Vishnepokromov, "isn't it remarkable?"

"Indeed, not bad at all, praise be to God. But we could do with a little rain for the crops."

"We do, we do, we need it badly," said Vishnepokromov, "it's good for the hunting too."

"Yes, a little spot of rain would be no bad thing," said Chichikov, who had no need of any little rain, but how pleasant it was to agree with a man who owned millions.

And the old man bowed to them all once again and departed.

"It quite makes my head spin," said Chichikov, "to think that that man has ten million. It's quite beyond belief, really."

"It's quite counter to the law, all the same," said Vishnepokromov. "Capital should not be concentrated in private hands. That's now discussed in treatises all over Europe. If you have money—well, share it with others: entertain, give balls, create the sort of beneficial luxury which gives bread to tradesmen and craftsmen."

"That I cannot understand," said Chichikov. "Ten million—and he lives like a simple peasant! After all, with ten million the devil knows what you could do. I mean, you could live the sort of life where you'd never have to mix with anyone but generals and princes."

"Quite so," added the merchant. "For all his estimable qualities Afanasy Vasilievich is sorely lacking in enlightenment. If a merchant has standing, he's no longer a merchant, in a sense he's already a negotiant. Then I will have to take a box at the theatre, and as for my daughter—no sir, I won't give her in marriage to some mere colonel: it will have to be a general or no one. What's a colonel to me? My dinner must be prepared by a chef, and not some common cook-woman..."

"You're absolutely right!" said Vishnepokromov. "With ten million there's nothing one can't do. Give me ten million, and see what I do!"

"No," thought Chichikov, "you won't do anything very sensible with ten million. Now, if I had ten million, I would most definitely do something."

"If only I had ten million now, after these terrible ordeals!" thought Khlobuyev. "I wouldn't make those mistakes now: experience teaches you the value of every single kopek." And then, after a minute's thought he asked himself: "Would I, in fact, order things more sensibly now?" And, with a wave of his hand he added: "What the devil! I believe I would have blown them just like before," and he left the shop, curious to know what news Murazov had for him.

"I'm expecting you, Pyotr Petrovich!" said Murazov, seeing Khlobuyev entering his house. "Please step into my little room."

And he led Khlobuyev into the room, already familiar to the reader, as plain a room as that of a clerk earning seven hundred rubles a year.

"Tell me, surely your circumstances are somewhat improved? Something must have come down to you after your aunt passed away?"

"Now, how can I put it, Afanasy Vasilievich? I don't know if my circumstances are actually better. All I received was fifty souls and thirty thousand in money, which I had to use to pay off a part of my debts,—and once again I am left with precisely nothing. But the worst of it is that there was something very fishy about the will. There's been some chicanery with that will, Afanasy Vasilievich. I'll tell you the story now, and you'll be amazed to hear what goes on. That Chichikov—"

"Forgive me, Pyotr Petrovich, before we talk about that Chichikov let us talk a little bit about you. Tell me now: how much, by your calculations, would be satisfactory and sufficient for you to extricate yourself completely from your predicament?"

"I am in terrible straits," said Khlobuyev. "And to get into the clear, to settle all my debts and to be in a position of modest comfort, I need at least a hundred thousand, if not more. So there's no hope, you see."

"Supposing, if you did have the money, how would you arrange your life?"

"Well, I would rent a small apartment, and attend to the education of my children because I could not go into service myself: I'm no good for anything now."

"Why should you be no good for anything?"

"But what could I do, judge for yourself! I couldn't start as a chancellory scrivener. Perhaps you have forgotten that I have a family. I am forty years old, I already have a bad back, I have grown slothful; but they will not give me a more important office; after all, my record is none too good. I admit it myself: I would not accept a cushy sinecure anyway. I may be worthless as a person, and an inveterate gambler, and everything you like, but I draw the line at bribes. I'm not going to join company with Krasnonosov and Samosvistov."

"But still, if you'll forgive my saying so, I cannot understand how you can do without following some road? How can you walk when there is no path; how can you go forward when there is no ground beneath your feet; how can you sail when your boat is not afloat? For what is life but a journey? Forgive me, Pyotr Petrovich, but those men of whom you speak, they are anyway following some path or other, they are doing their work. Well, let us suppose they might have strayed a bit, as happens with all us sinners; there is still the hope that they'll come back to the straight and narrow. He who walks cannot fail to arrive; there is always the hope that he'll find the road. But as for him who remains idle, what chance has he of getting on to any road? After all, the road will not come to me."

"Believe me, Afanasy Vasilievich, I can see the absolute reasonableness of what you say, but I must tell you that any sort of activity has totally perished and died in me; I cannot see how I could be of any use to anyone in this world. I feel that I am a totally useless log. Before, when I was a little younger, I thought that money was all that mattered, that if I could only get my hands on a few hundred thousand I'd bring happiness to many: I'd help impoverished artists, and found libraries and useful institutions, I'd collect works of art. I am not lacking in taste and I know I could have managed things much better in many respects than our rich men who do it all so stupidly. But now I see that this, too, is a folly, and there is little sense in this too. No, Afanasy Vasilievich, I am no use for anything, not for anything at all, let me tell you. I am incapable of being of the slightest use."

"Listen, Pyotr Petrovich! But you do pray, do you not? You go to church, you do not miss early or evening service, I know. You may not want to rise early, but you do rise and go—you go at four o'clock in the morning, when no one else is rising."

"That is quite another matter, Afanasy Vasilicvich. I do that for the salvation of my soul, in the conviction that in so doing I can at least to some extent expiate my idle existence, that for all my worthlessness my prayers will still count for something with God. Indeed, I do pray—even without faith, but I pray all the same. I can only sense that there is someone over me, on whom everything depends, just as the horse and the ox, which pull the plough, can sense the person who harnesses them to the plough."

"That means you pray to please Him to Whom you pray, to save your soul, and this gives you strength and makes you rise early from your bed. Believe me, if you were to undertake your duties in that same manner, believing that you were serving Him to Whom you pray, you would become active and no one would be able to cool your ardour."

"Afanasy Vasilievich, I must tell you again that it's quite another matter. In praying I can see what I am doing. I'm telling you that I am prepared to enter a monastery and I will perform the most arduous labours and duties I am charged with there. I am convinced that it is not my business to call for an account from those who impose these tasks on me; there I shall submit and I shall know that I am submitting to God."

"But then why do you not reason like that in the affairs of the world too? After all, in our worldly affairs we must also serve God and not anyone else. If indeed we do serve someone else we do so only because we are convinced that such is God's command, otherwise we would not do it. For what else are all our talents and gifts, which are so different in everyone? After all, those are the instruments of our prayer: there we pray in words, but here in deeds. And anyway you could not enter a monastery: you are bound to the world, you have a family."

Here Murazov fell silent. Khlobuyev was also silent.

"And so you suppose that if you had two hundred thousand, for example, you would be able to straighten out your life and henceforth live with greater prudence?"

"At least, I would undertake something I could do: I would see to the education of my children, I would be able to afford good tutors for them."

"And what if I reply, Pyotr Petrovich, that in two years' time you would once again be up to your ears in debt?"

Khlobuyev was silent for a moment, and then began, speaking slowly and deliberately:

"No, I don't think so, not after these experiences..."

"What have experiences to do with it?" said Murazov. "I know you only too well. You are a man with a kind heart: a friend will come to you to ask for a loan and you will give it to him; if you see a poor man—you will want to help him; an agreeable guest will call—you will want to entertain him a little better, and you will submit to the very first generous impulse and forget all about prudence. Finally, let me tell you in all sincerity that you are in no condition to educate your children. Children can only be educated by the sort of father who has already fulfilled his own duty. And your wife too ... she has a kind heart ... but she has not had the sort of upbringing that would enable her to educate children. I even think—forgive me, Pyotr Petrovich, but might it not be harmful for your children even to remain with you?"

Khlobuyev grew pensive; he subjected himself to a thorough mental examination, and felt that, to a certain extent, Murazov was right.

"Do you know what, Pyotr Petrovich? Trust everything to me—the children, your affairs, everything. Leave your family and your children: I shall take care of them. After all, your circumstances are such that you are in my hands; things have come to such a pass that you will soon be starving. You've got to be prepared to clutch at any chance. Do you know Ivan Potapych?"

"I do and I greatly respect him, despite the fact that he goes about in a peasant caftan."

"Ivan Potapych was a millionaire, he married his daughters off to officials, lived like a tsar, and then, when he went bankrupt—what else could he do? He became a shop assistant. It must have hurt to change from a silver dish to an earthen bowl: he seemed to lose heart and could not sct his hand to anything. Well, now Ivan Potapych can eat from a silver dish again, but he no longer wants to. He could have made a fortune again, but he says: 'No, Afanasy Vasilievich, I am now no longer working for myself, but because God has so ordained. I do not wish to do anything of my own will. I listen to you because I wish to obey God and not people, and since God only speaks through the mouths of the best people. You are cleverer than me, and therefore it is not I who answer, but you.' That is what Ivan Potapych says: and, truth be told, he is far, far cleverer than me."

"Afanasy Vasilievich! I am prepared to acknowledge your power over me, I am your servant and what you will: I submit to you. But do not set me tasks beyond my powers; I am no Potapych and I tell you that I am no use for any good work."

"It is not for me, Pyotr Petrovich, to set you tasks, but since you want to serve God, as you say yourself, here is a pious deed. There is a church being erected somewhere with the voluntary donations of pious people. The money has run out, more must be collected. Put on a simple peasant caftan... After all, you are now a simple man, a ruined nobleman, a pauper in fact; there's no point giving yourself airs now. So, with a record book in your hands, riding in a simple cart, make the rounds of the towns and villages. You will receive the blessing of the bishop and a book with threaded pages, and go with God."

Pyotr Petrovich was astounded by this new office. He, a nobleman of ancient lineage, to set off with a book in his hands to collect donations for a church, rattling along in a cart too! At the same time there was no way of getting out of it or declining the office: it was pious work.

"Giving it some thought?" asked Murazov. "Here you will be performing two services simultaneously: one service to God, the other to me."

"Which service to you?"

"This one: since you will be visiting places where I have never been, you are to ascertain everything there: how the peasants live, where they are better off, where they are needy, and the state of things generally. I might tell you that I love the peasants, perhaps because I myself am of peasant stock. But the truth of the matter is that all sorts of foulnesses are practised amongst them. They are troubled by sectarians and all sorts of vagabonds, incited to rise against the authorities, against law and order, and if a man is oppressed he will easily be incited to rebellion. Of course, it's easy to egg on a man who is in need. But the point is that chastisement should not begin from below. It will be bad when fists begin to fly: no good will ever come of that, only quick profit for thieves. You are a clever man, look around and discover where the peasants are really being oppressed by others, and where they are suffering from their own restless nature, and afterwards you will recount it all to me. In any event I shall give you a small sum of money to distribute among those who are really suffering guiltlessly. For your own part it will also be useful to comfort them with a word and still better to impress upon them that God bids us suffer without murmur and pray when we are unhappy, and not go wild and take the law into our own hands. I mean, talk to them without setting anyone against anyone else, try reconciling them all. If you see hatred in anyone for any other person whatsoever, do all you can."

"Afanasy Vasilievich, the task which you are assigning to me, is a holy deed," said Khlobuyev, "but you must remember to whom you are assigning it. It should be assigned to a man whose life is well-nigh holy, who himself is able to forgive others."

"But I am not saying that you should fulfil all this, only that you should do what is within your power. The fact remains that you will return with knowledge of those places and will have an idea of the state of affairs in that part of the country. An official will never come into contact with the populace, and anyway a peasant will never open his heart to him. But you, as you seek donations for the church, will have a look everywhere—you will visit the artisan and the merchant, and you will have an opportunity to put questions to them all. I tell you this for the reason that the Governor-General has need of such people especially now, and you, without going through any chancellery promotion scale, will receive the sort of position in which your life will not be useless."

"I shall try, and I shall exert myself, as far as I am able," said Khlobuyev. And a note of animation could be heard in his voice; his back straightened and his head lifted, as happens with a man in whom hope is awakening. "I see that God has rewarded you with understanding, and you know many a thing better than we, the near-sighted, do."

"Now let me ask you," said Murazov, "what about this Chichikov and what sort of swindle is he up to?"

"I shall tell you some really fantastic things about Chichikov. The tricks he is up to... Do you know, Afanasy Vasilievich, that the will was quite false? The real will has been found, in which the entire estate goes to her wards."

"What are you saying? And who fabricated the false will?"

"That's the whole point, that it's such a dirty business! They say it was Chichikov, and that the will was signed after her death: they dressed up some old woman in place of the deceased, and got her to sign it. In a word, the most scandalous business. They say thousands of petitions came from all over the place. Suitors are now flocking to Maria Yeremeyevna; two of them, men of high office, are already fighting over her. That's the sort of business it is, Afanasy Vasilievich!"

"I've heard nothing of all this, but the business seems certainly none too clean. I must confess I find our Pavel Ivanovich Chichikov a most enigmatic fellow," said Murazov.

"I also sent in a petition, just to remind them that there is a next of kin..."

"But let them all fight one another, for all I care," thought Khlobuyev, on his way out. "Afanasy Vasilievich is no fool. He gave me this commission, no doubt, after careful thought. I just have to carry it out, that's all." He started to think about the journey, at the same time as Murazov kept repeating to himself: "That Pavel Ivanovich Chichikov really does intrigue me! To think how much good could be achieved with will power and perseverance like his!"

In the meantime, in actual fact one petition after another did come to the courts. Relations popped up of whom no one had ever heard. They all swooped down on the vast estate left by the old lady like vultures descending on a carcass. Denunciations of Chichikov, of the spuriousness of the last will, even of the spuriousness of the first will poured in, and evidence was submitted of theft and embezzlement. Depositions were made accusing Chichikov of buying dead souls, and of smuggling when he served in the customs. Everything was dug up, all his past history became common knowledge. There's no knowing how all this had been nosed out. Evidence was even produced of affairs which Chichikov thought no living person beside him and the four walls knew about. For the time being all this remained *sub judice* and did not come to his attention, although a reliable note from the legal consultant, which he shortly received, gave him to understand that the fat was in the fire. The note was terse: "I hasten to inform you that there will be some bother in your affairs: but remember that there is no cause for alarm. The main thing is to be calm. We shall fix everything." This note quite set his mind at rest. "This man is positively a genius," said Chichikov.

Another good thing was that the tailor brought his new suit just then. Chichikov felt a strong desire to admire himself in his new tailcoat of Navarino smoke and flame. He pulled on the trousers, which hugged him on all sides in a wondrous fashion, wondrous enough to delight a painter. The cloth was pulled so splendidly tight on his thighs, on his calves too, it embraced every little contour, imparting an even greater elasticity to his limbs. When he tightened the buckle at the back, his stomach became taut as a drum. He tapped it with a brush and said: "I know it's silly, but it does complete the picture!" The tailcoat, it appeared, was an even better fit than the trousers: not a wrinkle anywhere, close fitting all round, moulded to show off his figure. It was a little tight in the right arm pit, but this only meant it hugged him all the tighter round the waist. The tailor, who stood by in complete triumph, only said: "Rest assured, no one could do any better outside St. Petersburg." The tailor was himself from St. Petersburg and his sign read: "Foreigner from London and Paris". He was not a man to be taken lightly, and by yoking these two towns together he wanted to put all the other tailors in their place once and for all, so that henceforth none of them would dare lay claim to such towns but would have to be content with some place like "Karlseru" or "Copenhara".

Chichikov magnanimously settled the tailor's account and, once he was alone, started to inspect himself in the mirror at leisure, like an actor, with aesthetic feeling and *con amore*. It transpired that everything was somehow even better than before: his plump cheeks more interesting, his chin more alluring, his white collar tips gave tone to his cheek, the dark blue satin necktie gave tone to the collar tips; the highly fashionable pleats in his shirtfront gave tone to his necktie, the sumptuous velvet waistcoat gave tone to the shirtfront, and the tailcoat of Navarino smoke and flame, sparkling like silk, gave tone to everything. He turned to the right—excellent! He turned to the left—better still! The line was that of a gentleman-in-waiting or of the sort of gentleman who rattles away in French in a way to shame any Frenchman, and who, even in moments of anger, will not defile himself with a Russian word, who does not even know how to swear in Russian and lets fly in the French dialect. Such delicacy! He attempted, by slightly inclining his head to one side, to strike the pose of one addressing himself to a lady of middle years and the utmost enlightenment: the result was quite exquisite. Artist, take up your brush and paint! In his pleasure he made a little leap, like an entrechat. The chest of drawers shook and a bottle of eau de Cologne tumbled to the floor; but this did not in any way discompose him. He called the stupid bottle a fool, as was quite befitting, and thought: "Now to whom should I pay my respects first? Best of all..."

When suddenly from the hall came the clatter of boots with jingling spurs, and a gendarme in full armour appeared, like the embodiment of an entire troop of soldiers. "You are ordered to present yourself at once to the Governor-General!" Chichikov was stupefied. Before him towered a dreadful ogre, with moustaches, a horse's tail on his head, a bandoleer across his shoulder, a bandoleer across the other shoulder, and a monstrous cutlass lashed to his side. It seemed to him that on his other side there also hung a rifle, and God knows what else: the very embodiment of a whole troop of soldiers! Chichikov opened his mouth to object, but the ogre declared roughly: "Orders are to go at once!" Through the open door he saw another ogre in the hall, he looked through the window— and there was a carriage. What could he do? Just as he was, in his tailcoat of Navarino smoke and flame, he had to take a seat in the carriage whereupon, trembling from head to toe, he was escorted by the gendarme to the Governor-General.

In the waiting-room he was not even given a chance to come to his senses. "Go in! The prince is waiting for you," said the official on duty. As in a fog, Chichikov saw the waiting-room where couriers were receiving packages, then a hall through which he walked, thinking only: "They're going to grab me and without a trial, or anything, march me straight off to Siberia!" His heart began to pound with a force that surpassed even that of the most ardent lover. A door opened before him: he saw an office with portfolios, cabinets and books, and a prince as wrathful as wrath itself.

"Destruction!" said Chichikov to himself. "He will destroy my soul, tear it to shreds like a wolf a lamb!"

"I spared you, I permitted you to remain in town, when you should have been in gaol; but you have again sullied yourself with the most heinous chicanery that has ever sullied any man."

The prince's lips trembled with anger.

"Which heinous act and chicanery, your Highness?" asked Chichikov, shaking from head to toe.

"The woman," declared the prince, stepping up a little closer and staring straight into Chichikov's eyes, "the woman to whom you dictated the will has been seized and will be brought to confront you."

Chichikov went as white as a sheet.

"Your Highness! Let me tell you the full truth of the matter. I am guilty, it's true, I am guilty; but not that guilty. I was slandered by enemies."

"No one could slander you, because there is more vileness in you than could be invented by the most accomplished liar. In all your life, I believe, you have not done a single deed that is not dishonest. Every kopek you have gained has been gained dishonestly, you have committed the sort of robbery and vile perfidy for which there is the knout and Siberia. No, this is the end! You will be taken to gaol this minute and there, together with the vilest scoundrels and robbers you will have to await your verdict. You are being mercifully treated considering that you are incomparably worse than those criminals: they come in rough peasant's coats and sheepskins, while you..."

He glared at the tailcoat of Navarino smoke and flame and tugged the bell-cord.

"Your Highness, have mercy!" cried Chichikov. "You are a husband and father. I plead not for myself. Spare my old mother!"

"You're lying!" shouted the prince wrathfully. "Before you implored me in the name of children and a family you never had, and now it's your mother!"

"Your Highness, I am a blackguard and the worst of rogues," said Chichikov in a voice... (*the sentence is left incomplete in the ms.*) "I did indeed tell a lie, I have neither children nor a family; but as God is my witness, I have always wanted to have a wife, to fulfil my duty as a man and a citizen, so that I would really earn the respect of my fellow citizens and the authorities... But circumstances so disastrously conspired against me! With my lifeblood, Your Highness, with my lifeblood I was forced to earn my daily bread. At every step I encountered enticement and temptation ... enemies, and destroyers, and usurpers. My whole life has been ... like a tempestuous whirlwind or a barque tossed on the waves at the mercy of the winds. I am a mere mortal, Your Highness!"

The tears suddenly gushed from his eyes in torrents. He
fell at the prince's feet—in his tailcoat of Navarino smoke
and flame, in his velvet waistcoat and new trousers, with
his satin necktie and carefully groomed hair from which
there emanated the fresh smell of eau de Cologne.

"Get away from me! Call the soldiers to take him away!"
said the prince to the servants who came running.

"Your Highness!" shrieked Chichikov, clutching the
prince's boot with both hands.

A violent shudder of aversion ran down the prince's
spine.

"Get away, I tell you!" he said, endeavouring to wrest
his foot from Chichikov's clutch.

"Your Highness, I shall not move from this spot until
I receive your pardon!" said Chichikov, without releasing
the prince's boot and being dragged across the floor in his
tailcoat of Navarino smoke and flame.

"Get away, I tell you!" the prince said with that inex-
pressible feeling of repulsion which one experiences at the
sight of the nastiest insect which he lacks the heart to
crush underfoot. He kicked out so sharply that Chichikov
felt the boot hit his nose, lips and round chin, but still
he did not release the boot and held the foot all the tighter
in his hands. Two strapping gendarmes forcibly dragged
him away, and taking him by the arms led him through all
the rooms. He was pale, broken, in that terrible insensible
state that a man enters when he sees before him the ines-
capable, black shape of death, that dread spectacle that is
so horrendous to our nature...

And suddenly Murazov came in through the door. A ray
of hope flashed before Chichikov. In an instant, with superhuman strength he wrenched himself free from the grip
of the two gendarmes and threw himself at the feet of the
astounded old man.

"Why, Pavel Ivanovich, what is wrong?"

"Save me! They're taking me to gaol, to my
death..."

The gendarmes seized hold of him and led him away,
without even letting him finish.

A dank, musty lumber room, smelling of the boots and
footcloths of garrison soldiers, a bare wood table, two
wretched chairs, a window with iron bars, a decrepit old

stove spitting smoke through a chink but giving off no warmth—such was the residence in which our hero was installed, a man who had already begun to savour the sweet things of life and to attract the attention of his fellow countrymen in his fine new tailcoat of Navarino smoke and flame. They did not even permit him to take his bare necessities with him, to take the little box in which he kept his money. The papers, the deeds of purchase on the dead souls—all that was now in the hands of officials! He collapsed on the ground, and the sarcophagous worm of terrible, hopeless grief coiled itself around his heart. It gnawed at this heart, reft of all protection, more and more greedily. Another such day, a day of such grief and Chichikov would have departed this world. But someone's all-saving hand had kept vigil even over Chichikov. An hour later the doors of the prison opened to admit old Murazov.

Even a man tormented by a searing thirst, into whose dessicated throat someone has poured a stream of spring water, could not have been so revived as was the wretched Chichikov.

"My saviour!" said Chichikov, and, suddenly seizing hold of Murazov's hand, swiftly kissed it and pressed it to his heart. "May the Lord reward you for visiting this poor soul!"

He burst into tears.

The old man gazed at him with a look of sorrow and pain and said only:

"Oh, Pavel Ivanovich, Pavel Ivanovich, what have you done?"

"I am a rogue... I am guilty... I have transgressed... But judge for yourself, judge for yourself, how can they treat me like this? I am a nobleman. To cast me into prison, without a trial, without an investigation, to take everything from me: my things, my box ... it contains money, all the property, it contains all my property, Afanasy Vasilievich—the property which I obtained through my sweat and blood..."

And unable to suppress another uprush of grief to his heart, he started to howl loudly in a voice which penetrated the thick walls of the prison and gave off dull, distant echoes, he ripped off his satin necktie and, gripping the collar of his tailcoat of Navarino smoke and flame, tore it in two.

"Pavel Ivanovich, it makes no difference: you must say farewell to your property and to everything in the world. You have fallen under the inexorable law, and not under the power of an individual."

"I myself wrecked my life, I know it—I could not stop in time. But why such terrible retribution, Afanasy Vasilievich? Am I a highwayman, or something? Have I caused anyone to suffer? Have I made anyone unhappy? I sweated, I sweated blood for every kopek. And what for? Only so that I could live out the rest of my days in contentment, so that I could leave something for the children I intended to acquire for the good of my country, for serving it. I fiddled a bit, I'll not deny it, I fiddled a bit ... what of it? But then I fiddled when I saw that you could get nowhere on the straight road, and that a crooked road was more of a short cut. But I did work hard, I did use my brains. Not like these scoundrels who take thousands from the Treasury in the courts, who rob poor people, who snatch the last kopek from those who have nothing! Afanasy Vasilievich! I was not a philanderer, I was not a drunkard. And if you knew how I toiled, what iron endurance I exercised! Yes, I can say that I paid for every kopek I earned with suffering. Let someone else suffer as much for his money, as I have! For that is the story of my life: fierce struggle, a barque tossed on the waves. And now what was gained through such a hard struggle has been lost..."

He did not finish what he was saying, and began to sob noisily from the unbearable pain in his heart. He fell on to the chair, ripped the rent skirt right off his tailcoat and flung it away from him, and thrusting both hands into his hair, which he had previously taken such pains to arrange, he mercilessly tore at it, relishing the pain with which he hoped to stifle the inextinguishable pain in his heart.

"Ah, Pavel Ivanovich, Pavel Ivanovich!" said Murazov, gazing at him dolefully and shaking his head. "I keep thinking what a man you could have been, if you had applied such strength and endurance to good works and to a better purpose! If any one of those people who love good had

directed such efforts towards it as you have to the earning
of your kopek! And if they had been able so to sacrifice
their egotism and ambition for good, and worked without
sparing themselves just as you have not spared yourself in
pursuit of your kopek!"

"Afanasy Vasilievich!" said the wretched Chichikov and
seized Murazov's hands in his own. "Oh, if only I could
be set free, if I could recover my property! I swear to you,
I would lead a quite different life! Save me, my benefactor, save me!"

"But what can I do? You want me to fight against
the law. Let us suppose I even presumed to do this, the
prince would not go back on his decision: he is a just
man."

"Benefactor! You can do everything. It is not the
law I fear—I shall find a remedy for the law—but the fact
that I have been thrown guiltless into prison, that I shall
perish here, like a dog, and that my property, my papers,
my box... Save me!"

He threw his arms around the old man's feet and rained
tears on them.

"Oh, Pavel Ivanovich, Pavel Ivanovich!" said old Murazov, shaking his head. "How you have been blinded by
this property! It has deafened you even to your own poor
soul!"

"I shall also think about my soul, just save me!"

"Pavel Ivanovich!" said the old man, and paused. "It
is not in my power to save you, you can see that for yourself. But I shall do my utmost to alleviate your fate and to
obtain your release. I do not know whether I shall succeed, but I shall try. If, however, beyond my expectation,
I do succeed, Pavel Ivanovich, I shall ask you for a reward
for my services: abandon all this seeking after gain. I tell
you in all honesty that if I were to lose my fortune—and
mine is bigger than yours—I should not shed a tear. No, no,
what matters is not the property which can be confiscated
from me, but that which no one can steal or take away!
You have lived long enough in this world to understand.
You yourself call your life a barque tossed on the waves.
You already have the wherewithal to live out the remain-
der of your days. Settle down in some quiet little corner,
close to a church and to simple, good folk; or, if you are so

set on leaving descendants after you, find a nice girl of modest means to marry, a girl accustomed to moderation and simple housekeeping. Forget this clamorous world and all its seductive whims: and let it forget you too. There is no peace in it. You can see: everyone in it is either an enemy, a tempter or a traitor."

Chichikov fell to thinking. Something strange, some feelings he had never known before, inexplicable feelings filled his heart: it was as if something was struggling to awake in him, something which had been stifled in childhood by harsh petrified sermons, by the lovelessness and dullness of his childhood, by the bleakness of his home, by his bachelor loneliness, by the poverty and wretchedness of his earliest impressions, by the stern gaze of fate which had glanced at him dully through some dingy window plastered with snow.

"Only save me, Afanasy Vasilievich!" he cried. "I shall lead a different life, I shall heed your advice! I give you my word!"

"You make sure now, Pavel Ivanovich, that you don't go back on your word," said Murazov, seizing his hand.

"I might perhaps have gone back on it, had I not received such a terrible lesson," said the wretched Chichikov with a sigh, and added: "But it's a hard lesson, a terribly hard lesson, Afanasy Vasilievich!"

"It's good that it's hard. You should thank God for that, pray to Him. I shall go and do what I can for you."

Having said this the old man departed.

Chichikov stopped weeping and rending his tailcoat and hair: he had calmed down.

"No, enough!" he said finally. "A different life, a different life. It's true, it is time I became a decent citizen. Oh, if only I were able somehow or other to extricate myself from this and to get away from here with at least a small capital, and I'll settle down far away from... But the deeds of purchase?.." He thought a moment: "Why should I? Why should I abandon all that which I toiled so hard to acquire? I shall not buy any more, but the ones I have I must mortgage. After all, the effort it cost me to acquire them! Those I shall mortgage, those I shall mortgage and buy an estate with the money. I shall become a landowner, because there I can do a deal of good." And in his thoughts there awakened those same feelings that had possessed him when he was on Kostanzhoglo's estate, listening in the warm evening light to his host's benign and wise words about how fruitful and beneficial it was to manage an estate. Suddenly in his mind's eyes he saw a village in all its beauty, just as if he were really capable of feeling the charm of village life.

"What fools we are, to pursue vain ambitions!" he said at last. "Honestly, we do it from indolence! Everything is close, everything is at hand, but we have to chase to the four corners of the world after nothing. For isn't that life, too, working with application, even if it is in some remote backwoods? Because pleasure really does come from toil. And there is nothing sweeter than the fruit of one's labours... No, I shall work, I shall settle in a village, to a life of honest toil, so that I shall also have a good influence on others. Am I really so utterly good-for-nothing? I have the qualities of thrift, and efficiency, and prudence, and even perseverance. I need only make a firm resolve to feel those qualities are really there. It is only now that I honestly and clearly realise that man does have a duty to fulfil on this earth, without tearing himself away from that spot, that corner in which he has been placed."

And a life of industry, far from the hubbub of the cities and from those delusions dreamt up by man in his idleness, in his estrangement from toil, took shape so vividly in his mind's eye that he almost completely forgot all the unpleasantness of his present circumstances, and he might perhaps have been prepared even to thank Providence for this hard-learnt lesson if only he would be released and have a part of his possessions returned to him. But ... the single door of his filthy cell opened to admit an official personage—Samosvistov, an Epicurean, a man-about-town, a boon companion, a debauchee and a thorough-going rogue, in the words of his own comrades. In time of war such a man would have performed miracles: he could be despatched somewhere or other to make his way across hazardous, impassable ground, in order to steal a cannon from under the very nose of the enemy—that would be a job for him. But in the absence of any martial arena, in which he might have been an honest man, he indulged in nastiness and filthy tricks. It was really quite baffling! With his friends he was a good fellow, he did not betray any of them and was always as good as his word; but any superior authority he regarded as some sort of enemy battery which he had to fight his way through, going for any weak spot, any breach or omission...

"We know all about your position, we've all heard!" he said after looking to see that the door was firmly closed behind him. "It's nothing, it's nothing! Have no fear: it will all be set to right. Everything will start to work in your favour and they will be your servants! Thirty thousand for the lot of them and that's all there is to it."

"Do you think so?" shrieked Chichikov. "And I'll be completely acquitted?"

"Totally and utterly! And you'll receive compensation for your losses too."

"And for the work?"

"Thirty thousand. Now that's for all of them—our chaps, and the Governor-General's, and the secretary."

"But, if I might ask, how can I do it? All my things ... my box ... all that is now under seal, heavily guarded..."

"In an hour's time you'll get the lot. Let's shake on it, shall we?"

Chichikov held out his hand. His heart pounded and he could not believe this was really happening.

"Farewell for now! Our mutual friend has asked me to tell you that the main thing is to remain calm and keep your presence of mind."

"Hm!" thought Chichikov, "I understand: the legal consultant!"

Samosvistov vanished. Alone again, Chichikov still could not believe what he had heard; then, no more than an hour after this conversation, his box was brought in: complete with papers, money—and everything in perfect order. Samosvistov had come to Chichikov's lodgings as though he were in charge: he roundly scolded the guards on duty for their lack of vigilance, he demanded extra soldiers to enhance surveillance, he took not only the box, but also removed any papers which could compromise Chichikov in any way; he tied all this together, sealed it up and ordered a soldier to take it at once to Chichikov himself, on the allegation that they were his essential night things and sleeping attire. And so together with his papers Chichikov received all the warm clothing he needed. This swift delivery delighted him beyond words. His hopes rose high, and once again he began to dream of various blandishments: theatre in the evening, a *danseuse* he was courting... The village and its quiet started to fade, the town and its tumult were again more vivid, more bright... Oh, life!

Meanwhile a case of infinite proportions got under way in the courts and chambers. The scriveners' pens scratched away, and, between nosefuls of snuff, the jurisprudential luminaries toiled away, admiring their pettifoggery with an artist's eye. The legal consultant invisibly operated the whole mechanism, like a concealed magician: he thoroughly confused everything before anyone had a chance to find his bearings. Confusion mounted. Samosvistov surpassed himself in valour and unheard-of audacity. Having ascertained where the arrested woman was being held under guard, he betook himself there directly and cut such a dashing and authoritative figure that the sentry leapt to attention and saluted:

"Have you been standing here long?"

"Since morning, Your Excellency!"

"How long till you're relieved?"

"Three hours, Your Excellency!"

"I'm going to need you. I'll tell the officer to dispatch someone in your place."

"Yessir, Your Excellency!"

He then drove home and, without a moment's delay, without involving anyone else so that none should be the wiser, dressed up as a gendarme, stuck on sideburns and a moustache, and the devil himself would not have recognized him. He returned to the house where Chichikov was being held and, grabbing hold of the first woman he saw he handed her over to two doughty young officials, and then—looking right and proper with his moustache and rifle—marched up to the sentry:

"You go along, the commanding officer's sent me to finish the shift." He took the sentry's place and stood there with his rifle.

This was all that was needed. In place of the previous woman the new one was installed, knowing nothing about anything and not understanding what was going on. The other woman was hidden away so successfully that even afterwards they never found out where she had got to. While Samosvistov was acting the sentry, the legal consultant was working miracles in the civil arena: the governor was confidentially informed that the public prosecutor was writing a denunciation of him; the gendarmerie official was informed that an official living amongst them incognito was writing denunciations of him; the incognito official was assured that an even more incognito official was writing denunciations of *him*—and everyone was reduced to such a state that they were forced to turn to him for advice. The upshot was the most unholy confusion: one denunciation came on top of another, and doings were uncovered the likes of which the sun had never seen, and even such as did not exist at all. Everything was dragged out and made use of: who was of illegitimate birth, what was the social standing of whose mistress, and whose wife was lusting after whom. The scandals, imbroglios and everything else got so mixed up and interwoven with Chichikov's own story and with the dead souls, that it was quite impossible to say which of these matters was the bigger nonsense: they all seemed of equal merit. When at last the papers started to arrive on the Governor-General's desk, the poor prince could not make head or tail of them. The exceptionally clever and efficient official who was charged with drawing up a résumé quite lost his wits, trying to follow the thread of the case. The prince was concerned about a great number of other matters at this time, each more disagreeable than the last. In one part of the province famine had struck. The officials sent there to distribute grain failed to organize things properly. In another part of the province the schismatics had come astir. Someone had spread among them the rumour that Antichrist had come, that he would not even let the dead alone and was buying up some dead souls or other. They repented and they sinned and, under the pretext of catching Antichrist, did away with many a non-Antichrist. In another area the peasants had revolted against their landowners and the local police. Some vagrants had spread rumours among them that the time was coming when peasants would themselves become landlords, dressed in tailcoats, while landlords would have to clothe themselves in coarseweave coats and be peasants—and an entire volost, failing to take into account that too many landlords and captains of police would result, refused to pay any taxes at all. Force had to be used. The poor prince was utterly distraught. And here the monopolist was announced.

"Show him in," said the prince.

The old man entered...

"So there's Chichikov for you! You stood up for him and defended him. Now he's got mixed up in the sort of affair that even the most hard-bitten criminal wouldn't contemplate."

"Permit me to inform you, Your Highness, that I do not fully understand this business."

"Forgery of a will, and what a forgery! A public flogging is what he deserves!"

"Your Highness, I say this not to defend Chichikov. But after all, the case has not been proved: the enquiry has yet to take place."

"The evidence is that the woman who was dressed up as the old lady who died, has been arrested. I specially want to interrogate her in your presence." The prince rang and gave orders for the woman to be brought in.

Murazov fell silent.

"It's a most perfidious business! And, to their shame, the town's leading officials, including the mayor himself, are mixed up in it. He should not keep company with thieves and scoundrels!" said the prince heatedly.

"It's true—the mayor is one of the heirs; he has the right to make claims; but as for the others latching on from all sides, that, Your Highness, is human nature. A rich woman has died, she failed to make sensible and fair dispositions, so the fortune-hunters descend in swarms: that's human nature..."

"But why play foul tricks like that? The scoundrels!" said the prince, seething with indignation. "I do not have one single decent official: they're all scoundrels!"

"Your Highness! But which one of us is really decent? All the officials of our town are people, they have their merits and many of them are highly competent, but everyone might succumb to temptation."

"Listen, Afanasy Vasilievich, tell me, you alone I know to be an honest man, what is this passion of yours to defend every manner of scoundrel?"

"Your Highness," said Murazov, "you call him a scoundrel, but no matter who he is, the fact remains he is a man. How can you not defend a man when you know that half the evil deeds he does he does out of his coarseness and ignorance? For we commit injustices at every step and at every moment of our lives, we occasion the misfortunes of others, even without intending to. After all, Your Highness has himself also perpetrated a great injustice."

"What!" exclaimed the prince in astonishment, quite taken aback by the unexpected course the conversation had taken.

Murazov paused, fell silent a moment, as if gathering his thoughts, and finally said:

"Well, if only in the Tentetnikov case."

"Afanasy Vasilievich! A crime committed against the fundamental laws of the state is tantamount to an act of treason against one's own land!"

"I am not vindicating him. But is it really just to condemn a youth, who in his inexperience has been seduced and led astray by others, as harshly as one of the instigators? Because the same fate has befallen Tentetnikov and these reprobates, yet their crimes were not the same."

"For God's sake..." said the prince with noticeable agitation, "do you know anything about this? Tell me. Just the other day I wrote directly to St. Petersburg seeking clemency on his behalf."

"No, Your Highness, I do not mean to imply that I know something you don't. Although, of course, there is one circumstance which would work in his favour, only he himself will not consent to its use, because it would entail the suffering of another. But I am only wondering whether you might have acted rather hastily on that occasion. Forgive me, your Highness, I am judging by my own feeble understanding. On several occasions you have bid me speak openly. Now, sir, when I was still an overseer, I had many workers, good and bad... I also had to keep in mind a man's previous life, because, if you do not examine everything calmly, and if you raise your voice at him right from the start, you will only succeed in frightening him and will not get a true confession out of him; but when you talk to him compassionately, as brother to brother, he will tell you everything himself and will not even seek any clemency, and he will feel no bitterness towards anyone, for he clearly sees that it is not I who punish him, but the law."

The prince grew pensive. At this moment a young official entered and stood waiting respectfully, holding a portfolio. The cares of office and toil were stamped on his young and still fresh face. It was clear why he had been chosen for special duties. He was a member of that rare breed who throw themselves into their work *con amore*. Burning with neither ambition, nor a thirst for profit, nor a desire to emulate others, he set to work only because he was convinced that it was necessary for him to be here and not in some other place, that he had been born for this. To investigate, to take to pieces, and, having grasped all the threads of an entangled affair, then to disentangle it: this was his job. His labours, his endeavours, his sleepless nights were all abundantly recompensed if the matter finally began to fall into place before him, if its secret springs were revealed, and he felt that he could put it all across in a few words, clearly and distinctly, so that it would be plain and obvious to any man. It could be said that even the joy felt by a pupil when some immensely difficult sentence is made clear to him and the real meaning of the thought of a great writer is revealed, is as nothing to his joy when a gravely entangled case was unravelled before him. On the other hand... (*the ms. breaks off here, and continues on a new page, in the middle of a sentence.*)

. . . .

...with grain in the famine stricken areas; I know this business better than the officials: I shall investigate who needs what in person. And if you permit it, Your Highness, I shall also talk to the schismatics. They will be more willing to talk with someone like themselves, with a common man. And perhaps, God willing, I shall help to find a peaceful settlement with them. But I shall not take any money from you because I should be ashamed to think about my own profit at a time like this, when people are dying of hunger. I have some grain in store; in fact I've also sent to Siberia for more to be brought by next summer."

"Only God can reward you for your services, Afanasy Vasilievich. But I shall not say a single word to you because—you know it yourself—words are powerless here. But permit me to say one thing regarding your own request. Tell me yourself: do I really have the right to turn a blind eye to this business, and would it be just, would it be honest for me to pardon scoundrels?"

"Your Highness, you cannot call them that, especially as amongst them there are many who are quite worthy people. Difficult are the circumstances of man, your Highness, very, very difficult. Sometimes a man seems to be unquestionably guilty, but when you go into the matter you find it isn't even him at all."

"But what will they say themselves, if I drop the matter? After all, there are some amongst them who will raise their noses still higher in the air after this and will even say they put the wind up me. They will be the first to lose any respect..."

"Your Highness, permit me to give you my opinion: gather them all together, tell them that you know about everything, and describe your own position to them exactly as you have been so good as to describe it here to me, and seek their advice: what would each of them have done in your place?"

"Do you think that they are capable of any more noble aspirations than double-dealing and lining their own pockets? Believe me, they'll only laugh at me."

"I do not think so, Your Highness. Every Russian, even one worse than the rest, still has his sense of justice. A Jew perhaps, but not a Russian. No, Your Highness, you have no need to hold anything back. Tell them everything precisely as you told it to me. As you know, they deride you as an ambitious man, a proud man, who does not want to listen to a thing, who is sure of himself—so let them see everything as it really is. What's it to you? After all, your cause is just. Tell them as if you were making your confession not before them, but before God Himself."

"Afanasy Vasilievich," said the prince, pensively, "I

shall give this some thought, but in the meanwhile I thank you warmly for your advice."

"But, Your Highness, please order Chichikov's release."

"Tell that Chichikov person to get himself away from here as soon as possible, and the further the better. He is someone I could never forgive."

Murazov bowed and went from the prince directly to Chichikov. He found Chichikov already in fine spirits, most composedly enjoying a fairly decent dinner, which had been served to him on china dishes from some very decent kitchen. From the very first sentences of their conversation the old man gathered at once that Chichikov had already spoken with some of the officials embroiled in this case. He even detected the intervention of the unseen hand of the expert legal consultant.

"Now listen to me, Pavel Ivanovich," he said, "I have brought you freedom on the condition that you remove yourself at once from the town. Gather together all your goods and chattels—and may God speed you on your way, do not delay for a single minute because the case has become even worse. I know what's going on, a certain person is giving you ideas; but let me tell you in confidence that yet another of his deeds has come to light, and no power on earth will save him. He, of course, is glad to drag others under, to keep him company, but the case is already nearing solution. I left you in a good frame of mind—better than the one in which you are now. I am giving you this advice in all earnest. No, no, it's not a question of property which is causing people to quarrel and cut each other's throats, just as if it were possible to order our lives on earth without thinking of the next world. Believe me, Pavel Ivanovich, until people renounce everything that makes them crush and devour one another on earth, and start to think about ordering their spiritual welfare, they will never be able to bring order into their earthly existence. Times of famine and poverty will set in, which will befall nations in their entirety and each individual separately... That is plain to see. For, say what you will, the body depends upon the soul. How then can things be expected to go in proper order? Think not about dead souls, but about your own living soul, and may God go with you along some different road! I shall also be leaving tomorrow.

Make haste! Or else disaster will strike when I'm no longer here."

With these words the old man took his leave. Chichikov fell to thinking. The meaning of life once again loomed large before him. "Murazov's right," he said, "it's time to follow a different road!" Saying this, he left the prison. One sentry followed lugging his box, another his trunk. Selifan and Petrushka were overjoyed at their master's release.

"Well, my good fellows," said Chichikov, addressing them graciously, "we must pack and be on our way."

"We'll whiz along, Pavel Ivanovich," said Selifan. "The road must be good and firm now: there's been enough snow. Honest, it's time we got out of this town. I'm so sick of it, I can't stand the sight of it."

"Run along to the carriage-maker and tell him to put the carriage on runners," said Chichikov, and himself headed for the town, but he did not wish to pay any farewell calls on anyone. After all this farrago it was even awkward—especially since such a plethora of highly disagreeable stories about him were circulating in the town. He avoided all possible encounters, and only called stealthily on the merchant from whom he had bought the cloth of Navarino smoke and flame, took another four arshins for a tailcoat and trousers and went back to the same tailor. For twice the fee the tailor agreed to redouble his zeal and kept his underlings hard at work all night, busy with their needles, their flat-irons and their teeth—the next day, albeit a little late, the suit was ready. The horses were all harnessed up. Still Chichikov took the time to try on the coat. It was perfect, exactly like its predecessor. But, alas! he noticed a bald spot in his hair and murmured sadly to himself: "Now why did I have to give way to such despair? There certainly was no cause to tear my hair." Having settled his account with the tailor he finally drove out of the town in a strange frame of mind. This was not the old Chichikov. This was but a ruin of the old Chichikov. His inner state could be compared to a structure, which has been dismantled in order that a new structure might be assembled from it, but work on the new has not yet commenced because the final plan has not yet arrived from the architect and the workers were left at sixes and sevens. An hour earlier old Murazov had departed on his way, riding in a bast-covered *kibitka* together with Potapych, and an hour after Chichikov's departure an order was issued that the prince, in view of his imminent departure for St. Petersburg, wished to see every one of the officials without exception.

The entire official estate of the town, from the mayor to the last Titular Counsellor,* gathered in the large hall of the Governor-General's residence: heads of chancery, counsellors, assessors, Kisloyedov, Krasnonosov, Samosvistov, bribe-takers, bribe-refusers, hypocrites, semi-hypocrites and total non-hypocrites—all waited in a not altogether tranquil state of mind for the Governor-General to make his entrance. The prince came out. He looked neither downcast nor uplifted: his gaze was firm as his gait... The entire assemblage of officials bowed, many of them from the waist. Answering with a slight bow, the prince began:

"Before departing for St. Petersburg I thought it fit and proper to receive all of you and even in part to explain my reasons. A most scandalous affair has occurred amongst us. I presume that many of those present know what I have in mind. This affair has led to the revelation of other, no less perfidious affairs, in which people whom I have hitherto regarded as honest are implicated. I am even aware of the secret aim of confusing everything so thoroughly that it should become quite impossible to disentangle it in a formal way. I even know the identity of the chief instigator and by whose subterfuge... (*the sentence is left unfinished in the ms.*), although he has very skilfully concealed his involvement. But the point is that I intend to deal with this not in a formal way, with an investigation of the papers, but with a swift court martial, as in time of war, and I hope that the Tsar will empower me to do so when I put all the facts of the affair before him. In a case, when it is impossible to conduct proceedings by civil law, when cupboards full of documents catch fire and, finally, when people attempt, with a mass of false testimony from outsid-

---

*Titular Counsellor—according to the Table of Ranks, a 9th rank official. As from 1845, officials of this rank were promoted to the noblemen's class, whereas until then this privilege was enjoyed by all the 14 ranks.

ers and with mendacious denunciations to throw a veil over an affair which is shady enough as it is, I regard a court martial as the only means and I wish to know your opinion."

The prince paused, as if waiting for an answer. They all stood, staring down at the floor. Many were pale.

"I also know of one other affair, although those behind it are fully convinced that no one could know about it. This will be investigated but not through documents, because I myself shall act as plaintiff and petitioner and shall submit irrefutable proof."

Some one in the assemblage of officials started nervously; several of the more faint-hearted were also abashed.

"It stands to reason that the primary instigators should be stripped of their rank and property, the others should be dismissed from their posts. It also goes without saying that many innocent persons will suffer amongst them. What can be done? The affair is too perfidious and cries out for justice. Although I am only too aware that this will not even serve as a lesson to anyone because others will appear to take the places of those dismissed, and those very same ones who have hitherto been honest will become dishonest, and those who are deemed worthy of trust will deceive and betray—notwithstanding all this I must act with severity because justice cries out to be done. I know I shall be accused of cruelty, but I know too that those people will also accuse me... (*the edge of the page is torn off in the ms.*) I must therefore turn myself into an unfeeling instrument of justice, an axe, which must fall on certain heads."

An involuntary tremor ran across all the faces.

The prince was calm. His face expressed neither anger, nor any emotion.

"Now that very same man, who holds in his hands the destiny of many others, and whom all entreaties and pleas were powerless to move, the very same man is falling at your feet and pleading with all of you. Everything will be forgotten, smoothed over, and pardoned; I shall myself intercede on everyone's behalf, if only my plea is granted. This is it. I know that it is not possible, by any means, by any threats, by any punishments, to eradicate corruption: it is already too deeply rooted. The dishonest practice of taking bribes has become a necessity and a prerequisite even for those people who were not born to be dishonest. I know that for many it is now almost impossible to swim against the general tide. But now I am bound, as at a decisive and sacred moment, when the safety of the fatherland is in jeopardy, when each and every citizen must endure everything and make every sacrifice, to appeal at least to those in whose breast there still beats a Russian heart and to whom 'nobility' still means something. There's no purpose in debating here which of us is most guilty! Perhaps I am most guilty of all; perhaps I treated you too severely at the beginning; perhaps I was too suspicious and repelled those amongst you who sincerely wished to be of service to me, although I, too, for my own part, could reproach them in equal measure. If they really cherished justice and the good of their land, they should not have taken umbrage at the haughtiness of my manner, they should have suppressed the stirrings of ambition within them and sacrificed their personal pride. I simply could not have failed to notice their self-sacrifice and exalted love of good, nor could I have failed, in the end, to accept their useful and wise advice. Surely it is more appropriate for a subordinate to adapt to the character of his superior than for the superior to that of his subordinate. This, at least, is more lawful and easier, because subordinates have but one superior and a superior has hundreds of subordinates. But let us not concern ourselves for the moment with the apportioning of blame. The point is that we are called to save our land; that this our land is being ruined not by the invasion of alien tribes, but by us ourselves; that, beside the legitimate powers that be, a new power has come into being, far more important than any legitimate one. It has established its own conditions; everything has been evaluated and the values have even become common knowledge. And no ruler, for all that he may be wiser than all the lawmakers and other rulers, is capable of correcting evil, however much he limits the activities of rotten officials by appointing other officials as their overseers. All efforts will fail until each and every one of us feels that, just as in wartime the people armed themselves against the enemy, so he must also rise up in arms against injustice. As a Russian, as one bonded to you by kinship of the common blood coursing through our veins, I now appeal to you. I appeal to those among you who have any understanding of the concept of nobility of thought. I invite you to recall the duty which faces man in every position he holds. I invite you to take a closer look at your duty and the obligations placed upon you by your service on this earth, because that is something of which we already have a vague conception, but which we can scarcely... (*at this point the ms. breaks off*).

Commentary

Volume One was first published in 1842 as a separate book under the title *The Adventures of Chichikov or Dead Souls. A Poem by N. Gogol*, Moscow, 1842.

Gogol began work on the poem in 1835. A letter to Alexander Pushkin of October 7, 1835, the same letter in which Gogol asked for a subject for what was to be *The Government Inspector* contains the first reference to *Dead Souls*: "Have begun to write *Dead Souls*. The subject has extended into a very long novel, and I think it will be highly amusing. But for the moment I have stopped at the third chapter. Am looking for a good pettifogger, one I could get to know well. I want to show at least one side of the whole of Russia in this novel." In informing Pushkin about this plan, with which Pushkin was already familiar, Gogol was, as it were, continuing the conversation to which he refers in his *Author's Confession*.

According to Pushkin, Gogol wrote, "The subject of d(ead) s(ouls) is good for me because it gives me complete freedom to travel the length and breadth of Russia with my hero and depict a mass of the most motley characters." This corresponds to the information contained in the above-mentioned letter to Pushkin. Gogol constructed his plot in such a way as to travel the "length and breadth" of Russia and portray a wealth of characters; due to the absence of a prototype for one of them, a pettifogger, the action was halted at the third chapter.

The work on *Dead Souls* begun in St. Petersburg was

resumed by Gogol in the autumn of 1836 in Vevey (Switzerland), and later continued in Paris. "I have rewritten everything I began," he wrote to his friend, the poet Vassily Zhukovsky, on November 12. "I have thought over the whole plan some more and am now writing it calmly, like a chronicle. Due to this Switzerland has grown better for me, its grey-mauve-blue-pink mountains lighter and airier. If I finish this work the way it should be finished, then ... what a vast, original subject it will be."

In this letter to Zhukovsky *Dead Souls* is called not a novel (as in the letter to Pushkin), but a "poem". A letter to the writer, historian and journalist Mikhail Pogodin of November 28, 1836 refers to the same changes: "The thing I am sitting and working at now ... is not like a story or a novel, it is very long enough for several volumes... If God helps me to fashion my poem as it should be fashioned, it will be my first decent work. The whole of Russia will be reflected in it."

Gogol's letters of this period to friends and relatives are full of requests for information about "legal cases", particularly those "associated with the buying of dead souls". "Tell Pushkin about it," Gogol asked Zhukovsky, "perhaps he will find something too." All this material was needed to continue the poem.

In February 1837 in Paris Gogol learned of Pushkin's death. "All my enjoyment of life, all my noblest enjoyment has disappeared with him," Gogol wrote to Pyotr Pletnyov from Rome on March 28. "I never undertook anything without his advice... This present work of mine was inspired by him. It was his creation..." Gogol now regarded *Dead Souls* as a "sacred behest" from Pushkin (letter to Zhukovsky of April 18, 1837).

By the end of 1840 Volume One was completed in the main and Gogol began to prepare it for publication. In December he wrote to the writer Sergei Aksakov from Rome: "I am now preparing the fair copy of Volume One of *Dead Souls*. I am revising, amending and completely rewriting a great deal..."

V. A. Panov, a relative of Sergei Aksakov's, who accompanied Gogol on his journey to Italy, and later Pavel Annenkov, the critic, prosewriter and memoirist, helped to copy out the poem. Annenkov has left a vivid account of how the poem was copied in Rome in the summer of 1841.

"Nikolai Vasilievich, having laid out the notebook in front of him ... would become totally engrossed in it and begin to dictate slowly and solemnly, with such feeling and fullness of expression that the chapters of Volume One of *Dead Souls* took on a special colour in my memory. It was like the calm, smoothly flowing inspiration which is usually engendered by profound contemplation of the subject."

When the copying of "The Tale of Captain Kopeikin", which evoked a feeling of evident satisfaction in the author, was completed, Annenkov expressed doubt as to whether it would ever be published. " 'Publishing's no problem,' Gogol replied confidently. 'It will all be published.' " The author's sense of satisfaction was even more strongly pronounced in the chapter where Plyushkin's garden is described. Never, I recall, did the fervour of dictation reach such heights in Gogol, retaining all its artistic naturalness, as in this passage. Gogol even rose from his chair (it was obvious that at this moment he could see before him the landscape he was describing) and accompanied his dictation with a proud, somehow imperious gesture. At the end of this remarkable sixth chapter I was so excited that I put my pen down on the table and exclaimed wholeheartedly: 'I consider this chapter to be a work of genius, Nikolai Vasilievich.' Gogol rolled up the small notebook from which he had been dictating and said in a thin, barely audible voice: 'Believe me, the others are not worse.' "

In October 1841 Gogol returned to Moscow via St Petersburg for the final copying and publication of *Dead Souls*.

On December 7 Gogol gave the manuscript to the censor I. Snegiryov, and asked him whether he thought the Moscow Censorship Committee would permit its publication.

Later, in a letter of January 7, 1842, to his friend the writer and journalist Pyotr Pletnyov, Gogol described what had taken place at the committee meeting: "As soon as Golokhvastov, after taking the chair, heard the title *Dead Souls*, he thundered in the voice of an ancient Roman: 'No, I shall never allow that: the soul is immortal, there cannot be a dead soul, the author is attacking immortality.' The explanation that it referred to registered serfs alarmed the censors even more: that certainly could not be allowed, it was an attack on serfdom." Nor did the intercession of

Snegiryov, who had read the manuscript, help. Not only did the "Asiatic" censors object, but the "European" censors too; one of the latter, N. Krylov, Professor of Roman law at Moscow University, said: 'I don't care what you say, the price which Chichikov pays ... the price of two-and-a-half-rubles which he gives per soul, is disgraceful... It would never be allowed in France or England or anywhere else. After this not a single foreigner will come here anymore.' "

Fearing that the manuscript would be banned, Gogol took it from the Moscow Censorship Committee and gave it to Belinsky who was leaving for St. Petersburg. Gogol hoped that in the capital the assistance of his friends Prince Vladimir Odoyevsky, Pyotr Pletnyov and Alexandra Smirnova would help *Dead Souls* pass the censors. And indeed on March 9 the poem was passed for publication with some minor amendments, but without "The Tale of Captain Kopeikin". "The Kopeikin episode turned out to be quite impossible to pass," Gogol was informed on April 1 by Nikitenko who was one of censors. "No one's authority could save it, and you will, of course, yourself agree that there was nothing I could do about it."

Gogol, however, decided to keep the Tale at all costs. He wrote to Nikitenko on April 10 that without it there would be a "hole" in the poem, which could not be "patched up". "This piece is essential not to connect the events, but to distract the reader for a moment, to replace one impression by another..." Gogol revised the tale, lowering the rank, so to say, of the characters in it: the aristocratic general became simply a "chief"; there was no reference to generals among his petitioners ("I have got rid of all the generals," Gogol informed Pletnyov on April 10); and even the name of the Palace Embankment was removed, to avoid associations with the Winter Palace there and the palaces of high-ranking officials. Qualities such as Kopeikin's obstinacy and fastidiousness were made more pronounced. Gogol even agreed to change Kopeikin's name ("if the name of Kopeikin does not suit them, I am prepared to call him Pyatkin or anything they like," he wrote to N. Prokopovich on April 15), evidently fearing associations with the figure of the folklore robber Kopeikin then well-known in Russia. There turned out to be no need for that, however; the revised version of the tale was passed for publication. Modern editions of the work, the present one included, contain Gogol's original version of the Tale.

The censor changed the title of the poem. Nikitenko wrote in red ink over the title *Dead Souls* "The Adventures of Chichikov or" (modern editions of the poem retain the original title).

While the book was being set up for printing, Gogol himself designed the cover for it. This cover is interesting as an example of grotesque ornament in weird combinations with everyday objects, figures of people and animals, and a large number of human skulls, which, on the one hand, fits in with the grotesque content of the poem and, on the other, goes back to the old traditions of grotesque wall ornament with its strange combinations of details from inanimate nature, flora and fauna.

The book came out at the end of May 1842. Public interest already aroused by readings of individual chapters (from at least the summer of 1837 Gogol frequently read extracts from the poem in various houses) and intensified by rumours of difficulties with the censors, focused on Gogol's new work. "All literary interest, all journal discussions are now concentrated on Gogol," Belinsky noted.

One of the first comments on the poem, an entry in the diary of the famous writer and Russian revolutionary Alexander Herzen for June 11, 1842, reads: "...Gogol's *Dead Souls* is a remarkable book, a bitter reproach to present-day Russia, but not void of hope." A little later Herzen added: "Great is the merit of a literary work which evades all one-sided views. To see an apotheosis is ridiculous, to see only anathema is unjust. There are words of reconciliation, there are provisions of and hopes for the future, a full and triumphant one, but this does not prevent the present from being reflected in all its revolting reality."

Vissarion Belinsky gave *Dead Souls* a rapturous reception in the journal *Otechestvenniye Zapiski* (Fatherland Notes), 1842, No. 7: "...Amid this triumph of paltriness, mediocrity, and triviality, amid these literary scriveners and rain bubbles, amid these childish pranks, infantile ideas, spurious feelings, pharisaical patriotism and sickly populism—suddenly, like a cleansing flash of lightning in the oppressive and putrid heat and drought, there appears a purely Russian, national work, drawn from the inmost depths of popular life, as true as it is patriotic, which mercilessly rips the veil off reality and breathes with a passionate, vigorous and vital love for the fertile core of Russian life; a work immeasurably artistic in conception and execution, in the characters of its personages and the details of Russian life—and at the same time profound in its ideas, social, national and historical..." (*The Adventures of Chichikov or Dead Souls*. A Poem by N. Gogol).

* * *

Volume Two of the poem was first published in 1855 in the form of an additional volume to the second edition of Gogol's works: "The Works of Nikolai Vasilievich Gogol Found after His Death. *The Adventures of Chichikov or Dead Souls*. A Poem by N. V. Gogol. Volume Two (5 chapters), Moscow, 1855. This book reproduced the extant rough draft of Volume Two of the poem, the fair copy of which was burnt by Gogol on the night of February 11, 1852.

We shall quote some extracts from memoirs which throw light on the content of those non-extant chapters.

Leo Arnoldi, who was present when the poem was read in the house of Alexandra Smirnova, recalled that the chapter which ended with General Betrishchev's laughter "was followed by another containing a description of a whole day in the general's house". On that day Chichikov at the general's request went to fetch Tentetnikov. "This is followed by their journey to the general's village, Tentetnikov's meeting with Betrishchev and Ulinka and finally the dinner. The description of this dinner, in my opinion, was the best passage in Volume Two." "...After this Ulinka decided to have a serious talk to her father about Tentetnikov... After praying, she went to her father's study, knelt before him and begged for his consent and blessing for her marriage to Tentetnikov. The general hesitated for a long while and finally agreed. On receiving his consent, Tentetnikov, beside himself with happiness, left Ulinka for a moment and ran into the garden... Here Gogol had two marvellous lyrical pages. On the hot summer day, at the height of noon, Tentetnikov stands in the dense, shady garden amidst a deep, all-pervading silence. The garden was described with the brush of a true master, each branch on the trees, the scorching heat, the grasshoppers in the grass, the insects and finally all the feelings of Tentetnikov, loving and loved in return. Chichikov, who has managed to become a friend of the Betrishchevs, takes part in the wedding preparations. At the request of the general he sets off to inform all the relatives about the betrothal. Naturally, with an eye to his own advantage, i. e., the acquisition of 'dead souls'."

The main twists of the plot to which Arnoldi refers find confirmation in the reminiscences of Alexandra Smirnova, and also in the editorial note by Stepan Shevyryov at the end of Chapter Two in the first edition of Volume Two of *Dead Souls*.

As for the subsequent development of the action, Alexandra Smirnova told Gogol's first biographer, Panteleimon Kulish, the author of *Notes on the Life of Nikolai Vasilievich Gogol* (St. Petersburg, Vol. II, 1856), that the extant fragments of the text did not include "a description of Voronii-Dryanoy's village, from which Chichikov moves to Kostanzhoglo. Nor is there a word about Chegranov's estate, which is run by a young man recently graduated from university. Here Platonov, Chichikov's apathetic companion, is fascinated by a portrait, and later they meet the living original of the portrait at the house of General Betrishchev's brother, and a love affair begins, from which Chichikov seeks to extract the utmost profit, as he does from all other situations, whatever they may be."

Some important information concerning the future fate of Tentetnikov, according to Shevyryov, was provided by Prince Dmitri Obolensky: "...Just when Tentetnikov, aroused from his apathy by the influence of Ulinka, is blissfully happy at being her betrothed, he is arrested and sent to Siberia; this arrest is connected with the essay he was writing about Russia and his friendship with a university student who had harmful liberal tendencies. As he is leaving the village and bidding farewell to the peasants, Tentetnikov delivers a parting speech (which, according to Shevyryov, was a masterly piece of writing). Ulinka follows Tentetnikov to Siberia, they get married there and so on."

We have very little information about the proposed contents of Volume Three. All that we know, from Alexander Bukharev's talk with Gogol, is that Chichikov was to be regenerated, that "his spiritual revival was to be brought about by the direct intervention of the tsar himself, and that the poem was to end with Chichikov's first breath in a true, decent life." Gogol himself made a fleeing reference to the fate of Plyushkin. In a letter to his friend, the poet Nikolai Yazykov, he wrote: "Appeal, in the form of a strong lyrical appeal, to a fine, but slumbering person... Oh, if you could but tell him what my Plyushkin is to say, if I ever get as far as Volume Three of *Dead Souls!*"

The publication of the surviving chapters of Volume Two produced a number of comments. Nikolai Nekrasov wrote to Ivan Turgenev: "What an honest son of his native land!" Gogol "may have violated his talent in many respects, but what self-sacrifice!" Turgenev, who read the chapters of Volume Two before they were published, wrote of October 19, 1853, that through them "runs a kind of unpleasant current ... in the characters of the fantastic mentor, Murazov, Ulinka, etc. But there are passages which grip and astound the reader's soul at the same time. Remember Petukh's boat ride—and the fishermen's songs— and Chichikov aroused—and the lifeless inertia of Platonov. That is a marvellous passage."

Several interesting remarks on Volume Two were made by Nekrasov in his "Notes on Journals for October 1855" published in the *Sovremennik* (No. 11, 1855). Thus, with reference to Koshkaryov he attacks Pisemsky's article on *Dead Souls* (*Otechestvenniye Zapiski* No. 10, 1855), writing that "the urge to elevate his private estate to the level of an administrative establishment ... the effort to make up for a lack of order not by rejecting the system, but by extending the same measures, Koshkaryov's obsession with this idea" all serve as "seeds" of a significant nature.

Most important was Nikolai Chernyshevsky's review in a long note on the first article "Essays of the Gogol Period in Russian Literature" (*Sovremennik*, No. 12, 1855). Noting the one-sidedness and "false idealisation" of several descriptions, the critic concluded that whatever some episodes in Volume Two of *Dead Souls* were like, the dominant character of this book, had it been completed, would nevertheless have been the same as that of its first volume and all the preceding works by the great writer."

Even during Gogol's lifetime *Dead Souls* found its way onto the stage. On September 9, 1842, a few months after the poem's publication, a play entitled *Comic Scenes from the New Poem "Dead Souls"* was put on at the Alexandrinsky Theatre in St. Petersburg. This dramatisation by the St. Petersburg producer N. I. Kulikov was of no artistic importance. *Dead Souls* has since been dramatised several times. The most interesting production was by the Moscow Art Theatre (stage version by Mikhail Bulgakov, produced by Vasily Sakhnovsky, première in December 1932).

The earliest foreign editions of the poem are as follows: German translation by F. Lebenstein, published in Leipzig in 1846, a Czech translation by K. Gavlichko-Borovsky which appeared in the newspaper *Narodni Noviny* in 1849, an English translation in 1854, a French one in 1858, etc. In the introduction to the Czech translation of *Dead Souls* the translator wrote: "May I express the hope that I shall earn the gratitude of our public for having introduced it to this fine work of Russia's major novelist..."

Yuri Mann

REQUEST TO READERS

Raduga Publishers would be glad to have your
opinion of this book, its translation and design
and any suggestions you may have for future
publications.
Please send all your comments to 17, Zubovsky
Boulevard, Moscow, USSR.

Николай Гоголь

МЕРТВЫЕ ДУШИ

Поэма

На английском языке

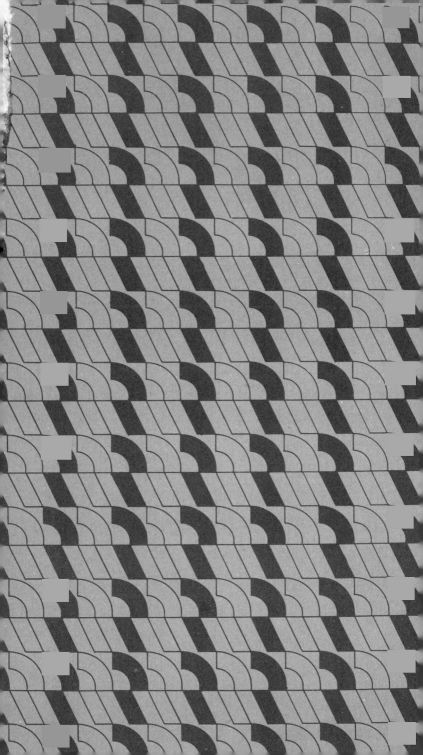